She's having his baby...

Caroline Adkins was looking forward to the
birth of her first child. Too bad she didn't
know which man would show up at her side
in the delivery room....

Abby Kildaire wasn't sure she was ready
for marriage, but she decided to give it a try.
Little did she guess that the pitter-patter
of little feet would follow her so closely
down the aisle....

THE BABY GAME

Sometimes a little bundle of joy
can cause a whole lot of trouble!

Relive the romance...

Two complete novels
by your favorite authors!

JUDY CHRISTENBERRY

has been writing romances for fifteen years because she loves happy endings as much as her readers. In fact, Judy recently quit her job teaching French just so she could devote her time to writing. She spends her spare hours reading, watching her favorite sports teams and keeping track of her two daughters. Judy is a transplanted Texan, who now lives near Phoenix, Arizona.

CATHY GILLEN THACKER

is a full-time wife/mother/author who began typing stories for her own amusement during "nap time" when her children were toddlers. Twenty years and more than fifty published novels later, Cathy is almost as well-known for her witty romantic comedies as she is for her ability to figure out what her now-grown children are up to almost before they know! Her books have made numerous appearances on bestseller lists and are published worldwide.

Judy Christenberry
Cathy Gillen Thacker

THE
BABY
GAME

HARLEQUIN®

TORONTO • NEW YORK • LONDON
AMSTERDAM • PARIS • SYDNEY • HAMBURG
STOCKHOLM • ATHENS • TOKYO • MILAN • MADRID
PRAGUE • WARSAW • BUDAPEST • AUCKLAND

HARLEQUIN BOOKS

by Request—THE BABY GAME

Copyright © 2000 by Harlequin Books S.A.

ISBN 0-373-21713-7

The publisher acknowledges the copyright holders of the individual works as follows:

WHO'S THE DADDY?
Copyright © 1995 by Judy Christenberry

MAKE ROOM FOR BABY
Copyright © 1998 by Cathy Gillen Thacker

This edition published by arrangement with Harlequin Books S.A.

Visit us at www.eHarlequin.com

Printed in U.S.A.

CONTENTS

Of all the things to forget…

Who's the Daddy?
Judy Christenberry

Chapter One

"Memorial Hospital, on line one."

James Adkins, one of the wealthiest men in Denver, reared back in his chair, ran a hand through his gray hair, slammed his bifocals onto the table and glared at his secretary. "I told you I was not to be disturbed."

"Yes, sir, but it's Caroline. She's in the hospital."

"That girl of mine is always running around getting involved in causes. Tell her we'll discuss it over dinner." He turned away, assurance in every ounce of him that he'd be obeyed. After all, he always was.

"Sir," the secretary persisted, desperation in her voice, "she's there as a patient."

He turned to stare at her, his frown of impatience turning to deeper emotion. "What? That's ridiculous. I saw her this morning."

"There was an accident," the secretary said quickly.

James Adkins moved faster than one would have expected from his less than sleek figure, overweight from rich foods and no exercise. He grabbed the phone and barked into it. "Who's speaking?"

The two men with whom he'd been meeting both stood and moved closer to the phone.

"She's what?" Adkins shrieked, and then listened

again. "Yes, yes, I'll be right there! Yes, I'll bring her mother." He slammed down the receiver and looked at the two younger men, for the first time unsure of his actions.

"Caroline's been in an accident. And...and she's got amnesia."

"Is she all right?" one of them asked.

"I just told you she has amnesia!" James snapped.

"But the accident— Is she hurt?"

"No, only bruised. Prescott, go to another phone and tell Lewis to bring the limo around. Adrian, you call Tucker and tell him he'll have to wait on my decision. I've got to call her mother and Chelsea."

As was their custom, the two men jumped to do his bidding. He growled to his secretary, "Find my wife. I believe she's attending the symphony auxiliary this morning. I'll try to reach my younger daughter."

The woman scurried from the room, as if grateful to have escaped.

"Chelsea? This is your father. Are you dressed?"

"Hi, Daddy. No, I'm still resting. Expectant mothers should get lots of rest, you know. Roddy agrees with me."

"I'm coming to pick you up. Your sister's been in an accident. She's not badly hurt, but she's lost her memory. The doctor thinks familiar faces will bring it back."

"But Daddy, why do *I* have to go? Pregnant mothers shouldn't get upset or go to hospitals. They have germs there."

"Chelsea, you have ten minutes to get ready. Don't keep me waiting," he warned in ominous tones.

"Your wife is on line two, sir," the secretary said softly from the door.

James nodded and told his daughter goodbye in the midst of another protest.

"Amelia? Caroline's okay but she's been in an accident."

"Oh, dear. But she's all right?"

He breathed a sigh of relief. Amelia might not be the perfect mother, but she loved her children. "Yes, well, she's lost her memory. It's temporary, of course, but—"

"Her memory? You mean she doesn't remember who she is? That's horrible. Why—why, she might think she's some—some common woman, not—"

"Amelia! We'll be there to pick you up in five minutes."

"Pick me up?" she asked in puzzled tones.

"Yes, the doctor said you should come. It might help Caroline's memory come back."

"But—but I'm in the middle of my meeting. Couldn't I come when I'm free? After all, I'm sure—"

"Five minutes, Amelia. I'll come in and drag you out if you're not waiting."

"James!" Amelia squealed as he hung up the phone.

Damn females! They drove him crazy. First Caroline with her independence, then Amelia with her social life. And he didn't know what to do about Chelsea.

He rushed out the door, hearing his secretary murmur, as he passed her, that the limo was waiting downstairs. Of course it was. The driver was a man and always did exactly what he was supposed to do. It was only females—three particular females—who gave James any difficulty.

When he reached the front door, he found both men who'd been in his office standing in front of the limo arguing.

"What's going on?"

"I think I should come with you, James. After all, Caroline and I have been seeing quite a bit of each other, and I might be able to help," Prescott Brownlee said at once.

"She was with *me* last night, at the opera ball," Adrian Meadows inserted, stepping closer to his boss. "Since we were just together, she might remember me more. Besides, James, you may need some help with details."

"Fine, both of you can come. I want her memory restored as soon as possible. I won't tolerate anything less. She's been acting strange lately. It's time for things to get back to normal around here. You hear me?"

Both men nodded and stood at attention as he got into the limo, neither daring to suggest that some things might be beyond James Adkins's control. They weren't sure *anything* was. Then they quickly scrambled after him, each one trying to enter first.

As the limo pulled out into traffic, James clenched his hands into fists. "If either one of you had convinced Caroline to marry him, she'd be home having a baby, like Chelsea, instead of running around having accidents!"

Both men protested their innocence, each assuring James he'd done everything in his power to court Caroline.

"Last night she really enjoyed herself," Adrian added, shooting a smug look at Prescott. "We danced all evening."

"Did you ask her?"

All three men knew what James was referring to. Adrian met neither of the others' gazes. "No. Uh, the time didn't seem right. But I'm sure she'll accept when I do."

Prescott snorted in derision, a knowing look in his eyes. James ignored both of them. "She'll make up her mind soon. I've sensed a readiness to settle down. We'll get her memory back, and then she'll marry one of you."

Neither of them argued with him. But then they never did.

"COME ON, MAX, give us a break. You've driven the entire crew like they were dogs the past few weeks. And they've done a good job. Let's give them tomorrow off, let'm have a four-day weekend for Labor Day."

Max Daniels pinched the bridge of his nose and closed his eyes briefly. His foreman, Jim Swensen, hadn't lied. He'd been a bear to work for, and he knew it. "Okay. That's a good idea, Jim. Give'm Friday off."

Jim slapped him on his shoulder. "Great. The guys'll be glad to hear it." He paused and Max tensed for what would come next.

"You still don't want to talk about what's buggin' you?"

He offered a brief smile to compensate for his negative answer. "No. But thanks for the offer. I'll see you on Tuesday."

"All right, man, but if you need to talk—"

"I'll know where to find you. Thanks, Jim."

Max watched as his foreman, also his best friend, headed toward the group of workers putting away their tools.

Slamming the truck in reverse, he backed out of the makeshift driveway, wanting to get away before any of the men came over to thank him for the extra holiday.

He knew he didn't deserve their thanks. He'd been impossible to work with for two months. No question. But he couldn't explain to them that he'd fallen in love and been abandoned by the woman with no explanation, no goodbye. One minute, bliss, the next, hell. And he was afraid that he'd demanded company in his personal hell, from everyone around him.

Man, he had to get a grip on himself. He'd never thought a woman would send him into such a tailspin. He still didn't understand why. She was beautiful, but he'd dated women more beautiful. She was intelligent, charming, but no more so than others. Her sense of humor delighted him, making him eager to share the events of his day with her, waiting to hear her warm chuckles. Her kisses—

A blaring horn reminded him the light had turned green and he stepped on the accelerator. Just as well. No sense following that line of thought.

He reached for the radio, seeking distraction. It was five after five and the national news had just ended.

"Now, in local news, Caroline Adkins, daughter of—"

Max almost drove off the road. Horns blared around him and the woman behind him sailed past, shaking an angry fist.

He pulled to a stop, reaching for the volume knob.

"...in an accident. A Memorial Hospital spokesman said she will be kept overnight for observation."

Without considering the consequences, he swung the truck back on the road and did an illegal U-turn at the next intersection. In two minutes, he was pulling into the parking lot at Memorial Hospital.

Please, God, let her be all right.

And if she was, he was going to break her neck for running out on the best thing that had ever happened to him.

"DID CAROLINE ASK to see me?" Amelia asked as the limo pulled into the hospital parking lot.

James sighed with impatience. "I told you, Amelia, she's lost her memory."

"Yes, dear, but if she didn't ask for me, I don't see why I couldn't have come after my meeting ended. Agnes told me I shouldn't always do whatever you say, you know."

James and his second daughter, Chelsea, groaned together. "That woman," James said through gritted teeth, "never agrees with me."

"Well, I know Caro didn't ask to see me," Chelsea said before her mother could respond. Her lips formed into a pout that seemed natural. "She never even calls me. You would think, now that she's to be an aunt, that she would show some interest in my baby."

"She told me last night how excited she was about your baby," Adrian assured Chelsea hurriedly, as if hoping to stem her complaints.

"Really? Well, she should spend more time with me, then," Chelsea said.

The limo pulled to a stop, and the chauffeur opened the door. All three men hurried out and then turned to help the two women.

"I think we should tell the doctor that I'm pregnant before I go into Caro's room, in case there could be any danger," Chelsea continued as they approached the front doors.

"Amnesia isn't contagious!" James snapped. He'd silently endured the complaints of both women for the length of the ride, but he was anxious for word of Caroline.

He would admit, though not to Amelia and Chelsea, that Caroline was his favorite. Not that they didn't fight. On the contrary, Caroline argued with him at every turn. She was too much like him not to.

Chelsea was like her mother.

"Chelsea!" someone called, and they all halted.

Chelsea's husband, Roderick Grant III, hurried up to them.

"What are you doing here?" James demanded. He didn't have anything against the boy, but Roddy wouldn't be of much help in a crisis.

"Daddy! Roddy's my husband!"

"I know that. I paid for that damned wedding, didn't I?" He muttered an apology when Chelsea and Amelia stared at him in shock. "I'm worried about Caroline," he added.

"Of course, you are, sir," Adrian said, patting him on the shoulder.

"Why don't we go right up," Prescott added. "I'll find out her room number."

"I know it. It's 482," James snapped, and strode for the elevators, leaving his entourage to hurry after him.

When they reached the fourth floor, the nurse on duty ushered all of them into the waiting room. "The doctor is with her now. I'll let you know when you can go in."

"Damn it, woman, I'm James Adkins. You go tell that doctor I want to see my child at once!" As the nurse calmly walked away, he bellowed, "Why won't any woman listen to me?"

"CAROLINE ADKINS, where can I find her?" Max had no idea how he'd gotten from the road outside the site to the hospital information desk.

"Is she a patient, sir?" the grandmotherly lady in a pink pinafore asked, smiling benignly at him.

"She was in an accident. They said they're holding her for observation."

"How would you spell that last name?"

Quelling the urge to grab the little old lady by the daintily tied bow at her neck, he spelled Caroline's name.

"She's on the fourth floor. Room 482."

Max was running for the elevator before the lady ever finished talking. After stepping into the first one available, he jammed the close door button after punching the number four.

He'd find Caroline—and this time she wasn't going to get away. Not until he had an explanation.

As soon as he got out of the elevator, he halted a nurse pushing a trolly of trays.

"Which way to 482?" he demanded.

"Just down the hall, sir."

With a hurried thank-you, he followed her direction and spotted the room up ahead of him. He pushed past a small group of people and reached the door.

"Just one minute!"

He looked over his shoulder to see a large man in both height and girth staring at him. "Yes?"

"Where are you going?"

"What business is it of yours?" he demanded.

"That's my daughter's room."

Max checked to see if he had the right room number. He did. "The desk said this was Caroline Adkins's room. I think you've made a mistake." He was sure Caroline didn't have anyone close by, much less a mob of people.

"I don't make mistakes!"

Max shrugged his shoulders and pushed open the door.

The man grabbed his arm before he could take more than a step into the room. "Who are you and why are you visiting my daughter? Are you the one who hit her?"

"I'm not visiting your daughter. I'm visiting Caroline Adkins," Max explained impatiently. "If this isn't her room—"

"Why would we come here if it's not Caroline's room?" Amelia asked plaintively.

"Sir, I think you're making a mistake," a younger man in an elegant business suit said, and Max glared at him. The young lady in the group began complaining about feeling faint. A man quickly supported her, and Max turned back toward the room only to find himself confronted by a man in a white coat.

"What is going on here?" he asked with quiet authority.

"I'm here to visit Caroline Adkins," Max explained.

Immediately behind him, several voices both protested his visit and demanded information about Caroline. What was wrong with these people? Max couldn't figure out why they were there. As far as he knew, Caroline had just moved to the area and had no one nearby.

"Quiet," the doctor commanded. The one word quelled even the older man who'd been protesting his presence, Max noted.

"You may all see Caroline, but she has a headache. Please keep quiet and don't ask her any questions."

Max frowned. He could wait for his questions to be answered, as long as he didn't lose her again. He *couldn't* lose her again.

THE SUDDEN NOISE at the door of her room had increased the pain in her head. The nurse touched her shoulder and smiled, silently encouraging her to relax.

Oh, sure. It was easy for the nurse. She hadn't lost her memory. She knew her name. And if she forgot, it was right there on her name tag.

The doctor had told her her name was Caroline. But there was no sense of recognition, no satisfaction. Just confusion. And, as much as she fought it, panic.

All she knew was what she'd been told since she'd awakened in the hospital. There'd been a wreck, a hit and run, and she'd smacked her head on the windshield even though she'd worn her seat belt. Her purse had been beside her, giving the doctor her name. He said he'd called her family.

If her family was making all the noise, she wasn't sure she wanted to see them. At least not yet.

Suddenly her bed was surrounded by people.

People.

But no one she knew.

She hadn't realized how much she'd hoped she would recognize her family when they arrived until that moment. You'd think she could at least recall her parents. Even though she could identify the two likeliest suspects by their age, her mouth went dry at the blankness that filled her.

Her gaze shifted to the first one who'd entered, seeking a distraction. He was somehow different from the rest of them. Rugged. And very attractive. *I don't know who I am, but at least I know what I like.*

She hurriedly looked away as a horrible thought struck her.

What if he was her brother?

The older man stepped forward and picked up her hand.

"Caroline, are you okay?"

She said faintly, "Yes, I'm fine."

As if he didn't believe her, he looked at the doctor.

"Are you Mr. Adkins?" the doctor asked.

"Yes."

"I'm Dr. Johansen. Your daughter is in good condition, considering the accident."

"Fine, fine. When can I take her home?"

She couldn't help the panicked gaze she sent to the doctor. These people were all strangers. She didn't want to go with them.

Before the doctor could answer, the older lady pushed through the crowd to the side of the bed. "You're fine, aren't you, Caroline? I know you wouldn't have asked me to leave my meeting. I told your father that, and Agnes agreed."

The younger woman groaned. "Mother, do you have to repeat everything Agnes says? Besides, I'm the one who shouldn't have come. After all, I'm expecting."

Caroline frowned. The young lady announced her condition as if she were the first pregnant woman in the world. As her lips quirked slightly, Caroline discovered something new about herself. She had a sense of humor. *Thank goodness. I'd hate to live with these people and not know how to laugh.*

She looked at the four men who hadn't spoken. Three of them were in expensive business suits. The other man, the one who'd first caught her attention, was dressed in jeans and a short sleeved shirt. He was slightly taller than the others, and his muscled figure was bronzed from the sun.

He opened his mouth, as if to speak, when the doctor said, "I understand how much you'd like to take her home at once, but, in her condition, I think we should keep her overnight for observation."

"I thought you said she was okay," the man in blue jeans snapped. Caroline liked the anxious look he sent the doctor.

"She is. But with the baby—"

"Oh, that's all right. I don't live at home anymore. She won't bother me," the young woman told the doctor with a superior air. "My husband and I have our own home, quite lovely, just a few blocks away from Daddy."

Dr. Johansen looked nonplussed, the first time he'd been stumped since Caroline met him after she'd awakened. Finally he said, "I think you misunderstood me. I wasn't referring to your baby, young lady, but Caroline's. She's pregnant."

In the silence that followed his explanation, Caroline moved her hand to her stomach, unable to believe the doctor's words. Pregnant? She couldn't be. Could she? Oh, dear, what had she gotten herself into?

And with whom?

A look at the shocked faces around her told her that no one else had known.

Then the young woman whimpered. "I should've known. I should've known you'd go out and get pregnant just to spite me. You always think you have to be better than me!" She broke into sobs, burying her face in the suit jacket of one of the younger men.

"Oh, no, dear, no. This is all my fault," said the woman she supposed was her mother.

The man who claimed to be her father turned to stare at the woman. "What are you talking about, Amelia?"

Amelia? Her mother's name was Amelia?

"I should never have asked Caroline to work in the unwed mother's home. It's my fault."

"Amelia, pregnancy isn't contagious, either!" the man ranted, his face turning red.

Caroline almost felt sorry for him. He seemed surrounded by some very strange people.

Dr. Johansen spoke again. "I apologize. I didn't realize you didn't know about the pregnancy. Of course, she's only two months along, but usually—"

"Two months?" Mr. Blue Jeans asked sharply.

"Yes, but—"

"I demand to know who the father is," the older man suddenly exclaimed, glaring at everyone in the room. In that tone of voice, Caroline was sure he was always obeyed.

She was right.

Three men stepped forward, each of them staring at her, and, in unison, as if rehearsed, said, "I am."

Chapter Two

She was sleeping with three men? At the same time? What kind of woman was she?

Caroline stared at each of those who'd claimed parentage to her child. No flicker of recognition arose. She was debating what her response should be when everyone else in the room spoke for her.

"I don't understand," Amelia said, a puzzled look on her brow.

"Well, I do! Caroline, how disgusting," her sister said, staring down her nose at Caroline.

"That's impossible!" James Adkins roared. "You couldn't be the father of her child!"

Caroline frowned as she realized her father was only speaking to the odd man out, the one in blue jeans. Her father didn't have a problem with the other two men claiming to be the father of her child? What qualified them? The fact that they were wearing suits?

After directing a glare at her father, the man turned to look at Caroline. She found herself swallowed up by his burning gaze.

"Oh, yes, I certainly could," he said, with no doubt in his voice.

If it were a matter of attraction, she'd accept his word,

hands down, she realized. But it wasn't. "Who are you?"
she asked.

There was a flash of disappointment in his gaze, but it
disappeared almost at once. "Max Daniels."

"We—we dated?"

"Briefly."

"Caroline, the man is obviously after your money. I'll
get rid of him," James Adkins promised, and then motioned to the other two daddy candidates.

She didn't know who she was, or who these people
were, but she did know she didn't take kindly to being
overruled. "I don't think that decision is yours to make."

The uproar her assertion of independence brought from
her father, the other two men, even her mother and sister,
was enough to make Caroline's headache feel like a vol-
canic eruption.

Even in pain, however, she noticed that the center of
the controversy, Mr. Blue Jeans, shot her a look of approval. Well, he needn't think he was home free. She
wasn't about to take a stranger's word about such an
important matter.

She was struck by the irony of calling the man a
stranger when he might be the father of her child.

"I asked you not to question or upset her," Dr.
Johansen interrupted. "You'll all have to leave now."

Though they didn't go quietly, the doctor herded the
visitors from the room and left Caroline in peace.

As much peace as one could have, pregnant without
knowing who the father might be.

Could she really have been sleeping with three men?
Was she the kind of woman who hopped from bed to
bed? Revulsion filled her and she wanted to believe that
was not possible. But then why were three men claiming
to be the daddy?

She recalled her father's remark, that Max Daniels was only after her money. Once the pregnancy had been revealed, she hadn't thought about her life before the accident. She was wealthy? Not that she objected. Not having to worry about paying hospital bills would be an advantage.

But she needed answers! She wanted to reclaim her life, to understand what was happening to her. And most of all, she wanted to know which man had made love to her two months ago. And heaven help her if it was more than one.

"ARE YOU ALL PACKED?" the nurse asked cheerfully, coming into her room the next morning.

Caroline murmured yes, not bothering to point out she had almost nothing to pack. She didn't move her head, however. Even after twenty-four hours, it felt fragile. "Is—is my father here?"

She still wasn't comfortable with James Adkins, or the other members of her family. Or even with herself, for that matter. She'd looked in a mirror and seen a stranger. A pregnant stranger.

That thought had been brought home to her when she'd gotten up this morning. Morning sickness, heightened by her concussion, the nurse had said, had attacked her. What little breakfast she'd eaten had come right back up.

Women go through this more than once? Voluntarily? The nurse had reassured her that her sickness was perfectly normal in the circumstances.

"He called earlier to let us know he was picking you up at ten. It's almost that now. I'll bring a cart for the flowers."

Her father had flooded her room with floral arrangements. Even more interesting had been the offerings from two of the men claiming to have fathered her baby. Long-stemmed red roses. Two dozen apiece.

Nothing from Max Daniels.

"Why don't you pass the flowers out among the sick?" Caroline said. "I think that might be easier than carting them all home." *Wherever that was.*

"That's very generous of you. I have several patients who never receive flowers." The nurse smiled.

"Then I hope they enjoy these."

Footsteps near the door had her turning around carefully. But it was neither the doctor nor her father. Her heartbeat picked up speed as she stared at Max Daniels.

How could she have forgotten making love to this man? He was certainly handsome, but there was something more—a connection she couldn't explain—that took her breath away. She noted he was again in jeans, this time coupled with a starched plaid shirt, and he held a bouquet of daisies in his hand.

"Good morning," he said.

She responded and waited, watching him. His eyes, as blue as the sky, looked wary, as if he weren't sure of his welcome. The nurse slipped from the room, murmuring something about fetching a cart. Left alone with him, Caroline's mouth went dry as she stared at the gorgeous man in front of her. The urge to touch him almost consumed her. When Max continued to say nothing, she asked in desperation, "Are those for me?"

He held the flowers out to her. "Yeah." His gaze took in the roses and carnations that filled the room. "You told me you liked daisies."

If she hadn't before, she did now. If Max Daniels delivered them. "I do, thank you. That's very thoughtful of you."

"Has your memory returned?" He took a step closer, his gaze intent.

She started to shake her head and then stopped. The headache hovering on the edge of consciousness edged closer with any radical movement. "No, it hasn't."

He thrust the flowers into her hands and stepped back. "Then how can I get a phone number where I can reach you? I'd like to stay in touch."

"You don't have it?" *Some relationship they must've had. If he was telling the truth.*

"No. If I'd had it, I would've found you a lot sooner," he said gruffly, a fierceness entering his gaze that had her stepping back.

Either the movement, or the puzzle that was her life at the moment, pushed the headache out of control. She reached for her forehead with her free hand, clasping the daisies to her breast with the other.

"Are you all right?"

"I need to sit down," she said faintly, and he guided her to the only chair. As she was sinking into it, her head lolling back against the top of it, the door to her room was pushed open.

"What are you doing to my daughter?" a booming voice demanded.

Caroline dropped the flowers into her lap and pressed both hands to her throbbing temples. "Please—"

Without answering her father's question, Max walked to the bed and pressed the nurse's button.

"I'm sorry, Caro, I didn't mean to make your head hurt," James Adkins hurriedly apologized, and then glared at Max, as if it were Max's fault he had yelled.

"Yes?" the nurse asked as she came back into the room.

"Ms. Adkins's headache has come back," Max said softly. "Is there anything you can give her for it?"

"It never went away," Caroline contradicted him.

"Because of the baby, we can't give her a painkiller. She just needs to have peace and quiet." The nurse glared accusingly at the two men.

"I'm here to take her home," her father said stiffly. "I don't know why *he's* here."

"Well, she needs to be back in bed as soon as possible. The doctor's on the way up to release her." She backed out of the room, still frowning at Caroline's visitors.

"He wants my phone number," Caroline told her father. "Would you give it to him, please? I don't remember it. And get his." Stupid statement. No one would expect her to remember a phone number when she couldn't even remember her shoe size.

But she didn't want to lose Max Daniels. Her reaction to him told her he had to be the one—the father of her baby. The love of her life? Frustration filled her—and not a little panic. What if she never remembered? What if—

Her father disrupted her fears by glaring at Max again and moving closer to her chair to say in a stage whisper obviously intended for Max's ears, "Caroline, I'm not sure that's wise. We only have his say-so that you two were—you know."

Caroline rolled her eyes. Great. Next her father would want to explain the birds and the bees. "Intimate. That's the word. Please give him my phone number."

Max stepped forward, ignoring her father, and extended a business card to her. "Both my work and home numbers are on this card. Call me if there's anything I can do for you—or anything."

"You've already done too much, according to you!" her father growled.

Max's lips—those enticing lips—flattened tightly against each other, and Caroline had the strangest urge to tease them into a smile. As attracted as she was to Max Daniels, if he was the father of her child, she felt sure she had put up no resistance whatsoever to any intimacy between them. In fact, *she* may have seduced *him*.

But what about the other two men who claimed to be the daddy? She wished she could rule them out, but she reluctantly admitted she couldn't. She'd read about women who carried on with more than one man, but— she had?

Distracted by a memory, even an insignificant one, she lost track of the men's conversation. It was such a relief to remember something, even though it was useless for solving her problems.

"Look, Mr. Adkins," Max said, moving closer to the older man, "what happened is between Caroline and me. What's her phone number?"

"It's unlisted."

"I figured that. I called all the Adkinses as I could find in the telephone book."

That remark snapped her from her thoughts. "You did?"

"You disappeared without saying goodbye. I wanted to know why." His expression said he blamed her for her unexplained departure.

She'd like to know why she'd gone away, too. Why would she leave someone she was obviously attracted to? Had she found out some deep, dark secret? Or was his entire story a lie?

"She probably realized she was in love with Prescott or Adrian. She came back to them, didn't she?" James offered.

Her father's interpretation of past events might not be

quite reliable, Caroline decided. He seemed intent on persuading her that one of the other men was the mysterious father.

"By the way, where *are* the Bobbsey twins?" she asked.

Max choked and tried to hide a chuckle behind one of his big hands. Her gaze remained fixed on his crinkling blue eyes, hoping for a glimpse of his smile.

"Caroline! You shouldn't call them such a thing. They're down in the limo, waiting. They wanted to come up here, but I assured them we'd be right down." James glared at Max again.

"They really came?" She'd only been teasing, hoping to lighten the moment.

"Of course. They're very concerned about you." He waved to the roses on each side of her bed. "After all, they sent you roses, a lot more expensive than those daisies."

In spite of her headache, Caroline smelled a rat and asked, "How do you know the roses came from them?"

"Well, I thought— I suggested— It was just a guess." He blundered to a stop.

As if it were a natural occurrence, her gaze flew to Max's and they shared a smile, a glorious smile that she'd been waiting to see. She took a deep breath of appreciation. The guy was as sexy as could be. She wondered what he'd look like without his shirt.

"Caroline!" Her father was obviously irritated at her distraction.

"Please, my head."

Both the doctor and the nurse returned to her room at that moment, the nurse pushing a flower cart.

"All ready to go, Caroline?" Dr. Johansen asked cheerfully.

"Yes, I guess so. But my headache is getting worse again."

"Hmm. Probably the excitement of getting out of here. I don't know why people react to hospitals that way," he teased as he picked up her wrist to take her pulse.

The door opened again to admit the two men her father called Adrian and Prescott. "James? We thought we'd better come up in case you needed help," Prescott said, his gaze sweeping the room. When it landed on Max, he stepped closer to James.

Interesting, Caroline decided. *He goes to my father's side, not mine.* Adrian, the second one, kind of hovered between her father and her, as if undecided about where his loyalties lay. As they moved, Caroline looked closely at them. They were both handsome, in a conventional manner. Adrian was blond, but a little too smooth for her tastes. Prescott was darker and slightly shorter, but neither stirred her as Max did.

"What's *he* doing here?" Prescott demanded, disdainfully waving his hand toward Max.

"He never left," Caroline rapidly answered, not happy with Prescott's attitude. What business was it of his if Max wanted to visit her? "We spent the entire night together."

Everyone except Max and the doctor gasped, staring at her. Then a babble of protests made her regret her short-tempered response. "Just kidding, just kidding," she said, raising her hand to halt their noise.

"Caroline's headache is back. Too much noise is bad for it," Max said calmly.

Prescott glared at Max, but Adrian moved closer to Caroline. "Is there anything I can do?"

"Yes. Do you know my phone number?" she asked.

"Why, certainly. Your private line or your father's?"

"Mine."

He said her telephone number, and Caroline smiled as Max took a pen from his shirt pocket and wrote it down on one of his business cards. His sexy grin was her thank-you.

"I'm not sure that was wise, Caroline," Prescott said, echoing her father's earlier warning.

"I may not remember too much about my past, but I know I don't like people bossing me around, whoever I am. If you know me well, Prescott, you must already be aware of that trait."

During their conversation, the nurse had pushed the flower cart out the door and returned with a wheelchair. "Is she ready, Doctor?"

"I believe she is. She may not be up to full fighting weight just yet, but I think she can handle this crew," Dr. Johansen said with a smile at Caroline. "I suspect you've already seen a doctor about your pregnancy, but if not, set up an appointment as soon as possible. And let me know if the headache doesn't gradually diminish."

"Gradually?" she protested.

"I'm afraid so, Caroline. Don't get too agitated for a while. Rest and sleep. That's the cure."

"Thank you, Doctor."

He excused himself and the nurse pushed the wheelchair to her side and then took her arm. "Okay, lean on me. On the count of three, we'll move to the chair."

Caroline would have preferred Max's help, but if she asked for it, Prescott would probably knock both of them over trying to reach her first. She stood and stepped over to the wheelchair. A sudden hand on her other arm needed no identification. The responsive surge of attraction told her it was Max. She smiled up at him once she was settled. "Thanks."

"I would've helped. You should've asked me," Prescott complained.

She almost groaned aloud. If Prescott was the father of her baby, she could expect a whiner and probably the biggest brownnoser in existence. What a depressing thought.

"Well, let's be on our way," her father said abruptly, swinging around to the door. His two satellites fell into step behind him.

Caroline wasn't quite ready. She wanted an excuse to touch Max one more time. Reaching out her hand, she said, "Thank you for the daisies."

He took her hand in his. "My pleasure." Then he leaned down and briefly caressed her lips with his. Her pulse throbbed. Good thing she was going to get some rest before she saw him again. Otherwise, she just might explode with all the excitement.

As if realizing something had occurred behind their backs, the other three men turned and stared at the two of them.

"Are you coming, Caroline?" James demanded.

"Yes, I'm right behind you, Dad," she answered, a smile on her face for Max Daniels. He remained in the room as the nurse pushed her out, her daisies clutched to her chest.

DAMN. Max stood alone in the hospital room and drew a deep breath. He shouldn't have kissed her. But he hadn't been able to resist. Even as pale as she was this morning, with a bruise on her forehead, Caroline was beautiful.

He'd only had two short weeks with her, but he'd missed her every day since she'd gone. Even though he called himself all kinds of a fool for still wanting her.

The two weeks they'd spent together seemed like a

dream now, with a nightmare ending when she disappeared. He'd already been making plans for their future together. Plans that were aborted when she left.

She'd told him she was from Kansas City and had just moved to Denver. At first, she'd said she was looking for a job. He'd offered to introduce her to the interior design firms he used, had even told her who to contact. It wasn't until after she left that he realized she'd never looked for a job.

Hell, he hadn't given her time. He'd spent every moment he could with her. He couldn't leave her alone. And he'd been making plans to keep her with him forever.

And now that he'd discovered she was an heiress, he knew they had no future together. Even if the baby was his. Her father wasn't going to let her marry him. Not when there were two superstar executives waiting with open arms.

Max wasn't even sure why he still wanted her. After all, everything she'd told him was a lie. Now he understood the old saying, ignorance is bliss. Those two weeks had certainly been blissful.

But if their two weeks had resulted in a baby, his baby, then he refused to be pushed out of the picture. He would not abandon his own child.

He shook himself from his misery. Feeling sorry for himself had never been his style. Instead, he formulated a plan and set about changing his circumstances.

Maybe that was what had frustrated him so about Caroline. He'd followed every lead he'd had, but he'd discovered nothing about her.

He reached the outer door of the hospital just in time to see a white limo pull away from the hospital. At least this time he had her telephone number. Now all he had to do was come up with a plan.

"WAIT!" PRESCOTT CALLED to the driver as they pulled out of the hospital parking lot.

Caroline rubbed her forehead. "Please don't shout."

"But we've forgotten your flowers. That damned nurse probably thought she could get away with stealing them. Turn around and go back."

"No!" Caroline contradicted. "Take us home, Lewis."

The chauffeur, much to Caroline's satisfaction, obeyed her.

"Caroline!" her father exclaimed. "How did you know?"

"What?" Her head hurt so much. She wasn't sure she could remain upright until they reached the house.

"His name. You knew his name."

"You must have said it," she replied, frowning, trying to think.

"No, I didn't. Your memory is returning!" he exclaimed happily. "That's wonderful. I'll give that doctor a bonus. Now," he said, pausing to lean toward her, "which of these gentlemen is the father of your baby?"

Immediately the headache increased.

"I haven't gotten my memory back. I don't know how I knew his name." She leaned her head back against the seat and closed her eyes. "I'm in so much pain."

"And I don't understand about the flowers. Didn't you like them?" Prescott grumbled.

"They were lovely. But there were so many of them I asked the nurse to distribute them to others who weren't going home. It seemed like the generous thing to do."

"It was, and just like you, Caroline," Adrian said as he smiled at her.

"Was it?" she asked coolly, leery of his friendliness. She decided his gray eyes were cold, even if his lips were smiling. And who knew if he was telling the truth? All she knew about herself so far was that she liked her own way, hated headaches, was pregnant, and apparently didn't mind sleeping with more than one man.

That couldn't be true. She never liked to share. In high school, her boyfriend had thought he could date her and her best friend at the same time. She'd shown him.

Another memory. She clutched it to her like a precious jewel. But when she tried to extend that grasp on the past, searching for other memories, she drew a blank. Frustration filled her.

"If you were so generous with the roses, why are you still holding those?" Prescott complained, gesturing to the daisies.

"Because I like them."

He turned to glare at her father. "You said roses!" he accused. He sounded like a little boy, but his thinning hair showed him to be considerably beyond his youth.

If she'd needed confirmation that the roses had been sent at her father's behest, his remark was it. She shot her father a knowing look.

"I was just trying to speed things up. I don't want my grandchild born a bastard, so I suggest you select one of these fine gentlemen to marry you. They're both willing."

"And are you going to speak the words for them as they mime a proposal?" she asked, growing tired of her father's arguments.

"That's not necessary, Caroline, darling," Prescott said, rushing in, as she should've known he would. She might not remember him, but she knew more about him than she wanted to already.

"I'm perfectly willing to marry you today if you'll agree," he continued, reaching for her hand.

She pulled her hands back. "No, thank you. I have a headache."

Not an original excuse...for a lot of things, but it was the best she could come up with right now.

"I'd prefer to make my proposal in private," Adrian informed her, sending a superior smile toward Prescott.

She'd prefer that he not make it at all. "Thank you, but I'm confused right now. I don't think I'm ready to make any decisions."

"Of course, but you won't forget?" There was an edge to his voice that irritated her.

"I hope not." It seemed to Caroline that a promise not to forget from an amnesiac victim wouldn't be worth much. *She* wouldn't believe her.

"Of course she won't forget," her father answered heartily. "And if she does, the three of us will be there to remind her. After all, she has to marry someone."

"No, I don't."

"Now, Caroline, no argument. I'm an old-fashioned man, and I expect my grandchild to be born on the right side of the blanket."

She ignored him.

"And if you don't cooperate, you just might find yourself written out of my will."

She might not have her memory, but the ease with which her father uttered those words made her suspect it was a threat he'd used before.

"Then call your lawyer, because *I* will decide what I do about *my* baby and *my* future. Not you."

The look of panic on Prescott's face that she might be written out of the will told Caroline her threat may have eliminated at least one potential daddy candidate. Whether her memory returned or not.

Chapter Three

Caroline stared in awe at the magnificent residence the limo stopped in front of, after having driven through a large gate flanked by brick walls. It must take an army of workers to maintain the lush grounds, she decided, her gaze traveling over the perfect flower beds, the exactly trimmed hedges.

She turned to compliment her father on the beauty of their home only to discover everyone staring at her. She felt like a bug under a microscope.

"No, I don't remember," she assured them dryly. "I'll let you know when my memory returns."

All three looked away.

"Why did Prescott and Adrian come with you to pick me up instead of my mother?" Caroline suddenly asked, struck by the presence of these men rather than family members.

"Friday is Save the Whales day," her father muttered.

"I beg your pardon?"

Adrian leaned forward to explain. "Your mother is quite involved in the local charities. On Fridays, she goes to the meeting for saving the whales."

Caroline remembered a curious remark from the day before. "And one of her charities is for unwed mothers?"

"Yes," her father snapped.

Caroline asked no more questions. Not yet.

Her father escorted her into the house and introduced her to the housekeeper, Mrs. Lamb, and then left for the office, accompanied by Prescott and Adrian.

"Welcome home, Caroline. Are you feeling all right?"

"I'm still a little shaky. If you'll show me to my room, I'll lie down for a while."

"Why, honey, there's no need to be formal!" the woman said with a laugh that sent a shooting pain through Caroline's head. "You know better'n me where your room is."

Her patience was wearing thin. Amnesia might play a large role in a lot of jokes, but she wasn't finding it funny. "Mrs. Lamb, I have amnesia. I don't remember ever seeing this house before."

"Oh, my stars. Of course, Caroline. You just come this way. Anything you want to know, you just ask me."

If her head weren't splitting into a chasm the size of the Grand Canyon, she might have taken the woman up on the offer. Later. She only had one question at the moment.

"If I want to invite someone to dinner, is that all right?"

"Of course it is. Just tell me when and how many."

Caroline took a deep breath before she clarified her request. "I meant if I wanted to have a guest for dinner and—and not dine with the family."

"Oh, of course, you want something romanticlike? No problem. It's nice out at night right now. I could set up a table for two on the patio. You'd be all alone there."

"That would be perfect. Thank you, Mrs. Lamb. I'll let you know when."

"Sure enough. I'm just having a little trouble with you

being so formal and all. When you wanted something real special from me, you always used to call me Lambie.'' The woman smiled with a warmth that struck Caroline as the kindest she'd seen since she awoke a lost person.

She reached out and touched Mrs. Lamb's arm. ''I'm sorry. I'm sure I'll remember everything soon. If you'll just be patient.''

''Of course I will. I'm just glad you weren't hurt bad.''

''Thank you.''

She followed the housekeeper up a wide staircase, down a long hall to the last door on the right.

''Your room looks out over the pool.''

She pushed open the door and Caroline stepped into the room. She stared around her, her eyes wide. ''Who decorated it?''

''Why, you did, Caroline, about two years ago. You don't remember? Oh, my stars, what a silly question. Forgive me, child. Now look, here's the phone and if you want anything, you just pick it up and press this button. Okay? I'll be in the kitchen.'' With a flush of embarrassment on her cheeks, Mrs. Lamb fled the room.

Though she moved about the room, searching for clues to who Caroline Adkins might be, she also recognized a sense of contentment gradually filling her. It felt as if she had finally found a sanctuary from the maze her life had become.

Maybe it's all the blue. I've always been partial to blue. She had taken several more steps before she realized she'd remembered something else about herself. Yes, she'd always liked blues. And bright colors.

With a sigh she pulled back the coverlet on the king-size bed and sank down amid a huge collection of pillows. She'd worry about who she was, what she'd done, later. Now, she needed to rest her aching head.

Caroline awoke several hours later, consciousness gradually returning. But not her memory. She let her gaze sweep the room, looking for clues to who she really was. With a sigh, she sat up.

The rest had given her the energy to indulge her curiosity a little more. After washing her face in the luxurious connecting bath, she returned to the bedroom and opened the closet door.

A ripple of pleasure ran through her as she examined the rows of clothes hung neatly in the large closet. *My, I have great taste...and expensive, too.* She recognized designer names on many of the dresses.

Since she couldn't remember buying or wearing any of the outfits, it was like having an entire new wardrobe. She wouldn't have to shop for months.

Wrong.

How could she forget the baby?

And the changes that would occur in the next few months. She groaned. Even the clothes she was wearing were a little snug, uncomfortably so. Before too long, they wouldn't fit her at all, and she'd have to start shopping all over again.

Not necessarily an unhappy thought, she realized with a grin. What woman didn't enjoy a little shopping? Sliding her hands into the pockets of her navy slacks, she felt the card Max Daniels had given her.

Resolution filled her. She had something more important than shopping to do right now. It was time to take back her life. And she would start with Max Daniels. She ignored the thought that she was starting with him because she *wanted him* to be the father of her child. She had to start somewhere.

She crossed the room to the telephone.

"Daniels Vacation Homes."

Caroline frowned at the sexy female voice that answered the phone. "I'm calling Max Daniels."

"Max is out of the office at the moment. May I take a message?"

"This is Caroline Adkins. I need to—"

"He just came in. One moment, please."

"Caroline?"

She released a sigh at the sound of his voice. It was as if she'd feared she wouldn't find him again. With no memory to support their relationship, she only had those few minutes at the hospital.

"Hi, Max. I—I wanted to invite you to dinner."

The silence that followed her request left a hollow feeling in her stomach.

"To dinner?" he finally asked.

"Yes." When he said nothing else, she asked, "Is that an odd request? Do you not eat?"

"Of course I eat, but you never even admitted you had family in the area, much less offered to introduce me." There was an antagonism in his voice.

"Look, I don't remember what I did…or why. I'm just trying to figure out what happened. I thought I'd start with you. If you don't want to talk to me, then say so." She could match his reluctance any day, she assured herself. Especially if she didn't think about him.

"Of course I want to talk to you. I want to know what happened as much as you do. And whether the baby is mine."

The doubt in his voice was like a blow. "You sounded a lot surer of that fact yesterday."

"That's before I realized I was one of a crowd."

Even as anger filled her, it was tempered by understanding. "It came as a shock to me, too." When he said nothing else, she asked, "Did I ever mention anyone else?"

"No. Like I said, I thought you had recently moved here. That you knew no one."

This discussion was going nowhere. She returned to her original question. "Will you come to dinner? I need to ask you a lot of questions." She didn't intend to plead, but she recognized a hint of persuasiveness in her voice.

"Tell me when."

"Tonight?"

"I can't. I've already made an appointment with prospective clients."

He could've sounded a *little* unhappy that he couldn't come right away. "Tomorrow night?"

Letting out a gusty sigh, he agreed. "What time?"

"Seven o'clock. And would you mind not sounding so put upon? I have no intention of torturing you!" she snapped, any patience she might normally have had having disintegrated between her headache and her heartache.

"It's too late. You already have." He hung up without waiting for a response.

"Oh yeah?" she yelled into the dead phone. "Well, just wait until tomorrow night!"

How dare that man act as if she'd intentionally hurt him? She was suffering just as much as him.

Recalling her bout with morning sickness, she decided she was suffering more. She strode to the closet and her wonderful new wardrobe. He thought he'd been tortured before? She'd make sure the torture continued.

"Caroline?" Mrs. Lamb called softly, rapping on the door before opening it. "Oh!" she exclaimed as Caroline appeared at the closet door.

"Hi. Did you need something?"

"I have a luncheon tray for you," the housekeeper explained, pushing the door open and stepping inside.

"I could've come downstairs," Caroline assured her.

"You're always so thoughtful, child, but you need your rest. What are you doing out of bed?"

"Trying to decide which outfit is my most killer one."

"Killer?" Mrs. Lamb's face was a perfect picture of puzzlement.

"Don't worry. I'm not plotting a murder. I don't think. I'm wanting to, uh, look my best. By the way, my dinner guest is coming tomorrow night. Is that okay?"

"Sure is. Do I know him?"

"His name is Max Daniels." Caroline studied the housekeeper's expression, but she saw no sign of recognition. "You've never heard of him?"

"No. Should I have?"

"He's one of the three... Has anyone told you I'm pregnant?"

Mrs. Lamb almost dropped the tray and Caroline rushed forward to support her.

"Oh, my stars. Are you serious? I can't believe it. Isn't that wonderful? You and Chelsea will have babies almost the same age. I—who's the father?"

Mrs. Lamb's abrupt question showed her sudden awareness of Caroline's situation. With a self-conscious shrug, Caroline said, "I don't know. The amnesia."

"Well, surely he'll come forward. I mean, a man should be responsible for his actions."

"That's the problem," Caroline replied. "Three men have claimed responsibility for—for my baby."

"Three? Oh, my stars! Caroline!"

Taking the shaking tray from the housekeeper's hands, Caroline set it on the lamp table. "Lambie, I need help."

"Why, I'll do whatever I—I don't see how—I mean, what are you going to do?"

"I need to find out what was going on in my life two months ago."

As if her knees had collapsed, Mrs. Lamb sank onto the bed. "Oh, my stars."

"What's the matter?"

"Two months ago? A little over two months ago, you had a fight with your father."

"A fight? What about?"

"I don't know. But the next morning, you called a taxi, and you left."

"A taxi? I don't have a car?"

"Of course you have a car. A Mercedes. Your father insisted, saying they were the safest. He buys you a new one every year."

She kept her feelings about her father's domination to herself. "Then why a taxi?"

"I don't know. You had a bag packed and you hugged me, saying not to worry, you were going on a vacation."

"Did I tell you where I was going?"

"No. You left a note for your father, but it didn't tell him anything, 'cause he questioned me."

She had some questions for her father the next time she saw him, too. "Did I call you after I left? And how long was I gone?"

"You called once and told me you were having a good time. And you left a message for your father."

"What message?"

Mrs. Lamb screwed up her face, as if trying to remember, and finally said, "You said you were proving him wrong."

Caroline stared at her. "That's it? Nothing for my mother?"

With a surprised look on her face, Mrs. Lamb said, "Why, no. You don't—I mean, you love your mother, of course, but Mrs. Adkins is so busy..." She trailed off and looked away.

"I see. And when I came back? Did I ever say where I'd been or what I'd done?"

"No. But you seemed sad. Once I found you crying, and that's unusual for you. Why, as a little girl, you'd fall and hurt yourself, but you'd never cry. Unlike Chelsea. Chelsea learned to shed tears whenever she wanted something. Tears just drive your father up the wall."

Caroline could believe that. But she wanted more information about herself, not her father or her sister. "Did I explain why I was crying?"

"No."

"Did I receive any strange phone calls? Or letters?" But she remembered Max asking for her telephone number. He wouldn't have called her.

"No."

"Did I date anyone after I came back?"

"You would go to social events with Adrian and Prescott. You did that before you left, too."

"Social events?"

"You know, to the Save the Whales dinner and dance, the opera, the symphony opening night. There was a real nice picture in the paper yesterday of you and Adrian."

"Why?" Caroline demanded, suddenly afraid she might have announced her engagement.

"You were dancing at the opera ball."

Caroline sat down beside Mrs. Lamb, feeling a little weak herself. And her head was beginning to ache. Again.

"You'd better eat some lunch, child. You don't look too well. And you've got a baby to think about now."

Caroline smiled faintly. It was too easy to forget that she was carrying a child inside her, since she couldn't remember the event that had brought it about. But Mrs. Lamb was right. She needed to eat.

"Let's take the tray back downstairs. I've had enough eating in bed to last me awhile."

And she needed to calm down again before she faced her father. He had some explaining to do.

SHE DIDN'T GET TO ASK her father any questions that night. Long before he'd returned from the office, she'd gone to bed, exhausted. Her mother had gotten home around four, but her vagueness made Caroline wonder if she even remembered that her daughter had come home from the hospital that day.

Even so, Caroline tried to question her at the dinner table that evening.

"Uh, Mother?"

"Yes, dear?" Amelia replied distractedly, examining the salad she was eating.

"Do you know why I argued with my father?"

"Did you? I have no idea, dear. You argue with him frequently, even though I tell you you shouldn't." She took a bite of salad and chewed it consideringly. "I don't think Mrs. Lamb is using a dietetic dressing, even though I asked her to."

"Please think, Mother. It's important."

"I know it is. I gained two pounds last month, and I'm sure it's the salad dressing."

"No, I mean arguing with—with my father." She had no idea what she normally called him.

Amelia looked at her blankly. "About what? Was he difficult when he picked you up?"

"No, not today," Caroline said, hoping her patience

could withstand more conversation with her mother. "Mrs. Lamb said that I had a fight with him a little over two months ago, and then I left."

"Did you? Where did you go?"

Caroline sighed. "I don't know. Didn't you notice I was gone?"

"Hmm. Two months ago? I think that's when I went to that spa in Arizona." She laid down her fork and rang the dinner bell that rested on the table by her plate.

Mrs. Lamb opened the door that led to the kitchen. "Yes, ma'am?"

"Mrs. Lamb, didn't I go to that spa at the end of June?" Amelia asked.

"Was that when I left, while Mother was at the spa?" Caroline added, hoping to clarify matters.

"That's right. Your mother left the day before you did."

"Where did Caroline go, Mrs. Lamb? She wants to know."

The housekeeper looked at Caroline and then her mother. "I don't know, ma'am. She didn't say."

"Thank you, Mrs. Lamb," Caroline said, dismissing the woman before her mother remembered the salad dressing.

A call to her sister didn't produce any better results.

"I have no time to keep up with your social schedule, Caroline. You disappeared just after I announced my pregnancy. I assumed you had left in a fit of jealousy. But I had no idea you'd go so far as to get pregnant yourself. Couldn't you let me be first in *something?*"

Having determined that her sister knew nothing about those lost two weeks, Caroline quickly smoothed her feathers and hung up the phone. Mrs. Lamb confirmed that her father had called and would be working late, which seemed to be a common occurrence.

No wonder no one knew anything. They barely saw each other. All of them together in her hospital room must have been their version of a family reunion. And not a very happy one.

Caroline crawled into bed and rested on the pillow, hoping its softness would soothe her head.

Tomorrow.

Tomorrow she would confront her father. Tomorrow she would ask more questions, find out about those elusive two weeks.

Tomorrow, she would see Max again.

Chapter Four

The first dress had to be replaced when she discovered it was too tight.

Fortunately, she made another discovery—an emerald green silk dress, with a V neckline that dipped dangerously low. The flowing skirt ended right at the knees and fluttered every time she moved. If he was a leg man, she'd definitely get his attention.

Max Daniels may have thought she'd tortured him before, but he hadn't seen anything yet.

After perfecting her makeup, she ran downstairs and poked her head through the kitchen door. "Everything okay?"

Mrs. Lamb, working at the huge sink, smiled distractedly. "Oh, yes."

"Thanks. I'll get the doorbell when it rings."

She didn't have long to wait.

Speeding to the front door, she threw it open, a welcoming smile on her face. It faltered when she discovered not one handsome man, but three, on the doorstep.

And none of them looked happy.

"Uh, come in," she muttered, stepping back.

Max glowered at her as he crossed the threshold, and the other two looked uneasy.

"Are you here to see my father?" she asked Adrian and Prescott.

Before either of them could answer, she heard footsteps behind her, and her father's voice answered.

"They're here as our guests for dinner, of course, just as Mr. Daniels is."

She turned to face him. "Max and I are dining on the patio."

Her father hadn't bothered with her since he brought her home from the hospital, but he smiled now as if they were perfectly in tune. "I know that was your plan, Caro, but I told Mrs. Lamb you'd changed your mind. I thought we'd all dine together."

Several responses ran through Caroline's head, the foremost of which was to kick her father in the shins and grab Max's hand and run. Definitely too immature. And if she challenged his decision and insisted on being served on the patio, it would cause Mrs. Lamb a great deal of trouble. And her father would probably just move his guests to the patio, also.

Leaving her no choice but to grin and bear it.

"I see. My apologies, Max. I'm afraid my plans have gone awry." At least she wanted Max to know she hadn't included her other—whatever they were—in the invitation.

"No problem," he murmured, but he was glaring at Adrian and Prescott, not even looking at her.

Determined to draw his attention, she slipped her hand into his. When he looked down at her, she leaned against him ever so slightly. "I'm glad you came."

His indrawn breath as his gaze fell to her neckline gave her some satisfaction. She grinned when his eyes met hers. At least he wasn't ignoring her now.

"Let's all go to the sun room and have a drink while

Mrs. Lamb finishes preparing dinner," James suggested, acting the genial host.

In the sun room, Amelia was sitting in a pool of light from a nearby lamp, industriously stitching.

"Good evening, Mother," Caroline said, wondering if she should offer her a kiss on the cheek. She concluded it probably wasn't a habit. This family, her family, seemed as disconnected as any she'd ever seen.

"Good evening, dear. How are you?"

It gave Caroline a warm feeling to know that her mother hadn't forgotten her physical problems, at least. Perhaps she was wrong to think her family was uninvolved.

"Much better. My headache is almost gone."

"You had a headache? That's unusual, Caroline. You should ask Mrs. Lamb for some aspirin."

So much for the warm fuzzies.

"Caroline is still suffering from her concussion, Amelia," James explained.

"Oh, yes. You were in the hospital. Nasty places, hospitals."

James seemed to suddenly realize everyone but Amelia was still standing. "Please, be seated. I'll serve drinks. Adrian, Prescott, your usual?"

Caroline resented her father's effort to make it clear that the other two were frequent guests. She turned to Max even as she tugged at his hand to lead him to the sofa where her mother sat. "What will you have, Max?"

"What are you having?" he asked.

"My usual," she assured him with a grin, "a club soda."

Her mother continued her stitching, but the men in the room stared at her as if she'd just revealed a national secret.

"What's wrong?"

"How did you know what you usually have?" James demanded, taking several steps toward her.

Realization of what she'd said set in, and she shook her head slowly. "I...I don't know."

Her father slapped his palm down on the bar. "Damn it, Caroline, why can't you remember the important things?"

"You think I'm doing it on purpose?" she retorted, irritated by his words. She was just as frustrated as her father at her inability to recall her life.

"Really, James, your behavior is inappropriate," Amelia said, still calmly stitching.

"Sorry."

"Is a club soda what I usually have?" Caroline asked in the silence that followed.

"Yes," Prescott said, speaking for the first time. "You always say alcohol gives you a headache."

Even Max nodded in agreement. "And I'll have the same."

"Mr. Daniels, are you sure you want a club soda? The rest of us are having Scotch," James said.

Max withdrew his hand from Caroline's and rose to walk over to the bar. "A club soda is fine." He picked up the two her father poured and brought them back to Caroline.

"Maybe I'll have a club soda, too," Prescott suddenly said, smiling at Caroline.

She couldn't resist sharing a smile with Max. Poor Prescott was so predictable. And Max's smile was heavenly. Just as she was searching for a reason to take his hand again, the doorbell rang.

"Who could that be?" she asked, looking at her father. He shrugged his shoulders.

"I would imagine it's your sister," Amelia stated as she continued to stitch. "She doesn't feel like cooking and they haven't found a housekeeper yet."

"How can they afford a housekeeper?" James snapped. "Roddy isn't the most successful stockbroker I've ever seen."

"I told them you would pay for her," Amelia said.

Caroline had to hand it to her mother. In her placid way, she had more effectively matched James than anyone Caroline had ever seen. Her father was gaping like a landed trout.

Chelsea and her husband entered the sun room, pausing at the entrance. "Hello, everybody."

When greetings were offered, Roddy moved forward but Chelsea grabbed his arm to hold him back. "Well? Aren't you going to say something?"

"What would you like to drink?" James asked, turning back to the bar.

"Not that, Daddy!" Chelsea said, pouting. "I'm wearing a maternity dress, my first."

"It's lovely," Caroline murmured, hoping her low-key compliment would satisfy her sister.

"Thank you. When you need maternity clothes, Caro, you'll have to ask me where to shop. I found some of the best places." Chelsea's superior air, while annoying, at least signaled she'd found a way to compensate for Caroline's pregnancy.

Apparently satisfied with the response to her new dress, Chelsea allowed Roddy to lead her to a chair. "Get me some white wine, sweetums," she cooed as she sat down.

"No," Amelia said calmly, but her word had the effect of an explosion. Everyone stared at her.

Even Caroline was taken aback. In the little she had

discovered about her mother, she assumed Amelia had nothing to say about anyone's life in her house.

"What? I always have white wine, Mother. And I should be pampered. After all, I'm pregnant." Chelsea pouted again.

"I'm sure your doctor told you to have no alcohol. It's not good for the baby."

"But surely one little glass of wine—" Chelsea began, but her mother cut her off.

"No. Have club soda like your sister."

"Oh, of course! Caroline is always right!" Chelsea huffed, sliding down in her chair and crossing her arms over her chest.

"Your mother's right, darling," Roddy began with such tentative tones that Caroline fought the urge to chime in with encouragement. It wasn't hard to decide who wore the pants in that family, even if they were maternity pants.

"I'm sure Mother heard that rule at the home for unwed mothers. And, of course, *they* shouldn't indulge because they have no self-control, but I—"

"Also have no self-control," James finished. "You'll do as your mother says and have club soda."

Caroline leaned toward Max. "I'm sorry," she whispered. "I'd planned on a private dinner. Then you wouldn't have had to endure this argument."

"No problem."

She stared at him in irritation. The least he could do was look disappointed at having to share her with this mob all evening. Instead, he seemed quite interested in Chelsea's performance.

Maybe he was attracted to Chelsea. Her honey blond curls, even if they were out of a bottle, gave her a little-girl look that some men found alluring. Caroline couldn't remember anything about her relationship with Max, but she knew she didn't want him attracted to her sister.

"Dinner is ready," Mrs. Lamb announced from the doorway.

Amelia put away her needlework and stood to lead the way into the dining room. Beside each plate was a charming china name plate. Caroline was unhappy to discover Max was to be seated at the opposite end of the table from her.

"I'm afraid a mistake has been made, Daddy," she announced, calmly exchanging Max's name with Adrian's. Instead of having her father's two favorites surrounding her, she would have Max as a dinner partner.

"I just thought I'd like an opportunity to visit with our guest, Caro," James protested.

"Some other time, Daddy." She took Max's arm and drew him to the chair at her mother's left. He courteously pulled out the chair beside him for her, in the center of the table, opposite her sister.

Max wasn't sure what difference it made where he sat at the big table. From the moment he'd met the other two men on the front porch, he'd realized the evening would be a disaster. He'd been an idiot to expect anything else, he decided.

An uneasy silence fell on the table as the housekeeper served consommé. Max may not have been brought up in a wealthy mansion, but he'd been taught good manners. He turned to his hostess.

"Do you do needlework for relaxation, Mrs. Adkins?" he asked politely.

His hostess looked surprised at his question, but she smiled. "Why, no. Actually, I'm doing it for an auction the home for the unwed mothers is having to raise money. It's so expensive to care for all of them."

"That's very nice of you," he said, and picked up his soupspoon. As if he'd knocked a hole in a dam, words poured forth from Mrs. Adkins as she described all the ways the money would prove useful for her charity.

An occasional nod or encouraging word was all Max needed to contribute for the next few minutes. That gave him plenty of time to think about the brunette beauty beside him. She'd been on his mind for the past two months. Their two weeks together had been wonderful. Since then he'd wondered if he'd ever see her again.

Maybe he would've been better off if he hadn't.

He sneaked a glance at her and decided that wasn't true. If he had a chance to be with Caroline, then he wanted that chance.

"Do you have brothers or sisters, Mr. Daniels?" Mrs. Adkins asked.

"Why, yes, ma'am. I have three brothers and two sisters."

"My, you come from a large family. Do they all work with you at your business? I believe my husband said you build homes?"

Max noticed Caroline leaned a little closer, as if trying to hear what they were saying. He grinned. She'd loved to hear him talk of his family. He'd assumed she had none of her own, but now he wondered if it was because hers seemed so distant to each other.

"Only my baby sister, Susan. She answers the phone when she's not in class."

"She's in high school?"

"No, Susan's a junior in college."

"Was she the one who answered the phone when I called yesterday?" Caroline asked, proving that she'd been listening to their conversation.

"Yeah."

"Did—did I meet her when we—while we were dating?"

"No."

He hadn't wanted to share her with his family. One introduction and they would've taken her in like a long-lost relative. So he'd put off taking her home to his mother. Until it was too late.

"Did I meet any of your family?"

"No."

Her hazel eyes, with their dark lashes, rounded in surprise. He wanted to lean toward her and kiss her soft lips and tease her about her reaction. Instead, he sat stiffly, unsure what to say. How could he explain the sweetness he'd wanted to hold close, keep private, as long as possible?

"And you had the nerve to complain that I didn't tell you about my family?" she whispered to him under her breath so her mother couldn't hear.

"At least I *told* you about my family."

"That's going to be a little hard to prove since I can't even remember *you*, much less what you told me!"

"Caroline," her father called, pulling her attention away from Max.

"Yes?"

"I wondered if you wanted to have lunch with me tomorrow? You haven't been to the office since the accident, and you used to come all the time."

"She can't," Amelia said as she rang the bell for the next course to be served. "Tomorrow is her day at the home for the unwed mothers."

"It is?" Caroline asked, seemingly surprised.

"I really don't think that's appropriate now, Mother," Chelsea said. "After all, they might mistake Caro for one of the inmates and not let her leave at the end of the day.'' She giggled, as if feeling her words were quite entertaining, but no one else laughed.

Max thought it best to ignore her remark. ''What do you do there?'' he asked Caroline.

The lost look on her face made him want to take her into his arms and comfort her, but that wouldn't be appropriate dinner behavior. Besides, anything she did got that reaction from him.

''I—I don't know. Mother, what exactly do I do there?''

''Why, Caro, you've done some wonderful things. You teach a cooking class, and you pay for a hairdresser to give free haircuts, and you teach them to read, too. Mrs. Brown is thrilled with your help.''

''A cooking class? I know how to cook?''

''Oh, nothing fancy. That's why it's so good. You teach them how to make easy, well-balanced meals. Mrs. Lamb helped you.''

In spite of the confusion on Caroline's face, Max wasn't surprised. She'd done a little cooking at his house. Nothing fancy, but good wholesome food. Even more interesting, she'd never acted as if she expected to be waited on. Maybe that's why he found her real identity so difficult to believe.

He'd dated one or two well-to-do young ladies after he'd begun to make his mark in the world. Any man making money drew that type of woman. In fact, Chelsea reminded him of them. And Chelsea, or anyone like her, would never fit into his family.

Caroline, on the other hand, would be adored by his sisters, and if it were anyone but him who introduced her, his brothers would be fighting over her. Just like the two jerks at the table.

Prescott, sitting on Caroline's left, leaned toward her.

"It shouldn't surprise you that you can cook, Caroline. You do everything well."

"I'm not sure Caroline should do anything so strenuous just yet," James said.

Max smiled in amusement as he watched Caroline's chin rise. Only once had he tried to tell her what to do. Her reaction had taught him a lot about her.

"I'm sure I'll be just fine. What time do I usually go, Mother, and—and where is it?"

"I'll send Lewis back home to drive you if you insist on going," James said, irritation in his voice.

Doubt darkened Caroline's hazel eyes. Max guessed she had just realized that the city she'd grown up in was strange to her, and she could easily get lost. In an attempt to comfort her, he took her right hand in his and squeezed it gently.

Her gaze as she turned to him reminded him all over again why he was here, dining with the ill-assorted group. The warmth in Caroline's eyes lit a fire in him that would never die.

Mrs. Lamb brought in the main course and everyone turned their attention to eating. About halfway through the meal, Caroline abruptly excused herself and fled the table, her hand to her mouth.

Max stood to go after her, but James Adkins ordered him back to the table. "Chelsea," he barked, "see about your sister."

"Me?" she asked in horror. "I can't, Daddy. If I do, I'll lose my dinner, too. She's just experiencing temporary morning sickness."

Max was willing to bet everything he owned that Chelsea hadn't been so calmly accepting of the nausea when it was happening to her. "I'll go," he said, as he stood again. "I've helped my sister a couple of times."

"But it's not morning," Prescott said, confusion in his voice as Max left the room. "Is that normal?"

While Max followed the sounds of someone throwing up, he marveled at his desire to help Caroline through her nausea. He was notorious in his family for his weak stomach. But he wanted to be at Caroline's side now, to share her difficulties. To experience the growth of his child in her.

The only problem was, he wasn't sure it was his child.

He shoved that disturbing thought aside and rapped on the bathroom door. "Caroline?"

She moaned before muttering faintly, "Go away."

Pushing the door open, he took in the pitiful sight of Caroline bent over the toilet. Without bothering to ask her opinion, he slid into the small room and wrapped one supporting arm around her waist and laid a hand on her forehead.

As another wave of nausea hit her, she sagged against him, moaning. When it ended, he held her to him and reached for a washcloth. After wetting it, he wiped her face gently. Then he offered her a glass of water to rinse her mouth.

"How did you know what I needed?" she asked afterward. "It was almost as if you've been through morning sickness before."

He ran a finger down the side of her beautiful cheek, enjoying the opportunity to hold her again, even in these circumstances. "That's because I have."

It didn't occur to him what she would think until she stiffened and her face clouded over.

Chapter Five

Caroline's heart sank. She'd wanted Max to be the father of her baby because of the strong attraction she felt for him. But his answer brought home to her how little she knew about Max Daniels.

Or herself.

"With my sister, Caroline, with my sister," he hurriedly said. "Her husband traveled a lot during the early months of her pregnancy and she stayed with us."

"Oh," was all she could think to say since she was overcome with relief. She still didn't know enough about Max, she warned herself, but the happiness filling her mocked that thought.

"Oh," she repeated. "I thought you meant—"

"No," he said hurriedly as he ran his hands up and down her arms. "I've never—I mean, you're the only—"

"I'm glad." Understatement of the year. She'd die of jealousy if he even so much as thought of another woman.

"There's not too many people I'd risk nausea for," he added. "You should count yourself lucky."

"Me and your sister? Is that all?"

"Maybe my mother or Susan. Or one of my brothers,

though they won't be experiencing morning sickness," he said with a laugh.

"You're very close to your family?"

"Yeah."

"Then why didn't you introduce me to any of them?" she asked. She couldn't ask that question in front of her mother, but she was dying to know the answer.

He sighed and linked his hands behind her back, bringing her body closer to him. "Because I didn't want to share you. What we had—have—is very special. My family kind of takes over, and I wanted you all to myself."

"Oh."

He frowned. "Don't you believe me?"

She wanted to. With all her heart she wanted to. But there was so much she didn't know, didn't understand, didn't remember. "I—I don't know."

"Then I guess I'll just have to show you," he murmured.

His blue eyes invited her to come closer and she met him more than halfway, leaning against his broad chest, loving his solid warmth, his all-male scent. His caring about her enough to face her sickness warmed her, but not nearly as much as the way his lips were coming closer and closer. She closed her eyes, anticipating his touch, her heart racing.

"Caroline?" Mrs. Lamb called out as she pushed the bathroom door ajar.

Caroline's eyes popped open and she saw the embarrassment she was feeling in Max's blue ones. He took his hands away and stepped back from her.

"Your mother sent me to see if you were all right," Mrs. Lamb explained, but her gaze was on Max.

"I'll—I'll go back to the dining room and leave you

to Mrs. Lamb's capable hands," Max said, and ducked out of the room.

"Thank you!" Caroline called out, wishing he was still there, holding her.

"What a nice man," Mrs. Lamb said, and then clucked in sympathy. "You do look a sight, and it's all my fault."

Caroline whirled to stare at herself in the mirror, concerned with how Max saw her, before Mrs. Lamb's words registered. "Your fault? Why is it your fault? I would've thought it was the baby's fault, or the fault of one of those three men sitting so calmly eating their dinner right now."

Caroline's nausea wasn't helping her temper. Nor the thought that Max had seen her when she wasn't at her best. Even more irritating was the frustration she was feeling because Max hadn't been able to demonstrate the magic they shared. "It's not fair that only the woman tosses her cookies in this pregnancy business. Why can't the man get sick, too?"

"Well, now, some men do experience a similar nausea, but not many. Anyway, I shouldn't have put jalapeño peppers in the beans, but that's your father's favorite and I just forgot about you being pregnant."

Caroline attempted to restore some order to her hair as she asked, "You think that's what caused it?"

"Oh, yes. I did the same thing to Chelsea before she even knew she was pregnant. Now, you just come back to the table and eat a little more. You've got to keep up your strength. But avoid the beans."

Mrs. Lamb left the bathroom and Caroline sat on the side of the bathtub to consider her options. She'd rather pass up a return to the dinner table. Except for Max.

Even though she knew she'd have little opportunity to question him, she couldn't resist being near him. Not that he'd feel any attraction for her now. How sexy can it be to lose your dinner at any moment?

But, she realized with a sigh, she was really hungry now. She had to eat something. Slipping up to her room, she renewed her makeup and hurried back to the dining room.

Max stood as she entered and everyone else stared at her. When she sat down again, he leaned over and whispered, "Better now?"

Though she appreciated his concern, her embarrassment kept her from showing him. She gave an abrupt nod and sipped the ice tea by her plate.

"Sorry, Caro, I should've warned you about the beans," Chelsea said, sincere regret in her voice.

Caroline looked up in surprise. She hadn't expected such sympathy from her younger sister. "Mrs. Lamb mentioned that you'd had an encounter with them, too."

"Yes. Miserable, isn't it? But after the first three months, it goes away."

"Not always," Amelia said. "Your father got quite tired of my dashing away from the table."

"I think he should've been grateful he wasn't the one having to do the dashing," Caroline muttered.

"Women are the stronger sex," Adrian said, speaking for almost the first time that evening. "I think that's why they bear the responsibility for continuing the human race." He smiled at Caroline, almost convincing her of his sincerity. Then he added, "Our child is going to have a wonderful mother."

Prescott immediately protested, but Max said nothing. Caroline stole a glance at him to see the steely glare he was directing Adrian's way. If she'd been Adrian, she would make sure she steered wide of Max.

"Are you the father of Caroline's baby?" Amelia asked, as if she were discussing the weather.

"Of course I am. I said I was from the beginning," Adrian replied, equally calm.

"You can't prove that," Prescott retorted, leaning across the table.

"Not until after the baby is born and we can do DNA testing," Adrian agreed. "But I intend to prove to Caroline that I'm the father long before that. I don't want my child to be born illegitimately."

Caroline stared at Adrian, her heart sinking. Could the man lie so sincerely? And could he be the father of her child? She didn't want him to be. Already she knew she wanted Max to be the father of the baby she was carrying. But what if he wasn't?

Sudden movement beside her drew her attention. Max, his expression grim, was about to say something. She slid her hand beneath the tablecloth to rest on his thigh, sending a pleading look his way.

He leaned back in his chair, his gaze resting on her, questioning her, and she silently shook her head. She didn't want a fight here and now, when she knew so little about her past.

Most frightening of all were the chills that raced up her arm from touching him. And the desire to continue to do so. How could she want one man so much when another was claiming to be her lover?

"I hope you prove you're the daddy immediately," James said to Adrian, satisfaction in his voice. "I expect to hold a wedding right away, before she has to start wearing maternity clothes like her sister. You hear me, Caroline?"

"I'm sure everyone heard you, Daddy," Caroline said, and forced herself to take another bite of her dinner.

Though Prescott continued to sputter, no one else challenged Adrian's assertion.

Max asked Roddy about his position as a stock broker and her brother-in-law talked for several minutes about the stock market. Caroline started to remove her hand from Max's warm thigh, but his left hand settled over hers, trapping it there.

Maybe he'd noticed her dress after all.

THE EVENING GREW increasingly strained. When dinner was finished, they returned to the sun room for coffee. But shortly after taking a cup, Max set it down on the coffee table and stood to leave.

"Thank you for your hospitality, Mr. and Mrs. Adkins, but I have an early appointment in the morning."

"We're glad you could join us," Amelia said politely, her interest again taken with her stitching.

"I'll walk you to the door," Caroline said, standing also. She hoped she might at least have a few minutes alone with him. To talk, of course.

"I'll go with you," James said, walking toward them.

"That's not necessary, Daddy," Caroline retorted.

"Oh, yes, it is. I wouldn't want to be thought rude to one of my guests."

The three of them left the others in the sun room and walked to the front door, Caroline fuming with every step. Once there, Max offered his hand to James and again said thanks.

James didn't take the hint. He stood there, a genial smile on his lips, watching them.

"Thank you for coming, Max, and for—for helping me," Caroline said, giving up on her father's departure. "It didn't turn out exactly as I planned."

"I know. But I enjoyed seeing you again."

Drat the man, he was turning to leave. Caroline grabbed the lapels of his blue suit and pulled him toward her. Ignoring her father's stare, she moved her lips over Max's until he abruptly took control of the kiss, wrapping his arms around her and lifting her up against him.

She released his lapels and encircled his neck, her heart thumping in her chest as she relished the feel of him against her. When he let her slide down his body until her feet touched the floor again, she almost cried out at their separation.

Before taking his arms from around her, he whispered a husky "Goodnight, Caroline," kissed her briefly again, and then walked out the door.

"Well, I didn't know you were so bold, Caro," her father commented, still standing beside her.

Reluctantly Caroline closed the door and turned to face him. "I suggested you remain in the sun room, Daddy."

"I'm glad I didn't. Who knows what advantage that man would've taken of you if I hadn't been here."

Or what advantage I would've taken of *him,* Caroline thought.

"Don't expect me to thank you for the protection, Daddy. It was unwanted."

"You'd better think seriously, young lady, about taking up with one man while carrying another one's child. Adrian might not be as understanding as me."

"We don't know that it's Adrian's baby," she snapped, her heart faltering at the possibility.

"He sounded pretty sure of himself tonight."

"They've all sounded sure of themselves."

"Max didn't protest. Only Prescott."

But he'd wanted to. She shivered as she remembered touching him.

When she remained silent, James said, "I want this

matter resolved right away. I was serious about getting you married before you start showing.''

''I'll marry when I've discovered who the father is, and not before.''

''I have your word on it?'' James asked.

''Of course!'' Only after her word was given did she have second thoughts. What if the father really was Adrian...or Prescott?

''Good,'' James replied with a smile, as if he'd won, and turned to go back to the sun room.

''Wait! Daddy, what did we argue about two months ago?''

He paused, as if frozen in motion, and then turned slowly. ''I don't know what you're talking about.''

''Oh, yes, you do. And I want an answer. Mrs. Lamb said we had an argument two months ago, or perhaps two and a half months. The next day I left and didn't return for two weeks. What did we argue about?''

''We're always arguing, Caro. And you frequently go on trips. It seems to me the argument was something about taking up a career. Or getting married. I don't really remember.'' With another smile, he strolled down the hall.

Caroline stared after him, her gut feeling telling her he was lying. And yet, either of those subjects might have come up. She had a feeling her father had been pressuring her about both of them. After all, she was twenty-seven. Her sister, three years younger, was already married.

Wearily she leaned back against the door. It had been a long evening, and she didn't feel up to returning to the sun room. She pushed away from the door and trudged to the stairs, taking them slowly.

Having a baby seemed to sap all her energy.

Or maybe it wasn't the baby's fault. Maybe it was the daddies. All of them.

Now that she'd given her word to her father to marry as soon as proof could be found, she had to make sure the proof featured a tall, dark-haired, blue-eyed man whose slightest touch sent her up in flames.

MAX OVERSLEPT the next morning, after spending most of the night alternating between reliving his night of passion with Caroline two long months ago and trying to figure out how to prove his identity as father of the baby.

The ringing phone brought him awake.

"Hello?" he growled.

"Max, where are you?" Susan demanded, her voice bright and wide-awake.

He checked his watch and groaned. "I was asleep."

"But you have an appointment with Mr. Lawson at the bank in ten minutes."

"Yeah. Call him and tell him something came up. Try to reschedule it for tomorrow."

"Okay."

Before she could hang up, Max said, "Wait, Susan."

"Yes?"

He pondered his question.

"Max? What is it?"

"Did I ever talk to you about Caroline?"

"Caroline Adkins?"

His heart leaped. Had he talked about her and then forgotten he'd done so? Would it convince Caroline that they'd spent two weeks together? "Yes," he replied anxiously.

"Nope."

"Then how did you know who I was talking about?"

"Jim mentioned something about her a couple of

months ago, and then she called yesterday." She paused and then, with sisterly cunning, asked, "Is she important?"

"Yeah. And if she calls, find me, wherever I am, okay?"

"Sure. Will I like her?"

"Suze, call the banker, and mind your own business." He almost hung up before he remembered one more warning. "And don't even think about mentioning her name to Mom or Karen, or your job is history."

As he showered and shaved, he thought back over the two weeks he'd shared with Caroline. He'd given her the names of his design firms. If she applied at one of those firms, using his name as a reference, that would be something, at least. Some proof that she knew him.

A few minutes later, he hung up the phone with a sigh. She hadn't called either firm.

After their first lunch together, he'd taken her out to dinner that same evening. He could get the waiter at Mario's to say she'd been there with Max, but that kind of proof was useless. They'd gone to the movies, to the theater one night. He'd taken time off for picnics in the foothills of the Rockies.

Thinking she was a newcomer to the area, he'd even taken her to tour the mint. He had the ticket stubs from that excursion. But they could've been used by anyone.

Ticket stubs didn't tell about the kisses he'd stolen at the back of the tour group. Or the leisurely dinner afterward when they'd laughed about people's reactions to cold, hard cash. Or the exquisite caresses they'd shared before he left her at her hotel room door.

The hotel!

Of course. At least he could prove she'd stayed in the

suburbs near his office. He showered and dressed, then grabbed his billfold and keys and hurried out the door.

A few minutes later, he arrived at the desk in the lobby of the medium-priced hotel he'd come to know well. "Excuse me," he said to the young man with his back to the counter.

"Oh, yes, sir. What kind of room do you need? A single?" The bright smile was perfect for PR, but Max wasn't interested.

"Look, about two months ago, the last week or two of June, a young lady stayed here. I need to see her registration card."

"I'm afraid that's not possible, sir. That's privileged information." The smile was gone and a frown took its place.

He hadn't expected high security. "Okay, I don't have to see the card. Just look and see if you had a Caroline Adkins registered during that time. She stayed in Room 210."

"I don't know," the man said, edging away as if he thought Max were a serial killer.

An older man came out of a door just behind the counter. "Yes, Mike, what's the problem?"

Realizing the clerk had called for reinforcements by some silent signal, Max put on his friendliest smile. "I just need confirmation that Caroline Adkins stayed in Room 210 the last week or two of June."

"I'm sorry, but we don't give out information about our clients."

"Look, I'm asking for *confirmation* of what I already know. I walked Miss Adkins to her room most evenings and waited until she took out her key and entered the room before leaving."

"If that's true, sir, why do you need us to confirm that information?"

Good question. Max was beginning to sweat. "Because Miss Adkins has amnesia from a car accident."

"You mean Caroline Adkins, daughter of James Adkins?" There was a flicker of interest in the man's eyes that Max regretted. "She stayed here, with us?"

"Yes. She did. Could you just check your records?"

"And all you want is for me to tell you you're right? I don't have to put anything in writing?"

The man still seemed reluctant, and Max eased his bill-fold out of his back pocket. The supervisor's gaze immediately flew to Max's hands and then to the clerk, ostensibly filing papers nearby. "Mike, go to the coffee shop and get me some coffee. I'll cover the desk while you're gone."

As soon as the clerk had walked away, Max slid a twenty-dollar bill across the counter. Without a word the supervisor pocketed the bill and turned to the computer.

"The end of June, you said. Room 210?"

"That's right."

The excitement faded as the man worked the computer keys. Finally he turned to Max with a frown. "I don't know what you're trying to pull, but we show no Caroline Adkins in that room."

"What?" Max wanted to grab the man by the throat. "Then who do you show registered?"

"I'm sorry. I can't—"

Max threw another twenty-dollar bill on the counter. "Yes, you can."

"We had a single woman stay in that room for two weeks. She paid in cash and registered under the name of Leslie McVey."

Max stared at him, stunned. "Leslie McVey? The end of June?"

"Yes. Otherwise, we've only had one- or two-nighters in there. We have a heavy turnover. It's not often a guest stays two weeks."

"Do you remember what Miss McVey looked like?"

"No, I don't. However—" he smiled at Max "—I might be persuaded to do so."

Great. All he needed was for the man to say Max had tried to bribe him to identify Caroline. "No thanks."

He strode from the hotel lobby, disappointed and frustrated. Why had Caroline registered under an assumed name? She hadn't hesitated to use her real name with him.

He looked at his watch and groaned. It was already lunchtime, and he'd accomplished very little. Climbing into his truck, he drove back to his office, only a few minutes away.

"It's about time you showed up," Susan greeted him cheerily. "I was just getting ready to beep you."

"Why? A problem on the job sites?"

"No. Caroline Adkins just called."

"Did you get a number?" he demanded.

Susan's eyes widened. "Hey, don't jump down my throat," she protested. "I asked and she said she'd have to call you later. Something about her not being able to tie up the phone."

"She didn't say where she was?" Even as he asked the question, he remembered her intention to do charity work today. "Bring me a phone book."

"But she didn't say where she was."

"I just remembered. The phone book!" he snapped and continued on to his office. He took a deep breath as he sat down behind the desk, hoping to curb his impatience. It wouldn't take much to make Susan suspicious. And when his little sister suspected a secret, she was hell on wheels until she uncovered it.

"Want me to help you look something up?" Susan offered as she entered his office, watching him as she held out the directory.

"No, I'll manage."

Several minutes later he shouted for his sister. He couldn't find any listing for the Home for Unwed Mothers. He was sure that was what Mrs. Adkins had called it last night.

"Yes, brother?"

"I can't find the telephone number."

She ignored his growl and took the directory with a laugh. "I knew you needed my help. What am I looking for?"

"I think it's called the Home for Unwed Mothers."

His thoughts were all centered on Caroline, but he looked up when his sister gasped.

"Your girlfriend is in a home for unwed mothers? Wait until Mom hears about this!"

Chapter Six

"Don't be ridiculous!" Max snapped.

"I'm not the one being ridiculous. Mom's gonna have a fit if one of her grandchildren is illegitimate. Don't you like this lady?"

"Susan, this is none of your business," Max advised her in stern tones. "Caroline is doing charity work at the home. She is not, I repeat, not living there."

"Oh, so I'm not going to be an aunt?" Susan teased, a big grin on her face.

Her words stopped Max cold. What could he say? Yes, she's pregnant. But no, it may not be his baby. That would make a good impression, sure to be passed on to his mother.

"Look, Susan, I want you to forget this conversation ever took place, okay?"

"Sure, no problem. But it'll cost you."

Long years of dealing with his baby sister told him to bargain. Threats would get him nowhere. "How much?"

"There's this gorgeous dress I found. I really need it for my date with Stephen."

"How much?" he repeated.

"A hundred and twenty dollars."

"For a dress? You must be kidding?"

"No, and it's worth it. One look at that dress and he'll be on his knees. Haven't you ever seen a dress like that?"

Yeah. Last night. He shook himself free from the picture of Caroline in the green silk. "Okay," he agreed roughly, pulling his billfold from his back pocket. After bribing the hotel man, now he had to bribe his sister. It was turning out to be an expensive day.

"I'll write you a check for a hundred and fifty if you'll go buy me some lunch before you do your shopping."

"Are you staying here the rest of the afternoon?" Her eyes were round with curiosity and Max had the uneasy feeling he should have protested more at her blackmailing him. It made him uncomfortable for anyone to know what a hold Caroline had on him.

"Just until I get a few things accomplished." *And until Caroline calls.*

He pretended to do paperwork until Susan returned with his lunch. Then he munched the barbecue sandwich and let his mind return to its one constant thought, Caroline.

When the phone rang half an hour later, he'd finished his sandwich but gotten almost no work done.

"Hello?"

"Max, it's Caroline."

Like he wouldn't recognize her voice.

"Yeah. Sorry I missed your call earlier."

"I couldn't leave a number because I'm calling from the home where I'm volunteering today. Anyway, I wanted to apologize again for last evening. Daddy can be difficult, you know."

"Yeah, I can tell."

"I wondered if you'd meet me for dinner this evening, so it would just be the two of us. And we could talk. My treat."

Max almost yanked the telephone cord out of the wall. "Are you trying to insult me? Do you think I can't afford a dinner?"

"No, I didn't think that. It's just that *I* invited *you*"

"Regardless. I ate at your house last night. Tonight I'll pay. I'll pick you up at seven."

"Uh, Max, I don't think that's a good idea. I think Daddy might even go so far as to have us followed. Or if not him, Prescott might think of doing that."

"Not Adrian? He's the one who's sure he's the father of your baby." That had been irritating him ever since last night. Had she slept with the man? And Prescott, too? He didn't usually feel he had the right to question his date's past experience, but this was ridiculous.

There was a pause before Caroline answered, and Max realized he'd hurt her feelings. "I'm sorry—" he began.

"Never mind. Maybe this wasn't such a good idea, after all."

"Caroline, I'm sorry. He upset me last night. We need to talk. I'd like to understand what's going on here."

"You know I can't explain it, Max. I've got amnesia!"

"Calm down. I know. Will you meet me at Mario's?"

Again she paused, and he held his breath for her answer.

"Okay. Where is it?"

"You don't know where it is? We always— Sorry, I forgot." He gave her directions, and they agreed to meet at seven. "And Caroline, I'm glad you called."

"Me, too," she whispered before hanging up.

Max sat with the receiver pressed to his ear until the dial tone became too annoying. Man, he had it bad if she could tie him into knots with a brief phone call.

Yeah, he had it bad.

"LEWIS, I REALLY appreciate your picking me up. I called for a taxi, but there was an hour's wait," Caroline explained as she slid into the front seat by her father's driver.

"You're supposed to ride in back, Miss Caroline," Lewis chided.

"I know, but I'd rather ride with you, like I usually do." She smiled at him until she saw the curious look that she was coming to hate. "No, I don't know why I remembered that. Things, unimportant things, just come to me." She sighed. "Ooh! This is so frustrating."

"Yeah, I guess so. Do you want to go home?"

"Yes, please. I need to change clothes before I go out."

"Will you need me to drive you?"

"No, I'm going to drive myself." She thought about asking him not to mention her outing to her father, but she didn't want to put him into such a difficult position. James Adkins could be harsh if an employee didn't do exactly as he wished. Better not to call attention to her plans and hope Lewis wouldn't think anything about it.

The rush hour in Denver had gotten increasingly heavy the past few years. Cars were backed up quite a way behind them. Caroline was looking over her shoulder at the line of traffic when the limo suddenly jerked and skidded before Lewis quickly corrected it.

"What's wrong?"

The chauffeur eased the limo onto the shoulder of the road and came to a stop. "I think we've got a flat tire."

"Will it take long to fix it?" she asked, automatically looking at her watch. She'd left the home later than she'd intended and it was almost six now.

"No. I'll hurry."

She felt guilty sitting in comfort in the limo as Lewis

did the dirty work. Opening her door, she swung her feet to the pavement and stood up.

"Uh, Miss Caroline, we have a problem."

"What is it, Lewis?"

"Two tires are flat. I must've hit something in the road, but I didn't see it."

Seeing the worry on his face, she quickly reassured him. "Don't worry about it, Lewis. I'm not running that late."

"I don't think you understand. I don't have two spares. Only one. I'll have to call for a tow truck, and there are only a few that can handle a limo."

Now she understood. And if she didn't know better, she'd think her father had planned this incident, too. He was determined to keep her away from Max.

"Okay," she said with a sigh. "So you call a tow truck, and then I'll call a taxi. It will be all right, Lewis."

Both of them made their calls, and they each discovered they would have to wait.

"I sure am sorry, Miss Caroline," Lewis said softly when they'd both returned to the limo.

"I know, Lewis." Her mind was dwelling on the man waiting for her at the restaurant, but it suddenly occurred to her that the flat tires provided her with an excellent opportunity to quiz Lewis.

"Lewis, do you remember when I left home two months ago? I was gone for about two weeks."

"Yes, Miss Caroline."

"Do you know why I left, or where I went?"

"No, I don't. I didn't drive you the day you left."

"Did my father say anything? Complain about me?"

Lewis grinned. "He's always complaining about you, Miss Caroline. You know how he is."

"I know," she agreed with a sigh. How she knew.

Suddenly she remembered a scene, a year or two ago, she thought, between her and her father. She'd been his son, the son he'd always wanted, following him into his business, acting as his right-hand man. Until she'd realized she wasn't enjoying her work. In fact she hated it.

When she'd told her father, he'd been heartbroken. That's why she was still living at home. He'd allowed her to return to school and pick up a degree in interior design if she promised not to move out.

"It would upset your mother," he had said gruffly, but she'd known he meant himself.

The memory faded and any more questioning was pointless, so she accepted Lewis's offer of a game of gin while they waited. The taxi and the tow truck arrived almost simultaneously. Caroline hoped she'd be able to depart without Lewis hearing her destination, but he walked her to the taxi.

"Where shall I tell the driver to go?" he asked.

"A restaurant in Golden called Mario's."

Without comment, Lewis gave the destination to the driver, apologized again for stranding her and stepped back. She waved goodbye as the taxi pulled out into traffic.

While the driver negotiated their way, Caroline pulled out her makeup bag. So much for the idea of having a quick shower, changing clothes. She'd have to make do with the contents of her makeup bag.

It was a little after seven when she arrived at the restaurant. Though it wasn't a four-star establishment, she liked the look of the place. It had a warmth and intimacy of which she approved, and she didn't feel terribly out of place in her denim jumper.

"Yes, ma'am?" the maître d' said in way of a greeting.

"I'm here to meet Max Daniels. He—"

"Of course. Right this way." The man showed no hesitation, so she figured either Max dined here often or he'd bribed the man outrageously.

The man led her to the back corner of the restaurant where the light was the dimmest. Max rose from the booth and moved aside for her to slide in. When he joined her on the same side, she looked up, surprised.

"If we're going to talk, I don't want to be overheard."

She didn't, either. And she certainly didn't mind close quarters with Max. As long as she could control the wild response he evoked.

"I'm sorry I'm late. Lewis was taking me home in the limo when we had two flat tires."

He gave her a wry look. "Was your father planting nails in the road?"

She tried to look stern, but an answering smile refused to be denied. "No. Though he might have if he'd thought of it."

"I'm not exactly his favorite person."

"No, you're not, but I'm not sure why. I think the two of you have a lot in common." She knew he didn't appreciate her comment by the ferocious frown on his face.

"What do you mean?"

"You both started out small and became a success. You're both very protective...and you like to get your way."

"You're one to talk."

They shared a grin.

"I know. That's one thing I've discovered about myself since the accident. I think I've been terribly spoiled all my life."

"Maybe. But I would never've guessed you were

James Adkins's daughter. You never acted stuck-up with me."

The waiter arrived with their menus and they paused to read them.

"What's good here?" she asked as she scanned the list.

"You don't remember?"

She lifted her gaze to his to discover the look she hated. The look that asked for the thousandth time if her memory had come back.

"Please, Max. Don't look at me like that."

"Like what?"

"You're wondering if I remember something, but I don't. And I hate that look. It's like I'm standing in the middle of the room in my underwear while everyone else is fully clothed."

Max's grin lit up his blue eyes.

"That's an interesting analogy."

She didn't think she was a person to blush often, but the mental picture brought heat to her cheeks. "I—I—"

"We'd better figure out what we're going to order. The waiter's on his way over here," he said, changing gears.

"Did we come here before?"

"All the time."

"What did I order?"

Max explained about all her favorites and they ordered. As soon as the waiter left the table, she drew a deep breath and began the question that had been bothering her for days.

"Max, how—"

"How did we meet?"

"No. Yes. Okay, how did we meet?" That wasn't the question she had in mind, but maybe it would be better to wade into these murky waters rather than dive in over her head. After all, they had all evening.

"You came into the model home I have. I happened to be there. We started talking and you told me you were an interior designer, looking for work."

Caroline frowned, thinking about what he'd said. It made sense, if she'd argued with her father about her future. But somehow, she wasn't satisfied. She shifted on the booth seat and brushed her leg against his. Immediately her pulse picked up speed.

"Something wrong?"

"No. I just—nothing." How could she explain that his slightest touch filled her with all kinds of fantasies? "What happened then?"

He didn't answer right away. She frowned, wondering why he was hesitating, when he reached over and took her hand. Raising it to his lips, he caressed it and then laid their clasped hands across his thigh.

"Nothing the hell should've happened, but I couldn't let you walk away. I hate to admit it, but you knocked me for a loop."

"I did?" She wanted to run her hand up and down his thigh, to feel his muscles tense under her touch. Instead, she let her hand rest in his, hoping he wouldn't notice her palm was sticky with desire. "Did you ask me out?"

He chuckled and she was amazed to see the blood surge beneath his tanned cheeks as he looked away.

"I did," he said and then added, "once I got up my courage."

She pulled her hand from his and grasped his chin to bring his face around to hers. "Wait a minute, Max, I may be gullible, but let's not take this to the ridiculous."

"What?"

"You were afraid to ask me out? I bet you have to

beat off the women with a stick, so don't give me this shy bit.''

He leaned toward her until their mouths were only inches apart, and said, ''None of them ever meant anything to me. You did.''

She gulped, her heart fluttering wildly. ''Even then?''

''Then, now and always,'' he whispered, and his lips reached for hers.

''Good evening.''

As absorbed as they were in each other, Caroline and Max hadn't noticed Prescott's approach. Without waiting for an invitation, he slid into the empty side of the booth.

''I hope you don't mind if I join you.''

''But we do,'' Caroline said, her voice stiff.

''Well, if you feel that way, I suppose I could leave, but all the tables are full. When I saw the two of you, I thought maybe you wouldn't mind if I sat with you. I've been on the road all day and it's almost an hour's drive home.''

Caroline wasn't sure she believed him, but after exchanging a glance with Max, she nodded. ''I suppose—''

''Thanks. Have you already ordered?''

After the waiter was summoned and Prescott placed his order, he turned to the two of them, eagerness on his face.

''What are you two doing? Having a secret rendezvous? That doesn't seem fair to me and Adrian.''

''You and Adrian can—'' she began, heat in her voice, when Max intervened, squeezing her hand under the table.

''Have you been working out of town today, Prescott? Just what kind of work do you do for James?''

Max's conversational gambit was far more successful than her anger. Prescott explained his responsibilities in great detail. Gruesome detail, Caroline thought. She really didn't care what Prescott did for her father.

Now if it had been Max explaining his job, she would've hung on his every word. As it was, she could only admire his skillful handling of Prescott. Before long, Prescott would think he and Max were best friends.

"I do most of the traveling for James. He doesn't like to go out of town as much as he used to. I scout the properties and make reports to him. When he's favorably impressed with something, he may take a trip to look at it himself. He, of course, makes the final decision, but he relies heavily on my expertise."

Caroline felt an urge to yawn, but the waiter's arrival saved her. He delivered plates of steaming pasta that made her mouth water. At least she would have something to do besides listen to Prescott.

Conversation floundered for a few minutes as they each enjoyed the meal. It seemed ages to Caroline since she'd shared lunch at the home. And it hadn't compared to what she was eating now.

Once her hunger was satisfied, Caroline paid more attention to the press of Max's thigh against hers, the strength of his shoulder as she leaned against him. He may have thought she knocked him for a loop, but Caroline had a suspicion the feeling had been mutual.

The question she'd intended to ask at once when he'd thought she wanted to know how they met was much more to the point. And she hoped she got an answer tonight.

And then again, maybe she didn't want to know.

But, she had to.

She had to know how soon they'd made love...and how often. She just hadn't realized how difficult that question would be. None of the men had offered the information.

It might go a long way in informing her just what kind of a woman she was. And if she was sleeping with three men at the same time, she had a lot of room for improvement.

Max, too, had finished eating. He spoke to Prescott again.

"Who supervises out-of-town projects? I should think that would be a lot of hard work. James wouldn't want just anyone to handle that."

Caroline frowned at the man beside her. He was buttering up Prescott as if he were a fat turkey, going into the oven for Thanksgiving. Why? What was he wanting?

"Usually, I'm the one who oversees those projects. James knows he can trust me. I've worked for him for eight years now," Prescott boasted. "And I can tell you he doesn't keep people around if they don't pull their weight. Right, Caroline?"

"Of course," Caroline agreed politely, but she rolled her eyes in disgust. How was she supposed to know? She couldn't even remember past four days ago.

"What are the recent projects you've been working on? Obviously you don't have one going right now."

"Aha. You're hoping to get some investment ideas from me, aren't you? I'll admit everyone wants to follow James. He is a genius."

Max shrugged his shoulders with a grin. "Okay, you caught me. Tell me about some of your past projects, then, if you won't talk about future ones."

Caroline frowned again. Max was up to something, but she couldn't figure out what. Maybe that was because she was too busy watching him, loving the expressions on his face, the grooves down his cheeks, showing how often he smiled. His blue eyes twinkled in the soft light, and she wanted all his attention on her, not Prescott and his boring conversation.

She almost jumped as his hand sought hers under the table. When his warmth flowed into her fingers, she relaxed again and leaned against him.

"Well, last year…" Prescott began, and Caroline almost groaned. The silly man was going to explain in incredible detail every project he'd overseen.

"If you'll excuse me, I'll be right back," she said, interrupting his nonstop spiel.

"Yeah, hurry back," Max whispered as he stood. She looked at him with a frown, but he didn't elaborate. Was he afraid she'd miss a single second of Prescott's career?

She really did hurry, much to her own surprise, but Max's words intrigued her. Had he discovered something about Prescott? Other than that he liked to talk about himself, of course. That's wasn't a difficult discovery.

She returned to the table, lipstick replaced and her hair combed, just as Prescott began to talk about this year's projects.

When Max took her hand in his again, she was content to sip her tea and wait Prescott out.

"Last June, we started building apartments in Cheyenne, Wyoming. James decided that that city is hitting a growth spurt."

"Cheyenne? Now that interests me," Max said, leaning forward. "How many units did you build?"

Prescott tossed out numbers and Max nodded his head. Caroline wiggled her toes, wishing she and Max were somewhere alone.

"How long did it take to build them?" Max asked.

"Oh, we had a tight deadline on that one. You wouldn't believe how quickly we put those up. Quality building, you understand. We don't skimp on anything. But we finished those apartments in six weeks. Worked straight through the weekends. I didn't get home the entire time," Prescott said, leaning back, as if waiting for accolades for his dedication.

Max squeezed Caroline's hand, but she'd already caught the significance of Prescott's words.

"You stayed there the entire time, Prescott? What dedication."

"Oh, I'm glad to do it, Caroline. Your dad's a terrific man to work for."

"Yes, but I do have one question."

"Sure. Ask anything you like."

His expansive mood almost made Caroline feel sorry for him.

Almost.

"Just how did you manage to get me pregnant if you weren't even here for six weeks?"

Chapter Seven

Prescott had leaned back against the cushion of the booth, his glass in hand, taking a sip of the red wine he'd ordered to accompany the pasta. Quite the sophisticated diner.

With Caroline's question, he almost jackknifed into his plate, sputtering wine everywhere.

"I—we—you—"

"*We* didn't do anything…together, that is," Caroline assured him. Even if he didn't admit he'd lied, after his reaction, she felt confident that he had. "So now I'd like you to explain why you claimed to be the father of my baby."

"You visited me!" Prescott gasped, his last-ditch effort undermined by his pale cheeks.

"Give it up, man," Max advised, a grim smile on his face.

Slumping back against the cushions again, Prescott sighed and avoided Caroline's gaze. "Okay. I lied."

"Yes, but why?" She leaned forward, eager for his response.

"Look, Caroline, I've always admired you. You weren't interested, I knew that. But you were in trouble, and...and it wouldn't hurt me in your dad's eyes if I helped you out.''

"Helped me out?" Caroline gasped. "Don't you think claiming to have fathered my baby goes a little beyond 'helping me out'?"

"Maybe," Prescott admitted, "but I had good intentions."

"What about the other guy?" Max asked.

Prescott's eyes narrowed and he asked cautiously, "You mean Adrian?"

"Have there been any others claiming my baby?" Caroline asked in exasperation.

"I don't know anything about Adrian and you. The two of you have gone out, like us, but mostly to social events your father or your mother insisted you attend."

"Where was he the end of June?"

"I don't know, Caroline, really, I don't. I worked my tail off on that project. Your dad's getting ready to make a decision about which one of us will be promoted to second in command. I thought I could sway his decision by bringing that project in on time."

"It sounds like a good plan to me," Max murmured.

"If you think efficiency would win out over a son-in-law, the father of his grandchild, I've got some swampland in Florida to sell you," Prescott said.

"Good point," Max agreed with a rueful grin.

Caroline stared at the two of them. "Great! Just great! I'm being discussed like a fringe benefit and you two are bonding! Men!"

Both of them hurried to assure her that they would never think of her as a Christmas bonus or a three-day weekend, at least that was her interpretation of their protestations, but Caroline had heard enough.

"I have a headache," she announced, and asked Max to let her out of the booth.

"Where are you going?"

"Home."

"You came in a taxi. I'll take you home."

"I can take her home. I live near her parents' house," Prescott assured Max. "It'll save you a long drive."

"I don't mind."

"You don't have to worry about me chasing after her now. She probably won't speak to me after tonight."

"Naw, she wouldn't hold a grudge that long."

"Excuse me," Caroline raged. "Why don't you two gentlemen flip a coin while I go powder my nose."

She really only intended to powder her nose, but as she reached the lobby of the restaurant, she saw a couple just exiting a taxi. It took only a minute to take their place. With a message to be delivered by the maître d', along with a healthy tip, she climbed into the taxi, gave her address and leaned back, closing her eyes.

She'd tried to do too much so soon after her accident. But at least she'd eliminated one suitor. Now if she could just find a way to get rid of Adrian.

And then she could decide what to do about Max.

"Sir, the lady said to tell you that she took a taxi."

"How did she find a taxi so quickly?" Max asked, staring at the maître d'.

"Some customers were arriving in one and she took it."

Max thanked the man for delivering the message and settled back with a frown.

"That's Caroline for you," Prescott muttered. "She's always been damned independent. She drives her father crazy."

"I can believe that, but I'm not her father, and it's about time she learned that." Max reached for his back pocket.

"What are you going to do?"

"I'm going to see Caroline home."

"But she just left."

"Uh-uh." Max signaled to the waiter. "By the way, you didn't turn up here accidentally, did you?"

"No. I was waiting for Caroline when the chauffeur returned, and he told me where you were."

"I thought as much." When he pulled out his credit card, Prescott stopped him.

"I'll take care of the bill, Max. After all, I horned in on the two of you. Go ahead and do whatever you're going to do. I wish you luck."

"Thanks," Max said, shaking Prescott's hand.

Then he was up and out of there, in pursuit of a very stubborn lady. He was determined to beat her to her house. If he didn't, he was afraid she wouldn't see him.

Once he turned off the freeway, he kept his eyes open for a taxi. When he spotted one just a block ahead of him, he breathed a sigh of relief.

He passed the taxi about two blocks before Caroline's house. In the darkness, he could see only one passenger. He hoped it was Caroline. Pulling into the driveway, he pressed the button, hoping someone would let him in.

"Yes?"

"Mrs. Lamb? This is Max Daniels. Caroline is on her way home and I'd like to come in and wait for her."

"Of course, Mr. Daniels."

Without any more conversation, the big gates swung open. He hadn't expected it to be that easy. When he stopped his car in front of the door, he got out and leaned against it, waiting for Caroline. He didn't want to wait inside.

And all the while, he worried that the taxi he'd seen might not have been Caroline's. He was going to feel pretty dumb if she didn't come home.

Two minutes later, he heard the gates swing open again. Tensing, he watched as the taxi pulled to a stop beside his car. He swung open the taxi door as Caroline was paying the fee. She gasped, obviously not having noticed that he was there.

"What are you doing here?"

"Waiting for you."

The taxi driver looked from him to Caroline. "Lady, if there's a problem, I can call the cops."

She shook her head, much to Max's relief. "No, that's not necessary."

Caroline got out of the taxi, after giving the driver what must have been a generous tip, from the delight on his face, and they both stood silently, watching the taxi depart. Then she faced him, her chin tilted at its most stubborn angle.

"Why did you follow me?"

"I don't think you can call it following since I got here first," he said, glaring at her.

She stamped her foot. "Max! Why are you here?"

"Because something I was about to do got interrupted, and I refuse to be put off any longer." He didn't wait to see if she asked for an explanation. He was tired of waiting. Tired of being interrupted. And most tired of not touching her. As she opened her mouth to protest, he pulled her into his arms and lowered his lips to hers.

The magic that always filled him at her touch returned full force. All he could think about was her. His hands caressed her back, circling her slim form while his mouth held hers captive.

When he finally came up for air, he muttered, as if in explanation so she wouldn't know how much she affected him, "I don't like my dates running out on me."

She tried to pull away but he held her tighter. "You're not going anywhere, Caroline, until you promise to stop doing that."

"I only did it once, Max. I don't think you could call that a habit," she protested.

Her body pressed against his made it hard to think, but he reminded her, "You ran out on me the morning after we made love."

"We only made love once?"

"Yeah." Though he'd planned on many more nights spent with her in his arms.

"Why?"

"Why what?"

"Why did we only make love once? Didn't you want to again?"

There was a quaver in her voice that almost brought him to his knees. She had no idea how much she affected him. Gruffly he replied, "I told you. You ran out on me."

As she stared up at him, her gaze puzzled, one hand slipped up his chest to caress the nape of his neck. Shivers ran down his spine and he tightened his hold on her as his lips took hers again.

"Max!" Caroline protested when he released her at last. "You—you shouldn't—"

"Yes, I should. I should take you to my bed and never let you out of it," he growled.

Before he could kiss her again, she put her hand between their lips. "But Max, why did I leave?"

"I don't know, damn it!" Frustration filled him for

several different reasons. "I didn't know why, and I couldn't find you. I still don't know why. But at least I know where to find you." And he showed her by claiming her lips again. As his hands caressed her, they encountered the buttons on her blouse. Though Max would have liked nothing better than to strip naked on the spot, both of them, some remnant of sanity, or the cool night air on her skin made Caroline corral his searching fingers.

"Max," she protested, breaking off their kiss, "Let's go inside." Slowly she pulled away from him, the clouds of passion gradually clearing in her eyes.

"Inside?" he asked, his desire unabated.

"Yes, come inside, Max." She took out her key and opened the front door. Mrs. Lamb appeared in the hallway only seconds after. "It's only me, Mrs. Lamb, with Max. We're—we're going to talk a little in the sun room."

Talk wasn't what he was interested in. He followed her into the sun room, wondering if she would let him touch her again. He felt like a starving man having only had his hunger aroused after ignoring it for too long. He needed to touch her again.

Much to his delight, she turned into his arms as soon as he closed the door behind them.

"Max, this feels so right. I can't—I don't want to hold back."

"You won't get any argument from me, sweetheart," he assured her as he held her against him. "No argument at all."

Just as he was lowering his lips to hers, however, she said, "I wish it had been more than once."

Max froze, puzzling over her words. When he could make no sense out of them, he asked, "Why?"

"Because it might explain why I ran away." She

backed away from him, as if she feared his nearness would undermine her resolve.

"What are you talking about?" he asked as he followed her.

"Think about it, Max. It's obvious I—I'm attracted to you. I can hardly keep my hands off you. Why would I run away from that?" She didn't wait for an answer, assuming he had one. "But if I'd had a fight with, say, Adrian, and run away, I might have felt that I'd betrayed him when you and I—when we—"

Max eliminated the distance between them in a flash and drew her against him again. "No! Look, we didn't just meet one day and fall into bed! That's not how I operate!"

"I don't think it's how I operate, either," Caroline said with a rueful laugh, "but I can't remember."

"Well, I can. And I know a classy lady when I see one," he added, his lips caressing hers again. He almost lost track of what he'd been going to say as remembered sensations filled him. Making love to Caroline had been like nothing he'd experienced before.

He broke off the kiss to continue before it was too late. "When I met you, you didn't come on to me, or even really flirt with me. Not then. We just talked. But there was something between us, some spark, or pull. I can't explain it, but I've never felt it before."

"Well, obviously, we're sexually compatible," Caroline offered, laying her head on his shoulder.

"I've been sexually compatible before," he said dryly, and felt her tense up against him.

"With whom?" she demanded, a fierce frown on her face.

He dropped a quick kiss onto her lips and stepped

away. "No one you'd know, but I'm thirty-four. Did you expect me to be a virgin?"

"Isn't that what men always want? Why can't I want the same thing?"

"You can, but you won't get it with me. Besides, that's a little unreasonable since you're the one with three men claiming your baby."

"Prescott lied," she hurriedly said.

"And Adrian?"

She turned away from him. "I don't know. I worry about it all the time." Turning to face him, she said, "That's why I thought—it would've been better if we'd had a—a relationship, not a one-night stand."

"Wait a minute, lady. It wasn't a one-night stand."

"Why not? It only happened once, you said. It was at night, wasn't it?" Though she was smiling, there was a worried look in her eyes that moved him.

"Do you always take things this literally?" he teased, stepping to her side and rubbing her shoulders. "It wasn't a one-night stand, at least on my part, because if I'd had a choice, I would never have let you out of my bed again."

"Never? You must have incredible stamina," she said, smiling at him even as she wrapped her arms around his neck, inviting his kiss again.

Max more than met her halfway, putting aside any idea of discussing their past. She was in his arms again and he never wanted to let her go.

She broke away from him. "Max, did—did you think about a future? For us, I mean?"

"Hell, yes! I told you I didn't ever intend to let you go."

"No, you said you didn't intend to let me out of your

bed. That's a little different from what I'm asking," she pointed out ruefully.

"You're asking if I had honorable intentions?" He pulled her closer to him again. "Yeah, I did. I didn't want to rush you, but I had every intention of marrying you."

"But you've never married before?"

"Nope."

"Why? Don't you want a family?"

"I want you. And whatever comes with you. And that's the reason I've never married. I never met a woman I couldn't live without. Until I met you."

He saw tears in her eyes and pressed her head against his shoulder. "Don't cry, sweetheart."

"It's okay," she said, her voice muffled. "I didn't even realize I wanted a family until I found out about the baby. But I do. I want a real family, a daddy, too. And, oh, Max, I want that daddy to be you!"

A YEARNING FILLED Caroline, so strong that it almost obliterated any restraint. She wanted to belong to this man, as old-fashioned as that sounded. She also wanted him to belong to her. Something deep within her shouted that he was her perfect mate.

But had she realized that fact before or after she'd slept with another man?

She shoved such destroying thoughts aside. Tonight, she only wanted Max to fill her mind. She wanted—

"Caroline?" Mrs. Lamb called through the door.

Caroline was greatly relieved the housekeeper hadn't entered, since Max was holding her tightly against him and her hair and makeup showed the signs of their embrace.

"Yes, Mrs. Lamb?"

"I just wondered if you two wanted something to snack on?"

"I'm only hungry for you," Max whispered in her ear, a melodramatic leer on his face.

She ignored him. "Thank you, Mrs. Lamb. That would be nice."

"I'll bring a tray, then."

She moved away from Max as Mrs. Lamb's footsteps faded down the hallway.

"Change your mind?"

He'd followed her.

"About what?"

"About us," he reminded her, slipping his arms around her again.

"Not exactly," she said, turning to face him within his embrace. "It's just that—that we have too many questions facing us to just forget about the past."

"I thought that was exactly what you'd done," he reminded her, a grin on his lips.

"Max, be serious. I did, but you know it wasn't on purpose. It's so daunting, having no past, no memories. I think what we've just shared is really special, but how do I know? I have nothing to compare it to."

"Just trust your heart, Caroline. Or trust me. I can assure you it's special."

She played with a button on his shirt, twisting and turning it, trying to figure out how to explain her confusion. He lifted her face up with a determined finger under her chin.

"Well?"

She laid her head on his shoulder. "I want to trust you, Max, but even if what we shared was special, we don't know if I found that out after I got pregnant, or before."

For the first time, *he* moved away from *her*. "Prescott was lying."

"I know, and it's a great relief to have eliminated *someone!* But as much as I want him to be a liar, too, I don't know that Adrian is. Apparently, I did go out with him often. And he seems quite sure that he's the father."

"Doesn't that strike you as weird? That he would be so sure that he's the father? You spent two weeks with me. Didn't he even wonder where you were?"

"I don't know! I've only spoken to him the night you all came to dinner. Last night. I haven't had time to investigate his claim."

"You sound like a damned insurance investigator, Caroline! We're talking about making love!"

"Oh, thanks for telling me. I was confusing being pregnant with a car wreck! Throwing up always does that to me!" She moved across the room, putting more distance between them, glaring at him.

"Caroline, you're not being very—"

Another knock on the door preceded Mrs. Lamb's entrance with a well-filled tray of snacks and drinks. "Here you are. I wasn't sure what Mr. Daniels liked, so I fixed a lot of different things."

Caroline turned with relief to the housekeeper. At least with Mrs. Lamb, everything was straightforward. Not like the maze her emotions were in concerning Max. "Thanks, Lambie. You shouldn't have gone to so much trouble."

"No trouble at all. With your parents at that city council banquet, it's been too quiet here this evening."

"Don't worry about cleaning up. Why don't you take the evening off, since they're gone. I'll bring the tray to the kitchen later."

"That'd be nice, honey, but I'll be available if you

need anything." With a nod to Max, the housekeeper left the room.

They stood as if frozen, with Mrs. Lamb's footsteps the only noise. Finally Caroline moved into the role of hostess. "Would you care for something to eat?"

"No."

"Then what do you want, Max?" she asked in frustration.

He stared at her, his gaze both hard and hot, a mixture of determination and desire. "You. I want you, and nothing else."

A part of her responded to his words, wanting to fling herself into his arms and throw care and truth to the winds. A large part of her wanted to do that. But that small nagging conscience kept tugging on her desire, telling her to wait. Damn her conscience.

"Max, until I know the truth about—about the baby, and what I was doing, I can't commit to anything."

"Then let's figure it out, Caroline, because I'm having a hard time holding back."

"You could try cold showers?" she suggested, hoping to lighten the tension as her gaze skimmed his impressive form, one few women would want to resist.

"I'm already a shriveled prune. What more do you want?"

He'd responded with teasing, as she'd offered her suggestion, but now she couldn't joke. "I want you, Max," she whispered. Then, before he could reach her, as he showed every intention of doing, she added, "But I also want, need, the truth."

He had closed the distance between them but he didn't touch her. The two inches between them could have been a mile, filled with frustration and confusion.

Max took a deep breath before saying, "Surely someone knows something, Caroline. We've just got to start asking questions.''

''Yes. I've tried, but…but I'll try again. Someone must know something.''

At that moment, the door to the sun room burst open and Chelsea, dressed in a silk maternity dress, holding a piece of paper in her hand, entered the room, followed by the faithful Roddy in a tux.

''Caroline, I must speak to—oh. I didn't know you had company. Hello, Mr. Daniels.'' She waited until Max acknowledged her greeting before saying, ''It's just as well you're here, however. Because I have something to say that you both need to hear. We can tell Prescott and Adrian later.''

Caroline and Max exchanged startled glances. Did Chelsea hold the key to their puzzle?

Chapter Eight

"What is it?" Caroline gasped, taking a step toward her sister. "Have you remembered something?"

"Remembered something? What are you talking about?" Chelsea demanded, staring at Caroline as if she were crazy. Roddy, meanwhile, had wandered over to the tray and was sampling the snacks.

"About my amnesia. About what happened two months ago," Caroline explained, her gaze glued to her sister.

"Don't be ridiculous. I told you I didn't remember anything. I want to talk to you about names." Chelsea moved over to the sofa and sat down. "Roddy, come sit with me."

As Chelsea's husband reluctantly followed her orders, Caroline exchanged a confused look with Max before she too sat down. She didn't think her shaky knees would hold her up much longer. "What are you talking about, Chelsea?"

"Names! Now, don't tell me you haven't been thinking about them. Why, that's the first thing I considered." She spread out the piece of paper on her lap and studied it.

"Names?"

Exasperation filled Chelsea's face. "For the baby, of course. I'm trying to be understanding, Caro. Daddy explained that you hadn't gotten pregnant to upstage me on purpose, so I thought the polite thing to do would be to give you a list of names that you shouldn't consider. That way you won't be disappointed if I select one of them for my baby, who will be born first, of course."

As if that would be a shock for me, Caroline thought. "I know, Chelsea. I can count."

Chelsea sniffed, as if dismissing her sister's sarcasm. "What names have you already thought of?"

The humor of the situation struck Caroline, fortunately, and she leaned back in her chair. "I've been too busy trying to name the daddy, Chelsea. I haven't had time to think about names for the baby."

"Well," Chelsea said, as if instructing the uninformed, "you need to consider them at once. People always ask, and you need an answer ready. Otherwise those questions will keep coming up, again and again."

"Like my breakfast," Caroline muttered. Max gave her a sympathetic smile as he pulled a chair to her side, then clasped her hand as he sat down.

"Caroline! That's most distasteful. You'll ruin Roddy's appetite."

Since Roddy had moved the tray to the coffee table in front of him and his wife and had continued to eat, Caroline wasn't too worried. Roddy, however, with a guilty glance at Chelsea, leaned back, away from the table.

"See? It's okay, Roddy. I'm sure Caroline didn't mean to be so unmannerly." Chelsea returned her attention to her list, and Roddy leaned forward to select another hors d'oeuvre.

"I don't think a week of intestinal flu could ruin his appetite," Max muttered, leaning close to her.

Caroline enjoyed the warmth of his smile as he exchanged looks with her. It made her want to turn into his embrace, to feel the comfort of his arms around her. She wanted to be alone with Max. But that wasn't wise.

"Now, I know it may not seem fair to you since you're the firstborn, but I've put on my list the name Etta Mae." Chelsea challenged Caroline with her gaze.

"Etta Mae?" Max gasped, bending forward in surprise. "Why would she not think it's fair? Why would she even—"

"Max!" Caroline exclaimed, stopping him from expressing his opinion about the name, though she had to struggle to hide her smile. "That's our grandmother's name."

"Oh. Are you disappointed?"

She loved the concern mixed with horror in his voice. He didn't want to hurt her feelings.

"No. That's all right, Chelsea. You can have grandmother's name."

"Well, really, Caroline, how can you just give up so easily? Haven't you thought about it? grandmother's sure to give a handsome gift to the great-grandchild named after her. She might even make special arrangements in her will for her."

Chelsea never noticed the look of amusement that passed from Caroline to Max. He relaxed against the back of the chair as he realized Caroline wasn't like her sister. Unfortunately, he apparently couldn't hold back his feelings.

"You would name a child Etta Mae for money?"

Chelsea glared at him. "An inheritance is important to a child, even if she's too young to realize. Besides, Etta Mae is a charming name. Old-fashioned."

"Definitely," Max agreed gravely, and Caroline covered her lips with her fingers, pretending to cough.

"That's not the only female name I've chosen, though. I might name her after Mother. Amelia is a charming name, also. Mother might even *notice* that she has a grandchild if I did that, instead of always thinking about her charities!"

The plaintive note in Chelsea's voice sounded all too familiar to Caroline, but she couldn't help responding to the need in her sister's voice. "Chelsea, she'll notice your baby. I'm sure she's excited about it."

"No, she's not," Chelsea said bluntly. "A friend called her the other day to discuss giving me a shower and Mother was too busy to talk." She blinked rapidly, as if dismissing tears, before looking at Caroline. "And that's another thing. I'm not sharing a shower with you."

Caroline remembered her first sight of her family. She'd wondered how anyone could love such a strange group. But she felt sorry for Chelsea, craving her mother's attention. Amelia only had eyes for the needy— but she was blind to the fact that her own daughter was one of them.

"That's all right. I'm not ready for a shower. And Mother won't notice my baby if she doesn't notice yours."

"That's true," Chelsea said, brightening.

Caroline almost chuckled. She guessed misery did love company. At least, Chelsea did.

"Now, the only other girl's name I'm going to reserve is Madonna Louise. That way she would be named after someone important and me, too."

Max erupted into a fit of coughing that tested Caroline's self-control. "I think I prefer Etta Mae," he whispered.

"Roddy, how do you feel about the names?" Caroline asked, curiosity filling her. He had said nothing since they arrived.

"Hmm? Oh, whatever Chelsea wants."

"I see." She carefully avoided Max's gaze, turning back to her sister. "I don't think we have any conflicts with those names."

"Oh, good. Now, about the boy's names. He will, of course, be named Roderick Grant IV, but I've put several other names on the list for the future. It's not fair for you to use all the good names just because you don't have a husband to name your baby after."

"Lucky me," Caroline agreed, unable to hold back the grin she sent Max's way. He was silently chuckling, shaking his head back and forth.

She was a little embarrassed at Chelsea's reaction and only hoped Max would understand. It occurred to her to wonder how Max's family would react to their announcement. Assuming, of course, there was anything to announce.

"So, I'm placing dibs on Daddy's name. After all, if I have a second boy, he'll need a good inheritance, too."

"Of course. Umm, what about Roddy's family? Aren't there any wealthy people on his side?"

Chelsea stared at her as if she'd lost her mind. "Don't be ridiculous. You know Roddy's family is one of the wealthiest in the state, along with ours. But I think Daddy should come first, after Roddy and his father. Don't you think so, Roddy?"

Roddy, with his mouth full of a chicken-salad finger sandwich, nodded quickly, muttering what might have been a yes. Caroline wasn't sure.

"Any other names?" Max asked innocently, and Caroline turned to stare at him. "I think Muhammad Ali Grant would be nice."

"Max," Caroline warned even as she grinned.

Chelsea, however, didn't take offense. "You're being frivolous," she said calmly. "We would never give our child an unchristian name, but it is important that they have a name of substance. You'd better think about that when you choose your child's name."

Max looked at Caroline, his gaze suddenly filled with realization, as if it hadn't occurred to him that her pregnancy would result in a baby. But then, he wasn't throwing up every morning.

"I think we still have a little time to decide," Caroline assured both her sister and Max.

"It's best not to wait—"

The opening of the sun room door interrupted Chelsea's warning. Amelia, James and Adrian entered.

"Good evening, children. Mrs. Lamb said you were all here. Any hors d'oeuvres left, Roddy?" James asked, heading for the tray at once.

"Yes, sir. Of course, sir," Roddy hastened to assure his father-in-law, reluctantly pushing the tray to the end of the table near the chair James chose.

"Good. I'm starved. From the meal they served this evening, one would think the city was on the verge of bankruptcy," he grumbled.

"I thought the chicken was delicious," Amelia commented. "I'm sure it had almost no calories, once I removed the skin. You should've followed my advice, James, and removed the skin. You never pay attention to your calorie intake."

While the two older members of the new arrivals were discussing food, Adrian drew a chair next to Caroline's other side and sat down.

"Good evening, Caro. I called earlier to see if you wanted to accompany me to the banquet, but Mrs. Lamb said you were out."

She gave him a brief smile. "Yes. Thank you for thinking of me."

He lifted her hand from the arm of the chair and drew it to his lips for a brief caress. Max was still holding her other hand and she could feel the tension emanating from his body.

"I always think about you, my dear. After all, we're going to be married."

His assumption set up her back, but it also disturbed her deep within. He sounded so confident. And he wasn't her choice.

"I'm not as sure about that as you are, Adrian. I don't think we've had a chance to discuss why you think you're the father of my child." She pulled her hand free, putting it in her lap, as far away from him as possible.

"Do you really want to discuss our affair here? In front of everyone? That's why I've kept quiet about it, of course, because you didn't want your father to know."

His words had such a ring of truth to them that she almost gasped. Of course she wouldn't want her father to know. Could she have been having an affair with Adrian before she met Max?

"If that's true, why did I go away for two weeks without telling anyone where I was going?"

Adrian's possessive gaze shifted from Caroline to Max and back again. "Is that what he told you?"

"That's what Mrs. Lamb told me, and Lewis, and my father and mother."

"Ah, but you didn't keep it a secret from everyone. *I* knew where you were going."

"I don't believe you," she whispered, panic filling her voice.

"I knew where you were going because you were going away with me. And that's why you didn't tell anyone. The secret, remember?" He leaned closer and smiled.

"That's a lie!" Max exclaimed, leaping up from his chair.

"Caroline knows it's the truth," Adrian said, standing to stare at Max.

Caroline, confused but worried Max might throw a punch at Adrian, stood also. "I—I don't know that! I can't remember anything!"

"What's going on?" James demanded, his interest drawn from the food.

"I was just explaining to this gentleman that I'm the father of Caro's baby," Adrian said, nodding at his employer.

"Great! Then we can get on with the wedding plans," James said, clapping his hands with pleasure. "I want a wedding right away. People will count, of course, when the baby is born, but the sooner the better."

"It's not that simple," Caroline exclaimed.

"You promised you'd marry the father of the baby, Caro," James reminded her.

"Yes, but Adrian has offered no proof that he's the father of my child." She turned to face Adrian and felt Max's hands come to rest on her shoulders as he stood behind her. "Do you have proof, Adrian?"

"I have plane tickets to Las Vegas for the day you left home, returning two weeks later."

"Do either of them have my name on them?"

"No, just my name and companion," he said, smiling a rueful grin. "Secrecy, remember?"

"I think I'm going to hate that word the rest of my life," Caroline muttered.

"You could've been accompanied by anyone," Max growled.

"Yes, I could've, but I wasn't. I was accompanied by Caroline. We've been, uh, dating about four months now. But she didn't want her father to know we were involved. She said he'd put too much pressure on her to marry."

"Damn right," James agreed.

"It's too late now, darling," Adrian assured her, taking both her hands in his. "The baby makes things too complicated for me to keep silent." His voice was filled with seeming concern and love.

With Max clasping her shoulders and Adrian her hands, Caroline felt torn in two. She didn't want Adrian to be the father of her baby. But wanting didn't make something so. The feelings he expressed touched her, even if she didn't want to hear them. Who was telling the truth?

"This is too frustrating! Why can't I remember?"

"You probably weren't getting enough vitamin B-6," Amelia murmured. "Or was it B-12? Or maybe another number, I'm not sure. But I was reading that it could improve your memory. I'll look for the article tomorrow."

Caroline pulled away from the two men's touch. "Mother, I have amnesia from a bump on the head, not from something I ate." She turned around to see both Adrian and Max staring at her.

"I need proof. My memory isn't going to work for me, so I have to have proof." She looked at Max. "Do you have anything to show me that I spent those two weeks with you?"

He stared at her, and she wished she could read his

mind. "Only this," he said quietly before closing the distance between them. Without another word, he pulled her against him and kissed her.

Caroline distantly heard gasps of outrage behind her, but she was too caught up in the senses Max inflamed. The man's touch was devastating.

He released her and stepped back. "I have no proof, sweetheart, except that we had something special."

Adrian stepped forward. "Anyone can kiss a lady," he said dryly. "Shall I demonstrate?"

Caroline moved away to stand behind her mother's chair. "No...no, I realize that isn't exactly proof." But Max had a point. His kisses were incredible. "Max, didn't you introduce me to anyone? Or—"

"What would that prove? I could bribe half a dozen people to swear they met you, but so could Adrian." Max was staring at her, tension on his face, but Caroline glanced at Adrian as Max spoke. There was an acknowledgment in his face, as if that had already occurred to him.

"True," she agreed, studying the two men consideringly. How could she figure out who was telling the truth?

Finally she faced her father. "Daddy, until someone offers me proof, I refuse to marry. If you're going to be embarrassed by the presence of an unwed pregnant daughter in your house, I'll move out."

"You'll do no such thing!" James exclaimed. "No one will criticize *my* daughter. But I'd rather you marry."

"We just had Chelsea's wedding last year," Amelia said. "I really think it would be better to wait another year for Caroline's. I told her she should've married before Chelsea, but she wouldn't listen to me."

"Amelia," James answered with open impatience, "if

we wait a year for Caroline's wedding, the baby will have already been born. Your grandchild will be illegitimate. I can assure you that is more socially unacceptable than having two weddings within a year of each other.''

"But, James, it would take at least a year to even plan a wedding.'' She peered around her distraught husband to stare accusingly at Caroline. "You should have given me at least a year's notice, dear.''

Hysterical laughter bubbled up in Caroline. Of course, she should've planned her pregnancy, and, for that matter, her amnesia, better, for her mother's sake. In fact, as long as she was planning, she should've left a note with the name of the daddy. It would've saved her a lot of trouble.

"I'm sorry, Mother, but I didn't exactly plan what has happened. *If* I marry, I think we can keep it simple and not need a year's preparation.''

"Of course you'll marry,'' James ordered.

"To me,'' Adrian added.

His insistence was getting on her nerves. "Not without proof,'' she reminded him coolly.

"I'll get proof.''

She turned her gaze to Max, trying not to plead with her eyes. She wanted him to assure her that he, too, would offer proof. That he was, indeed, the father of her child. That he loved her.

That thought hit her like a punch in the stomach. Loved her? Was she in love with Max? Of course she was if she went to bed with him, she assured herself. But did she? Or had she been sleeping with Adrian? Was she the kind of person who slept with a man because her hormones were in overdrive? And was Adrian a person who could arouse those hormones? She didn't have any doubt about Max's abilities in that area.

"I'm tired. It's been a long day."

"But I haven't explained about the names to Adrian," Chelsea suddenly said, having silently watched the drama unfold. "After all, it appears that he'll have more to say about it than Mr. Daniels."

"No, Chelsea. I'll decide the name of my child, or at least, I will until I'm sure who the daddy is."

"But he just said—" Chelsea began.

"I know what he said! That doesn't make it truth. Until I have proof, this is my child, and mine alone."

"I don't think that's physically possible, dear," Amelia murmured, staring at her daughter.

Caroline wondered if her mother could possibly be insane, but there was a twinkle in her mother's gaze that sent a sigh of relief through her. "No, probably not, Mother, but I'm beginning to wonder if it wouldn't be easier that way. Maybe I should discuss the topic in my prayers this evening."

"You could try," Amelia said, her voice filled with doubt, "but I've tried it before and nothing changed."

Chapter Nine

If they could put a man on the moon, the least they could do for women was find a way to eliminate morning sickness.

Or make pregnancy possible for men.

After starting the next day by throwing up anything she had consumed in the past century, that was the only thought that made Caroline laugh.

And also made her wonder if part of her sickness was caused by stress.

Why should she be stressed? Just because she had no memory of her life until five days ago, she was pregnant with a baby she had no memory of conceiving, and there were two men who wanted to claim that baby, she had no reason for stress. She groaned and staggered back to her bed just as someone knocked softly on her door.

"Oh, you're already up," Mrs. Lamb said as she entered to Caroline's call to come in, carrying a tray. "Here's some crackers to eat. They'll settle your stomach. I meant to bring them up last night so you'd have them first thing this morning."

"Do they really work?" Caroline asked, finding the idea of eating anything terribly unappealing.

"Most of the time. Have you already been sick?"

"Yes. Over and over again."

"Oh, my stars. You poor thing. Try a cracker and the carbonated water I brought. You're supposed to eat them when you first awake, before you even sit up."

Caroline lay on a pillow, munching crackers and sipping the water while Mrs. Lamb sat on the edge of the bed, watching. Much to Caroline's surprise, her stomach began to return to normal.

"It works, Lambie. I think I may survive."

"Of course you will. You always manage."

Caroline's mood darkened. "Do I? I don't seem to be doing a good job of managing my life right now."

"It's not your fault you got amnesia."

"No, but it's my fault I'm pregnant. At least I think it is. I can't believe I didn't insist on precautions."

Mrs. Lamb's cheeks flushed red, but she looked right at Caroline. "Even without a memory, I'm sure you know that sometimes a woman can be swept away by—by passion."

Caroline smiled at her. Clearly embarrassed, the older woman still had said what she felt needed to be said. As if it would—her thoughts skidded to a halt.

"Wait a minute, Lambie, I think you've got a point."

"Well, of course I do."

Sitting up, Caroline took the housekeeper's hand. "No, I don't mean—I mean, you may have found a clue about who's the daddy of my baby."

"I did? What clue?"

"If I was so swept away by passion that I didn't think of protection, which of the two men could arouse such forgetfulness?" She grinned because she already knew the answer and she liked it—a lot.

"Two? I thought there were three?"

"No, we eliminated Prescott last night. He was lying.

Just as one of the others is lying.'' To be fair, Caroline forced herself to consider Adrian and whether she might be swayed by him. She didn't have to give such thought to Max. Even being in the same room with him accelerated her pulse.

''Are you sure it will be so simple?''

Caroline stared at Mrs. Lamb. Talk about a bucket of cold water. ''What do you mean?''

''Maybe you wanted to get pregnant on purpose?''

''Why would I want to do that? Especially if I knew anything about it. Throwing up isn't a lot of fun.'' She rubbed her unruly stomach.

''That will pass. And you've always been the leader, between you and Chelsea.''

Caroline stared at her in horror. ''You think I might have wanted to get pregnant—without marrying—to show up my sister?'' Mrs. Lamb wasn't painting a very pretty picture of her behavior.

''I didn't say that. I just thought you should consider everything…with so much at stake.'' Mrs. Lamb wasn't meeting her gaze.

''Lambie,'' Caroline began, reaching out to take the lady's hand, ''was I really so spoiled that I would do such a thing?''

''No, not spoiled. I don't know. I just know that Chelsea always thought she had to compete with you. It might be natural for you to respond.''

''I think I like your first theory better. I can believe that M—that a man might have swept me off my feet.''

''So you think you know which one it is?''

''I hope so. And I'm determined to prove it. I'm tired of sitting around waiting to get back my memory. The doctor said it might be months…or never.'' She threw off the covers and slid from the bed.

"I'll go down and make you some breakfast, then."

Caroline started to protest but was surprised to discover that her stomach seemed to like the idea. Contrary thing! "Okay, but not too much."

Standing under the steamy spray a minute later, she thought about her hastily formed plan. It probably had all kinds of holes in it, but it appealed to her. She was going to get Max to retrace their steps for her. Maybe, just maybe, things she had seen only during those two weeks would bring back the memory she needed.

If it didn't, at least she would get to spend time with Max.

"BOY, ARE YOU A GROUCH this morning," Susan complained.

Max glared at her. "Just get me that file."

She returned in less than a minute, a file in her hand. "Here it is. So, what's bothering you?"

"Nothing."

"I didn't say anything to Mom or Karen about your girlfriend. If they found out, it wasn't from me."

"They didn't find out."

"Oh."

He pretended to study the file he'd asked for, hoping his little sister would take the hint. She didn't.

"So, are you still seeing her?"

"I don't know."

"Did she dump you?" Susan asked in astonishment.

"Susan," he warned, putting every threat he'd ever made toward her—and that covered a lot of territory—into his tone.

"Okay, okay, I'm going, but she's the one who made a mistake, if she did. You're one terrific guy, big brother."

Max held his sigh until she'd closed the door behind her. Sweet of her to try to make him feel better. But it didn't do much good. He *knew* he was the father to Caroline's baby.

But he couldn't prove it.

Without proof, things were at a stalemate.

And he didn't trust Adrian. The man might produce some kind of proof. Some kind of fake proof.

If the man had said he and Caroline had had an affair and then argued, causing her to run away, and Max had caught her on the rebound, he might have believed him. Caroline had been—not upset—but very cautious. Yes, that was the word, cautious.

But Adrian had chosen to lie about those two weeks. So Max knew Adrian wasn't the father of the baby.

The baby was Max's.

He was going to be a daddy.

He'd always intended to have a child, children. Somehow, it had never happened. Shrugging his shoulders, he admitted to himself that he hadn't made much effort.

But when Caroline had walked through the door to the model home, he'd known, as sure as he knew his own name, that she was the one. And while he wouldn't choose to marry her with a child already on the way, he didn't have a problem with becoming a father.

Did he want a boy or a girl? The sex of his child hadn't concerned him, but now he pictured Caroline holding their baby and somehow he just knew she'd be a girl. A baby daughter, just as beautiful as her mother. He'd teach her lots of things. How to defend herself. How to run a business. How to— He smiled even more. He wouldn't have to teach her how to flirt. Her mother would take care of that. Or how to knock a guy off his feet.

Yeah, his baby girl would be perfect. Just like her mother. And he couldn't wait to hold her.

He was lost in thought, contemplating the child, when Susan opened his door.

"Max, I'm going to go to lunch a little early, okay?"

"Yeah." Whatever. He didn't care what she did as long as she didn't ask any more questions about Caroline. She withdrew from the doorway but didn't close his door, so he had no difficulty hearing the outside door open.

"Hello. May I help you?"

"I'm Caroline Adkins. I'm here to see Max Daniels if he's available."

He leaped from his desk at the first word, knowing immediately who had arrived. By the time she finished her request, he was at Susan's side.

"Caroline," he said, trying to control his breathing. He didn't want to sound like an eager puppy.

"You're Caroline?" Susan asked, a smile breaking across her face. "I'm Susan, Max's sister."

"I'm delighted to meet you, Susan," Caroline said, smiling back at her. "I don't know if Max told you, but I have amnesia, so if we've met before—"

"No, we haven't. Max has kept you a secret."

"Oh."

He watched in frustration as disappointment filled her eyes.

"Come into my office, Caroline," he suggested, eager to get her away from his sister before Susan said something she shouldn't. "You can go to lunch, Susan."

"Oh, I'm in no hurry if you need me to do anything," Susan offered, smiling at Caroline.

"No. Go to lunch."

"Okay, okay. Nice to have met you, Caroline."

"Yes. I'm glad to have met you, too."

He slammed the door in the face of their niceties. He was too upset to tolerate them.

"Well, really, Max, what will Susan think?"

"She's already told me what she thinks, several times today. Do you want the exact words?"

He regretted his outburst as Caroline's eyes widened.

"Sorry. I seem to be in a rotten mood this morning."

"Is this the first time you've been angry with me, or have I forgotten the others?"

She tilted her head to one side, waiting for his response, and he wanted to close the distance between them and kiss her until she forgot everything but their passion.

"The only time I really got angry with you was when you walked out on me. And you weren't there to see it."

Caroline stepped away from him, moving over to the window behind his desk. "I know. I wish I could explain—or understand for that matter. And I'm tired of waiting for my memory to come back."

"I don't think you have a lot of choice there," Max replied, his bad humor still in place because of his frustration. When she continued to stare out the window, saying nothing, he asked, "Why are you here?"

She stiffened before turning to face him. "Not interested in company today? Afraid I'll chase away potential customers?"

Though she hadn't answered his question, he played along. "I'm always ready for your company."

Her gaze shifted away from him, making him suspicious. What did she have up her sleeve? And how well did he know her? He'd thought he'd known her, but recent days had proven him wrong.

"Did we come here often?" she abruptly asked, looking around his office.

"Never."

His answer seemed to surprise her. "Why?"

How could she ask such calm questions? Didn't she understand what was at stake? Their future depended on what happened in the next few days. He strode to her side and pulled her into his arms with all the energy of his pent-up frustration. "Because I don't consider this proper business behavior," he muttered before his lips took hers.

Last night had only aroused his passion more, not sated it. He pressed her body against his hardness, his lips insisting that she open to him. He was tired of standing by, waiting for her to acknowledge his role in her life.

"Max!" she gasped, wrenching her lips away. "We can't—"

"Can't what? Make love? We already have. And why the hell you can't remember the magic we make together, I don't know." He'd wasted enough time talking. He'd prove to her that they belonged together in the only way that mattered.

She responded to his kisses, her arms encircling his neck. When he stroked her, she pressed even closer to him, until he thought he'd lose control. Again.

It was the sound of the outside door opening that brought their frantic movements to a sudden stillness.

"Max?"

The masculine voice drew a gasp from Caroline, but Max recognized it at once. He shoved her toward the corner and left her in his office. As he moved, he struggled to button his shirt that had somehow come unbuttoned. "Yeah, Jim?"

"What are you doing? Dressing in the office?" Jim asked, grinning at him.

Max struggled to maintain his cool. "Yeah. What do you need?"

Jim unrolled a house plan and began pointing out some complications to Max. He tried to concentrate on the facts as his body did a slow descent from arousal. It was difficult.

"Well, what do you think?" Jim asked, and stood waiting.

Hell. He had no idea what the man had even asked. Now what was he going to do?

The outer door opened again and Susan walked in.

"I thought you went to lunch?" he growled. He didn't need any more complications.

"I did. I wasn't very hungry." Susan searched the room with her gaze. "Where's Caroline? And why is your shirt buttoned crooked?"

Max looked down at his shirt in embarrassment. Susan was right. He'd buttoned it wrong. He could feel his cheeks flaming.

Jim had never been a slow-top. After another look at the door to Max's office, he grabbed Susan by the arm. "Okay if I take Susan to see the new place?" he asked as he pulled her out the door.

"Great. That'd be great, Jim," Max assured him, silently promising the man a bonus. Intelligence should be rewarded.

Turning to his office, he found Caroline standing in the doorway. He was afraid she'd be angry with what had happened, but she appeared calm. Which was more than he could do.

"They're gone?"

"Yeah."

Without a word, she crossed to him and began unbuttoning his shirt. Before he could misinterpret her movements, she then placed the buttons in the proper holes.

"Thanks," he said huskily, but he couldn't help thinking he would have preferred her to reverse the procedure.

Then she surprised him by saying, "Let's go to your place."

Chapter Ten

Caroline was relieved to get Max behind the wheel of his truck. As long as he was driving, he couldn't distract her with his touch, his kisses. And distraction seemed to come easy for him. But she had some questions she needed answered.

There was no easy way to begin, so she broke their tense silence with the most important one.

"When we made love, why didn't you use protection? Don't you ever—I mean, with other women?"

She watched his hands tighten on the steering wheel, but his response was brief. "Yes."

She stared at him blankly before saying, "Yes, what?"

"Yes, I used protection with other women. I always use protection."

"Not always," she reminded him, several questions still unanswered.

He refused to look at her, keeping his gaze on the road as he swept his hand through his hair. She thought he wasn't going to answer her, but finally he said, "Look, Caroline, when I met you, I—you knocked me off my feet. I wanted to go to bed with you there in the model home where we met." He looked at her with eyes filled with hot passion.

"But we didn't," Caroline said hurriedly, pressing against the truck seat.

"No, we didn't. In fact, even though you were willing to go to dinner with me, you made it damn clear that dinner was all you were offering."

"What happened next?" She knew so little about herself, much less the man next to her. It was like working blindfolded. And she hated it.

"We spent the next two weeks falling in love." He made his blunt statement a challenge, daring her to contradict him.

She drew in a deep breath. "When—when did we—"

"The night before you left."

His responses were more and more brusque. Her inquisition wasn't pleasing him. *Well, too bad,* she thought huffily. She was the one pregnant. She had a right to ask a few questions. Particularly the one he hadn't yet answered.

"Why didn't you use protection?"

"Because I hadn't planned to take you to bed, okay?" he snapped.

"Are you trying to say I seduced you? Or are you blaming me for not having taken care of things, like most men?" She could get just as irritated as him.

"Hell! Caroline, how can you ask such stupid questions? It just happened. Don't you understand how it is between us? I can't touch you without going up in flames. And for your information, lady, you didn't do any holding back yourself."

She looked away, unable to meet his look. How could she argue with him after what nearly happened in his office? Just sitting beside him made her heart pound and her pulse race. "Where were we?"

"We were at my place." He stopped the truck and waved out the windshield with his hand. "Right here."

She ignored his house to finish her questioning. "You didn't have protection here?"

"Damn it, Caroline, what is the point? We didn't use protection. That's pretty obvious since you're pregnant."

"I want to know why."

Staring straight ahead, he said, "Yes, I had protection here. I didn't—hadn't used it in a while, but it was there. I preached too much to my brothers about always being safe not to have some condoms there."

Hadn't he cared enough about her to want to protect her? Was she wrong about him? "Then why?" she whispered.

He whirled in his seat suddenly and seized her by the shoulders. "How many times do I have to tell you? I lose control with you." His lips covered hers again in a demonstration that had her convinced at once.

Knowing she was going under for the count if she didn't do something quickly, Caroline pulled away from him. She clutched the door handle and muttered, "I want to see your house. It looks beautiful."

The glare he shot her didn't show any appreciation, but he wrenched open the door and got out. She quickly followed.

Max's home was his pride and joy. He'd rewarded himself with it a couple of years ago. Set in the foothills of the Rockies, it wasn't huge, with only three bedrooms, but it sported a back porch and patio with a mountain stream nearby.

He opened the front door and stood stiffly aside to let her enter.

"Do you take care of it yourself?" Caroline asked, looking around at the casual furnishings. His sisters had helped with the choices, but he'd made the final decisions, choosing bold, bright colors in comfortable, easy-care fabrics.

"No. The cleaning lady came today, so you shouldn't find any dirty underwear thrown under the bed."

Her eyebrows rose, a smile on her face for the first time since they left the office. "Oh. So that's the kind of person you are."

"I never tried to hide it."

His gruffness washed away her smile. "I know, but since I can't remember anything about those two weeks, it's like I'm meeting you for the first time."

"Not in one way."

"What are you talking about?"

"I'm talking about our bodies, Caroline. Your head may not remember me, but your body does. Surely you can admit that? Or do you want another demonstration?"

She licked her lips and he thought he'd die if he didn't touch her. He stepped forward and then stopped when she moved away from him.

"I want to believe that, Max, but you're a very sexy guy. Maybe you have that effect on every woman you date."

He leaned against the wall, trying to assume a casual pose. "Oh, yeah. You saw the line around the house, didn't you, just waiting to fall into my bed."

She grinned but shrugged her shoulders. "Just because they aren't here at the moment doesn't mean they aren't chasing you."

"Honey, once I met you, I haven't so much as talked to another woman except to order fast food."

She seemed pleased with his words but turned away to look at the living room. He watched her, his hands itching to pull her back into his arms, but he didn't.

Things had gotten a little intense, and he didn't want to frighten her away again. "Come on back to the den and I'll fix us a cup of coffee."

She followed him without saying anything.

As they passed the kitchen, Caroline dug in her heels. "Wow. I'm not a great chef, but I know a terrific kitchen when I see one. How perfect, Max."

Memory grabbed him and he blinked several times before explaining. "That's about what you said the first time you saw it."

She gave him a nervous smile and walked into the family room that connected. She moved to the huge windows that looked out toward the stream. "What a marvelous yard for children."

He walked up behind her and slid his hands over her stomach. "Yeah. For my kid." The idea of his being a father was becoming more and more real to him.

Her hands came to rest over his, but when she spoke, he heard the hesitancy in her voice.

"Max, I can't—I don't know."

He tensed again. He hated it when she refused to believe he was the father. When she didn't recognize what they shared. "Caroline, this child is mine. Mine."

"I believe—when you touch me, I have no doubts. It's only afterward, when I think about the past, that I get confused. What if the baby really is Adrian's? What then?"

He clenched his jaw until it ached. "It's not."

"But how can you know? How can any of us be sure until I regain my memory?" With an almost mournful air, she added, "And until I know whose baby this is, I can't make any decisions."

"Then why are we here?" he growled, wanting her, frustrated with her holding back.

"I want to see where we made love."

With his jaw set, he motioned for her to follow him as he led the way up the nearby staircase.

CAROLINE WANTED TO CLOSE her eyes, to run away, rather than face the possibility that this desperate measure wouldn't work. What if there was no recognition? There hadn't been so far.

And Max's house was distinctive, beautiful. She wouldn't forget it, would she?

They reached the top of the stairs with a spacious landing and three doors opening off it. Max led her to the farthest door. He swung it open and stood back for her to enter.

She gasped.

The entire back wall was floor-to-ceiling windows, framing the mountains in awe-inspiring beauty.

"Oh, Max, how stunning!" She turned around to smile at him, thrilled with the beauty of his house. He frowned back at her.

"You don't remember it, do you?"

His flat tones, devoid of emotion, stole her appreciation away. "I want to remember, Max! Truly, I do, but I can't lie to you."

He strode past her to stare out at the mountains. "I never asked you to lie."

"No, just to remember. But I can't do that, either. The doctor said I might never recover my memory."

He spun around to stare at her. "Never?"

She tried to smile as she shrugged her shoulders. "That's what the man said."

Unable to face the despair in his gaze, she moved around the large bedroom, dominated by a king-size bed. The room was decorated in shades of green, touched with rust, a very masculine room. As desperately as she searched for memory of the place, she found none.

He crossed his arms over his chest as he watched her. "Maybe you should look at the ceiling. I don't think you saw much of anything else the last time you were here."

"Max!" she protested automatically as the meaning of his words penetrated. Then a shiver ran over her as her eyes left the ceiling, where she'd automatically looked, to return to him. She could believe his words. Why look at scenery when Max Daniels was available? Only she wanted more than availability. She wanted to awaken every day with Max at her side, to go to sleep each evening in his arms. She wanted his love.

So far, Max had told her he wanted to make love to her, but nothing more. She met his gaze. "It's a wonderful house, Max."

"But you're not here to see my house...or me, are you? You're here to see if you remember anything. Right?" His voice was hard, accusing.

"So what's wrong with that? You want me to get my memory back, don't you?"

"Yeah. But I'd like a little honesty, too. Though that doesn't seem to be your strong suit."

"Max Daniels! How dare you!" It wasn't her fault she couldn't remember what happened.

"How dare I? It's easy, lady. Think about it. Everything you told me was a lie! When I got to that hospital room and found you, I thought I'd found Caroline Adkins, recently arrived from Kansas City, in need of a job, alone in the world. Instead, I find a room full of people, a family with more money than the rest of the state put together, and two other men claiming you."

Her teeth sank into her bottom lip. He was right. She couldn't deny a thing he said. Fighting back the tears, she stared at him, wishing her chin wasn't trembling. "What do you want me to say, Max? I can't remember. I've told you over and over again."

"Just don't say a damn thing," he growled, and turned his back on her.

Wanting to apologize, only she wasn't sure what for, she crossed the room to touch him. It seemed so natural to reach out to him. She wanted to believe she was remembering, but she wasn't sure.

"Don't do that!" Max snapped. "Don't you realize where we are?"

She was beginning to wonder if she'd stumbled into one of those houses of mirrors, where appearances constantly changed. After carefully looking around her, she said, "We're in your bedroom."

"Yeah, my bedroom, where we made love. Are you offering to repeat the experience? I need to know the limits before I kiss you."

Her eyebrows soared in exasperation. "Max! I just wanted to—I don't know what. I don't want to make you angry."

"Are you sure? Or are you still trying to remember?" He reached out and pulled her against him. "Maybe I need to refresh your memory. Do you want to know what really happened the night we made love? Do you, Caroline?"

The anger in his voice should've frightened her. But it didn't. The heat building in her, pooling in her stomach, only made her want his touch more.

"When we made love, I started by kissing you," he muttered, and then did exactly that, covering her lips, taunting her to open them as his tongue sought entrance. After an awe-inspiring kiss, he broke away to say, "Then, I slid my hands down here," and ran his hands down the seat of her pants, caressing her hips, pulling her more tightly against him, letting her feel his arousal.

She gasped and his lips returned to hers, taking the kiss deeper and deeper. One hand left her hip and moved to her breast, caressing it through her blouse. "Remember?" he whispered before his lips trailed down her throat.

Was she remembering? Or just wanting to remember so badly it felt the same? At that point she didn't much care. She just knew she wanted him.

They were both breathing heavily now. Caroline clung to him as if he were an anchor in a rough sea. His lips trailed his fingers as they began unbuttoning her blouse. When he took her bare breast in his hand, she almost cried out at the exquisite pleasure.

"That's right, Caroline. That's exactly how you reacted. You wanted my touch as much as I wanted to touch you. Do you remember?"

The anger in his voice had gone seductive, purring at her reaction, egging her on. As if she needed it.

She brought his lips back to hers and reached for the buttons of his shirt. His broad chest fascinated her and she wanted to run her hands over him. He was hard and unyielding but warm and inviting, and shivers swept over her.

He began to divest her of all her clothing, muttering as he did so, "At least we have an advantage this time."

She almost didn't hear his comment, as occupied as she was with his magnificent body. "What?"

"I can't get you pregnant."

She gasped, but before she could protest, his lips covered hers again. She gave herself up to the enjoyment they were both experiencing, concentrating on removing Max's clothes as efficiently as he was hers.

In a matter of seconds all restraints were gone, and Max swept her into his arms and carried her to the bed. Caroline didn't know if she remembered his touch or found it so mesmerizing she was confused. She only knew she didn't want him to stop.

As if reading her mind, he said, "Caroline, much farther and I can't stop. Do you want me to stop?" He gasped as he stroked her, caressing her breasts, her hips, every inch of her.

"Oh, no," she pleaded, and sealed his lips with hers. She wanted no more questions. She didn't want to think, only feel. They would be united, as she wanted them to be, forever and ever.

The next few minutes were filled with exquisite sensation. Max anticipated her wants almost before she knew them herself. Caroline writhed beneath him, spurring him on, loving his touch, returning each caress with more of her own. She had never felt as alive or as complete as she did in his arms.

His hands sliding over her body electrified her, and she stroked his muscled form, eager to learn every inch of it. She might not remember the first time they made love, but she was building new memories she hoped would last a lifetime.

"Caroline!" Max gasped as she touched him before his lips took hers in a kiss that was the ultimate in oneness, a union of breath and spirit that filled Caroline with joy. When, together, they reached completion, she collapsed, exhausted yet content from their lovemaking. For the first time since her accident, she felt at peace, happy.

Max lay without moving for several minutes, unable to think. Their lovemaking had been even more stupendous than he'd remembered, something he hadn't believed could be possible. Eventually he shifted his weight, concerned with hurting Caroline.

"Max!"

"What is it, Caroline?" he asked, recognizing something unusual in her voice.

"Max, I hope you have some crackers."

He leaned back and stared at her. "Probably, but we haven't discussed eating crackers in bed. Don't you think you're moving a little fast here?"

"Very funny," Caroline replied faintly. "If you don't get me some crackers quickly, I'm going to throw up my breakfast in your bed. Which do you prefer?"

He leaped off the bed and raced to the kitchen without bothering to pull on his jeans.

"CAROLINE?"

She was leaning back against the booth at the restaurant where they'd eventually gone for lunch, replete, her eyes closed. "Hmm?"

"Caroline, what are you going to do?"

Her hazel eyes popped open and she lost her satisfied look. "What do you mean, Max?"

"What are you going to do about us?"

"I—I don't understand."

"I just made love to you. You made love to me. Doesn't that mean something?" He could feel the frustration rising in his voice, but he didn't know how to control it. The thought of Caroline leaving him, perhaps even seeing Adrian, drove him crazy.

"Of course it does. It was the most wonderful experience in my life."

"That you can remember," he reminded her, his voice heavy with sarcasm.

Her cheeks flushed and she stared at him, her chin

raised. "Yes, that I can remember. Does that satisfy you?"

"No, it doesn't. We belong together. I don't want you to go back to your father's house. I want you to stay with me." He hadn't thought about the details. He just knew that she was his.

"Max, I can't do that."

She refused to meet his gaze and he felt he was fighting a losing battle.

"What do you mean?"

"I have to find out who the father of my baby is."

"Damn it, Caroline! I'm the father! I thought what we did was the proof you need," he growled.

Caroline looked around her as if she feared he'd be overheard. "Max, I loved what we—how we spent the past few hours, but that doesn't change the fact that you may not be the father."

"So what were we doing? Conducting a little test? Was that the real purpose of your visit? Comparison shopping? Are you going to try to remember with Adrian, too?"

He knew he shouldn't have said those things. He didn't even mean them. But he was frustrated...and afraid. He didn't want to lose her.

But it seemed he already had.

Since she'd left her car at his office, she couldn't leave without him, but she made her unhappiness obvious as she picked up her purse without a word and stood, waiting for him to join her.

Hastily paying the bill, he followed her from the restaurant. Once they were in his pickup, he tried to make amends.

"I'm sorry, sweetheart. What I said was out of line. I

didn't mean to be hateful. I'm a jealous snake. Please forgive me."

She said nothing.

"Come on, Caroline, that was a pretty good apology. I haven't groveled like that in a long time."

"Pretty good? You think pretty good will do after saying such hateful things?" she exploded, and then looked away, folding her arms over her chest.

"I guess not," he muttered, watching her out of the corner of his eye.

After several minutes taut with tension, she murmured, "Do you really think I planned—"

"No, of course not. I'm sorry I even suggested such a thing." When she remained silent, he added, "Especially if you're not going to speak to me again." They'd reached his office and he parked the pickup and leaned forward to force her to look at him. "Are you?"

"I'm thinking about it," she said, obviously trying to hold back a grin. His mother always said he would tempt a saint. And, thank God, Caroline was no saint.

"How about if I take you out to dinner tonight, as an apology for my boorish behavior?"

"Since it's an apology, do I get to choose the restaurant?"

"Man, you drive a hard bargain. Okay, okay," he agreed, holding up his hand when she would've protested. "You can choose the restaurant, but please don't make me wear a tux."

"A tux?" she repeated, perking up at the suggestion.

He groaned. "I knew it!"

She leaned over and kissed him. "Never mind. I won't torture you that much. Why don't we go back to that Italian restaurant we visited the other night when Prescott joined us?"

"Are you sure? I'll spring for something fancier if you want."

His arm settled around her shoulders and he pulled her closer to him. Leaning into his chest, she whispered, "I don't need fancy when I'm with you."

His response consisted of several kisses so hot Caroline thought she'd be consumed by fire. A honking horn interrupted them, or they might have embarrassed themselves.

"I think I'd better go," she said shakily, moving away from his magnetic presence.

"Yeah, well, I'll pick you up at seven."

"Don't be late," she whispered with a grin, sliding from the truck.

"Not a chance."

He walked her to her car, gave her one more sizzling kiss, and then sent her on her way with a smile.

CAROLINE FORGOT any other errands she'd planned that day and headed for home. She was exhausted and intended to spend the rest of the afternoon taking a nap before she made herself pretty for Max.

Though she still didn't have proof that Max was the father of her baby, she just knew he was. After Max, there could be no one else. No other man could compare to him. He was the father of her baby. She was sure.

She called out to Mrs. Lamb as she entered the house, then started up the staircase, her smile still in place.

"Caroline?"

She paused, a sinking feeling in her stomach as she recognized Adrian's voice. Leaning over the stair railing, she saw him emerge from the sun room.

"Where have you been? I've been waiting for you."

Frowning, she moved back down several steps. "I don't remember making any plans with you, Adrian."

"No, I didn't mean we had plans. But I think you'll be happy with what I do have."

"What do you mean?"

"I brought proof." When she stared at him, saying nothing because she couldn't speak, he added, "I've brought proof that I'm the father of your baby. Now we can be married."

Chapter Eleven

"No!"

One blond brow rose as Adrian stared at her, giving him a quizzical look. "No?"

"You can't have proof," Caroline said, her voice shaking as much as her knees. Suddenly she plopped down on the stairs.

"Are you all right?" Adrian inquired in studied concern. "Perhaps you should lie down for a while. We must take care of our child...and you."

"No! No, I need to see the proof. I need to—"

"There's nothing you need to do. Your parents have already gotten the ball rolling. In days we'll be husband and wife."

Now wasn't the time to be weak. Caroline grasped the banister and pulled herself to her feet. As she came down the stairs, she demanded, "Where is your proof? I want to see it."

"Well, of course, darling. It's in the sun room. I left it on the coffee table."

"Caroline? Is that you?" Mrs. Lamb called, her voice preceding her through the door that led to the kitchen.

"Yes, Lambie. I'm here. Could you bring me some tea to the sun room?"

The housekeeper walked over and placed the back of her hand against Caroline's cheek. "Of course, but you look pale. Shouldn't you lie down?"

"Not right now. I have something to do." She managed to dredge up a smile before she turned to the sun room. Adrian was right behind her, his hand coming up to rest against the small of her back.

How could Adrian be the father of her child? She couldn't stand his touch. Max, on the other hand—that didn't bear thinking about.

When she reached the coffee table, she stared at the large manila envelope lying on it. She was afraid to look at the "proof." What if she couldn't refute it?

He reached around her and picked it up. "I had forgotten that we ordered the picture. It came in the mail at the office this morning. I went at once to your father. He agreed that it was conclusive evidence."

Adrian's smile reminded her of the cat that had swallowed the canary. It made her sick to her stomach. "What picture?"

"One night at dinner in Vegas. You know how those photographers come around and offer to take a picture of a momentous event." He put his arm around her shoulders. "I thought what was going on between us was fairly momentous."

"Tell me again what was going on between us," she suggested, moving away from him, putting off the moment of truth.

"I told you the other night. We were having an affair. But you wanted to keep everything a secret. Your father is the master of pressure, and you wanted to avoid that."

Even without her memory, she knew that her father always wanted his way and would do whatever to get it.

That was what scared her. Adrian's story was so plausible.

Except for one thing.

She didn't want his touch.

Was it because she'd fallen for Max since she'd slept with Adrian? Could one extraordinary attraction wipe out the memory, the desire, for another's touch?

"How long had we been having an affair?"

"A couple of months. I'd been escorting you to some of the charity events, and one night we—well, we made love."

"Where?"

Both of his eyebrows shot up, as if the question surprised him.

"I can't remember!" she reminded him in frustration.

"My place, mostly. The first time, in the car."

"In the car? Like a couple of randy teenagers?" she demanded, horrified.

"Hey, there's nothing wrong with that. We were swayed by the moment." He leaned closer to say with a growl in his voice, "We're both passionate people."

She couldn't deny his assessment of her, not after her time spent with Max. But with Adrian? She stepped from his embrace to sit down in a chair. When Mrs. Lamb entered with the ice tea, she was grateful. She wasn't ready to look at the picture.

The cold drink revived her somewhat.

"Are you sure you shouldn't lie down?" Mrs. Lamb asked, hesitating before she left them alone.

"Maybe in a little while, Lambie. I'm fine."

Though she looked doubtful, Mrs. Lamb left the room. Adrian circled the coffee table and sat down on the end of the sofa nearest her.

"Don't you want to look at the picture? It's dated and everything."

"Dated?"

"Yeah. They do that on these professional photos," he explained, "kind of like they do on all the film these days." As he talked, he opened the envelope and slid out an eight-by-ten photograph.

Steeling herself for what she would see, Caroline held out her hand for the evidence. Adrian gave it to her and sat back against the cushions with a broad smile.

The photograph was of the two of them, her and Adrian. There could be no doubt of that, she realized, despair seeping into her heart. They were in a booth with the casino in the background, and she was snuggled against his shoulder while he had his arms crossed in front of him on the table. The date on the border of the photo read June 29.

"And you just received it today? Why did it take so long to send the picture?"

He shrugged his shoulders, undisturbed by her question. "Who knows? I figured we'd never see it. Some of these guys are fly-by-nighters. But you wanted the picture, so I paid."

He acted as if she should be grateful, she thought angrily. Instead, she'd like to tear the thing into small pieces. But that wouldn't erase the doubts the picture had put in her head. Or the despair.

"So, any more questions?" Adrian asked cheerfully.

"No, no questions." Not any that she could come up with at the moment. But something about the photo bothered her.

He leaned forward to take the picture, but she pulled back, pressing it to her chest. "No, no, I want to keep it."

"Now, come on, darling, let me have it. I'll get you a nice frame for it. We can show our child when he's older, explaining how the picture saved the day."

"I already have several frames. I'll take care of it."

"It's not the exact size. It'll need a special-sized frame," he explained, his smile not quite as relaxed.

"That's all right. I know a frame shop." The fact that he didn't want to leave the picture with her was the only encouragement she'd had the past ten minutes.

"Give me the name of the shop, and I'll drop the picture off on my way back to the office."

"Oh, no, it will be out of your way. I'll drop it off later." She watched with rising interest as frustration filled his face.

"You're going to be too busy, Caroline. After all, we have a wedding to get ready for."

"I don't think we have to be in a big rush. We have seven months before junior puts in an appearance."

The smile she was beginning to hate reappeared on his face. "Your father is much too impatient to wait any longer."

"I think it's my decision, not my father's."

Adrian laughed. "I guess you really did lose your memory if you think that. Your father is making all the arrangements right now. In three days, your wedding— our wedding will take place."

"Don't be ridiculous!" she exclaimed even as she believed what he was saying. How like her father! Without realizing it, she let the picture fall to her lap.

Instinctively, as she caught the rapid motion of Adrian's arm, she reached for the picture. It ripped in half, each of them holding a portion.

"Look at what you did!" Adrian exclaimed and reached for the other half.

Caroline pulled back, staring at the bottom half of the picture that she held in her hand. Suddenly, what had bothered her about the scene became obvious.

"I don't remember ever seeing this dress before."

"You lost your memory, remember?" His voice was heavy with sarcasm.

"But I've been through my closet. I didn't see a dress like this." In the photo she was wearing a tobacco brown linen coatdress with black trim on the collar.

"You bought it for the trip. That evening, the waiter spilled red wine on it. You ended up throwing it out."

"How convenient," she muttered, staring at the photo.

Adrian snatched it from her fingers, which she'd relaxed as she thought about what he'd said. "I'll have this mended. I know a good place. Then I'll buy a frame for it before I let you hold it again. That way it can't be destroyed."

He stood and walked over to the door. There he paused and said, "If I didn't know better, I'd think you weren't happy about our marriage. Fortunately, I haven't lost *my* memory."

His meaning didn't sink in until he'd left, closing the door behind him. Then she felt sick to her stomach. He was referring to their lovemaking. In a car, no less!

She couldn't imagine losing herself so much in a man that she'd— The sudden memory of those kisses Max had given her only a short time ago halted her protest. But that was with Max, not Adrian.

Could she respond to two men like that? At the same time? Of course, if Adrian was telling the truth, then today was the first time she'd slept with Max. And the last.

She buried her face in her hands.

Max.

Dear God, what was she going to tell him?

Afraid to put off calling him, in case she lost her nerve, she crossed the room to the telephone.

"Daniels Vacation Homes."

"Uh, Susan?"

"Yes?"

"This is Caroline Adkins. Is Max there?"

"No, Caroline, he's on a building site. Do you want me to beep him?"

She wasn't that brave. "No, just give him a message. I have to cancel our plans this evening."

"Okay. I bet he'll be disappointed. You sure did a lot to improve his mood today." Susan chuckled but Caroline didn't join in the laughter.

"Give him another message for me, please. Tell him— tell him Adrian has proof."

"Adrian has proof? Will he know what that means?"

Suddenly Caroline felt like crying.

"Oh, yes, he'll know."

MAX PULLED INTO the parking lot outside his office with a grin a mile wide. Life was good! He'd just sold another home and he was having dinner with Caroline.

After a terrific lunch.

As he got out of the truck, he remembered the kisses they'd shared on the same spot before she drove home. She felt what happened between them, just as he did. He'd convince her the baby belonged to the two of them.

"Hi, Suze. Unless there's an urgent message, just hold them till tomorrow," he said as he sailed past his sister's desk and into his office. He wanted to have plenty of time to shower and shave for this evening.

Susan followed him to the door of his office. "The only important one was from Caroline."

"She called?" he whirled around. "What did she say? Am I supposed to call her?"

"She didn't say. She just said she had to cancel your plans."

"What?" he snapped, disappointment filling him. "Did she say why?"

"No, but she left another message. It didn't make sense to me, but maybe it will explain things to you. She said you'd understand."

"What?" he demanded impatiently. Sometimes Susan could drive him crazy with her details.

"She said 'Adrian has proof.'" Susan stared at him, but he couldn't respond. He'd turned to stone. "Do you know what that means?"

Anger welled up in him. "It means that bastard is lying!" he yelled. He brushed past his sister and headed for his truck. He was getting to the bottom of this "proof" at once.

Why would she believe Adrian? She hadn't believed *him*, in spite of the magic that happened every time they touched. What had Adrian given as proof? He'd probably bribed someone to say he saw them together. Or manufactured a receipt.

His mind played endlessly with the possibilities until he screeched to a stop at the closed gates. Mrs. Lamb opened the gates from the house without question and he was knocking at the door in no time.

"Come in, Mr. Daniels. Are you here to see Caroline?"

"Yes, I am. Is she in?"

"Yes. If you'll just wait here, I'll go see if she's asleep. She wasn't feeling too well earlier."

Max wanted to bound up the stairs ahead of Mrs. Lamb. He wanted to find Caroline himself. He wanted to see if she was feeling okay. He wanted to love her until she admitted the truth. That she was his. And he was hers.

And Adrian…and his proof…didn't exist.

He was pacing the entry hall when footsteps alerted him to Mrs. Lamb's return. He whirled to the stairs to find Caroline had accompanied the housekeeper.

She didn't look well.

"Are you all right?" he demanded, starting up the stairs.

"I'm fine. What are you doing here?"

He drew back, stunned by her question. "What am I doing here? What the hell do you think I'm doing here? After the message you left? You thought I'd just quietly slink away?"

"Mr. Daniels, I don't think—" Mrs. Lamb began, stepping in front of Caroline, as if to protect her.

"It's okay, Lambie," Caroline said softly. "He has reason to be upset. We'll just go into the sun room and talk."

"Shall I bring you something to drink?"

"No. We just need to—to talk."

Her admission that he had reason to be upset calmed Max, somewhat. That and her paleness. She looked ready to faint. He suddenly remembered that she'd only been out of the hospital with a concussion for about a week.

"Should you be out of bed?" he asked as he closed the door behind him.

She turned to face him, her gaze troubled. "I thought you wanted to talk to me."

With a groan, he closed the distance between them and wrapped his arms around her, feeling her softness the entire length of him. It drove him crazy.

She rested against him for a brief minute and then pulled away, going over to sit down in a stuffed chair.

He followed her, standing over her like a disapproving father. "Tell me."

She twisted her fingers together in her lap, staring at them as she talked. "He brought a picture of the two of us in Las Vegas. It was dated June 29. He said we'd been having an affair for a couple of months and went away together. I'd asked him to keep everything a secret because of my father."

He slid a finger beneath her chin and lifted her face. Staring into her hazel eyes, he asked, "Do you believe him?"

"I saw the picture, Max. It was me. I was there in Las Vegas. And if that's true, then I couldn't have been with you."

Ah. There was the crux of the matter. One of them was lying, he and Adrian, and Adrian had a photo. He had nothing. He hadn't thought of taking a picture of her because he'd wanted to believe he'd never lose her.

Leaning forward, he captured her lips with his. Her arms slid around his neck and he pulled her up against him as his tongue enticed hers and he kissed her down to her toes. When he finally pulled back, they both were breathing heavily. "Do you believe that? Do you feel that with Adrian?"

He almost thought he'd won when a glimmer of a smile filled her beautiful eyes. "You know I don't, Max. At least, I don't think I do. The man hasn't kissed me since I've been out of the hospital, but I can't imagine he would affect me like you do."

They looked at each other, Max sharing with her the astonishment he felt each time they touched. It had never been this way before, with any woman. Only Caroline.

"But that doesn't make it impossible that I might have slept with him before."

"Before you slept with me?"

Her teeth sank into her bottom lip. "Max, if the picture is the truth, then I hadn't slept with you until today."

"Then that picture is a damned lie!"

She reached out and smoothed his ferocious frown with her fingertips. "I want it to be, Max, but I don't see how—"

"I want to see it."

"I don't have it. It got ripped and Adrian took it to have it repaired."

Max noted that she was avoiding his gaze. He pulled her chin back around. "What aren't you telling me?"

"What do you mean?"

"There's something you're not telling me."

She hesitated and then said, "He was extremely reluctant to leave the picture with me." Before he could speak, she added, "But that's just an impression. It isn't proof."

He shoved himself away from the chair and stood. "And that's what you have to have, isn't it? Proof. My word means nothing. My touch that drives you crazy means nothing. You have to have proof!" He made the last word sound like something dirty. And it was. Because without proof, she wouldn't believe him.

"Max! I can't go on my instincts. There's more involved here. He may be the father of my child! I can't just tell my child someday that I don't know who his father is. That I wanted to be with you, so I ignored the truth."

He stared at her, unable to deny the pleading in her gaze. Reaching out, he caressed her cheek briefly. Even that small touch set his blood racing. He stepped back, breaking contact with her.

"Okay. I'm trying to understand. Just give me a little time, and I'll find my own proof somehow."

He thought he was being magnanimous, exhibiting incredible patience, when what he wanted to do was punch out Adrian. Or anyone else who got in his way.

One look at Caroline's face as she sank back down into the chair, and he knew she wasn't impressed.

"Max—" She broke off and looked away.

"Spit it out, Caroline. If you want me to get lost, just say so." His heart would break if she did.

She leaped to her feet and then almost passed out. He clutched her and held her against him, hoping and praying it wouldn't be for the last time.

"Well?"

"No, Max, I don't want you to get lost. The thought of not seeing you again—"

"Then what is it? What were you going to say?"

"I—I can't give you much time."

"Why? What are you saying?"

"I promised my father I'd marry the father of my baby as soon as we found proof."

"And you always keep your word," he muttered, rubbing her back, imprinting the feel of her in his heart.

She buried her face in his neck even as she nodded.

"How long do I have before you marry this jerk?"

He waited tensely for her to answer. When she said nothing, he wondered if she'd heard the question. Finally she lifted her head and stared up at him, tears in her eyes.

"Three days. The wedding is in three days."

Chapter Twelve

"Three days?" Max repeated, drawing back to stare at her. Anger rose within him. "How could you agree to such a thing?"

She stiffened, the tears disappearing. "I had no choice, Max. I've embarrassed my parents enough as it is."

"A little embarrassment is more important than the truth?"

"Max Daniels, the least you can do is understand! I can't help it if I can't remember. I don't know who's telling the truth. But Adrian came up with proof."

"Probably manufactured. How about a lie detector test? How about if Adrian and I take lie detector tests?"

"I doubt that Adrian would agree," Caroline said, her anger leaving her like a deflated balloon.

"I doubt it, too. Since he's won."

She said nothing, but the sadness in her eyes cut him to the quick.

"You're really going to go ahead with it?"

"I have no choice...unless something turns up that says he's lying."

His heart aching, Max stepped to her side. He had to touch her one more time. Pulling her to him, his lips took hers until both almost forgot he was saying goodbye.

When he finally released her, he stepped back and said, "I'm not giving up, Caroline. That's my baby. I'll find a way to prove it to you."

Then he walked out of the house before he was tempted to carry her up the stairs to the nearest bed in a desperate attempt to convince her. Slamming himself into his truck, he burned rubber down the driveway.

Only as he headed back home did he calm down enough to think. She would marry that jerk Adrian unless someone found proof the man was lying.

Someone.

Who?

Him, of course. No one cared more than he did. It was up to him, Max Daniels, to find proof. Great relief filled him as he realized there must be something he could do.

His bubble burst when the next question occurred to him.

What?

What could he do?

He pulled to the side of the road. He had to figure out what to do and fast. There wasn't much time. He remembered reading an article in the paper recently about a private investigator. If he could remember the man's name, he'd call him. He pulled back onto the road and then off again when he reached the nearest gas station.

"Do you have a telephone directory, the yellow pages?" he asked the attendant.

The man readily handed over the thick book and Max thumbed through the listings.

"Damn! I'd better get help. I can't even find a telephone number," he muttered.

"What you lookin' for?" the attendant asked.

"A private investigator, but there aren't any listed."

"Sure there are. Look under 'detective.'"

Max briefly wondered why a gas station attendant would so readily know how to find such a listing. Then he dismissed that idea as he found the names of several detective agencies. He recognized the man's agency and wrote down the number on the back of an envelope he found in his pocket.

"Do you have a—" he began as he closed the book.

Divining his question, the man pointed to the telephone on the desk. "Use that one if it's local."

Much to Max's surprise, he received an immediate appointment with the detective in question. Getting directions, he rushed for his truck after thanking the gas station attendant.

The detective's office was modest but neat, nothing like the offices Hollywood always depicted. A sedate, middle-age woman greeted him and then announced his arrival to Don Knowles, the detective.

"Come in, Mr. Daniels. Have a seat and tell me what's on your mind."

After his eager rush to reach the man, Max found it difficult to explain his needs. The detective wasn't the problem. Like the receptionist, he was calm, quiet, middle-aged, redolent of respectability.

"It's difficult to explain."

"Just start at the beginning."

"A little over two months ago, I met a woman. Caroline Adkins." Max noted that the detective seemed to recognize the name. "We dated for two weeks. Then, one night at my house, we, uh, we got carried away."

Mr. Knowles didn't seem to need any amplification of that statement.

"She disappeared the next day."

"And you want me to find her?"

"No. I've found her. A week ago, I discovered she is the daughter of James Adkins."

"I thought so."

Max licked his lips. The story got a little more difficult to explain now. "Her name was given on the radio because she was in the hospital from an accident. She hit her head on the windshield and got amnesia." He shifted in his chair. "We all discovered at the same time that she is two months' pregnant."

The detective's eyebrows soared over his calm brown eyes.

"And three of us said, at the same time, that we were the father of her baby." Max paused, thinking about what he'd said. "I don't know if I said that correctly, but do you understand?"

"Yeah, I think I get the gist of it. You want me to find out who's the father?"

"No. I already know that. I'm the father. The other two both work for her father. They've got a lot at stake. Caroline and I eliminated one of them by his own admission. But the other one—he's come up with proof that he and Caroline were in Vegas the two weeks I *know* she was with me."

"What kind of proof?"

"A photo, taken by one of the professional photographers who roam the clubs. It's dated June 29."

Don Knowles leaned back in his chair. "Well, I think I've finally figured out what you want. You want me to prove the man is lying."

"Exactly. There are a couple of catches, however," Max added, wanting the man to understand the challenge he was giving him. "I don't have the photo, and I haven't seen it. And you only have three days."

CAROLINE FOUGHT HER WAY out of a deep sleep, something urging her to consciousness. Perhaps it was her stomach, but she had learned her lesson. She reached for the crackers and carbonated water Mrs. Lamb had begun leaving beside her bed every evening.

When she got her stomach under control, she turned her thoughts to the events of the previous day. After Max's departure, she'd had to deal with her parents' return and numerous questions.

Not about Adrian's revelation.

Her parents accepted the photograph as valid proof that she had been in Las Vegas with Adrian. And that he was the father of her baby.

She understood why her father wanted her to marry Adrian. And maybe it was guilt that kept her from refusing. Her father had counted on her to succeed him in the business. He'd brought her into the office right out of college, given her a lot of responsibility, shown absolute faith in her.

And two years ago, she'd walked out on him.

It had hurt to displease her father. She loved him. But she hadn't been happy working in the large corporation. The creative side of her was dying. She'd returned to school to get a degree in interior design.

Her father had never really forgiven her. Then he'd come up with the plan to marry her to someone who could take over the company. That's when he'd begun promoting Adrian and Prescott. At least, she thought so.

Between hating to disappoint her father a second time, and fearing that Adrian might be the baby's father, she couldn't simply dismiss her promise. Her child had the right to at least know his father, to bear his name. Even if it was Adrian's.

So she understood why her father was pleased that

Adrian claimed to be the father. And her parents' questions were about flowers, dresses, invitation list, preference of colors, and other inane questions that drove Caroline wild. How could she consider such ridiculous things when she was concerned with who the groom would be?

Without conscious thought, she wandered over to her closet. The dress wouldn't be there, Adrian had told her, because she'd thrown it out. But something about that dress bothered her.

She stared at the dual row of clothing, mulling over the picture in her mind. It finally struck her. There wasn't a single brown dress in her closet.

Not a single one.

Blue dominated the colors, a clear, bright blue. There were some reds, a couple of hot pinks, lots of shades of purple, an occasional green. Both white and black.

But no beiges, no browns, no yellows.

She turned to the phone and called down to Mrs. Lamb, asking for a breakfast tray. Slipping back into bed, with pillows propped behind her, Caroline waited.

When the housekeeper arrived, Caroline asked her to sit down and keep her company. "Mrs. Lamb, I've been looking at my wardrobe. I seem to like bright colors."

"Oh, my stars, yes, Caroline. You always pick bright colors. Chelsea likes pastels, but not you."

"Do I ever wear brown?"

"Only when you were in the Brownies," Mrs. Lamb said, chuckling. "I swear you quit because of the color of the uniform. I tried to persuade you to stay until you became a Girl Scout and could wear green, but you were stubborn, even then."

"So I never wear brown," Caroline muttered to herself.

"What is it, dear? Has something happened?"

"Do you know anything about photography, Mrs. Lamb?"

The lady stared at her. "Photography?"

"I know it doesn't seem connected to brown, but it is. Adrian showed me a picture yesterday of the two of us in Las Vegas, supposedly during those two weeks I was missing."

Realization dawned on Mrs. Lamb's face. "So that's why your parents are planning your wedding with him."

"Yes. But, Lambie, I was wearing a brown dress."

"Oh, my stars, that's impossible! You don't own a brown dress!"

"Adrian said I bought it for the trip and then threw it away after the waiter spilled wine on it." Mrs. Lamb's face reflected Caroline's own feelings. "It sounds rather convenient, doesn't it?"

"You think the picture is a fake?"

Caroline leaned back against her pillows and sighed. "I don't know. I don't even know if it's possible, because it was certainly my face."

"Of course it's possible. Why, those scandal sheets do things like that all the time."

"They do? Yes, I guess they do. I hadn't thought about it. I was so shocked—you're right. The picture is obviously a fake. And that's why he didn't want me to keep it."

"You don't have the picture?"

"No, he insisted on taking it with him." How she wished she'd been able to keep the picture.

"What are you going to do?"

Caroline set aside the tray and slid from the bed. "I'm going to find a way to prove Adrian is lying!"

After Mrs. Lamb took the tray and returned to the kitchen, Caroline picked up the phone and called her father's secretary. In minutes, she had the name of the security firm her father used.

She only had to give her name to be immediately put through to the head of the firm, Joe Perkins.

"Mr. Perkins, I have a personal job for you. Money is no object, but speed is."

When she finished the conversation, Caroline felt much better. After a quick shower, she searched her closet for an outfit that would allow for her gently swelling figure. It was too soon to be wearing maternity clothes, like Chelsea, but her own clothes were becoming a little uncomfortable.

Just as she was finishing buttoning her blouse, her mother knocked on the door.

"Oh, you're already up. Good. Chelsea can be ready at one for our shopping trip, so I suggested she come here at noon and dine with us. Before she arrives, we had better make some decisions. Otherwise Chelsea will want to offer her opinion."

Caroline noticed that her mother had a clipboard and appeared incredibly efficient, unlike her usual distant figure. Was this how she operated at the charities? No wonder she was so involved.

"Uh, Mother, I have to go out."

"Don't be ridiculous. We're planning a wedding. Besides, where would you go?"

"I have an appointment that's urgent. I'll try to be back by noon."

"But it's ten-thirty already. We haven't even chosen your colors." Amelia looked horrified at such a lapse.

"I love blue. See, that decision is already made." Caroline ran a brush through her hair, added a touch of powder to her nose and turned to leave the room.

"Neiman's is going to show us what they have in

gowns already in stock this afternoon. Mrs. Mason is pulling your size."

Caroline thought of the tightness of her clothes. "Better ask her to pull a size larger, Mother. I'm not a size eight anymore."

"Perhaps you should diet."

With a laugh, Caroline kissed her mother's cheek. "I don't think so. Pregnant ladies shouldn't diet."

"Oh, I forgot."

"Then you're not embarrassed that I'm already expecting a child before my wedding?" Caroline asked the question lightly, but she waited anxiously for her mother's response.

"Of course not."

"Thanks, Mother. Oh, I need a recent picture of me. Do I have any?"

"Yes, of course, but I've already taken care of the picture to the paper." She added huffily, "They said they weren't sure they could use it with such late notice."

Caroline almost groaned aloud. That's all she needed, publicity. "No, not for the paper. Where is the picture?"

"In one of the photo albums downstairs."

"Could you find it for me? I don't know where the albums are."

Her mother gave her an exasperated sigh and turned to leave the room, Caroline on her heels. As she walked, she muttered, "Honestly, Caroline, you really should take more interest in things. I've showed you those albums a thousand times."

As she followed her mother downstairs, a thought struck Caroline. Maybe losing one's memory was hereditary.

JUST A FEW MINUTES before noon, Don Knowles's secretary buzzed him. "Don, Mr. Perkins is on line one."

Don grinned as he picked up the phone. He and Joe Perkins were longtime friends and sometimes helped each other out.

"Hi, Joe, how are you?"

"Fine, Don. But I need a little help, so I naturally thought of you."

"Yeah, just because I owe you one for that missing wife case." They kept a running tab of favors done, though they both knew it meant nothing if either needed help.

"Right. But this one is kind of bizarre…and there's a real time factor."

"I'll help if I can. I've got a case kind of like that, too. In fact, I was thinking about calling you."

"Oh?"

"Yeah, it involves an employee of Adkins Industries."

"So we trade. Me, first. This is the weirdest case I've ever heard of. This woman, my client, was in a car wreck and hit her head. She got amnesia—"

"And she's pregnant and doesn't know who the father is."

There was a tense silence until Joe said, his voice filled with suspicion, "How do you know that?"

"Because the guy who says he's the father of her baby just hired me."

"Max Daniels?"

"She told you about him?"

"Yeah. She wants him to be the father. And the other guy is one of James Adkins's right-hand guys."

"That would be Adrian Meadows."

"So, what's your take on Daniels?"

"I believed him. I've been doing some calling around, and he seems to be legit."

"How about we combine forces? Would it be a betrayal to your client? I think they both want the same thing."

"I agree. What do you have?"

"A picture of Miss Adkins, the name of the casino, the dates. I wanted to hire you for a quick trip to Vegas."

"I'll get an afternoon flight. I wasn't sure it would be worth it with three days and not knowing the casino. My client didn't have that information. I'll be over to pick up the info you have as soon as I make a reservation."

"Great. I'll gather everything I've got. While you're gone, I'll work on Adrian Meadows. We did a background check a couple of years ago. He came up clean, but at least we have some info on him."

"Right. Sounds good. The only problem we've got is time."

"Yeah. Time."

Time.

It seemed to be racing by.

Max had done what he could, he decided, hiring Knowles. He'd liked the man. He only hoped he knew his business.

What else could he do?

Caroline was in the throes of planning a wedding. And he was trying to wreck her plans. Too bad all that work might go to waste. A sudden thought struck him.

It was bizarre.

Would Caroline agree?

He reached for the telephone.

"I'm sorry, Mr. Daniels," Mrs. Lamb replied to his

request for Caroline. "She's out shopping with her mother. May I ask her to call you when she returns?"

"Yes, please. I'm at the office." He gave her his number. "Do you have any idea when she'll be back?"

"I would guess around four o'clock, but sometimes shopping takes longer than you think."

"All right, thanks. Ask her to call as soon as she gets back."

He piddled around the office most of the afternoon, as he had all morning, wrestling with the desire to call Don Knowles to see if he'd made any progress. With only three days, he shouldn't pester the man. Knowles would need all the time he could get.

Finally, when he'd almost given up on Caroline calling, he heard her voice on the other end of the telephone.

"How are you?"

"Tired. Mother and Chelsea took me shopping for— for a wedding dress."

"Did you find one?" He felt masochistic, asking, but he had to know.

"Yes. I'm sorry, Max, but I don't have any choice."

He thought she did, but he wasn't going to argue with her. "I'm trying to work things out."

"Me, too. I'm hoping something will happen, but I have to prepare for the wedding."

"Caroline...I have a bizarre idea."

"What?"

He heard the eagerness in her voice and it warmed his heart. She didn't want to marry Adrian any more than he wanted her to.

"If I manage to prove Adrian is lying before the wedding, then all your work will go for nothing."

She gave an abrupt chuckle. "I don't think I'll complain."

"Me, neither, but it seems a shame."

"Max, what's your point? Do you want me to marry Adrian?" She sounded confused and a little outraged. "Do you think this is what I want?"

"Of course not. But I just thought—it makes sense to me for us to apply for a marriage license, too, to be prepared, in case I find proof that I'm the father of the baby." As he intended to do, come hell or high water.

"You want me to apply for *two* marriage licenses?"

Max heard her incredulity and laughed. "I know it sounds weird, but then, the past week hasn't exactly been normal for either of us. And if your parents are anxious for you to marry, I want to be prepared."

"I'm not marrying just to please my parents."

"And I'm not asking you for that reason," he assured her impatiently. Why was she being so difficult?

"I'm marrying Adrian because I owe it to my baby."

He squeezed the receiver, wishing it was Adrian's neck he held in his hands. "Don't expect a thank-you card."

"What?"

"I don't think the kid is going to be grateful. Whether he's his dad or not! You're making a mistake, Caroline!"

"You think I should just wait until the baby is born, when Adrian has offered proof?"

"No, I think you should marry me, no matter what."

"You're asking me to marry you?"

"Well, of course, I am." He'd been planning to marry her since he first saw her. "I told you I'm the father of the baby. Of course, we're going to marry. Just as soon as I can prove Adrian is a liar," he finished, a touch of sarcasm in his voice. He wanted her to believe him, without his having to produce proof. But however he had to do it, he was going to claim her and his child.

"Okay, I'll go with you to get a license," she suddenly

capitulated. A pleading note entered her voice as she added, ''Just one thing, Max.''

''Yeah, what's that?'' he asked, willing to promise her anything.

''Could you hurry with that evidence?''

Chapter Thirteen

After Max told her he'd leave at once to pick her up for their trip to city hall, Caroline hung up the phone with a sigh.

Another marriage proposal.

As much as she wanted this one, she found an important ingredient missing. Max had said he was the father of her baby. He had said he wanted her. He'd proven that one, actually. But, like Adrian, he'd never said he loved her.

She wanted to believe he did.

Some vague sense of recognition filled her and she grasped for a memory she sensed was close. Feeling as if she were searching for something important in a dense fog, she struggled, determined not to lose that elusive feeling.

A rap on her door disrupted her concentration. Chelsea walked in.

"Caro, have you thought about the napkins? What do you want printed on them?"

"Surely there's not enough time for that," she protested with a sigh for her lost memory.

"With Daddy's money, there's always enough time. Now, what shall we put on the napkins?"

"My name and a question mark seems appropriate," Caroline muttered.

"Whatever do you mean? Aren't you marrying Adrian? This is not something to joke about, Caroline."

"You're telling me."

"Caroline!"

She heaved a colossal sigh. "All right, Chelsea. My choice is to print nothing on the napkins."

"I told you there was time. Now, do you want Caroline and Adrian, Adrian and Caroline, or the Meadowses."

"None of the above. If I have to go through with this wedding, I can do without one thousand reminders on paper napkins." She crossed her arms over her chest and glared at her sister.

"You don't *want* to marry Adrian?" Chelsea asked, horrified. "But he's the father of your baby!"

"So he says. I'm not sure."

"Caroline! This entire situation is so distasteful. I can't believe you have embroiled us in such a mess."

Caroline glared at her sister in disgust. "Oh, really! What about the time you cheated on your spelling test and got caught? *You* embarrassed all of us then. So don't be so high and mighty!"

"I can't believe you're still bringing that—Caroline, you remembered!"

Her knees suddenly shaky, Caroline sank down onto the edge of her bed. "I—I guess so."

"Has your memory returned?"

As if testing a sore muscle, Caroline probed the inner recesses of her mind, seeking the elusive memory she'd lost a week ago. Nothing.

"No." She wanted to cry, but even that release eluded her. "No, I don't remember."

"Well," Chelsea huffed, "it doesn't seem fair that you remember *my* embarrassing moments but not yours."

She gave her sister a weary smile. "No, it doesn't, does it?"

An unexpected touch of sympathy filled Chelsea's face. "Maybe you'd better lie down. You look exhausted."

"Thanks, Chelsea, but Max is coming to pick me up."

The silence that followed her response brought her head up. Chelsea was staring at her. "What?"

"Well, I don't mean to tell you your business, Caro, but you're marrying Adrian in two days. Don't you think it's a little inappropriate to be dating Max?"

Hysterical laughter bubbled up in Caroline. If Chelsea thought her going out with Max was inappropriate, what would she think of them applying for a marriage license? "It's not really a date, Chelsea. We just have something we have to do."

"Does Adrian know?"

"I don't think so."

Chelsea crossed her arms and looked down her nose at her sister. "I know you're older than me, but since I've been married for almost a year, I think I should give you some good advice."

"Please, don't."

"Caroline! It's very important that you and your husband be honest with each other. Don't start your marriage by lying to Adrian."

"Why not? He's lying to me," Caroline muttered, irritation getting the better of discretion.

"What do you mean?"

"Have you ever seen me wear brown?"

Chelsea looked at her with concern. "Caroline, I think

you need to rest. I'll explain to Max that you're not well.''

"You'll do no such thing! I'm not crazy, which is what you're really thinking. The picture Adrian showed me! I was wearing a brown dress in it.''

"But you don't wear brown.'' The puzzlement in Chelsea's voice did Caroline's heart good.

"Exactly!'' When Chelsea still seemed puzzled, she added, ''I think he faked the picture. He was in Vegas with another woman, a woman who wears brown, and he had the picture altered!''

"But that would be lying.''

Caroline shook her head, a weary smile on her face. "I know, little sister, I know.''

"But why? I mean, you are attractive, Caroline, but there are other women who—I mean, you're pregnant! Why would he claim your baby if he's not— It makes no sense!''

"Yes, it does. Prescott admitted he'd lied because Daddy's going to select the second in command for his company very soon. Prescott doesn't think he'll have a chance if Adrian is Daddy's son-in-law.''

Chelsea's mouth dropped open and she sank down onto the bed beside Caroline. "Oh, my, how despicable.''

Caroline almost laughed. It wasn't often she and her sister were in agreement. At least she didn't think so.

"But why are you going to marry him if he's lying?'' Chelsea finally asked.

"Because I can't show he's lying. He's offered proof, which is more than Max has done.'' She got up from the bed to pace across the room. "Besides, Daddy wants this marriage so badly. And if Adrian is the father of my baby, it doesn't seem fair to him or the baby to deny him his legal right just because I've fallen in love with Max.''

"Can't you explain to Daddy? I know he's difficult but he loves you very much."

Caroline shrugged. "You can imagine Daddy's reaction if I told him I can't marry Adrian because I wore a brown dress."

"But you can't take sacred vows if you don't mean them!" Chelsea protested.

Caroline was coming to love her little sister in spite of her irritating ways. But sometimes her naiveté drove her crazy. "I'm going to do everything I can to be sure that doesn't happen."

"Good, because—"

The distant ring of the doorbell interrupted Chelsea. Caroline jumped up and then had to steady herself. Those abrupt moves reminded her of her pregnancy if nothing else did.

"Caroline, you must be more careful," Chelsea warned, supporting Caroline. "I always move slowly now."

Complacency was another of Chelsea's annoying traits.

"Thanks for the warning. I've got to powder my nose and comb my hair. That will be Max."

"I still don't think going with Max is right," Chelsea said, following her into the bathroom.

"Tough. I do, and that's what counts."

"But about those napkins?" Chelsea was back on that again. "Plain white, right?"

Caroline turned from the mirror and hugged Chelsea. "You get smarter every day, little sister."

"ARE YOU ALL RIGHT?" Max asked after several minutes of driving in silence.

Caroline continued to stare in front of her. "Yes. I was just thinking about something Chelsea said."

"She went shopping with you and your mother?"

"Yes."

"You were shopping all day? You must be exhausted."

"Not all day. But yes, I'm tired." She didn't mention how she'd spent her morning. What if the agency discovered nothing? Again she thought of Chelsea's words.

"Well, the license shouldn't take long, and then I'll take you to dinner and you can relax."

"Dinner? I'm not sure—"

"You owe me dinner, Caroline. You canceled last night, remember?" He reached over and took her hand, carrying it to his lips.

She shivered, reacting as she always did to his touch. Giving a halfhearted laugh, she said, "Chelsea said I shouldn't be dating you when I'm marrying Adrian."

"Maybe you won't be marrying Adrian. Maybe you'll be marrying me."

Maybe. Caroline sighed. Just one more question mark to add to her life. She only seemed to deal in question marks these days.

They had to rush to reach the office before it closed. When they entered, a gray-haired woman walked to the counter to greet them.

"My, you just made it. We close in fifteen minutes. How may I help you?"

Caroline was suddenly glad her father had taken care of the details of the marriage license with Adrian. She'd rather the woman not know this license would be Caroline's second in the same week.

"We need to get a marriage license."

The woman asked for their identification, gave them forms to fill out and then asked for the fee.

"Is that it?" Max asked.

"Yes, it is. You'll have your license just as soon as I enter your names into the computer."

"Computer?" Caroline asked nervously.

"Oh, my, yes, we're quite up-to-date. We have everything computerized," she explained as she typed their names into the computer. "Why, isn't that strange."

"What?" both Max and Caroline barked out.

"You're the second Caroline Marie Adkins to apply for a license this week." She hit several buttons and then turned to stare at Caroline. "You live at the same address. And have the same parents."

"I—I changed my mind."

"She hasn't made up her mind," Max said at the same time.

The woman stared at Max. "You knew about it? And it doesn't bother you that your fiancée has a license to marry another man?"

"It's a long story."

"But have you already married the man? Bigamy is against the law, you know."

"Of course, I know," Caroline said crossly. "I told you I changed my mind. There's nothing illegal about applying for more than one marriage license, is there?"

"Well, no, dear, I guess not."

The woman shot Max a sympathetic glance. Caroline looked the other way, unable to stand the embarrassment. The clerk took the opportunity to whisper to Max, "You really should reconsider before you pay for the license. There are lots of other women in the world. Especially for someone as handsome as you."

"Well, really!" Caroline protested, spinning around.

"Does counseling come with the license, or does he have to pay extra?"

The clerk gave her a glacial stare. "It's free."

"Thanks," Max said, and Caroline was incensed to see he was hiding a grin.

"Is the license ready?" Caroline prompted.

"Yes, of course." The woman muttered under her breath to Max, "But you'd better think about the step you're taking. Marriage is a serious thing."

"I couldn't agree more," Max said with a smile, taking the license and putting it into his shirt pocket. "Thanks for your help."

Caroline opened her mouth to tell the woman what she thought of her assistance, and Max leaned down and kissed her.

"My fiancée says thank you, also," he assured the woman, and pulled Caroline from the office before she could contradict him.

"You were laughing!" she complained as the door closed behind them.

He chuckled again as he held her close to him, his hand rubbing her shoulder. "Now, sweetheart, you'll have to admit it was kind of humorous."

"No, I don't," she insisted stubbornly, even as she enjoyed his touch. She slipped her arm around his waist and leaned against his chest as they continued to walk. "Well, maybe I do. I think I'm so tired I've lost my sense of humor."

He pulled them to a stop. "Would you rather go home and go to bed? I'll understand if you do."

"No. I want to have dinner with you, but I'd like to go home and change. I meant to do so before you got there, but Chelsea came up to talk to me and I forgot."

"Sure. We'll go back to your house and you can change."

Once they were in his truck and headed back on the freeway, Caroline said, "You know, that's another thing."

"Am I supposed to know what you're talking about?" he asked, squeezing her hand as he held it against his thigh.

"Sorry, I was thinking aloud. You always touch me."

"You're complaining?" he asked, startled.

"No! No, I love it, just as I love touching you. But Adrian doesn't touch me."

"He'd better not!"

His jealousy pleased her, but it wasn't her point. "No, Max, think about it. If we were sleeping together on a regular basis, as Adrian says we were, wouldn't he be used to touching me?"

He leered at her. "It's hard to sleep together and not touch."

She chuckled, as he'd intended, and leaned her head on his shoulder. "I mean when we're not in bed. We're touching. That's the first thing you do when we meet. You reach for me, whether it's my hand, my mouth, my shoulders, you touch me."

"You're pretty hard to resist."

"Adrian doesn't seem to have any trouble."

"You want him to touch you?" Max sounded jealous.

"Don't be silly. I'm just trying to think rationally about what's happening here."

"I agree with you, Caroline, but I don't think that line of reasoning is going to impress your father...or anyone else. And if you tell Adrian that, he'll just start touching you, to prove you wrong."

"I'll keep it to myself, then."

"Good girl," Max agreed, dropping her hand to put his arm around her shoulders and cuddle her close against him.

They pulled into the driveway and paused at the closed gate, Max pushing the button. While they waited for a response, he kissed her, a kiss that roused the desire simmering just below the surface every time they were close to each other. His hand was caressing her breast as the intercom came on.

"Yes?"

Max reluctantly pulled back, his gaze still on Caroline, as he answered Mrs. Lamb. After the gate swung open, he drove up to the house.

Just as he stopped the truck, Caroline said, "Oh, Max, I think I should tell you that there's a camera attached to the intercom system. Mrs. Lamb saw everything we did."

Like a schoolboy caught looking at dirty pictures, he flushed bright red up to his hairline.

"And that will teach you to laugh when *I'm* in an embarrassing situation," she teased before slipping from the truck.

With a growl, Max came racing around the truck and she scampered ahead of him into the house, laughing at his antics.

Until she almost bumped into Adrian.

And her father.

"Oh! Hi."

"Where have you been?" her father demanded.

Though he was speaking to her, James's stare was directed at Max.

"I had an errand to run."

"And you couldn't do it alone?" James demanded.

The seriousness of the situation eluded Caroline, especially when she applied his question to the past hour. "No, I don't think so."

"I find it inappropriate for my fiancée to be running around town with another man," Adrian said stiffly.

Caroline stared at the man she was supposed to marry in two days and remembered Chelsea's words. "Then perhaps I shouldn't marry you, Adrian."

Both her father and Adrian stared at her as if she'd just announced the outbreak of World War III. Max's hand came to her shoulder.

"Don't be ridiculous!" her father sputtered. "You promised to marry the father of the baby!"

"That's right," Adrian chimed in. "And I presented proof. That's more than *he* did."

"Adrian, I know I promised to marry the father of my baby. But I don't love you. I think it would be wrong for us to marry. I'd like you to release me from my promise." She wasn't sure when she'd made the decision, but Caroline felt she was making the right one.

Adrian's face took on a hurt expression that even convinced Caroline, making her uneasy. "I realize you don't care for me anymore, Caroline, but I think you owe me the right to make my child legitimate, to be its legal father. If, after it's born, you don't feel you can live with me, then we'll discuss a divorce. But at least give me the right to protect my child."

In spite of herself, his speech touched her. And made her angry. Even though she thought he was lying, he'd certainly made her feel like a despicable person, a fickle female, toying with his heart.

Before she could answer, Max said, "You aren't the father of her baby, Meadows, and you know it."

James answered before Adrian could. "I've seen his proof. Do you have any? Have you shown us anything to convince us that you're telling the truth and not just attempting to feather your nest with my fortune?''

"Daddy!" Caroline protested even as a sharp pain hit her between the eyes.

"I'm sorry, Caroline, but you have to be careful. I've warned you about men using you to get to me. And yet you still believe him."

"I don't care anything about you or your fortune!" Max roared. "All I care about is Caroline!"

"Easy to say, but like James said, I don't see any proof," Adrian taunted, triumph in his voice.

Chapter Fourteen

"What do you have?" Joe Perkins asked, gripping the telephone receiver tightly.

"Nothing so far. You?" Don Knowles asked in return.

"Nothing. This man covers his tracks well. I think there's another woman, but I can't find any proof of it."

"Several people have recognized the picture of Meadows you gave me. He was a tightwad tipper. But not the picture of Miss Adkins. They remember he was with a woman, but they're sure it wasn't her."

"Have you tried to find the photographer?"

"Yeah. There must be a million of them. I've looked at so many photos, I'm going crazy. I've got three more photographers to check out. Two of them are on vacation. The third one has disappeared."

"The wedding's tomorrow."

"Yeah, I know."

CAROLINE SLEPT LATE the next morning. The day before had exhausted her. And also frustrated her.

She was sure Adrian was lying, but his request to be the legal father of his own child, as he said, put her in a difficult position. And easily convinced her father her behavior was outrageous.

If she simply refused to marry Adrian, she would be alienated from her father. She didn't want that. Her family might not be like most families, but she loved them.

She reached for her crackers and nibbled slowly. How long before she got past morning sickness? Chelsea was six weeks ahead of her and she had no trouble with it.

Six weeks? Surely she wouldn't have to wait so long.

By then she supposed her fate would be sealed. All the mental debating would be over. And if she could find a way to avoid marrying Adrian, she'd just have to find a way to bring her father around.

"Too bad he's such a hardhead," she muttered. Though she really couldn't complain since she shared that particular trait.

And in spite of his great disappointment when she'd left his company, he'd supported her decision. Which made it all the more difficult to consider hurting him again. Which also explained why she was still living at home instead of having her own place, as she wanted.

With a sigh, she sank back into the pillow, covering her eyes. Too many decisions. Too many people to please. Too much she couldn't remember.

The phone rang. She checked her watch. Ten o'clock.

"Hello?"

"Good morning, Caroline."

Max's baritone warmed her to her toes.

"Mmm, good morning," she replied, snuggling into her pillow, wishing it was Max's shoulder.

"Are you feeling okay after yesterday?"

"Yes. I'm just not moving very fast."

"I guess Adrian hasn't confessed all?"

At dinner last night, they had discussed such a possibility, but they'd both admitted it wasn't likely.

"No. And Daddy is firmly entrenched on his side."

"Yeah. I gathered that. I think my first clue was the glares he kept shooting my way."

"It's not you personally, Max. He just wants me to marry Adrian. He probably already has the honeymoon planned."

"Without consulting you?"

"Given the choice, my father would plan my entire life without consulting me. He always thinks he knows best." Even as she finished talking, a sudden thought struck her. "Max! What about after the wedding?"

"That depends on whose wedding."

"No, Max, think! If we were getting married tomorrow, wouldn't you have made plans for afterward? Where we would live, where we would go?"

"We *are* getting married tomorrow, and I was hoping you'd want to live in my house. And I know what room we'll be spending all our time in."

Caroline shivered under the covers as she thought about the time already spent in Max's beautiful bedroom. "Oh, Max, I would love it, but that's not the point."

He chuckled. "It never seems to be with you."

"Max! Stop teasing. Don't you see? Adrian hasn't made any plans for after the wedding. At least, I don't think he has." Somehow she thought she was on to something here. "I think I should go to Adrian's apartment. Maybe I'll find something there that will give us proof."

"You're not going to that man's apartment alone!"

"Well, it wouldn't be appropriate to take *you.*"

"Look, sweetheart, I wasn't going to tell you because I didn't want to get your hopes up, but I hired a private investigator."

"You did?"

"Yeah. So let him do the investigation, okay?"

"I hired one, too." She waited for his response, but he remained silent. "Max? Are you there?"

"Yeah. I'm just surprised."

"Why? Did you think I wanted to marry Adrian?"

"No, but—have they found anything?"

"No. At least, they haven't called me. Yours?"

"No. I called this morning and his secretary said he was in Vegas, working on it."

"I'll call mine."

"Call me right back," Max insisted.

"Okay."

Two minutes later, she called Max. "He said they think there's another woman, but he has no proof. He sent a woman to the office this morning, hoping to get something out of his secretary, but she wouldn't tell her anything."

"Damn."

His forlorn tones made her want to put her arms around him. That and her desire to make love with him again. Were pregnant women supposed to think about such things? She'd better get her mind on important matters. "That's why I need to go to his apartment."

"Promise me you won't go alone."

Caroline promised and then hung up the phone reluctantly. She hated to break contact with Max. As long as she was with him or talking to him, she believed that they would somehow find a way to be together. And she desperately needed to believe.

Her body craved Max's. But even more importantly, her heart wanted him by her side. Forever and ever. She wanted to know that whatever she faced, Max would be by her side, sharing her life.

At least she'd found something she could do, and she

felt a sudden burst of energy. She called her sister, hoping to persuade her to accompany her.

"Well, of course, you should see where you're going to live. Do you want to start moving your things?"

"No, Chelsea. I just want to see his apartment. Will you come with me?"

"I suppose so," Chelsea agreed with a sigh. "But I must say, your wedding is consuming all my time."

"Sorry," Caroline apologized meekly, but she suspected Chelsea would've expected so much more had it been her wedding.

An hour later, with Chelsea driving, they arrived at the address her father's secretary had given them. Caroline was determined to see the apartment without telling Adrian.

The security guard in the lobby of the high-rise apartment building smiled at them as they approached.

"Good morning, ladies. May I help you?"

"Yes, you can," Caroline assured him, hoping her confidence would sway him. "I need you to let me in to my fiancé's apartment." She giggled and fluttered her lashes. "He forgot to give me the key, and we're getting married tomorrow."

The man's smile took on a paternal air. "Now, just who would that fiancé be?"

"Adrian Meadows."

The smile disappeared.

"Mr. Meadows didn't say anything about getting married. And I've never seen either one of you with him before."

Chelsea appeared affronted by his words. "Certainly not. I'm a married woman."

"You haven't ever seen me before?" Caroline asked. "Not even in the evenings?"

"I don't work the late shift."

"Oh. That would explain it." She'd hoped she'd maybe found more proof, since Adrian said they made love in his apartment most of the time. Maybe she could find the night man. "But it's all right. I'm his fiancée."

"I'll have to call Mr. Meadows for his approval."

"Oh, surely that's not necessary. After all, after tomorrow, I'll be living here, too." She hoped she wasn't, but so far she wasn't making much progress.

The man ignored her and picked up the phone.

"I think this man is rude," Chelsea complained in a whisper. "You should complain to Adrian."

"What's your name?" the security guard asked.

"Caroline Adkins."

He repeated the name to whomever he was talking. "Yes, ma'am. Just a minute." He held the phone out to Caroline. "His secretary wants to talk to you."

"Hello?"

"Miss Adkins, this is Mary Lambert. Mr. Meadows is out of the office at the moment. You needed to see his apartment?"

"Why, yes. Since we're being married tomorrow—" The sound of the phone hitting the floor stopped Caroline. "Hello?"

"I'm sorry, I dropped the phone. You're being married tomorrow, you were saying?"

"Yes, Adrian and I are being married tomorrow. I thought I should see where I would be living."

"I expect Mr. Meadows to return in an hour. I'll have him call you when he comes in." She sounded as if she was about to hang up the phone.

"Wait! Can't you just tell the guard to let me in? I don't want to have to make another trip over here."

"I'm afraid I can't do that, Miss Adkins. I'll have Mr. Meadows call."

Caroline was left holding the receiver, the dial tone in her ear. She looked at the guard, watching her intently, wondering if she could fake her way past him, but it didn't look promising. Finally she handed the phone back to him. "He's out of the office."

"Maybe he's with Daddy," Chelsea offered.

"Of course. Why didn't I think of that? May I borrow your phone again?"

The guard reluctantly handed over the phone and Caroline dialed her father's office.

"Daddy? Is Adrian with you?"

"Yes, he's here, but we're in the middle of a meeting. What do you need?"

"I want to see his apartment, to see where we'll be living, but the guard won't let me in." She hoped her voice conveyed some enthusiasm for the prospect of living with Adrian.

"Oh. Of course. Adrian, you need to give the guard at your condo permission to let Caroline in. She wants to see your place, though I guess she's seen it a few times, hasn't she?" he added with a chuckle.

Caroline wished she'd been able to see Adrian's face. Finding him with her father was so much better than him being in his office, alone. She heard a strangled protest.

"Why not?" her father asked, plainly puzzled. There was a mumbled response that Caroline couldn't understand.

"Adrian says the place isn't clean. He'll show it to you this evening."

"But aren't we having the rehearsal this evening? After all, the wedding is tomorrow night," Caroline insisted.

"No, your mother called and they've scheduled the rehearsal tomorrow at three."

"The day of the wedding?"

"Yes, Caroline, and I really have to get back to the meeting. Be a good girl, and Adrian will take you to his place this evening."

She hung up the phone. "I don't want to see it this evening!" she protested bitterly to her father, who could no longer hear her. Chelsea and the guard stared at her.

"Come on, Chelsea, let's go."

The guard said nothing as they walked away.

"What did Daddy say?"

"He said Adrian would show me the apartment this evening. After he cleans it. Can you see Adrian pushing a vacuum cleaner?" Just the thought cheered her, but she also knew that she'd lost the opportunity to surprise him. If she had to look at the apartment tonight, there wouldn't be a single shred of evidence.

"I'm not surprised you're irritated," Chelsea agreed. "Why, when Roddy and I were getting married, we made all our decisions together, picked out the house and furnished it before the wedding."

"Yes, but you had more than three days."

"Well, of course. It takes months to plan a wedding." Chelsea apparently realized she might have caused her sister concern. "I'm sure your wedding will be nice, too, Caro, but—but it would've been better if you'd had more time."

"Yes."

More time to catch Adrian in his lies.

More time to recover from her accident.

More time to remember.

MAX WAITED IMPATIENTLY for Caroline to call. She'd promised to do so as soon as she came back from Adrian's apartment.

There must be something he could do. He felt so helpless, letting others search for clues.

"Max?" Susan said from the door of his office. "While you were on the phone, a couple called to set up an appointment to see the house on Crider Lane. I made it for tomorrow evening at seven."

"Tomorrow? No, I can't make it."

"But Max, they sounded really enthusiastic. They've looked at it already. I think they'll buy it."

"See if Jim or someone can be there. I'll be busy tomorrow night."

"I didn't know you had anything planned. What are you going to do?"

Too bad she was his sister. Had Susan been a real secretary, he could have told her to mind her own business.

"Sorry, I should've let you know."

"You're going out with Caroline, aren't you? I don't know why you're keeping it a secret. I've already met her." Before he could say anything, she added, "First thing you know, the two of you will be looking at rings."

He stared at her. Rings. He'd never thought of that. Without another word, he got up and headed for his truck.

"Max? What did I say? Where are you going?"

"I'll be out of the office the rest of the day. And tomorrow, too."

He slammed the door of his truck and gunned the motor. Rings. He certainly was not going to use a ring purchased by Adrian Meadows. If he got the chance to marry Caroline tomorrow, she would wear *his* ring, not Adrian's.

Though his first impulse was to go to a jewelry store

and buy a ring at once, almost as a talisman to prove he had a chance of marrying her tomorrow, he reluctantly decided he should consult Caroline first. He would go to her house and wait for her to return.

Mrs. Lamb opened the gate and met him at the front door.

"Caroline hasn't returned?"

"No, she hasn't. Would you care to wait?"

"Yes, thank you."

She stood back to let him in. "I'm afraid we're a little topsy-turvy with all the activities for the wedding."

"Who was it, Mrs. Lamb?" Amelia asked, coming into the foyer. "Oh, it's you, Mr. Daniels."

"Yes, ma'am. I'd like to wait for Caroline's return if you don't mind."

"Of course not. In fact, you can make yourself useful. We need another pair of hands. You don't mind, do you?"

Good manners insisted he agree, but he wondered what he was getting himself into.

"Good. Come with me. I've ordered some things for Caroline and they've just arrived. You can help me open boxes to see if the order is complete. The women I hired this morning have been on the phone calling to invite guests, so they're too busy. And Mrs. Lamb is constantly having to open the door. Presents have already started arriving."

Somehow, Caroline's mother didn't feel his opening boxes of lingerie for Caroline, the woman he loved, that she would wear for another man, was inappropriate. He certainly found it interesting as he held up scraps of lace. His imagination worked overtime picturing Caroline in those garments.

And made him more determined than ever that *he* would be the husband, not Adrian.

"Well, the order is complete. And I don't think I've forgotten anything. Where is Caroline? She needs to start opening the gifts. We have to record them or she'll never get the thank-you notes right."

During their inventory of the lingerie wardrobe, Mrs. Lamb had brought in numerous deliveries of gifts. Max was astounded at how complicated things could become in three days.

"You'll just have to start opening the gifts, Max, and I'll write down who they're from. Let me get pencil and paper."

"Yes, ma'am."

"Oh, call me Amelia. You've been very helpful."

Max watched her leave the room and then stared around him at the neatly folded stacks of lace and satin. Caroline wouldn't need to buy lingerie for several years. Which was a good thing when he saw the price tags.

He picked up a teddy, one that had particularly intrigued him, in bridal white. Yeah, Caroline would look terrific in that.

"Max! What are you doing?"

The woman in his head had suddenly appeared in the doorway. He quickly dropped the teddy.

"Uh, inventorying your new lingerie." The stunned look on her face amused him. "It was your mother's idea. Next, we're going to open your wedding gifts."

"You can't be serious," she protested.

"That would be highly inappropriate," Chelsea chimed in, looking over her sister's shoulder.

Amelia appeared behind them. "Oh, hello, I'm glad you're back. There's so much to do. Caroline," she continued as she pushed past her daughters, "I bought you new lingerie as a wedding gift. Max has been so helpful. I believe they sent everything I ordered. Isn't that right, Max?"

"Yes, Amelia, every item." He grinned at Caroline.

"Mother, you shouldn't have asked Max to help with my lingerie."

Amelia turned to her in surprise. "Well, I had to have some help, Caroline. You and Chelsea certainly weren't available. Now, there's quite a lot more to do. We must begin opening the gifts and recording them so you can start on the thank-you notes. I'm sure Max will help. You've been such a dear, Max."

"Thank you again, Amelia, but I'm afraid I'll have to borrow Caroline for a little while." He'd like to do more than borrow her. The sexy lingerie gave him all kinds of ideas about what he'd like to do with Caroline.

The approving smile Amelia had been sending his way disappeared. "What? Don't be ridiculous. Caroline can't leave. She has too much to do."

"What is it, Max?" Caroline asked, crossing the room to his side.

He liked the concern in her voice, her instant attention. He took her hand in his and whispered, "We need to buy rings for the wedding tomorrow."

Staring up at him, she blinked several times, as if having difficulty understanding. "But, Max—"

"What are you two whispering about?" Amelia demanded.

"Umm, Max and I need to talk—alone. We'll be right back," Caroline promised, pulling him toward the door.

"I certainly hope so. I have several things for Max to do. He's such a helpful man."

"Thanks for being so helpful!" Caroline exclaimed in exasperation, raising her eyebrows at him as soon as they were in the foyer. He pulled her into his arms in spite of her protests.

"You wanted me to refuse to help your mother? I don't want to start off my marriage with my mother-in-law unhappy with me."

"Max, you talk as if we're—as if it's our wedding." Caroline looked away from him. "I may have to marry Adrian."

He took her chin in his fingers and turned her back to look at him. "No. You're going to marry me. Those detectives will find something. You've got to believe that, sweetheart." His lips briefly touched hers. He couldn't risk losing control at the moment. But, oh, how he wanted to.

"I want to believe, Max. But we're almost out of time."

"We'll make it. And when we do, I'm not about to use a ring purchased by Adrian. So, we've got to go pick out a ring now, so they'll have time to size it."

She stared up at him, unsure, and he hoped she wouldn't refuse his request. Ever since the idea of a ring occurred to him, it had been growing stronger in his mind. He wanted a ring, his ring, that would show that Caroline belonged to him. He breathed a sigh of relief when a grin slowly appeared on her face.

"Two grooms, two licenses, why not two rings? And one for you, too?" she asked. When he nodded, she added, "After all, I seem to be doing everything in pairs."

"I guess I should've told you twins run in our family," he said.

"Don't joke, Max," she protested, her grin still in place.

"Uh, Caroline, I'm not joking." And he wasn't. Hoping to distract her from his latest revelation, he pulled her against him and tasted her lips again. He couldn't stand to hold her and not kiss her. Especially after picturing her in that teddy.

"Caroline? What—" Amelia's voice intruded on the kiss, and Max slowly released Caroline.

"Well, really, Max, you've been very helpful, but I don't think that kind of behavior is appropriate," Amelia protested. "Why, it's almost as if you were the groom instead of Adrian."

His gaze still trained on Caroline, he said, "We have to keep our options open, Amelia. There could be a last-minute change."

"Oh. Does Adrian know?" Amelia asked, a confused look on her face.

Chapter Fifteen

"Does Adrian know what?" James Adkins asked as he entered the house.

Caroline turned to face her father, but she remained in Max's arms. It was her mother, however, who answered her husband's question.

"That there may be a change of grooms. I certainly was surprised, and I would imagine he is, too." She paused, studying Max. "But I must admit, Max, you have definitely been more congenial than Adrian ever is."

"What are you talking about?" James demanded in his normal roar. "Adrian is the groom. He had proof!"

"Daddy, I don't believe his proof," Caroline said, trying to keep her voice calm.

"Why not?" James set his briefcase down on the floor and put his hands on his hips. "Give me a reason."

"I was wearing a brown dress!" she replied in exasperation.

"What? What does your dress have to do with anything?"

"I didn't know you ever wore brown, dear," Amelia commented, looking at Caroline in continued confusion.

"I agree," Chelsea said as she came into the foyer.

"Caroline, don't tell me you're turning into your

mother? You've always been the sensible one," James moaned, slapping his forehead with his hand.

Chelsea was the only female to protest his criticism. Her wail about her father not loving her was background to the anger Caroline felt as she said, "I am sensible, but no more than Mother and Chelsea. They both realize something is wrong. Why don't you?"

"The only thing wrong is you won't do what you're supposed to."

"According to whom?" Caroline asked, moving closer to her father, challenging him.

"According to me! I'm your father! And you promised!"

"So, you don't care about my happiness?"

"I didn't say that!" James protested.

"I made you a promise, and I'm going to keep it, Daddy. Even though I know I didn't keep the promise I made you about work, I will keep this promise. But I want a promise from you." Caroline watched her father squirm. He loved tying others down, but he hated it himself.

"What promise?"

"If I find proof that Adrian lied, then you must be happy with my decision, whatever it is." She held her breath. Even if she didn't marry Adrian, that didn't mean her father would accept Max. Unless he made this promise. He kept his promises.

James met Caroline's gaze. "Very well. I promise. But it has to be good proof. I don't think Adrian would lie. He's an honorable man."

"Is he?" Caroline asked. "What was his reaction when I wanted to see his apartment?"

"He wants to make sure it's tidy for you. There's nothing wrong with that. We men aren't as neat as women."

James's voice sounded sure, but Caroline noticed that his gaze shifted from hers.

"*I* think he wants to get rid of evidence," she said with determination.

"Evidence? You're beginning to make this whole thing sound like an episode of 'Perry Mason.'" He stared at each of them before bringing his gaze back to Caroline. "Why? Just because of a brown dress? You put her up to this, didn't you?" James asked, swinging his gaze to Max.

"Not the brown dress bit," Max said. "I'm afraid I wouldn't have noticed anything like that. Besides, I didn't see the picture. Did you?"

"Of course I did. In spite of what she said, I care about Caroline's happiness."

His gruffness touched Caroline and she hugged him briefly. "I know you do, Daddy. But there's more."

"More what?"

"More evidence," Caroline assured him, taking his hand and pulling him toward the sun room.

"Adrian has more proof?"

"No, Daddy. *I* do."

Everyone followed them.

"Then why haven't you told anyone?" Chelsea asked.

"Yes," James agreed, "why haven't you produced this evidence? Where is it? I want to see it."

Caroline regretted her impulsive words. "Well, I can't exactly *show* it to you." She felt better when Max moved to her side, his arm going around her waist.

"Just as I thought. You don't have any proof," James said triumphantly.

"What about the fact that Adrian never touches me?"

"I've seen him touch you. He took your hand the other evening."

"That's not—"

"Besides," James continued, ignoring her response, "it's probably because this—this stranger is always pawing you."

Max stepped away from her, his arm falling to his side, as if guilty of some great sin.

Caroline swung around to glare at him. "Are you going to let him intimidate you?"

"No," Max answered in measured tones, as if he resented her question. "But I am a guest in his house and you are his daughter." He raked his hand through his dark hair. "Besides, I told you you couldn't convince your father with that."

"Aha! So, it's a conspiracy!" James exclaimed.

"Don't be ridiculous!" Caroline shouted, swinging back to face her father. "Men! Mother and Chelsea understand. Why can't the two of you?"

"Because men have to have facts," Amelia said calmly. "I learned that a long time ago."

"Some women do, too," Max murmured, reminding Caroline of how often she'd said she had to have proof.

"Daddy, I hired the Perkins Security Firm to find out if Adrian is telling the truth," Caroline said. "I will keep my word if he really is the father of my child, but I will not be trapped by some money-hungry liar!"

"You what? You can't hire them! They work for me!"

"Afraid they'll discover the truth?"

"No! There's nothing to discover!"

"Then you have nothing to worry about." She turned to Max. "Come on, Max. Let's go."

"Go where?" James demanded, catching her arm.

"Out!" She pulled her arm from his grasp, slid her hand through Max's arm and headed for the door.

"Will you be home for dinner?" Amelia asked, as if the past fifteen minutes had never occurred.

"No, I'll take her out to dinner," Max said.

"But Adrian is coming over to take you to see his apartment," James protested.

"I don't want to see it now. I wanted to see it this morning." She didn't care if she did sound petulant. She couldn't bear the thought of an entire evening in Adrian's company.

"What difference does it make whether it's morning or evening, Caroline? You're being ridiculous."

She ignored him and pulled Max through the door.

"What am I going to tell Adrian?" James asked, coming after them.

Swinging around, she glared at her father. "Tell him he'd better be sure he's telling the truth. If he's lying, he's going to be sorry."

After they reached Max's truck and drove away, he asked, "Have you calmed down yet?" He reached over and took her hand.

"Probably not. Did I scare you?"

"Nope. I just wondered if you and your father have a shouting match every time you disagree."

"How would I know?" she demanded, glaring at the man she loved.

"Hey, don't start on me. I'm the innocent party, here."

"Yeah, sure. That's why I throw up every morning."

He grinned. "I'll take credit for that, sweetheart, but not the mess we're all in. If you hadn't run away, we'd be planning our nursery now."

She smiled back at him, but he'd touched on the one point in his version of her missing two weeks that always bothered her. "You have no idea why I left?"

His smile disappeared. "No. I racked my brain for

hours, days, trying to figure it out. I alternately cursed you and called for you." He carried her hand to his lips. "I told myself, after a while, that I was glad you were gone. But the minute I knew where you were, I came running."

Whatever her reason for leaving, Caroline was happy he'd come. Even without her memory, she knew that Max Daniels was her soul mate, the one man in the world who could stir her senses, make her world complete. Leaning her head against his shoulder, she whispered, "I'm glad."

THE RING SELECTION didn't take long. They discovered they had the same tastes in rings. As soon as Caroline accepted Max's ability to buy the expensive ring she'd fallen in love with, their decision was made. Max chose a simple gold band, pleasing Caroline. She'd never liked diamonds on a man.

They enjoyed a quiet meal at a Mexican restaurant, another taste they discovered they shared. When the bill came, Max slipped out his charge card and laid it on the tray with the bill.

"I hope your ring didn't max out my card," he teased, and then laughed when she looked worried. "I'm just kidding."

"I shouldn't have chosen such an expensive ring."

He leaned over and kissed her, as if he had every right, and Caroline sighed in contentment. In her heart he did.

"Caroline, I'm not in your father's stratosphere as far as money goes, but most people consider me a wealthy man." He kissed her again. "In fact, now that I'm marrying you, I'd be considered very wealthy indeed."

Caroline smiled up at him, trying to hide the fact that his words disturbed her. They could so easily be interpreted the wrong way. Her father's claim about Max saying he's the father of her baby just to get to his money came back to haunt her.

"Is something wrong?"

"No! Nothing."

The waiter returned for Max to sign the bill. She watched him write in the tip with almost no pause. There was another difference between men and women. Men seemed to know how much to tip without ever stopping to calculate. When she signed for— "Max!" She grabbed his arm as the waiter walked away.

"What is it, sweetheart? You want something more? A sudden urge for a pickle?"

She ignored his teasing. "Max! I may have found a way to prove Adrian wrong."

"How?"

"Charge cards! I must have charged something during those two weeks. If the charge was here in the Denver area, instead of Las Vegas, then we'll have our proof."

"Brilliant," Max agreed, kissing her again. Then he took her hand and pulled her from the booth. "Come on. Let's go check your records."

They sat in tense silence as Max drove to her house. Too much rested on the result of their search for any idle chitchat.

"Where do you keep your records?" Max asked as they came to a stop in front of her house.

"There's a desk in my bedroom. Let's start there. If we don't find anything, we'll ask Mrs. Lamb."

Fifteen minutes later, Caroline called down to the kitchen. When Mrs. Lamb reached her bedroom door, Caroline was waiting for her.

"Mrs. Lamb? Where else would I keep my records? My bills, my files."

"Why, right here, child. Oh, my stars, you two have made a mess. What are you looking for?"

"We're looking for either of my charge card bills," Caroline explained.

Mrs. Lamb looked puzzled but she moved over to the bed to peer at the pile of paper. "Why, here they are, dear, right here on top."

"No, Mrs. Lamb, those are my current bills. I'm looking for the bills from late June, when I went away."

Mrs. Lamb looked from Caroline to Max and back to Caroline, slowly shaking her head. "Once you pay them, dear, you throw them out."

Caroline sank down onto the bed, not noticing the papers under her. "Surely not," she gasped. "Don't I have to save them for—for taxes or something?"

"They don't allow interest deductions anymore, you know, and you don't have business expenses since you don't have a business. Why save them?"

Caroline closed her eyes, fighting to keep the tears from slipping out. So close. She'd thought they would find proof.

"Caroline," Max said softly, his arms coming around her as he pulled her up into his arms. "It's all right. We'll find another way."

"I'm sorry," Mrs. Lamb apologized.

"It's not your fault, Mrs. Lamb," Max assured her.

Caroline lifted her face from his chest. "Max is right, Mrs. Lamb. You've done all you could to help. Can I call them in the morning, Max? Could they tell me over the phone if I made any charges then?"

"Good idea, Caroline. I'm sure they can. You won't get actual documents to back you up for several days, but your father would listen to reason, wouldn't he?"

Mrs. Lamb and Caroline looked at each other and

laughed. Suddenly Caroline felt better. "That's not a known trait for my father, but we'd convince him."

"Then maybe we still have hope," he said with a smile, kissing her forehead.

"Well, I'll just go back downstairs. You two probably want to be alone," Mrs. Lamb said, edging to the door.

"No, I have to leave," Max said, stepping back from Caroline. She looked at him in surprise.

"You do? Why?"

He looked at the bed before he looked at her. "You need to get a lot of rest tonight. And if I'm here, I don't think you will."

Caroline's cheeks burned a bright red. She knew exactly what he was thinking. And she liked it. But he was right. Tomorrow could be a difficult day.

"Then you walk him to the door, and I'll straighten up this mess. That way, you can get right to bed as soon as you come back upstairs," Mrs. Lamb suggested.

With a thanks sent the housekeeper's way, Max took Caroline's hand and pulled her from the room. After closing the door behind him, he wrapped his arms around her and kissed her.

"Oh, Max," she murmured, "maybe you should change your mind."

"I'd like to, but your father's house isn't the place. And tonight isn't the time. Tomorrow night we'll do our celebrating."

Caroline suddenly thought of the little boy whistling as he walked through the graveyard. She hoped Max's words weren't indicative of his fear that tomorrow night she'd be sharing her life with Adrian. A shudder seized her.

He pulled her tighter. "Something wrong?"

"No. I'm just missing you already."

Another kiss only made her want more.

"I have to go, Caroline," Max insisted, sounding desperate.

"You don't want to be with me?" she asked, surprised.

He gave her a bear hug. "Don't be ridiculous. I want to be with you too much. Now, walk me to the door," he insisted, tugging her toward the stairs.

They walked down arm in arm, not talking. Caroline was thinking about the next morning and how early she could call the credit card company. And how soon she'd see Max again.

The sound of the sun room door opening scarcely registered, but the voices that she heard shook her from her thoughts.

She started to say something to Max, but her father and Adrian came into view.

"Caroline! I didn't hear you come in," Adrian said, walking forward. He stopped when he got a good look at her and Max, their arms entwined.

"I really don't think your behavior is appropriate," he finally said.

"We've been over this subject before," Caroline said, keeping her arm around Max. "I don't believe your proof and I don't want to marry you."

"But you promised. It's my right as the father of your child."

Max turned loose of her and stepped down another step. "I'm tired of your statements like that, Meadows. You are not the father of this baby."

"I have proof."

"Yeah, and I'd like to see it. Just where is this proof?"

"I have it in safekeeping," Adrian assured him, but

Caroline noted he took a step backward. Max moved forward again.

"At your apartment?"

"No. It's being repaired. Caroline ripped it. And that reminds me, Caroline, I came to take you to my apartment. As you requested."

His attempt to make her feel guilty didn't work. "Didn't Daddy tell you? I wanted to see it this morning, not this evening."

"I don't understand what a few hours' difference could make."

"Oh, I think you do. Otherwise, you would've told the man to let me in."

"Don't be ridiculous. I just didn't want you to see the place before it was cleaned."

"By the way, Adrian, where are we going on our honeymoon?" Caroline suddenly asked.

"Honeymoon?" he repeated, as if he'd never heard the word before.

"Nowhere with him," Max growled.

She grinned, loving the jealousy in his voice, but she looked at Adrian, waiting for a response.

"Well, I haven't—there's been no time—I thought we'd go to Vegas. Kind of retrace our steps," Adrian finished with a rush, looking quite proud of himself.

Caroline stared at Adrian, a memory suddenly filling her head. She turned slowly to look at her father. "Why didn't you say anything?"

"What are you talking about?" James demanded.

"I remembered something. I hate Las Vegas. You took me there when I turned twenty-one, remember, Daddy?" She turned to grin at Max. "I had a miserable trip. I vowed I'd never go back to Las Vegas."

"And your father knew that?" Max stared at James.

"So what? Love can change a person's mind. Besides, she's older, now. Her tastes have changed since she was twenty-one," James blustered.

"Not that much. So that's another reason why I don't believe your 'proof.'"

Adrian had that bland expression on his face that she hated. "You have other reasons?"

"Yes, I do."

"What are they?"

Caroline started to answer and then closed her mouth. "No, I don't think I'll tell you. I have no physical proof, but I may have by tomorrow. So I'll just wait. But I wouldn't be counting on marrying me tomorrow, Adrian."

"You're bluffing," he said, a tight smile on his face. "You made a promise and I'll expect you to keep it tomorrow evening."

"I will," she agreed, without smiling in return, "unless the private detective I've hired finds something interesting."

"Or maybe the one I've hired," Max added, standing behind Caroline, his hands on her shoulders.

Adrian stared at them, his mouth open, his cheeks paling. "You—you've hired a detective?" He spun around to face James. "How could you let them do that? Make them call them off!"

"Now, Adrian, don't worry about it. After all, you've got proof that you're telling the truth. And once you're married to my Caroline," James added, "you'll be a member of the family."

"It could be a very costly membership, Adrian," Caroline said, determined not to ignore her father's blatant bribery. "You'd better be sure it's worth the price."

Chapter Sixteen

Her wedding day.

Somehow, Caroline hadn't thought it would be like this—nausea, fear, worry. The bridal magazines didn't describe wedded bliss that way.

As soon as her stomach was settled, she got out of bed and quickly dressed. She wanted to call the credit card companies as soon as their offices opened.

She was pacing the floor when Mrs. Lamb knocked on the door with her breakfast trey.

"You're already up?" the housekeeper asked, noting that Caroline was dressed in shorts and a T-shirt.

"Yes. I'm waiting to call about my credit cards."

"You can eat breakfast while you wait. Your mother is already up, too. She has a long list of things for you to do. And your dress was just delivered. The alterations have been made, but you should try it on as soon as possible. Your mother wanted me to remind you that the rehearsal is at three." She paused to take a deep breath. "I think that's all at the moment, but presents continue to arrive, and I think I'm going crazy."

Caroline gave the woman a hug. "I know, Lambie, but it will all be over soon. You've been a real trouper about everything."

Mrs. Lamb returned the hug. "I'm going to miss you when you're gone, Caroline. Oh, my stars, I will."

The housekeeper hurried from the room, whether to hide tears or simply to tackle all the chores waiting for her, Caroline didn't know. But that simple remark brought home to Caroline suddenly how much her life was about to change. Whether she married Adrian or Max, she would no longer live at home with her parents. She would no longer be independent. She would be part of a pair.

An unhappy pair, if the other one was Adrian.

If it was Max, she would be thrilled, but...but there were still some difficulties to work out.

She automatically ate her breakfast, thinking about her future, about the child she was carrying, the man she would share that child with.

When eight o'clock came, she put the tray aside and reached for the phone. Though it took several minutes to be connected to the right department, she persisted until she found someone who could answer her question.

"No, Miss Adkins. For that two-week period, you made no charges. There is a charge about three days after the date you gave me, but not during those two weeks."

"Thank you."

She dialed the second number, and again, after some delays, received the same answer. Depression threatened, but Caroline was getting angry. That emotion energized her as she paced the room. How had she paid for those two weeks? Surely she hadn't relied on the man, whichever one he was.

Her bank account!

She called the bank and asked for activities during that two-week period.

"Why, no, Miss Adkins. Well, on the day before the

date you gave me, you made a substantial withdrawal. Do you want that information?"

"Yes, please."

"You withdrew twenty-five hundred cash, here at the bank. Does that help?"

"Yes, thank you." No, thank you. At least she knew she had paid her own way, she thought, but it didn't tell her where she had spent that money.

Her hand was still resting on the telephone when it rang. She jumped as if she'd received an electrical shock.

"Caroline?" Max asked, his voice eager. "Did you call about your charges?"

"Yes. There were none."

After a painful silence, he simply said, "Oh."

"I know. I also called the bank. I withdrew a lot of cash the day before I left."

"That fits with what the hotel guy told me."

"What? What did he tell you?"

"That you paid in cash."

"They have a record of it? I registered there? Of course I did. Why didn't you tell me?" Hope filled her as she waited for his response.

"Yes, you registered, but not under your own name. I don't know why, since you told *me* your real name."

"Then how do you know it was me with the fake name?"

"Because I knew your room number. They only had one person stay for two weeks in that room during that time period. So I assumed it was you. But I can't prove it, and that's why I didn't say anything."

"What name did I use?"

"Leslie...uh, McBay, McKay, something like that."

"Leslie McVey?"

"Maybe. Does that name mean something to you?"

"Yes. That's Daddy's secretary's name."

"Well, it sure wasn't his secretary that I walked to the door and kissed good-night," Max assured her.

Caroline couldn't resist a chuckle at the picture of Max romancing the stiff and proper, elderly Miss McVey. She had been her father's secretary for more than twenty years.

"What's so funny?"

"Nothing, Max." Her amusement faded as she realized they still had nothing to show for all their hard work. "It's just—I'm getting scared, Max. What if we can't find any proof before—" She broke off, unable to voice the event scheduled for the evening.

"You could break your promise."

She almost chewed a hole in her bottom lip, trying to think of an answer to his statement.

"Forget I said that," he said gruffly. "That's frustration speaking. But Caroline, you're not going to live with this man, are you?"

"No. I'm only marrying him to—to give the baby its daddy's name," she assured him.

"Damn it, Caroline. I won't put up with you calling my baby his."

She covered her eyes, unable to face even the soothing blues of her bedroom. "Max, please. I'm sure my memory will come back soon. If—when I know the baby is yours, then we'll get married, okay?"

"And if you don't recover your memory?"

"I will! I know I will! It just may not happen before tonight." She drew a deep, shuddering breath and leaned back against her pillow. "Max?"

"Yeah?"

"Are you going to come to the wedding?"

Silence.

"I know I'm asking a lot, Max, but I'd like for you to be there."

"Of course I'll be there."

She knew those words cost him. But she needed him there in the church with her. She needed to be able to see him, to know that even if she had to marry Adrian, Max was there. And, according to him, would always be there.

"Thank you."

"No problem. I'll see you."

Caroline hung up the phone and slid back down onto the pillow, wrapping her arms around her and thinking about Max Daniels and the time they'd shared…that she could remember. How she wished he were here with her now, holding her, loving her. When Max held her in his arms, she believed nothing could go wrong.

She needed that confidence now.

Her mother knocked on her door. "Caroline? Are you awake? You need to get dressed," she added as she opened the door and found her daughter lying on the bed.

"What's the hurry? We're not having the rehearsal until three, are we?" Caroline asked, not moving.

"I guess I forgot to tell you that we're having a bridesmaid luncheon at noon. There's just so much to remember, it must've slipped my mind. And, of course, you have a hair and manicure appointment before that. They'll do touch-ups this evening, so you'll be perfect for the wedding. And then, you need to get started on your thank-you notes. After all, the sooner you do, the sooner you'll be finished. And, of course, to write your thank-you notes, you have to open your gifts. You'll receive a lot more this evening at the wedding. And—"

Since it seemed she had an unending list, Caroline interrupted. "Mother, I'll keep the hair and manicure appointment, but I thought Chelsea was going to be my only attendant, so what's the point of a bridesmaids' luncheon?''

''Dear, we couldn't have a proper wedding with just your sister as an attendant. Neiman's found four matching gowns and have expressed them here. And,'' Amelia paused, a triumphant air about her, ''I found four of your friends who are the right size.''

''I've heard of choosing bridesmaids for bizarre reasons, but it never occurred to me to choose them by dress size. Are you sure I know any of them?''

''Of course you do. There's Lilly, Ann, Sylvia...''

Caroline stopped listening. She didn't care who the attendants were. She just wanted the evening to be over, finished. And tomorrow morning she'd start divorce proceedings. She couldn't remain married to Adrian.

''Caroline? Are you listening?'' Amelia demanded, apparently recognizing her daughter's distraction.

''I suppose,'' Caroline responded, suddenly feeling very tired.

''Well, come downstairs and we'll get started. It's already nine o'clock.''

Nine o'clock. Only ten hours until the wedding.

MAX PUT DOWN THE PHONE and stared at the wall in front of him. What could he do now? The PI's secretary knew nothing. Well, almost nothing.

She'd said he had a line on the photographer. But the wedding was tonight. His heartbeat accelerated at the thought of Caroline meeting Adrian at the altar, taking the vows *he* wanted to share with her. She was his! His ring should be on her finger.

His arms should be around her. His lips should be caressing hers. His—if he didn't stop this kind of thinking, he'd have to take a cold shower.

But he wanted more than her body. He wanted to care for her, to share with her, to laugh with her. He wanted the right to be in her life.

"Max, a call on line two," Susan said through the intercom.

He snatched up the receiver, hoping it was Caroline or the detective he'd hired. Instead, it was a contractor working on one of his houses. And it was already eleven o'clock.

"YOU'RE NOT EATING anything," Amelia whispered to Caroline.

"I'm afraid if I do, it will come right back up," Caroline whispered in return.

Since they were in an elegant restaurant hastily hired for the bridesmaids' luncheon, throwing up would be highly inappropriate.

"Then don't try the eggplant," Amelia warned, and waved to the waiter hovering in the background. "My daughter would like some crackers, please."

She hadn't expected such understanding from her mother, but Amelia had tried to help her through the morning. Even Chelsea, now seated on her other side, had held her hand. But as the impending wedding drew closer, her stomach grew less reliable.

"Are you okay?" Chelsea whispered.

"I suppose," she answered as she had earlier that morning. "But I wish I could lie down for a while."

"As soon as we can get away, we'll take a taxi to my house," Chelsea said. "You can rest for an hour before the rehearsal. If you go home with Mother, there will be too much going on."

Caroline stared at her sister. "That's very sweet of you, Chelsea. I'd like that." She'd like even more to see Max, but at least, for just a little while, she would be out of the whirlwind that seemed to be consuming her. And she could use the telephone. To call the detective. And Max.

How she wished she could see him. Just a few minutes. To feel his arms around her. If she were preparing for a wedding with Max, things would be so different. She'd be feeling enthusiastic, not nauseous.

"Caroline," one of the bridesmaids called, "Tell us about your wedding gown. What's it like?"

Caroline went blank. She couldn't remember any of the details. Except that it was white, of course.

Amelia spoke, squeezing her daughter's hand beneath the tablecloth. "Oh, you'll just love it. The skirt is…"

Chelsea chipped in, describing Caroline's going-away suit, something else her mother had insisted she purchase, and she relaxed in her chair. Her mother and sister were taking care of her.

She surreptitiously checked her watch. Almost one o'clock.

She needed to talk to Max.

"HE'S NOT HERE, Caroline," Susan said cheerfully.

Caroline could have flung the telephone receiver across the room in frustration. "Do you know where he is?" she managed to say in civil tones.

"Nope. And, confidentially, he's been acting real strange today. All on edge, you know? But he left here about one o'clock, and he told me he wouldn't be back the rest of the day. That's unlike Max."

After ending the call, Caroline slumped against the pillow on Chelsea's guest bed. True to her word, Chelsea had gotten Caroline away from the luncheon to the relative quietness of her home. But Caroline had been unable to rest.

Instead, she'd increased her frustration by calling the security firm and then Max. And getting no response from either one. The wedding was in just a few hours.

"Caroline?" Chelsea poked her head around the door. "Yes?"

"Daddy's downstairs to take us to the rehearsal. Are you ready?"

No. She wasn't ready. She would never be ready to practice marrying Adrian. *Max, where are you?*

"Caroline?" Chelsea said again, and Caroline heard the concern in her sister's voice.

Wearily she pushed herself up from the bed. "Yes, I'm ready, Chelsea. As ready as I'll ever be."

When the two of them came down the stairs, her father was waiting.

"Ah, the beautiful bride and the matron of honor," he boomed, a big smile on his face. "What a wonderful day."

Caroline had seen better.

"SHE ISN'T HERE?" Max asked Mrs. Lamb as she opened the door to him. "Do you know where she is?"

"Well, I guess she's at the rehearsal, Mr. Daniels. It's supposed to start at three, and it's almost that time now."

He'd forgotten about the rehearsal. Which wasn't surprising since he was going out of his head. The thought of Caroline belonging to another man was unbearable, even if it was in name only, for a short time. She was his. Why couldn't everyone understand that?

"Can you tell me how to find the church?" he finally asked. Mrs. Lamb's directions were clear and the church was nearby, so he wasted no time getting back into his truck. He didn't know what he would say to Caroline when he found her. He only knew he had to see her. Now.

The limo, with Lewis leaning against it, was parked in front of the church. Max left his pickup by the curb and stopped to ask if Caroline was inside.

"Yes, sir. They're having the rehearsal."

With a nod of thanks, he hurried through the double doors of the church. The shadows, after the bright sunlight, made it difficult to see for a moment. But he had no difficulty recognizing the voice that called his name.

"Max!" At least Caroline sounded happy to see him.

"What are you doing here?" her father demanded almost at once.

He ignored James Adkins, reaching Caroline as she hurried to him, taking her hands in his.

"I had to see you."

"I've been trying to call you," she assured him, her eyes devouring him in a way that set him on fire.

"Any word?"

"No, you?"

He reluctantly shook his head.

"Caroline, come over here and get ready for the rehearsal," her father insisted as he approached them.

"I don't mean to interrupt, Mr. Adkins," Max said politely, though he was feeling far from calm. "I just need to talk to Caroline for a minute or two."

"The—the groom isn't here yet, Daddy, so I have time to talk to Max," Caroline assured her father.

James Adkins couldn't argue with that, Max realized, but he seemed determined to stand beside them.

"Alone, Daddy," Caroline insisted.

Max was grateful she was the one to tell her father to

go away. He was trying not to alienate Caroline's family any more than necessary. But the five steps James Adkins took didn't exactly give them a lot of privacy. Not when Max wanted to pull her into his arms.

"I'm sorry, Max, but I don't know where we could be alone," Caroline whispered.

"You must know I want to kiss you," he said with a rueful smile.

She smiled in return but shook her head no. "I just know I want you to kiss me. I want to feel your arms around me."

"Caroline," he protested. "Don't tempt me." He squeezed her hands, the most intimacy he could manage with a dozen people watching them. "Who are all these people?"

She looked over her shoulder, as if she'd forgotten their audience. "Mother rounded up some bridesmaids. Then there's the florist, and Daddy, and...I don't know who else. They don't matter. Did you call your detective?"

"Yeah. Several times. The secretary recognizes my voice now. Damn but you're beautiful." His gaze traced her hair as the curls tickled her brow, then moved on to her full lips. Hunger to touch her filled his gut and he had to fight to keep his distance.

"Max, I want *you* to be the groom!" she wailed softly, pain in her eyes.

"I want that, too. And if you say the word, I'll tell your father right now." He watched as tears filled her eyes. He knew what her answer would be. She felt obligated to keep her word, to offer the only man with proof the opportunity to give his name to her baby. But it was too high a price. And he was having to pay, as well as Caroline.

"I can't, Max. I can't."

One tear escaped and trailed down her beautiful face. He released one of her hands to gently wipe it away. The desire to pull her into his arms, to comfort, to love, was almost overwhelming. But he couldn't.

"Don't cry, sweetheart. Do what you have to do, and we'll work it out." It cost him a lot to offer such reassurance, but he loved her. He couldn't add to her difficulties.

She closed her eyes and then stared at him again, a brilliance in them that almost shattered his control. "I love you, Max Daniels."

"Damn, Caroline, you have to wait and tell me that now? With an audience, just before you marry someone else?" he demanded. "You must have a lot in common with the Marquis de Sade."

She gave him a watery chuckle that only made him want her more. "I just thought I should mention it."

"Thanks," he said dryly as he lifted her hands to his lips. Hand kissing should be all right, even if she was about to marry another man.

Wrong. The touch of her skin only made him want to continue right up those arms to her neck, her lips, her— he groaned as she licked her bottom lip.

"Caroline! Don't do that!"

She jumped and blinked rapidly. "Don't do what?"

"Don't lick your lips."

"But they were dry," she said, a puzzled look on her face.

"Sweetheart, I'm having a hard enough time keeping my distance without you making me think about—"

"Ah, this must be the lovely bride," an elderly man said, walking up to them. "I can always tell. They all look positively beaming with love. And that look in their eyes.'' The minister turned to Max. ''And this, I presume, is the lucky groom.''

Chapter Seventeen

"I have never been so embarrassed in my life," James Adkins said again, pacing about the bride's room.

"Daddy, you've told us that at least a hundred times since the rehearsal," Chelsea reminded him as she repositioned Caroline's veil.

"And I still don't think that's the truth," Amelia added. "I think you were even more embarrassed that time you lost your wallet and couldn't pay the bill at that restaurant in Philadelphia."

"Amelia, that's not the point!" he exclaimed, his irritation rising.

"Then what is the point, Daddy?" Caroline asked. She was hanging on to her patience by a thread, but she didn't know how much longer she could do so.

"The point is you shouldn't have been making goo-goo eyes with another man!"

"Goo-goo eyes?" exclaimed all three women at the same time.

"Well, whatever they call it these days. You know what I mean."

Caroline drew a deep breath and then turned to her mother and sister. "I need to talk to Daddy alone." She had rediscovered a kinship with her mother and sister that meant a great deal to her. But she had to face her father without their support.

When they were alone, she turned around to face him squarely, tugging the long satin train of her gown out of the way. "Daddy, you know I don't love Adrian. I'm not going to pretend I do."

"He's a good man, Caro. I wouldn't let you marry someone who would hurt you, but you're not giving him a chance. You keep hanging on to that other man, the one you're infatuated with."

"I'm not infatuated with Max, Daddy. I love him. And he loves me."

"Then why are you marrying Adrian? That's not fair to him."

She clenched her teeth in frustration. "I'm marrying Adrian because I promised you, and because he offered proof that he's the father of my baby. But I don't love him."

"But, Caroline, it's only fair that you marry him. After all, you've admitted that's his baby."

"No, I haven't. I said he offered proof. I don't know what to think. I want this baby to be Max's, Daddy. But—but I can't be sure. And I promised you."

"Baby," James began, calling her his pet name that he hadn't used in several years, "I only want what's best for you. Adrian is a good man."

"Caroline," Chelsea said, sticking her head into the room. "It's time. The wedding is starting."

With a sinking in the pit of her stomach, Caroline turned and looked in the mirror one more time. She would give anything to know that Max was waiting for her at the end of that aisle.

But he wasn't.

She hadn't seen him since that embarrassing scene in

the vestibule. But he'd promised he'd be here. Had he arrived? Was he sitting in the church, waiting to watch her marry another man?

Why hadn't they found something to prevent this disaster from taking place? Why hadn't they found proof that Adrian was lying? He had to be lying.

But it was too late.

Her father cleared his throat. "Ready, Caroline?"

No, she wasn't ready. But it seemed she had no choice.

Standing, she lifted her veil to cover her face. Her father hurriedly assisted her and then opened the door, waiting for her to precede him.

The bridesmaids had begun marching solemnly down the aisle. Chelsea, the last to go down, was waiting her turn and gave Caroline an encouraging smile.

She tried to smile back. She really did. But she couldn't. This should have been the happiest moment of her life. Instead, it was the worst.

Her father extended his arm and she placed her hand through it. The music changed, rising in sound, emphasizing the moment. They stepped through the double doors and began the long walk down the aisle.

But instead of looking at her groom, the bride was searching the audience, looking for a certain dark-haired, blue-eyed man who owned her heart.

As her gaze scanned those seated along the aisle, she saw a young woman she thought she should've recognized. Something was familiar about her, but Caroline couldn't think what it could be.

Then her gaze connected with Max's, and she forgot everything else. Max. The man she loved with all her heart. The man she wasn't marrying.

SHE WAS BEAUTIFUL. The most beautiful bride in the world, Max decided. But she wasn't his.

Since he'd left her at the church that afternoon, Max had paced various floors. He'd made every phone call he could think of to try to prevent what was about to happen. He had prayed a few prayers, hoping for divine intervention. He didn't know what else to do.

Except watch the only woman he'd ever loved marry another man.

Along with half of Denver. The church was full, which was amazing considering the short notice. Not that he cared. He would've married Caroline anywhere. In fact, he might prefer a deserted island, so there would be no one to interfere with his plans for after the wedding.

He forced his thoughts away from holding Caroline and watched with real pain as her father transferred her hand from his arm to Adrian's.

"Dearly beloved…"

She was his dearly beloved, more than he'd ever realized was possible. He wanted her with every ounce of his body. But he wanted, needed more. He needed her heart, her head, her soul. He wanted to protect her, to care for her, to love her for the rest of his life. In sickness or in health.

He'd already proven the sickness bit. A smile played across his lips as he remembered holding her as she threw up. She'd looked as beautiful then as she did now, in her white satin. She would look as beautiful nine months pregnant, her stomach swollen with their child, as she did now, all slim and curvaceous.

She was his, he promised himself, and always would be. No matter what words were spoken here today.

SHE FELT HIS GAZE ON HER. It warmed her and yet made her pain all the greater. She loved one man and was marrying another.

Sneaking a peek at her groom from under her lashes, Caroline thought he was the most repulsive man in the world. Others might think him handsome with his blond good looks, but she only saw the greed she thought motivated him. He wanted her father's empire. And he would do whatever it took to reach his goal.

Even marry her.

So why was she helping him?

She'd told herself she was being honorable, giving her child its due. But she'd always promised herself she wouldn't marry a man who wanted her father's money. Pain surged through her head at the thought. Pain and memory.

"IF THERE IS ANY REASON this man and this woman should not be joined in holy matrimony, please speak now or forever hold your peace," the Reverend Mr. Spencer intoned, a beaming smile on his face.

"Stop!" Caroline exclaimed hoarsely.

"Stop!" Max exclaimed, rising from the pew, to the amazement of those around him.

"Stop!" exclaimed two men standing by the double doors at the back of the church.

The guests gasped in unison before an excited buzz spread across the audience. The minister, shock on his face, stared at each of those who had responded to his question. "My, this is most unusual."

"Just ignore them," Adrian said through clenched teeth. "Get on with the ceremony."

"Sir, you may not have noticed, but one of those who spoke was your bride," the cleric gently informed

Adrian. "In good conscience, I cannot continue if the bride is unwilling."

"What's going on here?" James demanded, having left his seat beside Amelia and stepped to the altar.

"Mr. Adkins, there have been three objections to the wedding proceeding," the cleric explained. "I'm not sure what we should do, but I don't think the wedding should continue without discovering the reason for these interruptions."

"Caroline?" James demanded.

"I can't marry him, Daddy," she said, tears in her eyes. "He's not the father of my baby."

"You don't have proof of that," Adrian reminded her harshly.

"We do," a quiet voice said just behind him.

James, Caroline and Adrian turned around to face the strangers who had spoken last. At least they were strangers to Adrian, Caroline supposed. She knew one of them, the investigator she'd hired, and she was sure her father also knew him.

Just behind them stood Max. The man she loved, the man she'd hoped to marry. And the man she would have to walk away from.

And past Max, Caroline saw the entire church whispering, craning their necks, enjoying the show. They'd never seen a wedding like this one. And she hoped they never did again.

"I think it might be best if we retired to my office for a few minutes and sorted things out," the Reverend Mr. Spencer said.

James Adkins, his face growing redder by the minute, nodded in agreement. "All right." He turned to the audience. "There's a little confusion. If you'll just be patient, we'll resume the wedding shortly."

Caroline stared at her bouquet. She was afraid her father was promising more than he could deliver.

THE REVEREND Mr. Spencer's office was a large one, but it seemed small after everyone crowded in. In addition to the bride and groom, the pastor and the two detectives, James Adkins was joined by his wife and his younger daughter. And, of course, Max.

Caroline had taken one look at his determined face and turned away. Tears threatened and she didn't want to cry in front of any of them. Most especially Max.

"Now, I think we would all like to hear an explanation of what evidence you are talking about," Reverend Spencer said to the two men.

"Sir, we were hired by the bride and Mr. Daniels to determine if the picture this man showed them was valid. We have proof that it was not, and that he altered the picture to persuade Miss Adkins to marry him because he had gambling debts he couldn't pay."

As his audience stared at him, openmouthed, the man speaking, from James's security firm, extended his hand with a picture in it.

Even though Caroline no longer needed proof, she took the picture and stared at it. The woman in the church. It wasn't her face that was familiar. It was the tobacco brown coatdress, its lapels outlined in black, that was familiar. The dress in the picture. But in this photo, the head above the dress wasn't Caroline's. It was that young lady's.

"Who is she?"

"His secretary," Don Knowles said, stepping forward. "I'm sorry we didn't arrive before the wedding, but my flight was late."

"Mary?" James questioned, staring at his right-hand man. "You took Mary to Las Vegas?"

"There's more, Mr. Adkins," Joe Perkins said quietly. "But I think I should tell you in private."

James swiveled around to face Adrian again, his eyes narrowed, his jaw firm. The man stood frozen with fear on his pale face. James looked back at Perkins. "Okay. We'll talk after the wedding."

"There's still going to be a wedding?" the minister asked.

This time James turned to look at his daughter. "Yes, there's still going to be a wedding. I release you from your promise, Caroline. You can marry Max, as you wanted."

"Thank you, Mr. Adkins," Max acknowledged even as he moved toward Caroline.

"No!"

All eyes centered on her. At least her protest had stopped Max in his tracks. If he touched her, she wasn't sure she'd be able to continue.

"No, what? Caroline, this is what you wanted," James said.

"Yes, Caro, you said you wanted to marry Max," Chelsea added.

"I've changed my mind. I can't marry Max."

Her words were almost as astonishing as the interruptions in the church. Perhaps even more so to Max. James stepped closer to his daughter.

"Caro, it's okay. I want you to marry this man. He loves you. And since Adrian isn't the father of your baby, Max must be. I want my grandchild born on the right side of the blanket, remember?" When she didn't respond, he added, "And I want you to be happy."

She swallowed back tears. "Thank you, Daddy, but I can't marry Max."

"I think Caroline and I need some privacy to settle things," Max said quietly, sending a look to James, asking his cooperation.

"Yes, of course," James agreed, and began urging the others back into the sanctuary. There was pause as they encountered the eager stares of the audience, waiting for the next event in this singularly unusual wedding. Then James stepped forward and asked their patience, assuring them matters would be resolved very soon.

Caroline knew he was right. Only there wouldn't be a wedding. There couldn't be a wedding.

As the door closed behind the last of them, Max stepped toward her, and she backed away.

"Caroline, what's wrong? Why are you refusing to marry me?"

She looked at his beloved face and then turned away. It was too painful. How could she refuse when she loved him so much?

"Caroline?"

With her back to him, she said, "My memory returned."

"What? When? What do you remember? I'm the father, aren't I?"

She nodded her head.

The eager happiness she'd heard in his voice wasn't there when he asked his next question. "So what else do you remember? What is it that makes you say you won't marry me?"

Gathering her courage, she turned to face him. "I remember why I ran away."

There was no acknowledgment in his eyes, no shame,

no guilt. He still didn't know what had gone wrong. But there was a question there. He wanted to know.

"I woke up and you weren't there. I had pulled on your T-shirt and started downstairs when I realized you had company."

"It was Jim, my foreman," he agreed, still looking puzzled.

"Yes. He was reminding you of the need for more financing, for an influx of capital."

Max frowned. "I remember. So? Are you refusing to marry me because you're afraid I can't support you?" His incredulity was irritating.

"I'm not the one who's in the wrong here!" she snapped. "You're the one who's marrying me for my money. Or I should say my father's money!"

"What?" Max exclaimed in a roar that was probably heard in the sanctuary, adding to the audience's enjoyment. "You accuse me of marrying you for your money just because my foreman and I were discussing my company's finances?"

The tears drew closer. She loved this man so much. "No, that's not why. He—he said you should just get a loan from me because I was probably kin to James Adkins, and then you wouldn't have any troubles." She watched as memory came back to him. "And you agreed, saying that had been your plan all along."

She turned away, unable to face the guilt that she knew would be on his face. He'd been her knight in shining armor, her one true love. Now that he knew she knew, he'd probably slink out the door, and she'd never see him again. Tears rolled down her cheeks.

"Caroline Adkins!" Max exclaimed as he spun her around to face him. "I ought to wring your neck!"

She stared at him in shock.

"That was a joke! I didn't know who you were!"

A sob broke from her before she said, "Of course you would say that."

"I not only say it, I have proof," he insisted, "And I can't believe you ran away without even asking me about it. We've wasted two months we could've shared."

"Max, I understand, but I can't marry you. It's okay, I forgive you." She thought she was being magnanimous. He didn't seem to feel the same way.

"Wringing your neck is too nice! I'm going bury you in a nest of fire ants," he threatened, and pulled her against him, wrapping his arms around her.

"Max!" she protested, "I'm not going to change my mind. The reason I was there, with you, was because I'd had an argument with my father. He said no one would ever marry me without wanting his money. I intended to prove him wrong." More tears fell as she finished. "Instead, I proved him right."

Max pressed her head against his shoulder. "Don't cry, sweetheart, or you'll have red eyes for our wedding. Listen to me, you crazy woman. I love you! I don't care how much money your father has. It has nothing to do with us. I had made a loan at the bank the day before, and I have the papers dated to prove it. If you'd hung around a little longer, you would've heard me explain that to Jim."

"The day before?" she asked, looking at him, hope in her gaze.

"Don't you remember? You wanted to go on another picnic and I had to cut it short? That was my appointment with the bank."

"And you have papers dated that day?"

"Sure do. I can even go home and get them, but that means the wedding will last a little longer than planned."

He brought his lips to hers in a kiss that shook her to her very toes. Max loved her.

"It's your call, Caroline. What are we going to do now?" he asked huskily.

She raised her hand to caress his cheek and then draw his lips to hers again. When she finally, reluctantly, pulled away, she whispered, "I think we should get married. After all, we have to think about *our* baby."

Max didn't hesitate. He scooped her up into his arms and carried her into the sanctuary, to everyone's surprise. Setting her down in front of the pastor, he said, "We'd like to be married, please."

And they were.

Epilogue

Six months later Caroline wasn't feeling quite as exuberant. Her body was heavy and her patience frazzled. Twins. He'd warned her. But somehow, when the doctor had confirmed Max's prediction four months ago, she hadn't realized just how big she would get.

"I'm the size of the Goodyear blimp," she muttered as she tried to find a comfortable position on the sofa. Not that Max seemed to notice. His loving care was the only thing that was getting her through these last days.

The doctor had said the babies might come early. She wanted them healthy. But she also wanted—ah! Caroline held her breath, stunned by the pain she'd just felt. What was that? Surely it couldn't be—

She grabbed the phone and called her doctor. His orders were succinct and firm. She pressed the speed dial for Max's beeper. The phone rang only seconds after she hung up.

"Caroline?"

"It's time, Max."

He didn't even answer, just hung up the phone. In spite of the anxiety she was feeling, Caroline chuckled. The only person more worried than she about the birth was

Max. He'd hovered over her so much, even she had protested.

Chelsea had assured her birth wasn't so bad. At least, that's what she'd said last week. Immediately after giving birth to her pretty baby girl, whom she'd named Amelia Lynn, she hadn't been quite as sure.

Another pain struck her about six minutes later, and Caroline was glad she'd called the doctor. The sound of the front door slamming told her Max had arrived.

"Sweetheart! Where are you?" he demanded even as he ran to the back of the house.

"In here," she said, pushing herself up from the sofa. "Get the suitcase from upstairs, please."

He raced up the stairs and back down before she was able to stand, arriving at her side to pull her up. Before she could take a step, he carefully lifted her into his arms and headed to the front door.

"Remember when you carried me into the church?" she whispered, giggling.

"How could I forget it with so many people watching us? By that time, I don't know what they expected."

He got her into the front seat of his truck and then kissed her quickly before shutting the door and hurrying to his side. "Put on your seat belt," he warned as he started the motor. "I don't intend for my babies to be born in a truck. I'd never hear the end of it from your father."

Caroline laughed again. Her father and Max had developed a fine relationship, as long as James didn't try to tell Max how to run his business. Her father finally had the son he'd so desperately wanted. One just as stubborn as him.

"Did you call your parents?" he asked.

"Not yet."

Max picked up the phone in his truck and pressed a button. "Miss McVey? Tell James it's time. We'll meet them at the hospital."

"Where it all began," Caroline murmured, and closed her eyes.

"BOYS! TWIN BOYS! Can you believe it?" James patted Max on the back.

"How's Caroline?" Amelia asked anxiously.

"Pretty tired, but happy."

Chelsea and Roddy rushed into the waiting room, their baby daughter in Roddy's arms. He'd blossomed as a father, amusing everyone with his newfound authority.

"She had twin boys!" James exclaimed, a beaming smile on his face.

"Is Caroline all right?" Chelsea asked.

"She's fine."

"Well, congratulations. Of course, I think girls are sweeter, but I'm sure your boys will be just fine."

"I couldn't agree with you more, Chelsea. Girls are definitely sweeter." He winked at Roddy. "At least I hope so," Max added, a big grin on his face. "I'm going back inside with Caroline. The babies will be taken up to the nursery if you want to see them."

"Are they big enough?" Amelia asked.

Max smiled. Caroline had thought they were too big. "They both weigh more than five pounds, so they'll be able to go home with us when it's time."

When he stepped back into the comparative quiet of the delivery room, Caroline lay with her eyes closed. He bent over to kiss her cheek.

"Hi," she murmured sleepily. "Did you tell them?"

"Yeah. Your dad's jumping for joy."

She opened one eye. "And you?"

"Thrilled to pieces," he assured her with a grin. "But I think you should know Chelsea and I agree that girls are sweeter."

She studied him, a puzzled look on her face. "You're not happy we had boys?"

"Of course I am. I just don't want Chelsea to feel superior to us. Next time, we'll have a girl."

"Next time?"

He grinned at the note of exasperation in her voice. She'd been terrific in the delivery room and as much as he wanted a little girl, he wasn't sure he'd want her to go through labor again. "We'll discuss it later," he whispered before kissing her.

Caroline slid her arms around his neck. Maybe they'd have a little girl. After a while. Max could convince her to do almost anything.

And next time, she thought, she'd need no convincing about who's the daddy.

Nursery needed—pronto!

Make Room for Baby
Cathy Gillen Thacker

Chapter One

Moonlight bathed the luxurious hotel room in iridescent light as Tad McFarlane made one last thorough tour of Abby Kildaire's lips. When finally the kiss came to an end, he lifted his head. Still feeling as if he never wanted to let her go, he shook his head in heartfelt regret. "I can't believe we both have to leave here tomorrow."

"Neither can I." Abby sighed. As the spring breeze draped them in flower-scented warmth, the last thing Abby wanted was to return to her normal life.

Tad kissed her brow and traced his fingertip across her lips. His arms encircled her once again. He pulled her closer to his sinewy six-foot frame. "It's been the best weekend of my entire life," he whispered huskily in her ear.

And the most unexpected, Abby thought as she ran her hands across his broad shoulders. Who would've thought when she emptied her savings account to splurge on a trip to Paris that she—who never did anything on the spur of the moment—would also meet a handsome globe-trotting reporter and have a weekend fling that would change her life irrevocably? Because Tad had changed her life. He'd taught her that she could feel earth-shattering passion. He'd taught her that she could love a man in the most fundamental romantic way.

"It's been the best weekend of mine, too," Abby admitted wistfully, wishing their impetuous love affair could continue forever.

Tad framed her face with his hands and met her eyes. "I meant what I said before we made love, Abby. About having you with me—not just now, this weekend—but for the rest of my life."

How she wanted that, Abby thought as she inhaled the brisk citrus scent of his cologne. But like it or not, they had to be practical. They had to consider their responsibilities. "I have a job…" A good one. And so did he.

"We can work around that," Tad told her with the utter confidence she would've expected from one of the most respected reporters on the international beat. "I would never ask you to give up your profession just to be with me, any more than I would give up my life as a journalist."

Abby began to relax. Her career as the Home and Garden editor for *Trend* magazine was very important to her. She'd worked ten hard years to land such a coveted position. More important still, her work had sustained her through many a challenging time. Tad knew that. He accepted that. Just as he accepted that she lived in New York City and had for the past ten years.

Abby let her gaze drift over the arresting contours of his face and the perpetually rumpled state of his naturally curly black hair. At thirty-six, he was five years older than she was. And undoubtedly the sexiest, most easygoing man she had ever met. Everything about him—from his cleft chin, dimpled smile and deep blue bedroom eyes—appealed to her.

"What about your work?" she asked curiously, aware

that at the moment he had no regular home, just a post-office box. Home for Tad was whatever city he happened to be in, whatever hotel he happened to stay in. To him, they were all one and the same. A hotel room was not a home to Abby. Her apartment in New York City was home.

Tad shrugged. "The constant traveling is beginning to wear on me. I've been thinking about moving back to the States for some time. Now that I've met you—" he paused, his expression both thoughtful and content "—it seems like the time is right for everything. Like the two of us—this—is preordained somehow."

Abby knew exactly what he meant. She had never believed in love at first sight, either, but the moment she'd encountered Tad in the Paris airport, she'd known he was someone very special. "You'd do that for me?" she asked softly, realizing she had never met a man more generous or tender. Her heart filling with happiness, she studied him. "You'd give up the international beat?"

Tad nodded, his lips taking on a serious slant. "And so much more," he confirmed with a sincerity that went soul-deep, "if it means I could be with you." Abruptly his eyes darkened with a combination of affection and mischief. "Not that I don't have dreams of my own. I do. The difference is that now I know I want you with me when they all come true." He paused before adding, "I want to share my life with you, Abby. I want to share everything."

Hope for the future filled her. "Oh, Tad…"

"Say you want that, too, Abby," Tad demanded gruffly, drawing her close.

"I do," Abby said on a halting breath. *So much.*

"Then marry me, Abby." Tad sifted his hands through her hair. "As soon as we get back to the States."

Abby shut her eyes, the desire she felt for Tad warring with her common sense. How she wished they could keep the problems of their real lives at bay and stay locked in this moment in time until she'd had her fill of him and he of her. But she knew better. Didn't she? "It's not that easy," she murmured, distraught. She looked deep into his beautiful eyes. "I have to be at work on Monday morning." *So do you.*

"Then we'll do it Sunday night. In Tennessee," Tad told her confidently. "There's no waiting period there."

Abby grinned. Somehow she wasn't surprised Tad had gone to the trouble to find that out. He was a very thorough determined man. Never more so than when he wanted something. "You *have* done your homework," she teased.

Tad grinned. "I always do my homework." Many kisses and a long bout of leisurely lovemaking later, he asked her again.

Abby knew he deserved an answer. She also knew she shouldn't be naked, her heart pounding at his nearness, when she gave it. She knew what she wanted, but she had to think about this.

"I don't know. It's so impulsive." Abby threw off the covers and sprang from the bed. Her body still tingling from their lovemaking, she snatched up the satin-and-lace robe she'd left on the chaise. Pushing her trembling arms into the sleeves, she turned and walked toward the window. Outside the moonlight blanketed the city in sparkling silver. April in Paris. Was there anyplace more beautiful or more romantic in spring? she wondered as she belted the robe around her.

"I'm not impulsive, Tad," she told him as he moved to stand beside her. And yet she was here, with him.

Get 2

HOW TO GET YOUR
2 FREE BOOKS AND FREE GIFT

1. Peel off the 2 FREE BOOKS seal from the front cover. Place it in the space provided at right. This automatically entitles you to receive two free books and an exciting mystery gift.

2. Send back this card and you'll get 2 "The Best of the Best™" novels. These books have a combined cover price of $11.00 or more in the U.S. and $13.00 or more in Canada, but they are yours to keep absolutely FREE!

3. There's <u>no</u> catch. You're under <u>no</u> obligation to buy anything. We charge nothing – ZERO – for your first shipment. And you don't have to make any minimum number of purchases – not even one!

4. We call this line "The Best of the Best" because each month you'll receive the best books by the world's hottest authors. These authors show up time and time again on all the major bestseller lists and their books sell out as soon as they hit the stores. You'll like the convenience of getting them delivered to your home at our discount prices...and you'll love your subscriber newsletter featuring author news, horoscopes, recipes, book reviews and much more!

5. We hope that after receiving your free books you'll want to remain a subscriber. But the choice is yours – to continue or cancel, anytime at all! So why not take us up on our invitation, with no risk of any kind. You'll be glad you did!

6. And remember...we'll send you a mystery gift ABSOLUTELY FREE just for giving "The Best of the Best" a try!

MIRA ®

SPECIAL FREE GIFT!

We'll send you a fabulous mystery gift, absolutely FREE, simply for accepting our no-risk offer!

Books FREE!

HURRY! Return this card promptly to get 2 FREE Books and a FREE Gift!

The Best of the Best™

YES! Please send me the 2 FREE "The Best of the Best" novels and FREE gift for which I qualify. I understand that I am under no obligation to purchase anything further, as explained on the opposite page.

Affix
peel-off
2 FREE BOOKS
sticker here.

P-BB1-00
385 MDL CY2W

185 MDL CY2X

NAME   (PLEASE PRINT CLEARLY)

ADDRESS

APT.#   CITY

STATE/PROV.   ZIP/POSTAL CODE

The Best of the Best™ —Here's How it Works

Accepting your 2 free books and gift places you under no obligation to buy anything. You may keep the books and gift and return the shipping statement marked "cancel." If you do not cancel, about a month later we will send you 4 additional novels and bill you just $4.24 each in the U.S., or $4.74 each in Canada, plus 25¢ delivery per book and applicable sales tax, if any.* That's the complete price, and — compared to cover prices of $5.50 or more each in the U.S. and $6.50 or more each in Canada — it's quite a bargain! You may cancel at any time, but if you choose to continue, every month we'll send you 4 more books, which you may either purchase at the discount price...or return to us and cancel your subscription.

*Terms and prices subject to change without notice. Sales tax applicable in N.Y. Canadian residents will be charged applicable provincial taxes and GST.

If offer card is missing write to: The Best of the Best, 3010 Walden Ave., P.O. Box 1867, Buffalo, NY 14240-1867

BUSINESS REPLY MAIL

FIRST-CLASS MAIL   PERMIT NO. 717   BUFFALO NY

POSTAGE WILL BE PAID BY ADDRESSEE

THE BEST OF THE BEST
3010 WALDEN AVE
PO BOX 1867
BUFFALO NY 14240-9952

NO POSTAGE
NECESSARY
IF MAILED
IN THE
UNITED STATES

Didn't that tell her something? About the magic of the situation and the special something they shared?

Tad put both hands on her shoulders. He turned her to face him and flashed her a sexy grin. "I know you're not impulsive. Neither am I."

"Tad..." The breath soughed from her lips as he unbelted her robe, slipped his hands inside the silky fabric and tucked them around her waist.

"What?" he said, caressing her gently.

"I can't think when you do that," Abby protested as his hands moved lower toward her thighs, then swept upward across her ribs.

"I don't want you to think," Tad told her gruffly, dipping his head to hers. "I want you to kiss me."

And heaven help her, she did.

By Sunday morning he had her on a jet to Memphis. By noon Eastern time they'd located a justice of the peace who had everything they needed right down to the witnesses, bouquet and wedding rings. An hour later they were in their hotel, making love again.

If only things could always stay this simple, Abby thought as she melted in his arms.

But of course, as luck would have it, they didn't.

Three weeks later

TAD MCFARLANE strode into the offices of *Trend* magazine, knowing the moment of reckoning had finally come. He found his runaway wife right where he expected to find her—seated behind her desk, her silky golden-brown hair spilling to her shoulders, her long-lashed golden-brown eyes focused on the magazine layout in front of her.

She turned as he approached her desk.

Tad resisted the urge to take her into his arms and kiss some sense into her. Succumbing to passion, in lieu of talking, was what had gotten them into this mess.

"What's the meaning of this?" Making no effort to hide his unhappiness with her actions, Tad handed Abby the sheaf of legal papers that had finally reached him via registered mail.

Abby arched a delicately shaped brow at him and handed the documents right back. "I would think that would be glaringly apparent."

Tad refused to take them. He cleared a space and sat down on the corner of her desk. "Well, it's not."

Abby let the papers drop. She kept her pretty oval face level with his. "I want an annulment."

No, Tad thought, *you don't. You're just angry with me right now. And considering the giant misunderstanding we had, that's understandable.*

Determined to take whatever time they needed to work this out and salvage the marriage that had lasted barely a day, Tad folded his arms in front of him. "On what grounds?" he demanded, searching her wide-set eyes. "As I recall we consummated the marriage quite thoroughly."

Abby flushed, unable to argue that, and with good reason, Tad thought. They had made love repeatedly that entire weekend, both before and after the ceremony.

"That's just it, Tad," Abby snapped irritably as she stood and began to pace. Her willowy body was accentuated by a buttercup yellow jersey dress. Bone-colored stockings and matching shoes showed off her spectacular legs. Just watching her made Tad's blood run hot and quick. "We were driven by hormones. We weren't thinking clearly."

Speak for yourself, Tad thought irascibly. He'd been

thinking very clearly, then and now. He'd known the minute he'd laid eyes on her that he had to have her. And that desire—to make her his and his alone—had only increased over the past two weeks.

"You're still ticked off at me for buying the newspaper," Tad guessed as he tried not to think how good and right her soft mobile lips had felt beneath his.

Abby tossed her head, her hot-tempered movement filling the small elegant office with the intoxicating vanilla scent of her perfume. "You could have told me your plans before we married!"

"I did!" Tad replied, aware they'd covered this ground the morning after they'd gotten married—the morning she'd walked out on him and their new marriage.

"Funny, I don't recall you saying one darn word about the two of us moving to North Carolina."

Tad scowled. "I told you I spent summers there as a kid."

"Visiting your aunt Sadie, yes, I know," Abby said impatiently, obviously exasperated at having to go through this again.

"I also told you I wanted to own my own newspaper," Tad continued patiently.

"Right!" Abby aimed an accusing finger at him. "Someday!"

Tad cocked a brow, the hint of a smile playing around his mouth, even as he noticed Abby was still wearing the fourteen-carat-gold-and-jade ring that she'd selected to serve as both her wedding and engagement ring. That could only mean one thing—their impetuous union wasn't nearly as over as she wanted him to believe it was. "You didn't believe I was serious?" he chided, refusing to let her off the hook even for a second.

Abby rolled her eyes. "Of course I did. Your plan to

buy and revamp an ailing small-town paper sounded exactly like one of those irrational cockeyed retirement dreams that every man I know has. I figured you'd get around to it when you were sixty or something. And I'd happily go along with you at that point, twenty-five years from now, when I was ready to retire from the business, too!''

Abby'd never dreamed a journalist of Tad's caliber and fame would attempt to drop out of the mainstream at age thirty-six! Never mind literally the day after he'd married her. But that was exactly what had happened.

Unable to talk him out of it, unable to put the brakes on her formerly sedate but work-laden life that was fast spinning out of control, she'd promptly put a hold on everything and curtailed any plans to actually move in together, saying they needed time—at least three weeks!—to cool off and rethink what they'd done.

At first Tad had been adamantly opposed to such an arrangement. When she hadn't backed down, he'd eventually agreed to her request, but only because she'd given him no choice. Besides, he had some stories to finish and loose ends of his own to tie up before concentrating once again on her and their marriage.

Abby tried hard not to think what his nearness was doing to her or notice how fast her heart beat whenever he was near her. "Look, I'm sure what you are doing in Blossom is laudable," she said politely.

"But?" Tad said, sensing there was more.

Abby swallowed around the unaccustomed dryness in her throat. "If you'd told me you had already put a bid in on the *Blossom Weekly News* beforehand and were planning to move to North Carolina as soon as said bid was accepted—"

"*If* said bid was accepted," Tad corrected, letting her know that at that point it had been far from a done deal.

"—then I never would've married you," Abby concluded. Because that would have meant giving up her job at *Trend,* and she never would have done that.

Tad lounged against her desk. "So now it's over—just like that?"

"It has to be."

"No," Tad said heavily, looking very sexy in jeans that clung like a second skin, a white oxford shirt worn open at the throat, tweed sport coat and hand-tooled leather boots. "It doesn't."

Damn it all, anyway, Abby thought as she returned to her desk. She should have known a man like Tad, who was used to getting damn near anything and everything he wanted in life, would be difficult about this! She sat back in her chair, her forearms lying flat against the armrests. Hiking the skirt of her dress slightly, she crossed her legs at the knee.

"You're saying...what—that you're going to fight the annulment?" she asked tensely, wishing she wasn't still so attracted to him. Wishing she didn't recall in such exquisite detail what it had been like to make slow wonderful love with him.

He leaned across her desk. "I'm saying I want you to see what you're giving up before you actually give it up." He took two airline tickets out of his pocket and placed them in front of her.

"I can't go to North Carolina!" Abby exclaimed.

"Why not?" Abby's best friend, Yvonne Kirschner prodded, walking in unannounced. "Tomorrow's Saturday."

A weekend with Tad is what had gotten her into trouble in the first place, Abby thought darkly.

Sensing something out of the ordinary was up, Yvonne looked Tad over before returning her glance to Abby. "Who's the hunk?" she asked with a curious smile.

Unsure how to answer that, Abby looked at the forty-one-year-old Features editor for *Trend*. In her power suit and heels, her short red hair impeccably coiffed, Yvonne was not just the epitome of the New York City career woman, she was Abby's role model and mentor in the publishing world. The person Abby most frequently turned to for advice. But what could she say to Yvonne about this? Yvonne was—and always would be—married to her career. Yvonne would never have eloped on a whim the way Abby had.

Tad stepped forward. He stretched out his hand. "Hi. I'm Tad McFarlane. Abby's husband."

Yvonne did a double take.

"We got married in Paris at the end of April," Tad continued.

Yvonne's glance cut to Abby's left hand, lingering on the jade-and-gold ring she'd been wearing since her trip abroad. She looked back at Tad, who was wearing a plain gold wedding band. "You got married for the first and only time in your life and you didn't mention it?" Yvonne asked, aghast.

Abby lifted her hands. "Everyone was so upset about the magazine, the financial problems we've been having, that I…" Abby was blushing furiously.

"I still think I would have mentioned it," Yvonne retorted.

Not if you were getting an annulment, you wouldn't, Abby thought. "Look, don't tell anyone else," Abby insisted quickly, wanting her embarrassment to end here and now.

"Okay," Yvonne agreed, like the devout friend she

was. "But, uh…" Yvonne's glance returned to Tad, then focused on the sparks flying between Tad and Abby. "Maybe you should go ahead and go. It won't do any good to sit here wondering—"

"Good point," Abby interrupted, not about to let Tad know she—and everyone else at the magazine she had lovingly labored over for the past year and a half—was currently in jeopardy of losing her job, thanks to a recent takeover of the parent company by a huge conglomerate. "I do need a vacation," Abby said bluntly, vaulting to her feet. Even more urgently she needed to get Tad out of there. She snatched up the airline tickets he'd left on her desk, then grabbed his arm and her briefcase simultaneously. "Let's get out of here."

"Don't be a stranger," Yvonne called to Tad as Abby hurried him down the hall.

Tad glanced at Abby. "Don't worry," he promised softly, letting her know he wasn't giving up on them no matter how difficult she proved to be. "I don't intend to be."

"WELL, WHAT DO YOU think?" Tad asked Abby early the next afternoon after they'd completed the whirlwind tour of the brick building that housed the *Blossom Weekly News*.

"About what—western North Carolina?" Which was incredibly beautiful and heavily wooded. "Or Blossom?" Which was a charming little town of around ten thousand people in the Great Smoky Mountains, about sixty miles from the Tennessee border.

"About the newspaper," Tad said, gesturing around them.

Abby had the feeling he was talking about a lot more than that; he was talking about the prospects for renewing their marriage. Stubbornly she focused only on what she was prepared to discuss at that moment—the business he had just purchased. "It's a fine building. Well constructed. I'm not sure I like the bullpen atmosphere. I sort of like working in individual offices myself—find it easier to concentrate."

He picked up a copy of the newspaper. "What about this?"

Abby searched for something nice to say. "It's, um, compact."

"And poorly written and designed and limited in scope," Tad agreed.

Almost hopelessly so. "And yet you bought it," Abby observed, thinking Tad was more an enigma to her than ever.

"Precisely because it does need so much work," Tad confirmed. He gazed around them happily, taking in the four desks that had been scrunched together in the big uncarpeted room. "Can't you see the potential here, Abby?"

What she saw made her think he was nuts. A journalist of Tad's caliber and renown would never be happy here in the long haul. But he was going to have to figure that out for himself, Abby told herself firmly. It was not up to her to educate him.

"There are no computers," Abby remarked absently as beads of perspiration sprang up along her neck and chest. Was it hot in here, she wondered as she tugged at the jewel collar of her cotton sweater, or was it just her imagination?

"That's easily fixed," Tad assured her with youthful enthusiasm. He picked up a paperweight and tossed it from hand to hand. "I'll have some in by next week."

Abby continued to pace the office restlessly, noticing

that her knees felt a little wobbly, too. Why, she didn't know.

Nonplussed by her sudden wooziness, she rubbed at the back of her neck. "And there's only one section of the paper," she continued wearily.

Tad grinned confidently as he placed the paperweight on a desk and looked around. "I'm planning to expand. In fact, I'm looking for a Lifestyle editor for the new Lifestyle section as we speak."

Abby moved away from Tad. She drew a deep breath to see if that would help. "I'll let you know if I think of anyone," she said dryly.

Tad paused, his eyes on her face. "Actually I already had someone in mind."

Thinking maybe she'd feel better if she sat down, Abby eased herself onto the corner of the desk. "Really." She crossed her legs at the knee. "Who?"

Tad smiled. "You."

"Very funny, Tad," Abby drawled, trying hard not to let him know just how woozy she was feeling.

She'd been trying to ignore it, but the truth was she'd been feeling funny, sort of weak-kneed and dizzy, ever since he picked her up at her apartment in New York City to take her to the airport for the flight to North Carolina.

"You think I'm kidding?" Tad asked in a low sexy tone.

Abby's heart skipped a beat as she looked up into his eyes. *Saved by the bell,* she thought as the phone rang on the desk behind her. His eyes still on hers, Tad reached around her waist to answer it. "*Blossom Weekly News.* Yeah. Just a minute, Yvonne." Tad handed the phone to Abby. "It's for you."

Knowing something had to have happened for Yvonne

to call her here, Abby pressed the receiver to her ear. "What's up?" she asked.

"You picked the wrong time to go out of town, kiddo," Yvonne told her in a discouraged voice.

Anxiety hit Abby like a Mack truck. Aware her hands were suddenly trembling, too, Abby gulped. "What do you mean?" she asked with trepidation.

Yvonne continued grimly, "*Trend* has just been purchased by The Hindemythe Group in Great Britain. They're moving the magazine overseas, pronto."

"What about us?" Abby asked Yvonne as her heart began to pound. "And the rest of the staff?"

"We've all been fired."

"WHAT IS IT?" Tad asked as soon as Abby thanked Yvonne for the information, told her they'd talk soon and hung up.

Abby wet her lips and tried to make sense of her increasingly fuzzy view of Tad's handsome face. Sweat was gathering between her breasts and there was a roaring in her ears. What was wrong with her? Was it the altitude? The fact Blossom, North Carolina, was five thousand feet above sea level? Or was it just being around Tad, knowing he wanted to continue their hasty marriage, that left her feeling so dizzy and disoriented? Whatever was causing it, Abby decided firmly, she had to get a grip.

"I just lost my job, as did everyone else at *Trend,*" Abby told Tad calmly.

"I'm sorry." Tad took her hands in his. He rubbed his thumbs across the insides of her wrists. "But maybe it's not such a bad thing, after all."

Abby blinked, stunned Tad did not see the development as the calamity it was. Her career was the one thing—the only thing—she had counted on through thick and thin. She'd put her heart and soul into her job at *Trend.*

"If it gives us a chance to be together," he soothed, wrapping a comforting arm about her shoulders, "maybe it's even a good thing."

His analysis was so hopelessly optimistic, so far off the mark, Abby didn't know whether to laugh or cry. She only knew, with the room taking on an increasingly precarious tilt, and her whole world crashing down around her, that she couldn't hold it together any longer.

She stopped trying to fight it, pitched forward into Tad's waiting arms and let the swirling dizziness overwhelm her.

Chapter Two

"What'd you say to make her faint?" Doc Harlan said as Tad carried his new bride into the doctor's office just down the street from the newspaper.

"What makes you think it was something I said?" Tad asked as he eased Abby onto the examining table. "It could have been something I did. Or something someone else said."

Doc grinned as he listened for her heartbeat and checked her pulse. "Always gotta see all the angles, don't you, son?"

Tad tried not to show his fear. It had scared the life out of him when Abby had collapsed in his arms. "That's the way I've been trained—the way all journalists are trained."

Fortunately he'd had Doc nearby. The sixty-year-old physician had taken care of the people in Blossom for the past thirty years. His kind eyes and comforting smile were as well-known to residents as the plaid sport shirts, khaki trousers and suede loafers he wore beneath his starched white lab coat. Tad searched Doc's face anxiously, taking solace in the fact Doc was such a capable family physician. "Is Abby going to be all right?" Tad asked as Abby began to moan and come around.

"Yes, but I'd like to know why she fainted. Does this happen often?"

Tad shrugged as he turned his attention back to Abby's pale oval face. She hadn't fainted in Paris. Or when they got married in Memphis.

"Not that I know," Tad said. "But we've only been married a little over three weeks."

Doc nodded, accepting that information as he broke open an ammonia capsule. "Did she just have a shock?"

Tad nodded, recalling the precipitous phone call from her friend Yvonne. "She just found out she lost her job."

Doc gave Tad a compassionate look. He waved the capsule beneath Abby's nose. "That's probably it, then, but just to be safe, I'd better examine her."

Catching a whiff of the ammonia, Abby coughed. Her golden-brown eyes fluttered open. Bewildered to find herself lying prone on an examining table, she looked at Tad, then Doc, then Tad again. Embarrassed color highlighted her delicately sculpted cheekbones, and the tip of her tongue snaked out to wet her soft pink lips. "What...?" She tried to raise herself slightly, abruptly lost all color and lay back down again.

"You fainted," Tad told her, taking her hand.

Remembering, Abby groaned.

"I caught you," Tad continued.

Abby moaned louder and covered her face with both hands.

Doc grinned. "That'd be my reaction, too, if I was married to him." Doc angled a thumb at Tad.

Abby's eyes widened. She peered at Tad through her splayed fingers as if to say, *You told him?*

Tad shrugged. If it were up to him, he'd be shouting it to the world.

"Since you were in no shape to do so, I had to give

him permission to treat you,'' Tad said to Abby. To Doc, ''She's not really used to being my wife yet.''

''So I gather,'' Doc said.

His nurse came in, patient gown in hand.

Hand on his shoulder, Doc ushered Tad toward the door. ''There's a good selection of magazines in the waiting room. Make yourself comfortable.''

''But—'' Tad protested.

''I'll call you when I know something,'' Doc promised.

''IT CAN'T BE,'' Abby whispered hoarsely, tears glimmering in her eyes as she sat on the examining table, still in her pale blue patient gown.

''Honey, it is,'' Doc said gently.

Silence filled the small room as Abby tried to absorb all he'd just told her.

''I'll get your husband.'' Doc patted her knee. ''The two of you can talk, then if you have any questions, you can ask me together.''

''What is it?'' Tad asked seconds later as he rushed into the room, looking worried.

Abby drew a deep breath and shot him an accusing look. This was all his fault! ''I'm pregnant.''

Tad stared at her, evidencing much the same gut reaction she'd already had. ''That can't be.''

Which was, as it turned out, exactly what she'd said.

''We used—''

''Protection, I know,'' Abby said grimly. ''But as Doc says, every kind of protection fails sometime. We just happened to hit one of those sometimes.''

''In Paris.'' Tad swiftly pinpointed the time and place.

''Or our wedding night in Memphis,'' Abby supposed, remembering how jubilant and uninhibited their lovemaking had been just after they'd eloped. "Either way, I'm due approximately eight months from now."

"A baby," Tad repeated in a low stunned voice as he sat down beside her and took her hand. Slowly his deep blue eyes filled with joy. "We're going to have a baby."

"Looks like," Abby said, still feeling as though she'd just had the wind knocked out of her.

She had always sworn she would never get pregnant until the man and the moment were right, until she could provide her child with the kind of loving stable home her oft-married-and-divorced parents had never given her.

Yet here she was. Trying to annul her marriage to Tad at the same time she discovered she was carrying his child. Could it get any worse?

"This changes things," Tad said firmly.

"Yes," Abby agreed, "it does." It made them much more complicated.

Tad smiled at her. "Looks like we have a lot to talk about."

"Yes, I'd say so." Such as, what were they going to do? She wanted this baby—Tad's baby—so much. But she was afraid, too, that in the end neither she nor Tad would be able to do right by their child and give him or her the peaceful loving two-parent home every child deserved. She did not want to hurt her child the way she'd been hurt when her parents had split.

"Do you need any help getting dressed?"

Just the thought of him helping her take off the examination gown and put on her clothes made her skin burn. Abby drew an unsteady breath. "I can handle it." She met his eyes. "I'm feeling fine now. Honest."

"All right." Tad rose reluctantly. "I'll be waiting for you in the reception area."

Abby nodded.

"And, Abby?" Tad came back to cup her shoulders warmly and kiss her brow. "This is good news."

"READY TO GO?" Tad rushed to his feet as a pink-cheeked Abby came out into the waiting room, several samples of prenatal vitamins and a prescription in hand.

As ready as I'll ever be, Abby thought, nodding.

"Good." Tad flashed a sexy grin that brought his dimples into prominence. "'Cause I've got a surprise for you."

Abby dug in her heels as they moved through the clinic doors and headed toward his Jeep. "I'm not sure I can take any more surprises."

"You'll like this one. I promise." Tad helped her into the passenger seat, climbed in himself, then drove across the center of the small town to a shady residential street of older Victorian homes. He parked at the curb in the center of the block in front of a house with a Sold sign in front of it. With a feeling of dread, Abby looked over and saw plenty of room, crumbling gray-white paint, windows smeared with years of grime, shrubs badly in need of a good trimming and a yard overgrown with weeds.

"Don't tell me..." Abby began, with a sinking feeling of dread.

"I bought it along with the newspaper," Tad announced proudly. He was already out of the car and sprinting around to her side. "You're going to love it."

Somehow Abby doubted that.

"It's the perfect place for rearing kids. Once it's fixed up of course."

Abby looked at the sagging steps leading up to the front porch. "It would take years."

Tad remained undaunted. He braced his hands on his

hips and looked around with satisfaction. "Not with someone like you running the show."

Abby was the first to admit she had a lot of talent. She could spot an idea that would excite readers and compel them to buy a magazine in an instant. But this? Just the thought of tackling it made her feel overwhelmed. "Tad, I'm an editor, not—"

"A home-and-garden editor." Tad unlocked the door and opened it wide.

"I've never personally supervised the renovation of a home. I just okay the ideas behind different projects and oversee the articles written about such endeavors."

Wordlessly Tad picked Abby up in his arms and carried her across the threshold. He closed the door behind them, strode over to the ugliest olive green Naugahyde sofa Abby had ever seen in her life. He set her down gently and then sat beside her. "Our life together is going to be full of firsts, Abby," he told her gently, taking both her hands in his. "The first marriage, first child, first home, first newspaper, first lifestyle section…"

His enthusiasm made her want to grin. Holding on to the grim reality of the situation with effort, Abby replied, "Back to that again?"

Tad lifted her hand to his lips. He kissed it soundly, then laid it against his face. "I need you, Abby," he told her softly. "Together we can make all our dreams come true."

Abby wanted to believe that; she couldn't. Her life thus far had taught her to take nothing for granted, to depend only on what she knew to be a concrete basis for her life.

She rose and moved away from him. "My dream has always been to climb to the top of my profession," she reminded Tad.

Together they walked through the downstairs, viewing

a large imposing entryway, living room, den, dining room and kitchen. All of which looked as if they'd been decorated by a color-blind two-year-old and furnished at a swap meet.

"You can still climb to the top of your profession if you work with me," Tad pointed out as they went up the stairs and toured the four bedrooms and two full baths. "It'll just be in a different format."

The third floor was an attic, and it was as filled with junk as the rest of the house. Feeling she'd seen enough, Abby turned and headed back down the stairs.

"Magazines and newspapers are very different. Just as your career dreams are very different from my career dreams, Tad."

"I'll concede that." Tad followed close on her heels. "But fate has taken a turn we didn't anticipate and can't change." Tad cupped her shoulders and turned her to face him. "And until you do find another job at a magazine, why not work here with me?"

Her skin warming to his touch, Abby sighed.

"It could take months to find another position on par with what you had at *Trend*," he went on.

"I know that!" The fact she'd been fired still rankled.

"You're going to need to be busy in the meantime. You're going to need to be someplace good for the baby. And I want you nearby so I can take care of you and the baby both."

It didn't take a genius to see where this was heading. Abby crossed her arms and stepped back, away from him. "You're talking about continuing our marriage?" she said, angling her chin at him.

He studied her with a fiery determination that set her pulse to racing. "Yes."

Despair swept her. "Tad..." As utterly romantic, as

optimistic, as Tad's proposal was, she did not want to prolong the agony of defeat, and she had already conceded defeat in her marriage to Tad. He, however, had other ideas.

"Our baby deserves to be born legitimately, to two parents who love him. Our baby deserves the very best start we can give him." Tad drew her into his arms and held her against him. "I know this is unexpected—" he soothed.

Tears burned Abby's eyes. "You've got that right!"

"—but it's not that far off course, either," Tad said gently. "You already know I love you and you love me."

That Abby could not dispute. It was what came after the love that worried her. How many times had she seen her parents fall madly and passionately in love, marry, only to divorce mere months later?

Abby flattened her hands on Tad's chest and pushed away from him. "It takes a lot more than a whopping jolt of love at first sight to make a marriage work, Tad." She paced in the opposite direction.

"But love is the basis on which all good marriages are built," Tad reminded her. Again he crossed to her and took her in his arms. He threaded his hand through her hair. "I told you in Paris that I wanted you to share everything with me, including my dreams."

Abby recalled that night. It had been oh, so romantic. She'd been enthralled. The problem was his proposal wasn't *practical*.

"Having a baby is one of my dreams. And yours," Tad stated persuasively.

"But not now," Abby protested in heartfelt agony. "Not when everything is so messed up." Not when she didn't even have a job!

"It doesn't have to be messed up." Tad gently

kneaded the tense muscles in her back. "Stay here with me. Help me fix up this house and breathe new life into the newspaper. Wait out the birth of our baby with me by your side."

Abby reluctantly admitted she did not want to go through pregnancy alone. Plus, Tad was the father. He deserved to participate in the event as much as she did. And aside from the fact they wanted very different things out of life—he a chance to revive a small-town newspaper and a home in the mountains of North Carolina, she a career as a magazine editor in a big city—they did get along very well. Any child would be lucky to have him for a father.

"You understand I can't—won't—give up looking for work in my field in the meantime?" Abby said bluntly, wanting no more misunderstandings between them on this score.

Tad nodded.

"Because after the baby is born," Abby continued, "I intend to go right back to work." Work was the sustaining force in her life. It had seen her through a lot of good times and bad. It was the one thing in her life she had always known she could count on. Yes, getting fired was a setback, but it hadn't been her fault, and with time she knew she would bounce back stronger than ever.

"What about after the baby is born? Are you proposing we split up?"

"From a practical standpoint, we'll probably have to, if we get jobs in different states. But that doesn't mean we couldn't both participate actively in our child's life. Commute. Have him or her spend time with both of us. I'd be more than amenable to working things out on that score. I'd just want to know…I'd want you to promise me that when that time comes—"

"If it comes," Tad interrupted.

"—that we'll part gracefully and both do whatever it takes to work things out on a practical level."

Tad's kneading hands stilled. "All right," he said eventually, "as long as you're here with me in Blossom when the baby is born and agree to share every moment of our baby's development and birth with me, then I promise I'll be supportive of your efforts to get back into the magazine business, no matter what that entails. But in return," he said in a low intense voice, "you have to do a favor for me."

Abby's heart skipped a beat as she lifted her gaze to his. At that moment she felt she could drown in his sexy blue eyes. "That favor being...?" she asked on a halting breath.

"I don't want anyone in Blossom to know our marriage is being held together only by the baby," Tad warned her. "People talk, especially when the subjects involved give them something to talk about." Compassion gilded the handsome features of his face. "I wouldn't want anything hurtful coming back to haunt our child later on."

"Like the fact his parents were about to divorce and had to stay married," Abby guessed. She recalled the gossip she'd endured as a kid about her own parents and their oft-changing love lives. There was no getting around it. It had hurt.

"Right." Tad kissed the inside of her wrist. "Let's just let it be known we eloped in Memphis after spending the weekend in Paris. We'll tell people the truth—that we're both delighted to be having a baby, and for the moment, anyway, you're going to be helping me out with the newspaper, with the intention of one day going back to magazine work."

Abby couldn't fault Tad's thinking; it seemed he had covered everything. "That sounds fair."

"Good." The set of his broad shoulders relaxed.

"In return for my cooperation, however, I'd like to ask yours."

His expression sparked with masculine interest. "On what?"

"The sleeping arrangements."

Tad's dimpled grin broadened and his eyes twinkled sexily. "As I recall, we never seemed to get much sleep."

"Exactly my point," Abby said, flushing, reminding herself it was the unbridled passion flowing between them that was responsible for all their miscommunication and had gotten them into this mess. They needed to be a lot more circumspect in the future, and there was no way they could do that if they were making love to each other like there was no tomorrow. "I don't think we should be sharing a bed. We should be talking instead. Besides," she hurried on, aware how ridiculous she sounded, but not about to back down now that she'd laid out the rules, "I'm pregnant. I need my sleep."

He lifted a dissenting brow. "You also need to be loved."

Abby pushed the memories of their ardent lovemaking from her mind. It was rushing headlong into bed with Tad that had gotten her into this situation in the first place. She swallowed and tried not to think about his lips on her skin. "Things are complicated enough as it is without bringing sex back into the mix, Tad," she told him sternly.

He studied her, but the passionate argument, the insistence on having his own way in this that she expected, never came.

"You want us to concentrate on getting to know each other, instead," he guessed, stepping back and mulling over the idea.

Abby nodded and folded her arms. She didn't know why—the day was quite warm—but she suddenly felt chilled. And oddly bereft. "I think it'd be a good idea, since we're going to be rearing a child together, don't you?"

His expression impassive, Tad continued studying her. Finally he let out a long slow breath and allowed, "I have to admit there's a lot I want to learn about you."

"Same here."

"And a lot more you should know about me," he concluded just as the phone rang. With a last backward look at her, he went to answer it. He listened intently, then frowned, promising, "I'll be right there."

"Trouble?" Abby asked as soon as he hung up.

Tad nodded. "It's my aunt Sadie."

"Is Aunt Sadie one of the reasons you moved back?" Abby asked as, minutes later, they climbed back into Tad's Jeep.

"She's my only living relative, and—"

"She's ill?"

"Not exactly."

Abby waited as Tad started the engine and pulled the Jeep away from the curb. "What do you mean, not exactly?"

"That was one of her neighbors who called. Said she's been worried about Aunt Sadie ever since she retired last year. That she'd been acting a little strange."

Abby frowned. This did not sound good. "You think she's getting senile?"

Tad shook his head. "She's always been sharp as a tack."

Abby heard the reservation in his voice and knew there was some sort of problem, even if he wasn't coming right out and telling her so.

As they turned onto the next street, loud music filtered out to greet them. Wordlessly Tad pulled up in front of a small tidy brick house with tons of gingerbread trim.

In tandem they turned their gazes in the direction of the commotion. Abby blinked and did a double take. "Oh, my heavens," she said.

Chapter Three

"Let me guess—Aunt Sadie," Abby murmured as the two of them approached the spry-looking woman in full flapper regalia, doing the Charleston on her front porch while her bassett hound lay prone beside her, watching.

"One and the same," Tad confirmed with a grin.

"Come on up and join me!" Aunt Sadie beckoned them with a wave, then went back to kicking up her heels and crossing her hands over her knees.

Before Abby could guess Tad's intent, he had taken her by the hand and swirled her around to face him. The next thing she knew they were both kicking up their heels to the lively beat of the music for which the dance had been named. While Sadie threw back her head and laughed, the three of them danced round and round in the warm May air, till finally the music on the old Victrola stopped.

"Whew!" Sadie put a hand to her perspiring forehead, adjusting the vivid blue band that encircled her head, and peeked out beneath the thick silvery bangs of her wedge-cut hair. Sadie turned sparkling eyes on them. "That'll get the old blood pumping!"

"And then some," Tad concurred, laughing.

Taking Abby's hand, he led her to a seat on one of the

white wicker chairs on the front porch. She sank into the cushions gratefully while Sadie moved to a table to pour three glasses of icy lemonade.

Tad reached down to pet Buster, then also took a seat. "Did you forget your doctor's appointment this afternoon?" Tad asked his aunt.

"No, not at all," Sadie said breathlessly, as she settled opposite him on the porch swing. "I just had more important things to do."

Abby wondered what could've been more important than an appointment with Doc Harlan, the town's only physician.

"Dancing," Tad guessed, no expression readily identifiable on his face, though Abby sensed inwardly he was a little piqued about the blown-off appointment.

"Cheering up Buster," Sadie corrected. She pointed to her bassett hound, who was still lying on the porch, his head resting between his paws. "He's been very depressed," Sadie continued.

Tad looked at Buster, then turned back to Sadie. "How can you tell?"

Sadie sighed, exasperated. "That face!"

Tad laughed and shook his head. "Aunt Sadie, Buster always has that mournful look."

"True, but usually he doesn't just lie there like that all day long, and that's all he does these days," Sadie complained, fanning herself.

"Have you taken him to the vet?" Tad put his lemonade aside, then hunkered down in front of Buster and scratched him behind the ears.

"Yes." Sadie sniffed indignantly. "They can't find a thing."

"Then maybe he's just tired," Tad suggested, straightening. "He probably hasn't been sleeping much, either, if *you're* not sleeping nights."

Sadie sighed and scraped her teeth across her lower lip. "I hadn't thought of that."

"Which is why, as you recall, you have an appointment with Doc Harlan—" Tad consulted his watch "—twenty minutes ago."

Abby noted Sadie looked less than eager. "I think I should let someone else go," Sadie said. "Someone who's really sick."

"Oh, no." Tad strode toward his aunt. "You're not getting out of it that easily. So c'mon." He held out a hand and assisted his aunt out of the swing. "Let's go."

"Oh, all right, just let me freshen up," Sadie grumbled. She slipped into the house.

Abby turned to Tad. "You're taking her to her appointment?"

Tad nodded. He looked at Abby, his eyes filled with concern. "It's the only way to make sure she'll show up."

Sadie sailed through the door. Abby was amused to see that Sadie was still in her flapper outfit. "Now you listen to me, Tad McFarlane," Sadie scolded as she led the way down the steps to Tad's Jeep. "This is the very last doctor's appointment I am letting you make on my behalf. There is absolutely no way I am going to let you or anyone else turn me into a hypochondriac just because I retired from teaching last year."

Tad held the door for his aunt. "Aunt Sadie, no one is calling you a hypochondriac," he said wearily.

"Might as well." Sadie snorted, incensed, as she accepted Tad's help getting up in the Jeep. "Insomnia! Whoever heard of going to the doctor for that?"

AS IT TURNED OUT, Tad was disappointed to hear, there wasn't a whole lot Doc Harlan could do for Sadie.

"I don't want to put you on sleeping pills if we can avoid it," Doc told Sadie. "I'd rather you increase your activity during the days and cut out all naps no matter how drowsy you get. See if that doesn't get you back on a normal sleep pattern. Meantime you can try some of these."

He gave her a list of things to do that included, among other things, sleeping in a dark quiet room and drinking a glass of warm milk before she retired. "You might also buy some eye shades down at the pharmacy," Doc said. "They don't work for everyone, but they might work for you."

While Abby walked down to the pharmacy with Sadie to get them, Tad stayed behind to talk to Doc. "She really is okay?" he asked anxiously.

Doc nodded and gave Tad a comforting smile. "Fit as a fiddle as far as I can tell." Doc made a final notation on Sadie's chart, then handed it to his receptionist/nurse for filing. "It may be she just has something on her mind."

That much Tad had guessed, too. "Any idea what?" If it wasn't an illness or the possibility of one keeping Sadie awake nights, then what was?

Doc shook his head. He looked equally baffled. "You're a lot closer to her—you'll need to figure out what. But my guess is your aunt probably just needs to stay busier during the day. I gather she hasn't been all that active since she returned from her last cruise in February."

"That's true." Tad shook hands with the gray-haired physician. "Thanks, Doc."

"Anytime." Doc winked. "Take care of your new bride now, you hear?"

If she'll let me. Thus far, Abby had one foot—no, make that half her body—out the door.

He went to join Sadie and Abby, who were just leaving the pharmacy. Together, they climbed back into the Jeep.

"I want the two of you to stay for dinner," Sadie told them firmly. "Abby and I have a lot to catch up on."

When they returned to Sadie's, Buster was still lying on the porch. His expression remained mournful and his tail barely lifted as he followed them inside.

"Poor thing," Sadie murmured compassionately. "I don't think he likes me being home all day."

Buster didn't? Or Sadie? "So this blue mood of Buster's has just happened since you retired," Tad said as Sadie led the way into the homey confines of her peach-colored kitchen.

Sadie brought out a mesh bag of baking potatoes and carried them to the sink. She thought about Tad's question as she rummaged around for aprons for herself and Abby. "Actually it didn't start right away. At first he was happy to have me home."

"When did he begin acting so listless?" Tad asked as Abby began scrubbing the three potatoes Sadie had picked out.

Sadie returned to the refrigerator and pulled out an armful of salad fixings. "It didn't happen overnight. It was more of a gradual thing, since last...oh, March."

Tad watched her bring out several pots and a large cast-iron skillet. "Is it possible he's picking up on your mood?"

Sadie paused, caught off guard. Her glance lifted to Tad's. "You think he knows I've been a little blue?"

Tad shrugged and exchanged concerned looks with

Abby over Sadie's head. "Well, Buster's been with you nigh on twelve years now, Aunt Sadie," he said gently. "He has to know you better than practically anyone. If he thinks you're unhappy..." Tad bent his knees and scrunched down so they were at eye level. "Are you unhappy?"

Sadie straightened her slender shoulders and folded her arms. Her chin took on a militant tilt. "Well, as much as I absolutely loathe to admit it, yes, I am."

Abby looked sympathetic, too. She wrapped an arm around Sadie's shoulders and said, "Your retirement not all it was cracked up to be?"

Sadie nodded miserably. Moving away from both Tad and Abby, she threw up both hands and said in exasperation and disappointment, "It bothers me to admit it, but I'm no good at this!" She shook her head. "All those years I saved and scrimped, only to find out I got tired of traveling after just three overseas trips, and I'm no good at hobbies. And now that I'm home again the days are too long and I'm lonely here, rambling around this house on my own. I've tried volunteer work, but with everyone in these parts looking after their own, there's not a lot to do. The bottom line is, I no longer feel useful. And that makes me feel crabby and just plain bored and I hate feeling this way!" she stated vehemently.

Buster perked up, hearing the passion in his mistress's voice. The droopy-eyed hound looked from Tad to Sadie to Abby and then back again, then sank back down, looking more mournful than ever.

"Then we're going to have to fix that," Tad told his aunt firmly.

"How?" Sadie returned glumly. She clearly saw no solution.

"By making use of your talents," Tad told her, moving forward to wrap his arm about Sadie's shoulders just the way Abby had. "I'm expanding the newspaper. I'm going to need someone else to help proofread all the copy, and I can't think of anyone who'd be better at it than you, Aunt Sadie."

Tad caught Abby's confused look and explained, "Aunt Sadie taught high-school English lit for thirty-nine years."

Abby smiled, impressed. "Wow. You did have a long career."

"And a very distinguished one," Tad added.

"You're sure I wouldn't be in the way?" Sadie asked, her blue eyes narrowing in concern.

Tad shook his head. "The only problem is limited budget. Until I can increase revenues at the newspaper, I'm not going to be able to pay you much more than minimum wage."

The diminutive Sadie waved off his concern. "Don't worry about that." She stood on tiptoe to kiss his cheek. "It'll be a pleasure just to be active again."

THAT SETTLED, the three of them quickly set out to make dinner in earnest. "So, Abby, tell me a little about yourself," Sadie said as she slid floured chicken into the frying pan while Tad and Abby worked together on the salad. "How did you end up working as a home-and-garden editor for *Trend* magazine?" Sadie asked as she moved the sizzling pieces of chicken around with a long-handled fork.

"I majored in English when I was in college," Abby replied. Still standing shoulder to shoulder with Tad, Abby lined up the carrots on the cutting board and began to julienne them. "Between my sophomore and junior year I got a job as a summer intern for a home-decorating magazine. Which was probably the last place I ever expected to be working, since neither of my parents were really into decorating. My mother's a fashion photographer and my father's a documentary-film producer. They divorced when I was a baby and agreed to split custody, so I shuttled back and forth between the two. Anyway, they moved around a lot and went wherever the work was.'' Abby smiled. ''And they both really loved their work—still do. So we lived in hotels and rented houses and little efficiency apartments, none of which were decorated in anything but hotel chic.''

Finished cleaning the lettuce, Tad paused to regard Abby affectionately. ''Sounds like a challenging life,'' he said.

Reminding Abby that although they might be husband and wife and expecting a baby together, they still knew very little about each other. If they were going to coparent a child successfully, Abby knew that would have to change.

''It was.'' Abby paused, remembering what it was like, going to a new school nearly every semester. ''Anyway, I'd always been fascinated by the little touches that made a house a home, so working as a gofer for renowned interior designers was really exciting. When I went back to college in the fall, I added interior design and gardening courses to my course load. And when I graduated, I got hired at a magazine in the home-and-garden department.'' Abby tried but could not discount the respect she saw in Tad's eyes.

''Did you always work for *Trend?*'' Sadie asked as Abby checked the potatoes and found them fork-tender.

''Oh, no.'' Abby grabbed a couple of pot holders and carried the steaming pan over to the sink. With Tad's help, she poured the potatoes into the colander to drain.

"I worked for half-a-dozen magazines before landing there. But it was at *Trend* that I really found my niche and was given the responsibility to lead a department on my own. Only now I've been fired." Abby set the empty pan aside.

"Oh, dear." Sadie clucked sympathetically as she got out the electric mixer and handed it to Abby.

"Everyone else was, too. Hostile takeover."

"Well, you'll land on your feet," Sadie soothed.

"Actually she's going to help me at the newspaper," Tad told his aunt as Abby began to mash the potatoes, "by creating a Lifestyle section for the paper."

"Oh, my. That sounds exciting."

It was a challenging proposition. One Abby looked forward to tackling. "And Tad's going to give me free rein," Abby said, tongue in cheek, as she measured milk, butter, salt and pepper into the mixing bowl.

Tad's eyes glimmered with humor, too, as he gave her a look reminding her exactly who was editor-in-chief of the new and improved *Blossom Weekly News*. "Oh, I am, am I?"

Abby nodded, grinning and continuing in a light but completely serious manner. "'Cause he knows that's the only way I'll take the position." *Even temporarily.* She was used to calling her own shots. She was going to continue to call her own shots. Temporarily still married or not.

"See that, Buster? Those are sparks in their eyes. All newlyweds should have them," Sadie murmured.

"So what do your parents think of Tad?" Sadie asked Abby as they sat down at the table minutes later.

As they began to add generous portions of southern fried chicken to their plates, Abby looked at Tad uncomfortably before answering his aunt. "Um, they haven't met him yet. They're both rather inaccessible at the moment. Mother's in Europe compiling photos for a book on reigning royal families. Father's in Tibet, beginning work on a new documentary."

"But they do know you're married," Sadie questioned as she added gravy to her mashed potatoes.

Abby nodded, doing her best to keep her expression neutral. "I dropped them both a line."

"And they were happy about your marriage?"

Not exactly, Abby thought, as she ladled succotash onto her plate. "After five divorces, Mother no longer feels marriage per se is a valid institution. Father just thinks I should have waited till I was a little older, say fifty or sixty, before taking such a big step. He's been divorced six times." Abby's lips curved wryly as Tad passed her the bowl of tossed green salad. "Both have vowed never to marry again, and frankly I think that's wise. The ability to stay married just isn't in their genes." Each time her parents had gotten hitched, they'd thought they were marrying The One. Each time they'd come out of the failed union more disillusioned than ever.

Sadie looked at Tad. "Goodness!" she exclaimed. "You're lucky you talked Abby into matrimony at all."

"You don't have to tell me," Tad drawled, looking at Abby in a way that made her think he intended to stay married to her come what may.

Sadie turned back to Abby. "What do they think about the baby?" she prodded.

Abby flushed uncomfortably. She watched Tad break open a fluffy golden biscuit. "I haven't had a chance to tell them yet."

Sadie gently patted the back of Abby's hand. "You should tell them as soon as possible, dear. I'm sure they'll both be very excited."

About being grandparents? Not bloody likely, Abby thought. Nevertheless, she promised, "I'll write them tonight." As far as the rest went, she and Tad might have made a child together, but there was so much she still did not know about him. Like how he'd chosen his career.

It was time she'd found out. "How did you end up covering the international beat?" she asked Tad casually as they began to eat. "You never said."

Tad's shoulders tensed. "I moved around a lot as a kid, too."

A tinge of almost unbearable sadness and compassion entered Sadie's eyes. "Especially after Houston and—"

Tad cut his aunt off with a look that warned her to say no more. A curious silence fell. Tension still flowing between Tad and Sadie, Tad turned back to Abby and continued explaining matter-of-factly, "That was when my dad started taking on international assignments. He was a geologist. He worked for an oil company."

What didn't Tad want her to know? Abby wondered. Until now she hadn't been aware of any deliberate secrets between them. But this clearly was one. "Where all did you live?" Abby asked casually, determined to find out more.

"All over the Middle East, Alaska, Central and South America. We were never in any one place for more than four or five months."

"That sounds rough." And a lot like her own childhood, Abby thought.

"It was. But it was good for me, too," Tad said, smiling reminiscently. "It made me more adaptable. And it's what first fostered my intense interest in the news."

Sadie shook her head in silent admiration. "I never

saw a child insist on reading so many different newspapers every day!''

Tad shrugged off the compliment. ''That's how I caught up with all the news on the places I'd been and acclimated myself to whatever city or country I was in. I read the newspapers.''

''So you knew when you entered college that you wanted to be a reporter,'' Abby guessed, admiring his single-minded ambition, so like her own.

Tad nodded as his dazzling blue eyes met and held hers. ''Once I got my first job, I was a natural for the international beat.''

''And he's been traveling nonstop ever since,'' Sadie recounted proudly. ''Which is why I'm so glad he's settling down here. Sad and difficult as it was, it's high time he got over it,'' Sadie said firmly. ''And moved on with his life.''

High time Tad got over what? Abby wondered, putting clues to his past unhappiness together, an unhappiness she'd heretofore known nothing about. What had happened to Tad and his family in Houston?

''Anyone else want coffee?'' Tad asked. Abruptly leaving the table, he headed for the kitchen. ''Sadie, why don't you help me in here for a minute?'' Tad commanded from the adjacent room.

Her curiosity mounting, Abby started to rise.

Her expression concerned with something a lot more important than coffee, Sadie shook her head and lay her hand across Abby's wrist. ''No, dear, you stay. I'll take care of this.''

Sadie exited the room.

Abby looked down at Buster, who was reclining next to the sideboard. Face on paws, he looked as mournful as ever. ''They're hiding something from me, aren't they?'' Abby murmured. It was up to her to find out what.

Unfortunately Tad was not going to make her fact-finding mission easy.

As soon as they got back to the white-elephant house where she and Tad would be living as long as they were in Blossom, Tad carried in her suitcase.

''You must be tired,'' he said.

Not too tired to ask a few questions.

''Tad?'' Abby followed him upstairs to the master bedroom, not sure where to begin, just knowing she was going to, come hell or high water.

''Hm?'' He set her suitcase down on the narrow double bed and turned to face her.

''What happened in Houston? What are you not over yet?''

Chapter Four

"Look, Abby," Tad said tiredly, the reflection of a thousand sleepless nights in his eyes, "the time my family spent in Houston was not a happy time for us. Beyond that, I don't care to discuss it." A muscle clenching in his jaw, he brushed by her brusquely. "So if you've got everything you need for tonight..."

Everything except a few moments of intimacy with you. How were they ever going to really get to know each other, Abby wondered in mounting frustration, if he kept pushing her away? Didn't he realize it was situations just like this that would doom their marriage for even the short time they planned to stay together? "That's it?" she asked, propping her hands on her slender hips and mocking his abrupt tone to a T. "That's all you're going to tell me?"

"Like I said." Tad turned around to face her and pushed the words through clenched teeth. He gave her the once-over, making no effort at all to hide his impatience with her. "I don't want to talk about it."

"Maybe you should."

Tad closed the distance between them, not stopping until they stood toe-to-toe. Tilting his head down at her, he gave her a smile edged with a weariness that seemed to come straight from his soul. "So now what? You want to be my shrink, is that it?"

Abby tried not to think how much she liked the tantalizing scent of his aftershave. "I want to understand you," she said quietly but emphatically.

He shrugged and slid his hands into his back pockets. His eyes connected with hers and held for a breath-stealing moment. "You do understand me."

"Not enough."

Grinning devilishly, Tad wrapped his arms around her and urged her close with the flat of his hand, until their bodies fit together with the smooth familiarity of a lock and key. She could feel his arousal and remembered without wanting to what a demanding and yet fantastically giving lover he was. With an unrepentant grin, he whispered playfully in her ear, "Oh, I think you know enough."

Abby burned everywhere they touched. Her breasts were tingling. Her thighs were fluid, her knees weak. Abby pulled away from the evidence of his virility. "Oh, no. You are not going to distract me that way." No matter how long it had been since they'd made love.

Tad slid his palm from her shoulder to her wrist, eliciting even more tingles of awareness. He smiled at her wickedly. "How would you like to be distracted, then?"

"Not—" the fluttering in her tummy slipped a little lower "—the way you're thinking."

Tad sighed regretfully and made no effort to hide his disappointment. "Then we both lose out, don't we?"

Heat started low in her body and welled up through her chest, neck and into her face. He wanted to lose himself in lovemaking, forget the things that should be discussed, things keeping them apart. When he knew—had to know—that it was their hasty foray into bed, before they had learned all they should have learned about each other, that had gotten them into this situation in the first place.

"You're infuriating," Abby said, still angry he wouldn't confide in her. Whether he wanted to admit it or not, Tad was shutting her out of the most intimate revealing details of his life, letting her get only so close. And Abby wanted no part of that kind of man.

Tad studied the resolve in her eyes, showing her in an instant he was as frustrated by their situation as she was. Finally he shrugged and stepped away. "Yeah, well, as much as I'd like to stand here chatting with you about things I have no intention of ever sharing with you—or anyone else for that matter—I've got things to do."

"Like what?" Abby demanded.

"Like the editorial meeting I've set up for first thing tomorrow morning," he announced glibly as he headed out into the hall, his strides long and confident.

Abby let out an exasperated breath. Tad turned. Their glances meshed.

Since they'd known each other, they'd covered the range of emotions. Now, for the first time, it seemed to Abby that a wall had gone up between them, one he wasn't about to let her scale, now or ever.

"Get some sleep, Abby," Tad advised, his expression gentling slightly. "You and the baby both need it." He disappeared from view, continuing on down the stairs.

What she needed more, Abby thought moodily, was the straight scoop from Tad. Sadie had hinted that whatever was haunting Tad was something he'd been running from for many years.

Common sense told Abby Tad needed to explore his feelings on whatever had happened in the past. Maybe, with time, and a lot more trust on his part, she'd be able to help him do that.

She dug out paper and pen from her suitcase. She'd promised Sadie she would write to her parents about the baby tonight, so she might as well get started on that, difficult as it was going to be.

"EVERYONE, I'D LIKE YOU to meet my wife, Abby. She's going to be the editor of the paper's new Lifestyle section and will feature our own house renovation as her first series," Tad began the next morning, as all six people— himself included—gathered around the conference table for the first official meeting of the entire newspaper staff.

"Most of you already know my aunt, Sadie Mc-Farlane," Tad continued, after Abby had greeted everyone. "She's going to be doing all our proofreading."

Sadie smiled and said hello to everyone, too.

"Raymond Burke is going to run our printing press. He's just moved here from Charlotte."

Everyone sent the older man with the amiable grin and salt-and-pepper buzz cut a smile and soft hello.

Tad nodded at a slim young woman in denim overalls and an appliquéd T-shirt. She had short curly red hair and dangling blue-and-white earrings shaped like a Tarheel footprint. "Cindy just graduated from Chapel Hill," Tad told the group. "She's going to be in charge of the classifieds and head up a major drive for new advertisers."

Tad gestured at a preppy blond kid not much older than Cindy. "And last but not least, I'd like to introduce Sonny to everyone. He's our roving reporter and photographer rolled into one. He's the lone old hand among us, since he's worked here off and on since high school. He just graduated from North Carolina State."

"It's nice to meet all of you," Abby said.

Cindy grinned enthusiastically. "We're glad to meet you, too. Ever since Tad took over a couple of weeks ago, he's been hoping you'd agree to work on the newspaper with us."

Yet he'd only just now mentioned it to her, Abby thought.

"We didn't know the two of you were married until the day before yesterday when he called to let us know you were coming back with him," Sonny chimed in.

Abby knew exactly why Tad hadn't said anything about the two of them being married. He hadn't known if they were even going to give their whirlwind relationship another chance.

Sensing some explanation was required of them, Abby said, "It all happened rather suddenly."

"As did the news we got yesterday," Tad said, glad to change the subject and grinning like a proud papa to be. Giving her no chance to stop him, he went on, "If you haven't already heard, Abby fainted while we were looking around here." His smile widened all the more as he announced happily, "Doc confirmed she's expecting."

Abby felt herself flush as congratulations were offered all around. "When is the baby due?" Cindy asked.

"January twenty-ninth, give or take."

"Meanwhile," Tad said, rolling up his sleeves, "we all have a lot of work to do if we want to make the *Blossom Weekly News* into the acclaimed regional newspaper I envision it as being."

"Speaking of the next edition, have you seen this?" Frowning, Sonny gave a handwritten note to Tad. "What do you think about this letter to the editor? It was under the door when I came in this morning."

"'Dear Editor,'" Tad read aloud to the group, "'I hope now that we've got a world-famous reporter running the paper here in Blossom that we'll finally get some decent investigative reporting done, because there are some real crooks operating in this town who need to be put out of business and fast!'" Tad stopped reading abruptly.

"Who are the crooks?" Abby asked, intrigued.

Tad frowned. "It doesn't say. The note's not signed, either." He looked up at the group. "Any idea who the writer is talking about?"

Everyone shrugged. No one ventured a guess.

Tad turned to his aunt. "Aunt Sadie, you've lived here for the past forty-some years. Do you have any idea who the writer might be talking about?"

Sadie colored slightly. "I've heard stories, of course, about this and that. Everyone has. But I make it a policy not to speak ill of people without proof. So you'll just have to smoke them out."

If anyone knew how to do that, Abby thought admiringly, Tad did.

"FIND OUT ANY MORE about the identity of the town crooks?" Abby asked Tad later that evening as the two of them sat down to their first official dinner in their new home.

His eyes gleamed in a way that let her know he was up to something. "I'm working on it. Meanwhile, you can say it if you want to," Tad told Abby frankly as he spread a napkin on his lap and passed the peas.

"Say what?" Trying not to notice how cozy it felt to be there with Tad that way, or think it could be that way for them forever if she wanted it to be, Abby ladled take-out mashed potatoes, cranberry sauce and rotisserie chicken on her plate.

Tad gave her a cocky grin that belied the hurt in his words. "You didn't like my idea about using the renovation of our white elephant of a home as the centerpiece of a series on home remodeling." Tad added some coleslaw to his plate.

Circumventing her mixed emotions about the way he'd pretty much announced his idea as a done deal during the staff meeting, Abby shrugged. She knew she shouldn't be annoyed. In the end this was going to be his home, not theirs. She was only staying there temporarily.

Keeping her expression carefully neutral, Abby dug into their hot almost-as-good-as-home-cooked meal. "Living room one week, dining room the next. Who wouldn't want to see what we do to jazz up the master bedroom?" And the narrow double bed that Tad had not slept in the night before. But that had been her choice, she reminded herself sternly. He'd only been following her lead.

"Plus," Abby forced herself to continue enthusiastically, "it will be great for the baby if we can get your house completely fixed up before he or she is born."

Tad continued to study her. If he'd noticed the way she'd referred to the house as his, not theirs, he didn't show it.

"You're right. It will be good for the baby," he said calmly. "Which is why I don't understand why you're so ambivalent about the project." Tad's deep blue eyes searched hers. "As the new Lifestyle editor and the parent here with all the decorating expertise, it's going to be your show from start to finish."

He was acting as if they were going to be a real family,

at least until their baby was born. Struggling to retain her equilibrium, Abby pushed back her chair and headed for the refrigerator. She rummaged around for the strawberry jam. "You were very generous, giving me free rein in the decorating. I mean, who knows?" Moving the three gallons of milk around, Abby finally found the jam and pulled it out. "My taste could turn out to be horrendous, to say the least."

Just the way their living together before the baby was born, as a sort-of-married couple, could also be a mistake. For Abby, the lines between reality and fantasy and wishful thinking were already becoming blurred. Was the same thing happening to him? she wondered as Tad got up and lounged against the opposite counter.

One corner of his mouth lifted at her prediction of doom in the decorating department. "I don't think so," Tad retorted dryly as he watched her peel the protective plastic seal away from the jam jar and toss it into the trash. "So what gives, Abby?" he asked bluntly, folding his arms. "What is it about this setup you don't like?" He hesitated only a moment before he asked, "Are you ticked off because I told everyone we were expecting a baby?" He reached out and plucked the jam from her hands.

Abby gave him a deadpan look, then turned away from him stiffly and sat back down at the table. "I would have waited a bit, if it had been left up to me."

"Okay." Tad opened the jam for her and sat down, too. "Next time I'll ask," he promised as he handed her the jam. "And together we'll decide on the timing." Beneath the small cozy table, their knees touched. At the contact little lightning bolts of warmth surged through her. Abby tensed beneath the onslaught; she did not want to feel desire for him.

"Now what?" Tad asked, watching the play of emotions across her face.

Abby swallowed and concentrated on her meal. "Nothing."

"It's not nothing when your cheeks get pink like that."

She'd thought the two of them could be just friends. But she was beginning to see this was going to be much harder than she'd thought. Every time she was around him, she was reminded how good it had been between them. And then she started wanting him and yearning to be close to him all over again. And she knew what a trap that was. If she let herself rely on him too much, it would hurt all that much more the next time he refused to confide in her or insisted on living out his dreams, not hers.

Abby's temper flashed as he continued to study her. She did not want him seeing into her heart and mind. "Stop being so solicitous!" she snapped. She felt like he was humoring her, and she did not want to be humored, any more than she wanted to be pampered just because she was pregnant.

Tad's face broke into a grin. "Oh, I get it. This is one of those moods, isn't it, that comes with the fluctuations of hormones?"

Abby fumed. She was definitely not moody! And she was definitely not the follow-him-anywhere wife he wanted her to be. She gave him a dark look, aware she would've rather died at that point than ask him for any favors. "I would not go there if I were you," she warned as she pushed her empty plate away.

"Fine." Tad's eyes took on an amorous sheen as he stood and carried both their plates to the sink. "What would you like to do tonight?"

What a loaded question, Abby thought on an unaccountably wistful sigh.

If she wasn't pregnant...

If they hadn't rushed into marriage...

But she was, and they had, Abby realized uncomfortably. And there was no denying that if she felt his lips on her skin again, there was no telling what would happen.

Assuring herself her caution was for the best, Abby kept her distance and regarded him cheerfully. "Since you brought home dinner for us, I'll do the dishes. Then I plan to go back to work." Knowing how much work she had to do to get the Lifestyle section launched in the time frame she'd set for herself, she'd spent most of the afternoon setting up a temporary home office for herself in her bedroom upstairs where she could work as much as she wanted, undisturbed.

"You don't have to do the dishes alone," he told her pleasantly.

"It's okay," Abby said, bracing her hands on either side of her and staking out her territory by the sink. "I don't mind."

His expression inscrutable, Tad crossed his arms again and continued to study her. "You're sure about that?"

Abby nodded, never more aware of the agreement they'd made not to bring sex back into the mix. Given the way things were, the fact that their marriage was not going to continue after the birth of their baby, she did not want to fall for him any more than she already had. "Positive," she told him.

He returned her smile with one of his own. "Okay then," he said as he grabbed a pocket-size notepad and pen and slid them into his shirt pocket.

Watching him head for the door, Abby asked, "Where are you going?" She wondered even as she spoke why it mattered so much to her. Or why she should feel so lonely without him.

"Back down to the newspaper to grab a camera, then over to the Rotary Club meeting, the softball games at the Little League fields and then maybe the local tavern." Tad came back just long enough to give her a brief kiss on the brow and a hug goodbye. Turning, he headed straight back to the exit and said over his shoulder, "We have a helluva lot of news to gather if we're going to put out our first edition of the *Blossom Weekly* by Saturday."

So it was back to business as usual.

Why was she not surprised?

TAD STOPPED SHORT at the bedroom door. "Sonny's gonna be here any minute to photograph the Before pictures of the house and you're not—"

"—dressed," Abby grumbled, as she rummaged madly through her closet. "I know," she said, uncomfortably aware of the way her short and silky kimono-style robe clung to her suddenly too-plump breasts.

"What's the problem?" he asked sympathetically as she held up one garment after another to her and then promptly hung it back up.

The problem was, Abby thought as she sorted quickly through her collection of highly sophisticated summer business attire, in an effort to avoid prolonged contact with Tad, she'd been working out of the house the past four weeks. Challenged to build a new Carolina Life section of the paper with minimal resources and an even more minimal budget, she'd been on the telephone nonstop. That being the case, it had made sense to work at home, away from the often chaotic bullpen atmosphere of the *Blossom Weekly News*.

Thus far, she'd had a fair amount of success contacting

the journalism departments of all North Carolina universities and recruiting freelancers to submit samples of their work. From there she'd doled out assignments to capable writers, their fees due upon acceptance of their articles.

The problem was, in deference to the warm and often muggy June weather, she'd been wearing shorts and T-shirts, and she hadn't realized until too late how her body had changed by the end of her second month.

"I'm just running a little late," Abby told him as she plucked out a sky blue suit that had always been a little large on her, stepped over a sliding stack of old editions of the *Blossom Weekly News* and headed for the adjacent bath.

Very much aware Tad was waiting on the other side of the closed bathroom door, Abby slipped off her robe and draped it over the rim of the old-fashioned claw-foot bathtub. With a slight prayer she stepped into the pale blue knee-length skirt. She tugged it up over her hips and found—just as she'd feared—that the zipper was a good inch away from closing.

Hoping against hope that the jacket would cover what the skirt did not, Abby reached for the long tunic jacket and slid her arms into the sleeves. Swiftly she buttoned it up the front and found—to her delight—the jacket would close. It was a little snug around her hips and breasts, but otherwise okay.

Breathing a huge sigh of relief, Abby ran a brush through her hair and stepped out of the bathroom. She was shocked to see Tad shifting her clothes to the other side of the master-bedroom closet and putting in a bunch of his own.

"What are you doing?" she asked, trying not to notice how good he looked in the dark green polo shirt and jeans.

"Putting my clothes in here."

Abby blinked, not aware that anything in the current platonic nature of their relationship had changed. "Why," she asked drolly, "when you have so much room in the other closet?"

"Because I don't want everyone in Blossom to know we're sleeping in separate bedrooms," Tad told her practically as he reached over to the other side of the double bed where he should have been sleeping had theirs been a normal marriage and rumpled the covers there, too.

"Shouldn't you be making that bed, not mussing it up? Since it's going to be photographed and all," Abby questioned him.

Tad inclined his head at the ringing doorbell. "No time. Besides, this is a Before picture and we want it to look as bad as possible so that the After one will look even better," he told her. "What time is the designer you selected to supervise this project supposed to get here?"

"Same time as Sonny." Abby glanced at her watch. "Right now." Abby lifted the hem of the bedspread. "Have you seen my beige pumps? Never mind." She knelt to get them and heard the first tiny rip of a skirt seam. "Here they are."

Better not bend down like that again, Abby thought just as the doorbell rang again.

Oblivious to the damage Abby had done to her skirt, Tad stepped around another huge stack of files, three unpacked suitcases and several boxes of her belongings that had been sent from the New York apartment she'd had to let go and headed for the door. "I'll get it."

Abby nodded. Praying her skirt would hold through the photo session, she said calmly, "I'll be right down."

"WHOA, THIS IS SOME MESS you got here," Sonny said as he extracted the camera from the case and looked around.

"Tell me about it," Tad agreed grimly as he led Sonny into a living room packed with an assortment of his and hers moving crates.

Call me a fool, Tad thought, but when he'd asked Abby to share his dream with him, he'd expected them to be together twenty-four hours a day. The reality was they rarely saw each other. Abby was always on the phone, out of the office, working at home or off on appointment, lining up freelancers and even a dietitian to do a cooking column. And while he appreciated the gusto with which she was doing her job, as her husband and the man who'd once made passionate love to her—and was dying to do so again—he felt very neglected.

Sonny snapped several pictures of the disorganized heaps of carpet, tile, wallpaper and paint samples that covered much of the spacious front hallway. "Abby really likes to get into her work, doesn't she?" he remarked.

"You got that right," Tad murmured, aware it was taking a real effort on his part not to feel completely disgruntled.

The truth was if he'd known how thoroughly Abby would throw herself into the job as Lifestyle editor, he never would have offered it to her. As it was, she worked until she crawled into bed, exhausted, and then slept for ten or sometimes even twelve hours straight, only to wake and start the same routine all over again. When they did talk, it was about business and little else.

And while part of him admired her dedication, another part was increasingly frustrated and ticked off. He wanted to kiss her and remind her what it was like to be really married to him, the way they'd been married that first glorious night, but he'd made a promise to allow them to get to know each other first. The only problem was she wasn't letting him get close to her. In fact, he felt more removed from her than ever.

Delicate feminine footsteps sounded on the stairs. Seconds later Abby swept into the room, looking more beautiful than ever. "Hey, Ab," Sonny said, "ready to get those pictures taken?"

"Sure." Abby grinned warmly. "Just make sure you're focusing on the rooms, not us."

"Easier said than done," Sonny said, looking down into his lens, "'cause the camera loves you."

That, Tad could believe. Just as he could imagine what Sonny was clearly so struck by. From her glowing tresses, sparkling eyes, graceful movements and luminous skin, there wasn't an inch of Abby that wasn't both gorgeous and compelling. It didn't matter what she wore or how she did her hair, whether she was in shorts and a T-shirt, with her hair drawn up in a bouncy ponytail on the back of her head, or—like now—wearing crisp tailored clothing and high-heeled pumps that showed off her spectacular legs. She was sexy as hell. So sexy, in fact, that he was in a constant state of arousal whenever he was around her. The knowledge she was carrying his child made it even more difficult to control himself.

Politically correct or not, he wanted to take her and make her his, again and again and again. And he was still thinking about it as Abby led a madly photographing Sonny through the entire first floor, then up the broad front staircase to the master bedroom and bath.

"Whoa. Is this a bedroom or an office?" Sonny asked, stepping around the piles of work, a half-dozen as-yet-unpacked boxes of Abby's stuff from New York and two open overflowing suitcases.

"Both," Abby said.

Sonny quirked an amazed brow. "Some honeymoon, huh?" he said, guessing—correctly—that not much besides work went on here.

Which was, Tad noted, exactly what Abby wanted him to think. That was not, however, the impression Tad wanted to leave. Nor was it a situation he wanted continued.

Knowing it was bound to tick off his wife, yet feeling bound to provoke things a little, anyway, since she'd already done the same, Tad laced a proprietorial arm about Abby's shoulders. Ignoring the way she stiffened almost imperceptibly at his touch, he tucked her close to his side.

Watch it, her simmering look said.

No, you watch, his look said right back.

Planting his other hand on the small of her back, he trapped her against him. "Hey, there's no rule that says you have to make love in a bed," he said, lowering his head to hers. Caressing her lips with his eyes, he continued softly, "Red-hot loving can happen anywhere." *Like Paris.* Wanting to remind Abby of that, lest she forget everything good that had happened between them before they'd quickly and foolishly jumped into marriage, Tad threw caution to the wind and kissed her soundly. At the touch of their lips, she melted in his arms, just the way he'd thought she would.

"Now that's a honeymoon." Sonny sighed enviously, snapping photos of that, too.

Ignoring the flash and whir of the camera, Tad gave in to the bittersweet pangs of desire and the urge to be close to her again. How long had it been, he wondered, shifting his hands to the soft skin of her upturned face, since he'd wanted anything even half as much as he wanted Abby? How long since he'd ached with pleasure and been more drawn to the present and the future than haunted by the past?

As Sonny came closer, still snapping photos manically, Abby groaned low in her throat and pushed against Tad's chest.

Reluctantly he broke off the kiss. Abby's eyes were liquid pools of fire, reminding him that she had not agreed to have another honeymoon with him here. Which was just too bad, Tad thought, on yet another whisper of regret. Because he wanted one and thought they should have one.

"Back to the tour," Abby ordered.

She could hold him—and the possibility of making love again—off for a while. But not, if that scorching kiss was any indication, forever, Tad knew.

"So how much of this stuff is going to stay and how much is going to be hauled to the junkyard?" Sonny asked as he wandered into the bedroom-turned-study across the hall and paused to take an up-close-and-personal-photograph of an ugly brown Naugahyde recliner.

"That's yet to be decided," Abby said, knowing that was one piece that was definitely going to have to go.

"But the chair'll go to the dump, right?" Sonny said.

If she had her way? "Absolutely," Abby said.

"Not on your life," Tad said. "This chair stays. It has history." It was not only where he'd been sleeping ever since he'd been back in Blossom, it was also his first ever furniture purchase. He'd had it all through his college days, and it had been in storage ever since. Now that he finally had a home, after all those years as a roving reporter, he wanted it with him; he wanted it in a place of honor. Abby, however, refused to understand that. To her it was just a piece of furniture that was hopelessly out-of-date.

"I'm thinking attic or garage," Abby said.

Tad smiled, as willing to wage war on this as she was. "I'm thinking main-floor living room," he countered.

"There isn't an interior designer in the world who'd agree to that," Abby replied hotly, "never mind consult for free and put her name to a room with that piece of history in it."

Tad had the sense Abby wanted to pick a fight with him. More surprising, he wanted to pick one with her, too. He kept his eyes level on hers. "The chair stays," he said firmly.

Abby glared at him. "Not it if messes up my first big series for the new Lifestyle section, it doesn't."

"Hey," Sonny said, grinning, as he snapped a couple of photos of the two of them squaring off toe-to-toe. "A lovers' tiff. Great. Maybe we can put this in the paper, too!" he crowed victoriously.

"Like hell we will," Tad growled as the doorbell sounded again downstairs. "There are some things, kid, that stay private."

On that, Abby quite agreed. She didn't want any of her private life played out for the newspapers the way her famous parents' various highs and lows had been. Glad to be able to change the subject, she glanced at her watch. "That's probably the interior designer," Abby said.

"You finish showing Sonny around. I'll bring the designer up." Tad hurried off.

"He's a little testy about the chair, isn't he?" Sonny said as he walked into the room that would one day be their child's nursery and took photos of that, too.

"Tad's putting a lot of pressure on himself to make

this paper a success,'' Abby explained. Worse, she had the feeling that this living-together business was not exactly how either of them had envisioned it.

When she'd agreed to stay, she'd expected them to live together but still go their own separate ways. And while that was true to a point—Tad had been busy covering various community events, introducing himself and his plans for the paper via editorials, and penning much of the routine news—he had also been reveling in his newfound status as brand-new husband and father to be in a way that surprised her. For on that score, Abby knew, much to her own discomfiture, he had the unabashed envy of many of the men in town.

Worse, newlywed jokes—like the one Sonny had just made about the lovers' tiff—had abounded wherever they went, and Tad did nothing to discourage them. Instead, to her mounting exasperation, he seemed to welcome the kidding around with an audacious smile and a twinkle in his eyes that left no doubt as to the libidinous nature of his thoughts. Or his joy over the baby they were expecting.

Abby felt a mounting joy and anticipation, too. It went without saying that the day she and Tad welcomed their baby into the world would be among the happiest in their lives. But the fishbowl atmosphere of the small town reminded her of the past and made her want to bury herself in her work all the more. There was safety there, in the acquisition, writing and editing of various articles. There was no safety in their relationship when she knew—because of the hurried way it had come about and because he would only let her get so close to him—that it was doomed to end.

Not that this stopped her from fantasizing about what might have been if only they'd shared the same dreams and aspirations, Abby mused while Sonny took photos of the attic. She often found herself wondering what it would take to get Tad to give up this pipe dream and go back to New York so she could find another job and resume her career as a magazine editor. With his experience and reputation, she knew Tad would have no trouble finding a job at a big-city newspaper. And if they were both living in the same area, they could stay together permanently, just as they'd originally planned.

But he wasn't willing to compromise, Abby reminded herself grimly. Instead, he expected her to give up everything to follow his dream. And that just wasn't fair. And there were other things that bugged her, too, she thought as she led Sonny back downstairs. Like the way he was always pushing milk and vitamin supplements on her. And while he'd said he would give her free rein over the house decor, he hadn't told her that he wanted to keep every ragged piece of furniture and memorabilia he'd had in storage since his college days. A fact that made her job overseeing the redecoration of their home all that much harder.

But maybe, Abby thought, as she strode toward the lovely thirty-something woman in red standing in the front hall chatting with Tad, Donna Delaney would be able to help.

Tad looked up at her, surprised. "You didn't tell me you'd hired Donna."

"Do you two know each other?" Abby said, amazed at the camaraderie between them.

Donna threw back her head and laughed. "Do we!"

Chapter Five

"We're old fishing buddies," Tad explained.

Donna nodded. "We met one year when Tad was on one of his solo summer visits to see his aunt Sadie."

"I used to spend a couple of weeks here with Sadie every summer no matter where my parents were living at the time," Tad said.

"And those visits became even more important after…" Donna caught Tad's look and the subtle but unmistakable wish she not confide more. An understanding that eluded Abby passed between them, then Donna shrugged and—to Abby's frustration—continued in a low friendly tone, "Well, anyway, we lost touch about ten years ago when Tad stopped coming around for those long visits with Sadie and my folks moved to Charlotte."

"And let's not forget your marriage," Tad said, grinning. Arms braced on either side of him, his ankles crossed in front of him, he relaxed against the banister. "Donna was just showing me pictures of her husband, Ron, and their three kids." He cast Donna an admiring almost envious glance that reminded Abby how much he wanted the baby she was carrying inside her. "You've got quite a crew there."

"Thanks." Donna beamed. "They really keep me

hopping. You and Abby will have to come by sometime and meet them."

"Look forward to it," Tad said. He straightened and turned to Sonny. Suddenly both men were braced for action. "Ready to go out and get the pictures of the garage and that wilderness we call a backyard?"

Sonny nodded. The two men left, talking about what Tad proposed they shoot.

"You didn't tell me you knew Tad," Abby said as she began to walk Donna through the main floor. As she stepped over a stack of papers, she heard another little rip and felt her skirt seam widen another inch.

Donna acknowledged this was so with a glittering smile. "I wanted to get this job on my own merit if I got it. I didn't want anyone accusing me of pulling strings." She paused and gave Abby a woman-to-woman look. "I hope you don't mind."

"Not at all," Abby said, respecting the path Donna had taken even as jealousy stirred inside her at the thought of Tad with another woman, even way back when. Which meant what? she wondered, stunned by the unfamiliar emotion. That she was more possessive of Tad and the brief passionate affair they'd had than she knew?

Abby swallowed as her skirt slipped a little lower on her hips, thanks to the ever-widening rip in the seam. Discreetly Abby pressed a hand over the tear. "So were you as surprised as everyone else when Tad bought the *Blossom Weekly News?*" Abby asked Donna as she tried, through the fabric of her jacket, to keep the unraveling side seam of her skirt together.

"Not really." On the other side of Abby, Donna smiled as she removed a pen and pad from her briefcase and began to take notes. "Tad's always been the kind of guy who wants to try everything once. That's why I wasn't surprised when I heard he'd become a roving reporter years ago. The job suited him perfectly. He could see every part of the world, get clued in to what was happening there and then move on to the next adventure.''

And then move on to the next adventure. Was that what she and the baby were? Abby wondered. The next adventure?

"Were you surprised to hear he was married?" Abby asked, praying her skirt would stay together long enough to get through this meeting. Like it or not, she was really going to have to get some maternity clothes.

"No." Donna's green eyes sparkled with an almost sisterly affection. "He was always a big hit with the babes. And he absolutely adored kids. Still does. But then, you probably know that from the amount of articles he's done on children and children's issues around the world."

Actually Abby hadn't known that. Which just went to show, she thought as she led the way upstairs to the second floor and felt her skirt slip another inch, how little she and Tad really knew about each other.

The next few minutes were taken over by talk about the house. To Abby's delight, Donna's view of what could and should be done matched hers to an enviable degree, and they were still bubbling over with plans when Tad and Sonny came back in looking equally satisfied with the way things were going.

Tad smiled at Donna. "So, we'll see you at the open house at seven o'clock, then?" he asked her.

"Absolutely," Donna said. "And I'll bring my portfolio, too."

Was she the only one who hadn't a clue what they were talking about? Abby wondered, confused. She shot a look at Tad, then turned to Sonny and Donna. "What open house?"

"You know, at the paper tonight," Sonny said. "We're all supposed to be there with bells and whistles on."

"No, I didn't know," Abby enunciated carefully.

"We've been talking about it all week at the staff meetings," Tad explained.

Most of which Abby had missed in her attempts to avoid spending too much time with her new husband. Nevertheless Tad could have told her about it, couldn't he? Unless he'd been trying to make a point by deliberately leaving her out.

"That's right," Sonny said thoughtfully as he put his cameras away. "You weren't there, were you?"

"No, I wasn't." Abby forced a smile and saved face as best she could. "But it sounds like a good idea."

"We thought it would help drum up advertising," Tad said as their eyes connected briefly.

Donna glanced at her watch. "I want to take a quick look at the backyard and then I've got to head over to the pool to get the kids before I swing on home." She dashed off.

Sonny said, "I've got all I need."

Seconds later both had exited and Abby and Tad were left alone. Tad held her glance. And suddenly saw just how steamed she was at having been left out of the loop. He grimaced unhappily. "I've done it now, haven't I?" he said.

Knowing she had to get her ripped skirt off before it slid down her hips and fell off, Abby turned on her heel and headed for the stairs, her high heels making a sharp staccato on the polished wood floor.

"What, no comment?" he said, following.

Abby turned and shot him a sharp look over her shoulder, then raced up the stairs, her hips swaying provocatively beneath her skirt. "I don't know what you're talking about."

"I thought you knew," he told her grimly.

Abby gritted her teeth and stared around her morosely. The house that had seemed so full of possibilities only minutes earlier, now seemed like a metaphor for the confused state of her life. She kicked off her heels, stepped out of her ripped skirt, tossed it on the bed and folded her arms. "Obviously."

Outwardly Abby looked calm, but Tad knew her well enough to realize she was about to explode. He was sorry he was responsible for the stress. He wasn't sorry he had asked her to work with him on the newspaper. It was not only a good challenge for them both professionally, it was an activity that was guaranteed to give them much satisfaction and bring them much closer probably by the time the baby was born. But for the moment they had this calamity to work through.

Reluctantly he tore his eyes from the sight of her shapely, stocking-clad legs. He could still recall how they'd felt wrapped around his waist. He wanted to feel them there again.

"It's not as if you've missed anything," he told Abby calmly as hot excited color poured into her cheeks. "Nothing's happened yet. You can still be there—"

"How do you know?" Abby interrupted, her golden-brown eyes flashing as she tore off her jacket, too.

They squared off in silence as Abby slipped back into the short kimono robe. "Can you be there?" Tad asked finally, reminded by the way she was standing, feet planted slightly apart, fists propped on her hips, that his wife never gave an inch without a major battle of wills.

Luckily he liked a challenge. And if there was one thing Abby Kildaire McFarlane was, he thought admiringly, it was a challenge.

"Does it matter?" Abby glared at him, the pouting thrust of her lower lip letting him know she felt furious, humiliated and embarrassed by the oversight.

He cleared a place on the rumpled covers of the bed and sat down. "Don't be like that."

Abby didn't want to, but given what had just transpired, she was unable to help feeling hurt and a little left out. Plus, like it or not, there was the larger problem of what to wear. Business attire was called for. And she had just ripped the very last skirt she could fit into.

"The open house is in two hours," she reported grimly. Worse, the closest maternity store was a good forty-five-minute drive away. Not that this was all Tad's fault. She really should have taken the time to shop before this situation came up. But it was too late now for regrets.

Tad continued to look perplexed. "Do you want to skip it?" he asked. "Because if you do, I'll cover for you."

The fight went out of Abby as swiftly as it had come. Exhausted, she sat down next to Tad on the side of the bed. "No, I don't want to skip it," she said wearily. "But unless I suddenly find myself able to conjure up a dress out of a bed sheet, I really can't go. I don't have anything I can fit into except a pair of jogging shorts, and that would hardly do."

"The suit you just had on was a knockout."

Wordlessly Abby handed him the skirt and pointed out the rip. "Why didn't you say so?" Tad folded her skirt neatly and handed it back to her. "I can solve this problem for you." It was one of the few things he could do.

"I don't know how," Abby retorted.

Tad winked. "I'll show you," he told her confidently. Five minutes later he revealed the "surprise" a little early. "Luckily Aunt Sadie had already finished the first dress," he told Abby. "She's bringing it over right away."

"She's really planning to sew a whole wardrobe for me?" Abby asked, amazed by the surprise Tad's aunt had been planning. Her own parents had never done anything for her themselves they could hire out.

Tad nodded. "This is her first grandnephew or niece. She's very excited. And she wanted to welcome you into the family."

Abby told herself it was the unexpected thoughtfulness of the gesture—not the idea of really becoming a part of his family and spending a lifetime with Tad here in Blossom—that had her head swimming and her heart beating triple time. "That's really nice," Abby said appreciatively. Incredibly nice.

"No doubt about it. Aunt Sadie is one fine lady." Tad slipped his fingers beneath Abby's chin, lifted her face and studied her eyes. His own eyes softened as he leaned forward and gently kissed her cheek. "And in case I haven't told you lately...so are you."

TWENTY MINUTES LATER Abby stood in front of the mirror. As Abby had anticipated, Aunt Sadie was an excellent seamstress. The only problem was, as far as maternity dresses went, Aunt Sadie was stuck firmly in another era. The bright pink dress was covered with fat white polka dots and featured a white Peter Pan collar, puffed sleeves that threatened to overwhelm the entire dress and a huge bow. Made to be worn right up until the day of delivery, the tea-length dress fell in voluminous folds that literally threatened to swallow Abby whole. She looked both fat and ridiculous. So ridiculous she didn't know how she was going to muster the courage to model the garment in her own home.

Tad shut the bedroom door behind him. He headed straight for her. As he neared her, he rolled his eyes. "It's hideous, isn't it?" he whispered bluntly.

Abby was unable to take her eyes off her reflection. "Oh, I wouldn't say that," she murmured, her humorous expression mirroring how they both felt. "If I were Lucy Ricardo or June Cleaver," she quipped, "this would have been a great dress."

Tad continued to regard her skeptically. "Look, you don't have to wear it. I'll just go down and talk to Aunt Sadie."

Abby thought about the hours of work that had gone into this and curled a hand around his biceps before he could depart. "No, Tad, don't," she said, her fingers warming to the solid feel of his flesh. "You'll hurt her feelings." And that was the last thing in the world Abby wanted.

"I know, but—"

"But nothing," Abby said firmly, already thinking of ways to accessorize the dress to make it a little more current. "She's your aunt. And she did this out of love for both of us." Abby smiled at him warmly. "I'll wear it."

"THERE'S SOMETHING your husband needs to understand and, quite frankly, doesn't," Joe Don Jerome told Abby at the open house. Dressed in an all-white summer suit, white boater-style hat, white shirt, white shoes and black bow tie, the only used- and new-car dealer in Blossom was as flamboyant in person as he was in his humorous television commercials. "It isn't good for business when he prints inflammatory letters to the editor like the one he ran last week."

"There are no crooks in Blossom," Nowell Haines, a buttoned-up banker in a three-piece suit continued, sweat glistening on his brow.

Cullen Marshall, who was known as much for his bad toupee as the insurance policies he sold, said smugly, "Your hubby never should've started that Troubleshooter hot line, either."

Nowell Haines nodded as he mopped his face with a handkerchief. "Businesses around here don't need to be investigated."

There Abby disagreed, as did the rest of the *Blossom Weekly* staff.

"Particularly when those same businesses supply a lot of his advertising revenue for this newspaper," Joe Don Jerome told Abby flatly.

"And, as the little woman in this situation," Cullen Marshall continued, "you undoubtedly have a lot of influence over that new hubby of yours." Well, that, Abby thought, was a matter of opinion. She couldn't think of a single thing she could dissuade Tad from doing if he really had his heart set on it.

"And now that you know how things are done by those in the know here…" Cullen began when Tad sauntered over to join the four of them. He wrapped an arm around Abby's waist and tugged her close. Everywhere they touched, Abby felt solid male muscle.

"Gentlemen." Tad nodded at Joe Don, Nowell and Cullen, then looked at Abby as though she was the only woman in the world. "What's going on, darlin'?"

Cullen Marshall adjusted his toupee, elbowed his way forward and cut in before Abby had a chance to answer.

"We were just explaining to your wife here why it'd be smart of you not to stir up any more trouble, running unsigned letters to the editor in the town newspaper."

"'Cause if you do," his buddy Nowell Haines warned, "we might be forced to pull our advertising."

Tad smiled like a shark in a wading pool and studied the trio of businessmen skeptically. "Is that so?" he countered pleasantly, a warning to back off—now—underlying his low tone.

"You better believe it," Joe Don Jerome replied, stepping forward and flashing Tad a crocodile grin of his own. His eyes narrowed maliciously as he continued threatening Tad with grating Southern charm. "'Cause we know you put your life savings into this. And we'd all just hate to see you lose your shirt."

Tad remained unimpressed. "I wouldn't worry about it," he drawled.

"Do the right thing and you won't have anything to worry about," Cullen Marshall warned smoothly as the three businessmen moved off.

As soon as they did, Abby released a long breath. She hadn't realized until the three businessmen left how tense they'd been making her.

Tad kissed her head just above her ear. "Are you okay?" he asked.

There was no doubt she felt a lot safer in his arms. Staying cozily within his protective grip, Abby turned to him. "You're the one who should be worried," she murmured, looking up into his handsome face.

"About the Three Stooges?"

As Abby watched them leave the building, a shiver ran through her. "They're angry, Tad."

"They are also most likely crooks. Otherwise they wouldn't be so worried."

Abby bit her lower lip. Aware she didn't know quite as much about Tad's financial situation as she'd like, she continued to regard him steadily. "Can they put you out of business?"

"Not unless I let them," Tad told her confidently as he led her toward the refreshment table and paused to pour them both some lemonade. "And I don't intend to let them."

"How much revenue do you get from the ads they place?" she asked quietly.

Tad helped himself to a flaky cheese puff from Audrey's Bakery and Café down the street. "In the past their ads have paid for nearly twenty percent of every issue." He handed Abby one, too.

"Ouch." Abby bit into the fragrant flaky appetizer.

"Yeah," Tad said, now helping himself to a stuffed mushroom cap. "But I don't want their dirty money. Besides, I had two new advertisers sign up this evening already."

"That's great." Abby sampled the quiche squares.

"And we'll have even more signing on when we get the Lifestyle section up and running."

The rest of the evening was a blur of introductions and question-and-answer sessions. By the time Tad and Abby picked up a pizza and salad and got home at ten-thirty, she was exhausted. Tad poured the milk while she brought out the plates. Both kicked off their shoes. They settled down on the sofa and dug in.

Tad playfully nudged her thigh with his. "Did I mention how pretty you looked tonight?"

Abby blushed and rolled her eyes. She'd done her best to accessorize the outfit, but even with her hair down and a white summer sweater over her shoulders, she was acutely aware she'd still looked like the heroine out of a fifties TV sitcom.

"I'm serious," Tad said gently as they clinked their milk glasses together in a silent toast. "Most women couldn't have managed to look thoroughly competent and professional in a dress like that, but somehow you did. Whenever you talked about your plans for the Lifestyle section, you just glowed."

"You looked and sounded pretty excited yourself," she said. In fact, it was impossible not to get excited about the prospects for the future when Tad spoke about his plans for the newspaper.

"It was really nice of you to wear that dress," he continued.

Abby shrugged. "No nicer than Sadie making it for me," she said as their eyes met.

"Speaking of Sadie—" Tad grinned "—she got a promotion tonight. She's going to be doing some writing for the newspaper, too. So she's not going to have time to sew any more dresses for you. I told her that was okay because I'm driving you to the closest maternity shop first thing tomorrow morning. And I'm going to do my husbandly duty and make sure you're outfitted properly from head to toe."

Abby considered this while she munched on her pizza. "And she wasn't hurt?"

"No, excited." Tad smiled. "I also told her we needed some hand-sewn quilts and blankets and sheets for the baby's room. So she's going to talk to you and Donna about color schemes and get right on that."

Abby shook her head in silent admiration. "That was really nice of you," she said softly at last.

Tad put his plate aside and pulled her onto his lap so that her bottom was nestled snugly in the warm hard cradle of his thighs. "Don't you know there isn't anything I wouldn't do for you?" he said tenderly as he sifted his hands through her hair.

"Tad..." Abby groaned as his sexy bedroom eyes met and held hers again.

"Abby..." He mocked her lightly, then lowered his head and took her mouth in a searing kiss. Abby moaned. Tad deepened the kiss and wrapped his arms around her, the pressure of his hands on her back bringing her intimately close. A torrent of need swept through her, sending all her senses into an uproar. It felt so good to be wanted and touched again, Abby thought. Desire trembled inside her, making her insides go all warm and syrupy.

Tad made a low contented sound in the back of his throat. "I'm ready to make love anytime." He brushed the hair from her nape. His warm breath caressed the skin of her neck, sending yet another shiver of desire coursing through her.

"All you have to do is let me know you've changed your mind, and we'll turn this into a real marriage."

But was that true? Abby wondered without warning, a tidal wave of conflicting feelings surging through her. Whether she wanted to admit it or not, there was still so much she didn't know about Tad. Things that Sadie— and perhaps even his old friend Donna—knew. Like what had happened in Houston. If they wanted to have a chance of making things work for the long haul, the two of them had to get to know each other first and form a friendship that was so strong, so enduring, it would last the lifetime of their child. She knew Tad well enough now to realize that wouldn't happen if she let them be distracted by passionate sex.

"I'll just bet you are." She sighed wistfully, a part of

her wishing she could still be as foolish and impetuous and driven by passion as they had been in Paris. But with a baby on the way—their baby—that was no longer possible. Like it or not, Abby told herself sternly, she had to be responsible. Her child's happiness—and hers and Tad's—depended on it.

"But?" Tad prodded as his black brows drew together.

Reluctantly Abby reminded herself they were only in this predicament because she'd rushed into bed with Tad. She was far too savvy to make the same mistake again. "But we have to get up very early tomorrow if we're going to go clothes shopping together before we head to the paper."

Tad tensed from head to toe. "So no go," he guessed, disappointed.

"No go," Abby confirmed, delivering a look meant to quell him into submission even as she wished she weren't so damn susceptible to his kisses.

He loosened his hold on her. While he accepted her decision, clearly he was not giving up. "You know where I'll be if you change your mind," he told her as he lightly, triumphantly kissed her forehead one last time.

Yes, Abby thought, sighing wistfully as her still-tingling body continued to telegraph its regret. That was the problem—she did.

Chapter Six

"You're not playing fair," Abby told Tad late the next morning as she cornered him in the supply room at the rear of the building.

Figuring this was one conversation the rest of the staff did not need to hear, Tad shut the door behind him and put down the package of yellow legal pads he'd been about to tear open. He took his time getting to her side. "What do you mean?"

Abby tossed her head imperiously. Color swept into her cheeks. She pursed her bow-shaped lips together. "Asking everyone how to sex up the copy during the staff meeting."

"I think the word I used was jazz," Tad corrected, amused and pleased to see he'd gotten under her skin just as he'd hoped. "Jazz things up."

"Then you went on to say sex sells."

Tad braced his shoulder against the wall and tilted his head down at her. "It does. Everything from toothpaste to cars to beer."

Abby rolled her eyes in exasperation. "I'm not arguing that."

"Furthermore," Tad continued, more aware than ever how pretty and pulled-together she looked with her golden-brown hair fastened by a stylish silver barrette at the nape of her slender neck, "no one else seemed to mind."

Abby folded her arms militantly and leaned back against the wall. "That's because they were full of ideas about features on the most romantic places to dine, what kind of mattresses were best and where to go on dates in the good old summertime."

Tad stepped close enough to inhale the intoxicating vanilla fragrance of her perfume. "Cindy's idea about starting a G-rated Personals column was a good one, don't you think?"

"Yes. I'm sure it'll cause quite a stir."

He looked into her eyes, deliberately holding her gaze, daring her to look away. "Then what's the problem?" He was tired of putting his desire for her on hold, and yet he didn't want to hurt her. He didn't want her thinking that the only reason he wanted them to stay married was the baby they were expecting, because it just wasn't true. He'd wanted her from the first moment he'd laid eyes on her and he still did. The question was, how could he make her believe it? Not just in her head but in her heart.

"Like you don't know exactly what I'm so fired up about."

His expression all innocence, Tad flattened his hands over his chest. "I don't." And it was true.

"Then I'll spell it out for you, my dear husband." Abby propped both her hands on her trim hips. "It was the way you've been looking at me all morning long!"

Ahhh. Now they were getting somewhere. He touched her face with his callused palm, cupping her chin in his hand, running his thumb across her lower lip. "Like I wanted to put my arms around you and kiss you again?"

"Yes!"

"Can't help that." Tad shrugged and dropped his hand. "It's the way I feel."

Abby glared at him, refusing to back down. "Tad, this was a staff meeting," she admonished with a weariness that went all the way to her soul.

"We're all one big family here. I thought I'd made that clear." Plus, everyone—except Abby, it seemed—knew he was head over heels in love with his wife and always would be, no matter how this hasty marriage of theirs turned out.

Abby turned away from him stubbornly. "Yes, you did."

"Then you also know that no one else seemed to mind if every once in a while there was a spark or two between us."

"A spark!" Abby echoed. "More like a bonfire!"

So, Tad thought, pleased he was getting to her. Maybe more than he'd realized.

"Did I tell you how much I like what you're wearing?" That morning, before they'd gone shopping, she'd asked to borrow one of his shirts and a tie. Curious to see what she was going to do, he'd opened up his closet and given her free rein. She'd selected a jade green twill dress shirt and a jade, black and amber necktie and later paired both with a pair of dressy black maternity slacks and leather flats.

Abby sighed and fiddled with the hem of his loose-fitting shirt. "You probably think I should be wearing one of those maternity blouses we purchased for me this morning."

Tad grinned and shook his head. That wasn't the case at all. He loved the idea of her in his clothes. The buttoned-up look was damn sexy on her. He even liked the way she'd rolled up the cuffs twice to make the sleeves the proper length for her. "You look a lot better in that shirt and tie than I ever did," he said. And he understood Abby's reluctance to make the leap to total maternity wear just yet, when she was showing only a little bit. He curled a hand about her waist and guided her close. "You look…very sexy in a Katharine Hepburn sort of way," he said, kissing her cheek. "What's even sexier is this." He slid a hand beneath her shirt and caressed her tummy.

Abby sighed and melted against him. Tad gave in to a whim and touched her face with the back of his hand. It felt like hot silk beneath his flesh, softer than the petals on the bouquet of roses he'd bought for her their first night in Paris. He let his hand slide beneath her hair to the nape of her neck. He tilted her face up to his. The way she looked at him then—all soft and wanting and vulnerable—made his heart pound even harder. This was tough on her, too. Tough on both of them. He knew she needed him, even if she wouldn't yet let herself admit it.

"I meant what I said last night," he told her softly, guiding her closer still. "There isn't anything I wouldn't do for you." He knew damn well there would be hell to pay later, but right now he couldn't help himself. Abby was his wife, she was carrying their child, and he wanted her more than life itself. He lowered his lips to hers, slanted his mouth over hers and poured everything he felt, everything he wanted, into the slow leisurely caress.

Abby moaned, soft and low in her throat. Her hands came up to ineffectually push at his chest, then ended up wrapped around his neck. He felt the need pouring out of her, mingling with the desire and the tenderness that was so much a part of her, too. And knew no matter what happened, he would never get enough of her.

Abby hadn't meant this to happen. But then, she

thought, as Tad kissed her with a thoroughness that shook her to her very soul, she never did. The yearning that swept through her was almost unbearable. Her breasts ached and burned for the nimble play of his fingers while lower still she longed to be as one. Moaning, she chalked up her wantonness to pregnancy hormones and surrendered to the need pouring through her. She stopped fighting him, fighting this, and let herself go. Threading her hands through his hair, she kissed him back passionately, wildly, until everywhere their bodies touched, liquid fire pooled.

And that was when it happened. When the door swung open behind them and an unsuspecting Sadie barged in.

"Whoops!" Sadie said, laughing and clapping an astonished hand to her face.

"Honeymooners," said Raymond, who was standing behind her and chuckling, too. He shook his head. "When we noticed the two of them had disappeared, we should've known."

"YOU CAN STOP blushing now," Sadie told Abby as they went over the layout for the next edition of the paper. "It was only a little kiss."

Using her computer mouse, Abby changed the positions of two of the articles. "There's no such thing as a little kiss from Tad," she grumbled. Each one knocked her socks off.

"So? I know we're at work, but no one here minds," Sadie was quick to reassure her. "In fact, we all kind of enjoy watching the sparks fly between the two of you." She looked at Abby closely. "The question is, why are you holding that nephew of mine at arm's length?" She held up a hand, silencing Abby's protest. "I'd have to be an idiot not to notice the yearning looks and touches and near kisses. Yet he doesn't seem to act on any of those very often."

"It's complicated" was all Abby could say.

"Not that complicated," Sadie replied firmly. She pulled up her chair so the two of them were sitting knee to knee and took Abby's hands in hers. "Listen to me, sweetheart. When I was your age, I thought just the way you're thinking. But now I know. True love comes along so rarely. Maybe once in a lifetime." Sadie sighed wistfully. "I've never had it, much to my regret. But if I had ever felt the magic that you and Tad are feeling," she said firmly, laying a hand across her heart, "I sure as heck wouldn't squander it."

Was that what she was doing? Abby wondered uncomfortably. Or was she merely being practical and saving them all from more hurt?

"Is it my imagination or are Sadie and Raymond attracted to each other?" Abby asked Tad that night as they sifted through the three proposed decors for the entryway and living room—the first rooms Donna was proposing they redo for the newspaper.

Tad picked up a swatch of wall-to-wall Berber carpet and compared it to a sketch of an Oriental rug over a hardwood floor that dominated another sketch. As he studied both thoughtfully, he said, "I think there's definitely something going on there. Raymond's been a widower for the last ten years, you know. He never had any kids, either, and he said something to me the other day about being really tired of the bachelor life."

Abby dropped a swatch of drapery fabric meant to go with the Oriental rug. "You think he was talking about getting something going with Sadie?"

Tad shrugged and sat back on the sofa. "Wouldn't

surprise me. Every time I turn around those two are making up some excuse to go talk to each other.''

Abby discarded a third sketch that favored a stark modern decor. She'd noticed Tad didn't like it much, either. ''Hmm.''

Tad studied her. ''What are you thinking?''

Probably the same thing you are. ''I hope Sadie finds some romance.''

Tad took Abby's hand in his. He turned it palm side up on his knee and absently stroked her open palm from fingertip to wrist. ''It'd be nice, wouldn't it,'' he mused aloud, a hopeful light coming into his eyes, ''if she didn't have to spend her golden years alone?''

''Very.'' Abby clasped Tad's hand in hers, squeezed. ''Although there's the age difference. Raymond is... what?''

Tad frowned. ''Nine years younger than she is.''

Abby sighed. ''Think that might be a problem?''

''I don't know.'' Tad's worried scowl deepened. ''But there's no use borrowing trouble since they don't have anything but a friendship at this point.'' He nodded at the trio of sketches in front of them. ''So what do you think? Should we go with the carpet and the oak furniture, the wood floors and Oriental rugs, or the stark ultramodern look?''

Abby hesitated. ''If you still want to keep your lounge chair and use it to a build a reading corner in the living room—''

''I do,'' Tad said firmly.

''—then I suggest you recover your chair and go with the oak furniture and Berber carpet. But,'' Abby amended quickly, feeling a little guilty for taking such an active part in decisions that were mainly going to affect him, "it really should be your decision since you're the one who's going to be living here for the long haul."

Tad's face changed abruptly. "Right." He let go of her hand and stood abruptly.

Guilt flooded her anew, adding to the confused welter of emotions deep inside her and the disturbing feeling that her life was spinning way out of control. Abby bit her lip. She hadn't meant to hurt him. Neither was she willing to lead him on. She pressed her lips together, able to feel a massive tension headache coming on. "I didn't mean—"

"I know what you meant, Abby," Tad interrupted gruffly.

Abby swallowed and tried again. "I just don't think we should lose sight of our agreement." She forced them both to deal with what she knew they'd both rather leave unsaid. "We have to be practical here," she insisted firmly. *We have to protect ourselves from getting hurt.* And in this one instance her parents were right. Given the hasty impulsive way it had happened, her marriage didn't have a snowball's chance in hell of surviving. Odds were it would be over as soon as their baby was born, if not before.

"Of course. Why didn't I think of that?" Tad grabbed his jacket and headed into the front hall.

Abby followed him. She was determined to get an answer about the decorating details even if he was being difficult. "I have to tell Donna tomorrow if you want this done, photographed and in the paper two weeks from now."

"Then you decide," Tad told her as he grabbed his car keys. "It doesn't really matter to me, anyway. One decor is as good as any other. Just make sure my chair stays—and if it is recovered, it has to be recovered in brown!''

Her heart sinking at the thought of how she'd hurt him when all she'd been doing was trying to protect him, Abby watched him stride out the door. She leaned against the jamb, all too aware that it was late, nearly ten-thirty. ''Where are you going now?'' There wasn't much open in Blossom at that time of night, except one fast-food restaurant and the tavern.

Tad stopped and gave her a look. ''Why should you care? As you've pointed out on more than one occasion, this marriage is only a temporary convenience.''

His angry words hit her like a stab to the heart. She held out a beseeching hand. ''Tad, please,'' she said. ''I don't want to fight with you.''

''I don't want to fight with you, either, which is exactly why I'm leaving.''

Just like her parents had left each other and every spouse they'd had since, Abby thought, as feelings of hurt and disillusionment came back to haunt her anew.

''Don't wait up,'' Tad said indifferently over his shoulder as he climbed into his Jeep.

TAD DROVE AWAY from the white elephant and headed for the outskirts of town. He hadn't told Abby where he was going because he didn't *know* where he was going. He only knew he didn't want to be around people at this moment, and he didn't want to face what was, more and more, looking like the inevitable end to his marriage to Abby.

He knew she felt unstable due to their impulsive marriage, the loss of her job, their relocation to North Carolina and the baby. The truth was, Tad acknowledged to himself as he left the Blossom city limits and headed out into the countryside, he felt the same. His feelings for Abby were not going to change, but that did not mean he could make her love him the way she needed to love him to make their marriage last.

Tad sighed as he turned his Jeep onto yet another winding country road. He was just going to have to find a way to convince her they did belong together, after all, and he was going to have to do that by finding a happy medium and not moving too fast or too slow. The one thing they weren't going to do, he decided firmly as he eased his foot off the accelerator, was talk about it anymore. They had done that enough as it was, to unhappy result.

Tad slowed as he came upon a shiny red pickup truck pulled over to the side of the road. Ernest Lee Scruggs, the head mechanic over at Joe Don Jerome's car dealership was standing with his head under the hood.

Tad parked behind the disabled vehicle and got out. "Hey there, Ernest Lee," Tad said.

The mechanic nodded. "Hey there, yourself," he said grimly.

"That's a new truck, isn't it?" Tad asked.

"You better believe it." Ernest Lee wiped his grease-stained hands on a rag. "It's less than a month old. And it just up and quit on me. The durn thing is deader than a doornail."

Tad regarded the mechanic sympathetically. "Want me to call for a tow truck on my cell phone?"

Ernest Lee sighed and banged the hood down. "Might as well. Thanks, Tad."

Tad made the call. Figuring this was as good a chance as any to see what he could find out about Ernest Lee's boss and whatever sleazy deals Jerome and his two cohorts might be in, Tad leaned against the side of the truck and prepared to wait it out with Ernest Lee.

"I guess you heard I'm not too popular with your boss," Tad said.

Ernest Lee rolled his eyes. "Ain't that the truth."

"They want me to take out my Troubleshooter phone line down at the paper."

"Yeah. I heard."

"Any idea why Joe Don and his buddies would be so opposed to it?"

Ernest Lee continued looking at the side of the road. Was it his imagination, Tad wondered, or was Ernest Lee beginning to look a little tense?

"They probably just don't want you stirring up trouble."

"I wouldn't be creating trouble, Ernest Lee. Just reporting on trouble that already exists. There's a difference."

Ernest Lee was silent. Finally he said, "Joe Don has the only car dealership in town. He talks to Nowell down at the bank and Cullen over at the insurance place and makes sure people that might not otherwise qualify for loans or be able to get insurance get it. That's a good thing."

"If he's running an honest business, it's a good thing," Tad agreed as a pair of headlights appeared in the distance. "If he's not, that's something else again."

"There's my tow truck," Ernest Lee said.

The conversation was over. Tad had managed to get one thing out of Ernest Lee. The Three Stooges were— at the very least—bending the rules to help local residents buy cars. And while that might have been laudable in some cases, Tad had the feeling that there was more going on than just that. And whatever it was, was probably not only benefiting the Three Stooges, but also illegal or unethical as hell. As the only newsman in town, it was up to him to find out what that was. And damned if he wasn't going to do just that, Tad decided firmly, with or without Ernest Lee's help.

"If it was me, I'd forget about Tad's lounge chair, relegate it to some unseen unimportant area of the house, like the attic or the garage, and go with the design scheme that includes the Oriental carpet," Yvonne told Abby over the long-distance line. "But I'm not a home-and-garden editor, who instinctively knows what readers want to see in their homes and yards at any given time. And I'm not the one who's going to be living there. So what gives, kiddo? Why do you really need my advice? And for the record, I don't for one minute buy the story that you need my help with the decor decision."

Abby let out a breath. "Okay, here it is. I feel guilty making a decision on the house since I'm not going to be living here permanently. And yet I know it's what I'm expected to do...on some wifely level." And she had no idea at all about how to be a good wife to Tad or anyone else. She only knew, from watching her parents' numerous marriages fall apart, that when the passion faded and people were left with the reality of a disintegrating relationship, it could get ugly. Ugly enough to destroy everything good and decent that had gone before. Baby or no baby, she did not want that to happen to her and Tad.

Yvonne paused. "Then you're going back to magazine work?"

Like there could be any doubt about that! "Yes," Abby said. "As soon as possible after the baby is born."

Another silence on Yvonne's part, though somewhat briefer. "Have you started looking for a job?"

Abby went to the freezer and got out a pint of Chunky Monkey ice cream. "No. But maybe it's time I got back to that." Maybe that would make her feel like her life was back under control, she thought as she searched in the silverware drawer for a spoon. "Do you know any headhunters?"

"Absolutely. One in particular, too."

Abby put down her ice cream long enough to grab a pen and paper. "Give me her name and number."

They talked a few minutes more, then Abby hung up the phone. Carton of Chunky Monkey in hand, she looked at the trio of designs one more time, realized she'd eaten half the ice cream in one sitting and reluctantly put it away, no decision made. Her stomach still growling hungrily—what was it about pregnancy and these eating binges? she wondered—she went upstairs to bed.

The truth was, she thought as she slipped into her nightgown, part of her very much wanted to see this marriage through. Part of her wanted to know if she could do what her parents had never managed—build something lasting and true in the marriage department. And, had she and Tad not had a baby on the way, had they both still been living their career dreams and working in New York City, maybe she could have risked everything falling apart and them detesting each other in the end if the passion that tempted them now eventually fizzled.

But with their baby coming, their marriage continuing only because of her unexpected pregnancy, common sense dictated she take a much more practical approach. She and Tad had to stay friends; they had to build a lifelong relationship that would enable them to coparent their child effectively. Their baby's happiness depended on it.

So, Abby thought, tears slipping down her cheeks as she climbed into bed, she would have to put aside the remembered passion and nagging temptation and do what she knew to be best—continue to hold Tad at arm's length.

THE HOUSE WAS SILENT, the light in the master bedroom on when Tad finally got home at midnight. Wondering if he was the only one feeling bad about the tension between them earlier, he paused to look in on Abby. She was curled up in the double bed fast asleep. Not wanting to disturb her, he walked soundlessly across the floor to turn off the bedside lamp. And that was when he saw the tracks of tears on her face and knew she'd cried herself to sleep.

Wondering if it was due to the words they'd come close to exchanging earlier or something much deeper, Tad pulled up the cover, and switched off the light.

Maybe she thought he didn't care. Well, he'd fix that first thing tomorrow morning.

"I LIKE THE DECOR with the hardwood floors and Oriental rug for the living room," he told her over breakfast.

Abruptly Abby looked as though she might break into tears. But she didn't. "Good." She drained her milk and stood. "I'll call Donna from the office."

"Want to drive in together?" Tad asked.

Abby shook her head. "I think I'd rather walk." She grabbed her briefcase, headed for the door and slammed the door behind her. Touché, Tad thought. *I walked out on you last night. You walked out on me this morning.* Maybe, if he was really lucky, tonight neither of them would walk out on the other.

Unfortunately it did not look as if that was going to

be the case when he got to the office. Abby was by turns stressed and surly. Midmorning she just got up and grabbed her briefcase. She stopped by his desk on the way out, waited until he got off the phone. "I'm going home."

Tad stood and reached into his pocket for his car keys. He handed them to her, feeling as though he could step on a land mine any second. "You feeling okay?" He studied her face. She seemed awfully flushed.

Abby's golden-brown eyes flashed. She shoved a hand through her hair. "Can't I be in a bad mood every once in a while?" she snapped.

Tad shrugged as activity in the office stopped and all eyes turned their way. "Well, sure you—"

"Good." Abby cut him off autocratically. "Because I am." She handed him back the car keys and said, "Thanks, but I'd rather walk." Then she waved to the rest of the staff. "Later, guys." As she strode toward the door, she tossed off a last parting shot with a wry smile and self-deprecating humor. "Maybe by tonight my hormones will settle back into the nonlethal range."

"If you ask me, that was more than hormones," Sadie said worriedly as soon as Abby had left.

"She's definitely not herself this morning," Cindy said.

Tell me about it, Tad thought. He'd been as nice as he could be all morning and still felt like he was dealing with a lioness on the prowl.

"Are you sure she's feeling okay?" Raymond asked.

No. Tad wasn't. More to the point, he realized uncomfortably, he didn't even know what to look for when it came to danger signs. He found himself in Doc Harlan's office ten minutes later.

Doc listened intently while Tad quickly brought him

up to date. He knew if anyone would know what to do, it was Doc, who'd been married thirty-five years, had six kids and sixteen grandchildren and, according to local lore, handled every moment of it like a pro.

"Sounds like your first instincts were right," Doc conceded. He sat back in his chair and steepled his hands in front of him. "It probably is hormones causing Abby's mood swings. Or it could just be the fact that she's pregnant. Her body and indeed her whole life are both undergoing tremendous changes right now. We men think we understand, but I have a feeling we don't, since we aren't the ones carrying the little one around inside us. So I'm going to give you a few simple rules to follow that should help even things out a bit. Okay?"

"Okay," Tad said. At this point he was willing to try anything. He didn't want Abby crying herself to sleep again or leaving the office in a huff.

Doc held up the index finger on his right hand. "Rule number one—agree with her about everything, no matter what."

Tad leaned forward in his chair. "But—"

"No buts," Doc said from the other side of the desk. "Just agree with her. You'll both be a lot happier. Rule number two—give her presents for no reason, frequently." Doc smiled encouragingly. "You'll be surprised how much that'll help her mood if she knows you're thinking of her. And last but not least, rule number three—and this is very important, Tad—you need to let her know you love her."

Tad knew he did love Abby. But if he told her that now, in her current peevish mood, she'd probably burst into tears. Either that or she'd explain to him that he really didn't love her.

"Because she needs to know you love her whether

she's pregnant or not, young or old, fat or thin, tall or short, already married or just engaged. Once she does, once she feels that in her heart, my guess is she's gonna calm down pretty quickly.'' Doc stood. The advice-giving session over, he clapped him on the shoulder. ''Think you can handle all that?''

Tad nodded. Agree with her, give her presents, tell her that he loved her. It sure sounded simple enough. ''Thanks, Doc.'' Tad shook Doc's hand. ''I really owe you for this one.''

''DID DOC KNOW what to do?'' a worried Sadie asked Tad the moment he walked back through the newspaper doors.

Tad nodded, distracted. ''Yeah,'' he said thoughtfully, sitting down behind his computer. The more he thought about it, the more it made sense to him.

Abby was already a little ticked off at him because he'd kept trying, however subtly, to preempt their agreement and get her back into bed with him. That had seemed—to him—a logical and speedy way to get them feeling close again.

Judging by what Doc had told him about pregnant women needing lots of reassurance and husbandly understanding, that had probably been a mistake. Abby already felt pressured by the many changes in her life. She probably thought sex was all he wanted from her. And though Tad knew nothing could be further from the truth—he wanted Abby in his life, baby or no baby, sex or no sex—he resolved to stop putting the moves on her until she gave him a signal that she wanted them to resume the physical side of their relationship.

Doc was right. Maybe if Abby realized he loved her

for herself and not just the shape of her body or the incredible passion between them, she'd begin to have trust in him, in them, and see they had the potential to make their marriage last a lifetime, after all.

Chapter Seven

Tad tried calling off and on the rest of the morning. Abby was either not there or not answering or talking on the phone and ignoring the call-waiting beep. Whatever the case, Tad had to check on her or go crazy. When lunch hour came, he delegated a breaking story about a potential salmonella outbreak at the Mighty Fine Restaurant to Sonny, then hopped in the Jeep and drove home.

The red, white and blue express-mail truck was just pulling away from the curb as he turned into the driveway. Abby was standing in the doorway. She looked pale and wan and had what appeared to be a receipt in her hands. In deference to the warm and sunny July day, she'd changed into an oversize navy blue T-shirt and matching running shorts that deftly disguised her pregnancy. Her feet were bare and her golden-brown hair had been caught in a bouncy ponytail on top of her head. Color flooding back into her cheeks, she waited while he approached.

"Everything okay?" Tad asked as he followed her into the house.

She shrugged her slender shoulders, her expression noncommittal. The pink spots in her cheeks deepened. She swallowed hard and took a deep breath. "I could ask you the same thing.'' Their eyes met as she folded her arms beneath her breasts. ''What are you doing home?''

''I left some papers here,'' Tad fibbed as he moved close enough to inhale the intoxicating vanilla fragrance of her perfume. He wasn't sure what he'd expected from her today. Recriminations for walking out on her the night before, not telling her where he was going or letting her know when he'd be back. At this point he'd even take the silent treatment. Instead, she seemed determined to let him know she couldn't care less what he did. And that left him feeling panicked.

Determined not to let her know that, however, Tad sauntered into the living room and stepped around his favorite recliner. Recalling his purported mission, he looked around for papers—any papers. ''I tried to let you know I was coming home to pick them up—'' he paused to retrieve a folder of papers from the coffee table he was half-afraid she knew he didn't need ''—but the phone line was busy, I guess.''

Abby put her express-mail receipt and several new copies of her résumé in her briefcase. ''I've been on the phone all morning talking to a headhunter Yvonne recommended.''

The news Abby was now actively pursuing a job hit Tad like a sucker punch to the gut. He was irritated with Abby, but remembering Doc's advice not to upset her, Tad lounged against the back of the sofa and pretended an amiable attitude he couldn't begin to feel. ''Yeah?'' He studied her with growing curiosity. ''What'd she say?''

''She thinks she can get me something, but it'll probably take at least six months,'' Abby replied. ''Meanwhile, she wanted copies of my résumé ASAP, so I printed them out and sent them to her.''

Again Tad feigned approval of her actions. She hadn't left yet, he reassured himself. He still had months to get her to change her mind. Tad spotted the ginger ale and saltine crackers on the coffee table. "You feeling okay?"

Abby tossed her head. "If you must know, no. At least I wasn't earlier." She pivoted on her heel and headed for the kitchen. "I'm starving now."

Now was not the time to be noticing how sexy her legs were or that she was not wearing a bra.

"Feeling better, then?" he asked gently.

"Yeah." Abby smiled. "Plus," she continued happily, "I think I've *finally* figured out why I've been so depressed and moody lately."

Tad had to admit he was very curious about why she'd cried herself to sleep the night before. Aware once again of the overpowering need to comfort her, he watched as she pulled a package of linguine off the shelf and put some water on the stove to boil.

"I'm listening," he said, all the compassion he felt for her reflected in his eyes.

"I think it has to do with the fact that I hadn't started my job search." Her golden-brown eyes serious, Abby moved away from him. "I told myself I'd delayed it because of the pregnancy, because I was so busy here, but I don't think that's why I hesitated at all," she confided as she bent down to get a skillet from the storage bin beneath the stove. As she straightened, she seemed to lose her balance. He moved forward and put out a hand to assist her. The feel of her soft hand in his was enough to make his heart pound, and he longed to kiss and hold her all the more.

Removing her hand from his, Abby turned to put the skillet on the stove. For a moment her eyes narrowed reflectively and her mood turned brooding again. Finally she shook her head, let out a soft self-deprecating sigh, then turned back to him. "I think I was just afraid that I wouldn't get another editing position on par with what I had. I know." She held up a hand before he could interrupt. "It's silly of me to even think that way, not to mention self-defeating, so I've decided to stop," she told him happily, looking up at him with new resolve, "and just have a more positive attitude."

No question, Tad wanted her to feel good about herself and her work. "That's smart," he told her, knowing even as he encouraged her to shoot for her dreams, too, that he still did not want her to leave. Could he help it if he wanted her in his life? he wondered guiltily. For now, forever?

"You're right, it is smart," Abby replied, squaring her shoulders. "Because the future is coming whether I want to think about it or not and I've got a baby to support."

"We both do," Tad reminded her. He only hoped one day soon she would see that this was also something they could do together.

"Right." Abby smiled, relieved to find he understood. "Anyway, I need my work to sustain me, always have, always will, so knowing I'm eventually going to pick up where I left off is a big morale booster." She strode past him and headed for the refrigerator.

What about the work we're doing here? Doesn't that count? Tad wanted to ask. He recalled Doc's advice, the fact Abby had already admittedly been sick once today, and knew he had no choice but to agree with her. "I'm sure it is."

Abby got out the makings for clam sauce. She put butter and garlic in a saucepan and turned the burner up to moderate heat. "In fact, I think if I'd just made finding a new job in my field my number-one priority from the

beginning, I would've felt a lot better from the get go."
Abby paused to add flour and then clam juice, blending
the mixture with a wire whisk.

Tad had known their marriage ultimately might not
work the moment he'd told Abby he'd purchased the
newspaper and intended to move to North Carolina. But
it still stung to see her acting as if they were already on
the road to divorce when they still had a good six and a
half months ahead of them before their baby was born to
try to make things work.

The doorbell rang. Abby looked at Tad. "Are you expecting anyone?"

Tad didn't know if he was glad or sorry about the
interruption. He only knew he didn't want to talk about
her leaving anymore. "No. You?"

She shook her head. Tad went to get it, and a moment
later Sonny and Tim Grau, the owner of the Mighty Fine
Restaurant, came barreling in. Tad knew before one word
was spoken what the visit was probably about.

"You can't do this to me," Tim shouted at Tad angrily, his face turning almost as red as his rust-colored
hair. "Not after all the advertising dollars I gave your
paper."

"Look, I'm sorry if you have a problem down there,
but one thing has nothing to do with the other," Tad said.
The scent of simmering clam sauce filled the air and a
perplexed Abby came out to join them, wooden spoon
still in hand.

"The hell it doesn't!" Tim countered as Abby walked
over to Tad and stood next to him. "I just opened three
weeks ago," Tim continued. "If you lead with a story
on food poisoning, I'm finished."

"Not necessarily," Tad said.

"Oh, yeah?" His expression grim, Tim looked at Tad.

"Would you want your pregnant wife eating there if you read in the *Blossom Weekly News* that six people got sick after eating the chicken special last Thursday?"

Tad understood why Tim was upset, but there was no way he was censoring the news to protect some people and expose others. The truth was the truth. The news was the news. And that was the way it was going to be.

"Six people did get sick, according to the health department," Tad said matter-of-factly.

"It wasn't my restaurant's fault! The poultry was tainted when I got it!"

"If the facts bear that out," Tad said, knowing full well that the investigation by the health department had not yet been completed, "then the article will say that."

Tim Grau glared at Tad. He looked mad enough to punch something. "You know, I heard from some of the other merchants in town that you were going to be unreasonable," he said, a muscle working in his jaw. "But pulling stuff like this is going to do you in, McFarlane. In fact, unless you adhere to the local creed and give more favorable coverage to those who place the bigger ads as a sort of professional courtesy, from one merchant to another, I'll bet you go out of business faster than I do."

Tad was betting he wouldn't. "I've never purposely held back on a story and I'm not going to start now," he told Tim as Abby slipped her hand in his and gave it a squeeze.

"Then you're going to be sorry." Tim Grau turned on his heel and left in a huff.

Sonny looked at Tad apologetically. "I tried to stop him, but in a town this size, it wasn't hard to figure out where you were. Since he was headed over here, as the reporter covering the story, I figured I'd better come over here, too.''

"It's okay," Tad reassured Sonny.

"It certainly is." Abby smiled at him, too.

Relief flooded Sonny's youthful features. Once again he looked to Tad for advice. "So what should I do about the story?"

"Write it. Talk to everyone who got sick, including Doc and the health department, and then put it on my desk. It's going in the next edition."

"Are you sure that's wise?" Abby asked after Sonny had left and she and Tad sat down to steaming plates of linguine with clam sauce.

Tad liked the idea of coming home to have lunch with his wife, even if it had been sort of a spur-of-the-moment deal. It was cozy and intimate, sitting here with her like this. So much so that he wanted to take her in his arms, cement their conciliatory words with a hug. He knew he couldn't, not without being tempted to do more, so he sat where he was.

"I purchased my own newspaper because I was disgusted by the increasing bias in the news and the pressure put on me by the brass to slant certain stories certain ways and forget others entirely. I'm going to give fair balanced reporting or none at all."

"I admire the way you're sticking to your convictions," Abby said with a smile as she got up to get out dill pickles and chocolate syrup. While Tad watched in amazement, she added chocolate to her milk and pickles to the edge of her plate. "That was one of the things I always hated about magazine work. We were so dependent on advertising."

"Well, you won't have to do that at the *Blossom Weekly News*," Tad said as he dug into the delicious pasta. "If there's a story of interest to our readers, we'll cover it, and we'll leave the editorializing to the editorial page."

He held her gaze, amazed as she continued to down her food with all the gusto of a hungry linebacker. "You're really going to eat that dill pickle with the linguine?"

"Disgusting, isn't it?" Abby replied cheerfully as she ate one spear and then helped herself to another.

Tad remembered Doc's advice to agree with his pregnant wife at all costs. "No, actually it looks pretty good." Tad pushed aside his revulsion and downed a couple of tart dill pickles, too.

"You're nuts, you know that, don't you?" Abby said.

He had to be, Tad thought, to be living here with her, and not making love to her. But that was the agreement they had struck, he reminded himself, and until she believed he loved her just for herself and nothing else, that was the way it would have to be.

"THAT'S THE FOURTH present this week, isn't it?" Donna said as the finishing touches were put on the living room in late July.

"Yes, it is," Abby said, bringing in the dozen red roses that had just been delivered from the local florist. Before that, there'd been a box of Godiva chocolates, a CD she'd been wanting and an array of scented hand soaps. The two weeks before that had been equally rife with gifts. Not a day went by, it seemed, that Tad didn't come in at night with her favorite food or beverage or even a newspaper or magazine he knew she liked to read. At first it had been nice to be the object of so much thoughtfulness. Now...well, now Abby didn't know what to think.

Sonny loaded film into his camera. "So what'd Tad do to land in the doghouse?" he asked.

It was possible he felt guilty about working so much. Since the brouhaha over the publication of the article on the salmonella outbreak at the Mighty Fine Restaurant, he had worked increasingly long hours, as had she.

"Nothing. He's not in the doghouse—at least not with me."

"Right." Sonny's lip curled with suppressed amusement as he got down on one knee to photograph the interior of the two rooms. "Maybe someone should tell him that."

Donna plumped the pillows on the long cream-colored tuxedo sofa just so while Abby adjusted the white plantation shutters to let in the maximum amount of light. The newly refinished wood floors gleamed beneath the beige-brown, cream and marine blue Oriental rug. Gleaming white trim and crown molding put the finishing touches on the handsome marine blue walls. And last but not least, Tad's recliner sat in a corner, in a place of honor, newly covered in a beige-brown jacquard that coordinated well with the two other overstuffed armchairs in the room.

"I know where Sonny is coming from." Donna chuckled as she straightened the bookcases and the streamlined laptop computer on the antique writing desk. "My husband, Ron, gives me gifts for only two reasons. A special occasion, like my birthday or our anniversary, or when he's trying to make up to me for something he's done." Donna paused to open a door of the armoire, to show the stereo and television set hidden within. "The size of the gift is usually directly proportionate to the degree of guilt he's feeling."

"Amen to that," Sonny said, directing both Donna and

Abby into the next picture. "It didn't take me long to discover that the right pair of earrings or bottle of perfume can go an awfully long way toward making up."

Abby smiled for the camera. As they moved into the finished entryway to photograph that area, she wondered what was going on with Tad.

"DID YOU GET my flowers?" Tad asked, immediately seeking her out when he came in about ten o'clock that evening.

Aware work would begin on the formal dining room in the morning, Abby was in there standing on a chair when Tad strode in. In a vivid blue cotton sport shirt worn open at the throat, casual khaki slacks and loafers that had seen better days, he looked casual and at ease. His naturally curly black hair was agreeably rumpled, his jaw shadowed with evening beard and scented with aftershave. And there was a seductive smile tugging at his sensual lips.

"Yes, I got them."

Trying hard not to react to his presence or think how much she'd begun to miss his once-persistent passes, Abby turned her eyes from his handsome profile and continued taking down the threadbare flocked-velvet drapes that had come with the house. How long had it been since he'd kissed her, she wondered, or even wanted to kiss her? The answer was easy. It had been weeks. Meanwhile, her waist was thickening by the day.

Tad glanced around. "Where are they?"

"The kitchen."

He studied her. "You like red roses, don't you?"

Actually they were her favorite. Which, in Abby's estimation, made it all the worse. She stopped what she was doing and turned to face him. Figuring they might as well get it all out in the open, she told him, "You don't have to do this, you know."

Tad blinked in confusion. "Do what?"

Feeling depressed and disappointed, she let her arms fall to her sides. "Try and buy your way into my good graces."

Tad hooked his hands around her waist and helped her down from the chair. He kept his hands there even after her feet touched the floor. "I was trying to show you how much I appreciate you."

Abby shrugged and said nothing.

"Obviously you think there's another reason."

Abby extricated herself from his grip. "Look, let's not talk about this."

Tad caught her by the shoulders and ever so gently spun her around to face him. His eyes glimmered with barely suppressed frustration. "Too bad, 'cause I think we should."

"Have it your way," Abby muttered, as he motioned her to sit in the chair she'd just been standing on.

"So what's up?" Tad pulled up another chair, turned it around backward and sat, folding his arms over the top. "What's got you so upset?"

When she didn't answer, Tad prodded, "C'mon, Ab, just tell me."

"Why do you feel guilty?" Abby blurted out.

Tad nearly choked. "Excuse me?"

"You heard me," Abby retorted grimly. "All the gifts have to be for some reason, so what have you done?"

"Nothing!"

Abby had half expected he might react this way. "I knew this was a waste of time!" she said, bolting to her feet.

Tad followed. Started to speak, stopped, then thought

for a long tense moment in which he seemed to change his mind and, in fact, change courses completely. "You're right of course," he said finally in a smooth cultured tone she didn't believe for a moment. He smiled and held out a hand. "I have been feeling guilty for not spending enough time with you. The gifts were just a way of showing you that I appreciate you. If they upset you in any way, I'm sorry."

He was much too agreeable, Abby decided. The Tad she knew and fell in love with, the Tad who reported the unvarnished truth come what may, would never have backed down so readily.

Which meant, of course, Abby thought, fuming all the more, he had to be feeling really guilty about something! It was up to her to find out what.

An idea began to form. And she knew it was a doozie. Knowing he wasn't the only one who could change tacks rapidly, she smiled at Tad sweetly. "Have you eaten dinner?"

"Yeah." Tad regarded her with the caution one approached a skunk who was about to spray. "I grabbed something earlier when we were putting tomorrow's edition of the *News* to bed."

"Well, I'm famished. I was just going to have a snack. Want to join me?"

"Uh...sure."

Abby led the way into the kitchen. This was going to be the test. "A sandwich okay with you?" she asked, already knowing what his answer would be. Her back to him, she mouthed, *Whatever you're having.*

"Whatever you're having," Tad said.

Well, Abby thought, revenge very much on her mind, *you asked for it.* With Tad lounging against the counter watching her every move, she brought out pumpernickel

bread, strawberry-flavored cream cheese, sardines, on-
ions, green and black olives and chili sauce.

Abby saw him swallow and it was all she could do to
repress a giggle. "This looks disgusting, I know, but
you're going to love it, I promise," she said enthusiastically as she quickly put together a sandwich he would
never ever forget. "Here you go." A scant minute later
she motioned him to the table and put the plate in front
of him.

Tad watched as she began to put the ingredients away.
"Aren't you having any?"

"I changed my mind." Abby touched her middle.
"Heartburn." *And you caused it, you scoundrel.* "But
you go right ahead. I'll just sit with you and watch."

Tad looked at her and again seemed to really struggle
with himself and whatever it was he was thinking.

"Well, maybe just a bite," Abby said, reaching over
and cutting off a wedge of his sandwich. She popped it
into her mouth. "Mm-mmm." Ignoring the hideous taste
in her mouth, she sighed and laid a hand across her chest.
"This is so-o-o good. Try it."

A smile on his face, Tad lifted the sandwich to his
mouth. For a moment she thought he was going to
chicken out, but finally he took a bite. Swallowed. Took
a long long gulp of water.

"Now," Abby said cheerfully, as the nauseating mess
made its way to his stomach, "look me straight in the
eye, you scoundrel, and still tell me everything I do is
wonderful. I dare you."

Very, very slowly, Tad set down the sandwich. He
wiped his hands and his mouth with his napkin. And
looked her straight in the eye. "What do you want from
me?" he demanded, a muscle clenching in his jaw. Suddenly he seemed every bit as near his limit as she was.

Hot angry color swept into her cheeks. "How about a little honesty?" Abby snapped, pushing her chair back and vaulting to her feet.

"Fine. You want honesty!" he said in a voice that was so low it sent shivers down her spine. "I'll give you honesty. That was disgusting, but I tolerated it."

"That's what I thought." Abby stomped forward until they stood toe-to-toe. She tilted her head back and glared up at him. "Then why did you eat it? No. Don't answer. I think I know. Darn it all, you're humoring me, aren't you? *Aren't you!*"

Tad grimaced. He slid his hands into his back pockets. "Yes. I am. On doctor's orders."

"What?"

"Doc told me just to agree with you on everything."

"Oh, he did, did he?" Fuming, Abby began to pace. She hadn't been this angry since…well, since she didn't remember when.

Tad continued, his words as calm and deliberate as hers were furious and emotional. "He said your pregnancy would go a lot smoother for both of us if I humored you, and he should know. He has six kids and sixteen grandkids and a beautiful loving wife who still worships the ground he walks on after thirty-five years of marriage."

Abby sent Tad a withering glance. "The gifts?" she prodded coolly.

Tad drew a deep breath, then confessed, his jaw set. "He told me to do that, too. He said what you're doing for me—for us—carrying our baby is nothing to be taken lightly. He said I should make sure you knew that, and gifts are one of the easiest ways."

Abby raked both hands through her hair, not sure whether to laugh or cry, just knowing she felt like doing both. "Not to mention the fact that it would probably get you in my good graces."

"But it didn't," Tad said.

"One or two probably would have." If they'd been given of his own volition, Abby thought. "But a dozen?" Abby stared at Tad, shaking her head, as her eyes filled. Did he think she could be bought? Was that it? "That's overkill, don't you think?"

"Not really, no." Tad's expression gentled as he stepped even closer. He put his hands on her waist. "If it were up to me, I'd be giving you presents every day the rest of our lives," he said softly. "If it were up to me—as long as we're being honest—we'd still be making love and you'd be sleeping in my arms every night. If it were up to me…"

Letting the ardent thought hang in the air, he scooped her up in his arms and carried her toward the stairs.

"What are you doing?" Abby demanded.

Tad smiled down at her and kept moving. "It just occurred to me, it *is* up to me." He sailed through the door to her softly lit bedroom and lowered her gently to the bed.

"You mean it, don't you?" Abby asked breathlessly as he gazed at her with the passion she'd ached to know again. "You really want to make love to me."

"With all my heart and soul." Tad stroked her hair. The next thing Abby knew, his lips were on hers. He kissed her with the abandon they'd discovered in Paris, and she reveled in the hot insistent demand of his mouth over hers, the urgent thrust and parry of his tongue. He kissed her until they were lying on their sides, sprawled length to length in the middle of the double bed. Until she moaned and melted against him, her hands curling around his shoulders.

He drew back, the misty lights of desire and tenderness in his fathomless blue eyes as he scored his thumb across her lower lip. "What would ever make you think I didn't want you?"

Abby blushed. "My ever-expanding tummy, for one."

He smiled and slid lower, bent to kiss her tummy through the satin fabric of her pajamas, then touched and rubbed and stroked. "Your tummy is beautiful, and so is the rest of you."

Abby swallowed around the growing knot of emotion in her throat. "Tell me you missed me, Abby, as much as I've missed you," Tad whispered fervently as he shifted her onto her back and slid upward. Lying alongside her, he tucked one leg over hers. "Tell me you've missed this," he said.

He teased her tongue with the tip of his until her breath was as short and shallow as his. And though Abby's mind was still fighting him, fighting the surrender, her body had stopped long ago. Heaven help her, she wanted him to make love to her. She wanted to feel everything it was possible to feel. She did not want this moment to pass either of them by, because she knew, even if she didn't want to admit it, that it had never been like this for her. So intensely pleasurable and out of control. And it never would be again. For her, Tad was just it.

"Oh, Tad…" Abby whispered, already trembling from head to toe, and he hadn't even started to undress her yet!

As she whispered his name, Tad's eyes darkened with pleasure. Swiftly, still watching her face, he unbuttoned her pajama top.

"You know I desire you," Abby said, her voice filled with longing as Tad divested her of her pajama top and whisked off her bottoms, too. That had never been the problem between them. "But—"

"No conditions, Abby," Tad said as he impatiently tugged off his own clothes and, naked, joined her on the bed. She moaned as he circled her breast, then cupped the weight of it with his palm. "Not tonight and not ever again." He bent to pay homage with his lips and his tongue until her nipples were tight and achy. "Just love me," Tad said as he rolled her slightly onto her side, slid one arm beneath her hips and arched her lower body against him. "Just let yourself go and love me."

As he continued to kiss and touch and caress her, dizziness swept through her in waves. The hot melting feeling in her abdomen grew, and a need unlike any she'd ever known built within her. No one had ever loved her so fiercely, so possessively, Abby thought, as she returned his kisses passionately and her hips rose instinctively to meet him. No one had ever loved her in such a fundamental way.

Needing to touch him, too, she ran her palms across the smooth hard muscles of his back, across the hard muscles of his stomach and up across his chest, until she could feel his thundering heart. As she touched lower still, she marveled at the velvety hardness and the depth of his need, a need only she could ease.

As she looked into his eyes, the intensity and tenderness of his dark blue gaze held her mesmerized. When he looked at her that way, she felt beautiful, inside and out. And she knew he was right—they did need to love each other again, physically and in every other way.

The next thing she knew he had shifted her onto her back again and nudged her legs apart. She opened herself up to him as gently and irrevocably as a flower blooms in the spring. He caught her by the hips to steady her and then he kissed her. Again and again and again, commanding everything she had to give until she no longer knew where her body ended and his began, until she had never felt so much a woman nor been so aware of a man. She surged against him, loving the touch and taste and smell of him, loving the way their bodies automatically came in contact in all the right places as he satisfied one hunger and fed another.

Tad had always wanted a spirited woman. A woman who was strong but soft, feisty but giving, a woman who wouldn't be afraid to experience pleasure to the max. He knew she'd been hurt badly in the past. So had he, he thought as he trembled with the need to hold back his own release. That didn't mean they had to spend even one more day as husband and wife in name only. In six months they'd be having a child together. Starting now, they could really be a couple and have a life together, too.

Abby trembled from the fit of her body against his, from the pressure nudging her feminine cleft. His whole body was quaking as he stretched out on top of her, spread her knees and slipped between them. The soft V of her thighs cradled his hardness, and his sex throbbed against her surrendering softness. Again, he bent to kiss her, loving her an inch at a time, going deeper and deeper. She rocked against him, taking him inside her, closing tight. Sensations swept through him. He could barely control himself as she shuddered and writhed beneath him, her insides clenching around him, urging him on to release. He heard her moan and felt her tremble, and then it was just too much. Going deep, he followed her over the edge. And then they were both gone, floating, free, feeling a peace they hadn't felt in weeks.

AN HOUR LATER, as they lay wrapped in each other's arms, Tad shifted so that she was beneath him. Bracing his weight on either side of her, he said, "Let's make a promise to look to each other for pleasure—at least until after the baby is born. I know, I know, you're worried us making love every night will complicate things."

"It will," Abby told him sternly.

"But it'll also make things all the more bearable," Tad said, kissing her brow. "Admit it. You want me, too."

Abby sighed. "You know I do."

Tad grinned. Getting her to admit that was a major victory. "Then stop worrying about what's going to happen six months down the road," he told her gently. "We can't predict the future, Abby." Reaching for her hand, he turned it palm up and kissed the middle of it. "We can live in today."

The fight to keep him at arm's length faded as quickly and unexpectedly as it had come. "All right," Abby said. She touched a finger to his lips, compelling him to silence. "I'll do it on one condition." Her golden-brown eyes flashed an ardent warning.

Tad would have given her anything if it meant having her back in his life again. He grinned. "Fire away."

"No more fibbing to me, even if you think it's for my own good," she said as their ragged breaths meshed as one. "And no more gratuitous gifts. Okay?"

Relief flowed through Tad. These were conditions he could meet. He kissed her again, knowing, even if Abby didn't yet, that this was just the beginning. They would find a way to make this work over the long haul. He would see to it.

"Okay."

Chapter Eight

Two weeks later

"Why didn't you tell me?" Abby asked Tad after everyone but the two of them had gone home.

Tad looked up from the computer printout in front of him. Outside, a drenching rain continued. Knowing it was his job to protect his pregnant wife as much as possible from all of life's difficulties, yet knowing he owed her honest question an honest answer, he stood his pencil on end and met her eyes. "I didn't want you to worry." *And let's be honest, I didn't want anything to interfere with the immensely satisfying, immensely passionate turn our relationship has taken.*

Since Abby had surrendered to her feelings, they'd made love every night with as much passion, if not more, than they'd discovered in Paris, and selfish father to be and husband that he was, he didn't want anything putting a damper on their love affair. And who knew? Maybe, if things were good enough before the baby was born, she would decide to stay with him after the baby was born, Tad thought.

Abby's golden-brown eyes flashed and her chin took

on a stubborn tilt as she continued taking him to task. "I should know when the newspaper is in trouble."

"We're doing okay," Tad defended himself.

Abby began to pace. Because she'd always preferred to wear skirts and dresses to work, she'd taken to wearing a variety of slimming above-the-knee maternity skirts with his shirts and ties. Tad knew he wasn't the only one who thought she looked as fetching as could be. In fact, now well into her fourth month of pregnancy, she was one sexy lady.

With a concerned glance out at the rain and another in his direction, Abby reminded him gravely, "Five of the major advertisers have pulled all their ads because of the final article on the salmonella outbreak at the Mighty Fine Restaurant. None of them have any plans to reinstate with us in the future."

Tad sighed, knowing, even if he'd been able to predict this calamity, he still wouldn't have done things any differently. "They may change their minds," he said evenly, "particularly if Tim Grau changes his mind and turns this unfortunate situation to his advantage."

Abby paced closer, her suede flats moving soundlessly across the polished wooden floor. "Did he get back to you on your offer to use the situation to further public awareness?"

Able to see they were going to be here for a while, Tad kicked back in his chair and propped his boot-clad feet on the corner of his desk. He folded his hands behind his head. "You want his exact words or the general idea?"

"That bad, hmm?"

Tad shrugged. "Tim doesn't want the general public to know that some of his help were chopping raw vegetables on the same cutting boards they used to cut up the raw chicken.''

Abby groaned and started to run her hands through her hair. Remembering belatedly she'd put it up with a barrette on the back of her head, she began to take it down. ''If only they'd all known to keep the two items separate and use a lot of hot soapy water on any surface the raw chicken touched,'' she lamented as she ran her fingers through her silky mane.

''My point exactly.'' Still enjoying the way the overhead lights hit her hair, making it sparkle with golden lights, Tad crossed one ankle over the other and steepled his fingers on his lap. ''The *Blossom Weekly News* could have made him and his staff out to be heroes for educating the public and reassured everyone at the same time that it wasn't going to happen again.''

''Instead—'' Abby stopped pacing and perched on the corner of his desk ''—Tim tried to bury the incident and now may go out of business as a result.''

Tad lifted his eyes to hers. ''While I can't fathom his shortsightedness, I do sympathize with him. I know what it's like to follow your dream.'' He knew what it was like to want something—someone—so much that nothing else mattered.

Abby raked her teeth across her lower lip. Her eyes lifted to his, held. ''Word on the street is that Tim has enough capital to keep going until Thanksgiving. That still gives him time to change his mind and take you up on your offer.''

Tad nodded. He could only hope Tim Grau came to his senses and did so.

''Meantime—'' Abby sighed deeply ''—we have our own problems to solve.'' She picked up the computer printout of figures from Tad's desk. She frowned as she studied the bottom line. "Like how we're going to replace the lost revenue."

Confronted by the aggravated longtime customers and the sudden loss of advertising revenue, he'd been thinking about that all day. "One way to go would be to cut back."

"But you don't want to do that," Abby guessed.

"No." Tad lowered his feet to the floor. He stood and now it was his turn to pace. "I want to expand the paper as rapidly as possible and try to pick up the slack with additional sales and subscribers."

Abby regarded him thoughtfully. "It might work."

Tad stared at the fast-running river of water moving along the curb to the storm drain. "Unfortunately for the two of us that's going to mean things are going to be tight." He turned away from the sight of the rain splattering the top of his Jeep and leaned against the glass. "I pay myself a percentage of the profits, and for the month of August, at any rate, there are none."

Abby smiled at him reassuringly. "I can live on a shoestring. Underwriting the costs of the white-elephant redecoration are another matter entirely, however. We've promised the readers a room every other week."

"And I'd like to up that to once a week," Tad said, thinking a move like that would boost readership more than ever. He rubbed his jaw. "The question is, where are we going to get the money?"

Abby's eyes lit up as she crossed to his side and stood on tiptoe to kiss his cheek. "Why don't you leave that to me?"

"IT'S ALL SET," Abby told Tad early the following afternoon as Sonny went out on assignment and Raymond went to the rear of the building to work on a minor printing-press problem that had just cropped up. "I got a list of craftsmen from Donna. They've all agreed to do the rest of the work on the house for free in exchange for in-depth interviews by me on how they work and learned their trades and so on. It's sort of a barter thing. We give them free publicity that will hopefully generate a lot more business for them, and they do a great job for us. Sonny is going to do the photo essays. So we're going to need a lot more space to fit all this in, because now we'll be focusing on donated materials, expertise and labor for every room."

Tad cast her an admiring glance. "Maybe we should make this a regular series even after we finish the white elephant," he suggested. "Perhaps even raffle off chances to have a kitchen face-lift or master-bedroom redecoration."

"Sounds good to me," Cindy said, setting a big paper bag on the counter.

Tad looked at the UNC grad. She'd just come from a run to Audrey's Bakery and Café down the street. "How are we doing with the classifieds?"

Cindy shrugged off her rain slicker, hung it on a hook by the door and returned to lift containers of milk, café lattes, a variety of sandwiches and freshly baked banana-nut muffins from the bag.

"I wanted to talk to you about that. I think we could do better if we lowered the cost of the ads by at least ten percent and started an aggressive campaign to get people to advertise using copy like this." As everyone picked up their snack orders, Cindy dashed to the ad counter. She returned swiftly, handing Tad and Abby two cartoon ads urging people to buy space in the newspaper.

"These are cute," Abby said.

"Definitely eye-catching," Tad agreed, as he took the

top off his café latte. He sat back in his chair. "How big did you want to make the ads?"

Cindy regarded him hopefully. "Don't shoot me, but half a page at the beginning and end of each advertising section. I also thought we could put copies of the ads up on bulletin boards around town."

"Okay. Give it a try," Tad said with a smile, just as a rain-drenched Sadie burst through the door.

Tad had only to look at his aunt to know something was up. "What's happened?" He got immediately to his feet.

Sadie clapped a hand over her heart. "Buster ran away!"

"What?" Abby and Tad both rushed to the older woman's side.

Sadie removed her dripping rain hat and reported breathlessly, "I went home for lunch to walk him—you know how he hates to go out in the rain—and he wasn't there. I looked everywhere."

"Meaning what?" Abby asked.

"He went out his doggie door and dug a hole beneath the fence."

"Buster?" Tad asked, amazed. He had never known Aunt Sadie's mournful-looking bassett hound to do anything anywhere near that energetic or mischievous.

"I know." A red-faced Sadie threw up her hands. "I couldn't believe it, either." She began to tear up. "Tad, I don't know what I'm going to do…"

"Sit tight, Aunt Sadie." Tad enveloped his diminutive aunt in a hug. "He probably hasn't gone far. I'll find him."

"I'll help."

Tad looked at Abby. She knew exactly what he was going to say. "I'm pregnant, not water soluble. Besides, it'll do me good to get out of the office. You can drive and I'll look out the window.''

"Bless you both," Sadie said, dabbing at her eyes.

"They'll find him, Sadie," Cindy said, patting her arm.

Tad and Abby grabbed their raincoats and took off. He carried the umbrella as they hurried out to the Jeep. Tad shook his head. "What a day to run away."

"The question is why," Abby said as she climbed into the passenger side. "Buster hates rain."

They found out soon enough—almost a mile away. Buster had a girlfriend. A cute little cocker spaniel. The two were cuddling beneath the front porch. They were also covered with mud and wet as could be. Abby and Tad groaned in unison as they contemplated how best to remove the lovesick canines.

"This ought to be fun," Abby said.

"Who lives here, anyway?" Tad asked.

"I don't know." Abby bit her lip. "We'd better ring the bell."

Unfortunately there was no answer at the door.

A neighbor, pulling into the driveway next door, stopped to roll down her car window. She cupped a hand around her mouth and shouted to be heard over the rain and her car.

"Problem?" the neighbor shouted, nodding at the two dogs, who looked very unwilling to come out from the bed they'd made under the front porch.

Tad nodded.

"Unfortunately Raymond's not home. He works at the paper during the day."

"WELL, THE GOOD NEWS is," Tad told Aunt Sadie via cell phone from the front porch, "we found Buster."

Briefly he went on to explain. "The bad news is I think it's going to take both you and Raymond to coax the dogs out from under there."

Short minutes later Sadie and Raymond arrived. "Belle's in heat," Raymond told Abby and Tad.

"Oh, dear," Abby murmured.

"And Buster can still be a papa," Sadie explained.

"Make that double dear," Abby—who'd never more acutely appreciated the miracle of life than she did since she'd been pregnant herself—teased. Wouldn't it be fun, she thought, if Belle and Buster had puppies?

"The question is, how did they find each other?" Tad knelt down in the mud and helped pull a mud-caked Buster out. "They weren't exactly living on the same block."

Sadie and Raymond exchanged looks and colored deeply.

"Okay," Tad prodded, "what am I missing here?"

"They've, uh, met before," Sadie told Tad and Abby reluctantly.

"We got them together," Raymond explained a little less self-consciously. "Took them both to the park last week just before Belle went into heat."

Sadie's color deepened even more. "We just never thought they'd try to get together on their own!" she exclaimed.

"A little romance going on here, hmm?" Tad asked as he wrapped a drenched and muddy Buster in the towel Raymond provided and prepared to carry the mournful-looking bassett hound to his Jeep.

And not with just the lovesick pups, Abby thought as she studied the heightened color in both Sadie and Raymond's faces. She'd thought they were getting a little chummy at the newspaper! How nice for Tad's aunt.

Maybe, Abby thought optimistically, Raymond would be the one for Sadie, and vice versa. "Well, the puppies—if there are any—will certainly be unique," she said cheerfully. "I wonder what they'll look like, given they'll be a bassett hound-cocker spaniel mix."

In unison everyone imagined it. And everyone groaned.

"I WAS GOING to ask you how things were going," Yvonne said from the doorway of the *Blossom Weekly News* an hour later. "But maybe this isn't the time."

Abby checked the impulse to hug her old friend and let a grin suffice, instead. She waved a hand down the length of her, then cast a look at her husband, who looked just as bad, if not worse. "We're a little muddy, huh?"

"And then some." Yvonne took off her trendy black silk raincoat and hung it up "What happened. Did you get caught in a mud slide?"

"My aunt's dog was lost. So we tracked him down..." Tad began.

"And then had to coax him in out of the rain and mud and give him a bath for Sadie," Abby explained.

"Which Buster absolutely did not appreciate," Tad continued.

"Finishing each other's sentences. I like that," Yvonne teased.

"What brings you to Blossom?" Abby asked, ignoring Yvonne's comment.

"I was en route home from a job interview in California and thought, what the heck, why not take a little detour and see how you were doing? That was, of course, before I knew it was raining here. Sheesh." Yvonne shook the dampness out of her coiffed flame red hair.

Abby smiled at her friend. "August is hurricane season

around here. Even this far inland, we get some ferocious storms off the coast.''

Tad looked at Yvonne and said, ''Abby and I were about to close up here, go home and get cleaned up, then fix some dinner. Want to join us?''

''Actually,'' Yvonne said, ''I'm looking for a place to spend the night first. Any recommendations?''

Abby looked at Tad and knew they were in sync. ''Just one. With us,'' Abby said. '''Cause, girlfriend, I've really missed you.''

Yvonne's eyes glittered warmly. ''Ditto.''

An hour later Abby had showered, put on a pair of maternity jeans and a long tunic top and gone down to the kitchen where Yvonne was seated, chatting away with a still-muddy Tad. He looked at Abby. ''My turn?''

She nodded, aware of how easy and comfortable they'd become with each other, how very much a couple. It went a lot deeper than just finishing each other's sentences or making love. ''Any thoughts on dinner?''

''Well—'' Tad took a deep breath and looked out at the rain still coming down in sheets ''—I don't think we should use the barbecue.''

Abby rolled her eyes. ''Very funny.''

''You ladies decide,'' Tad said affably. ''When I come back down, let me know what I can do.''

As soon as he was out of earshot, Yvonne asked, ''Can he cook?''

''You mean something besides beans and franks out of a can?'' Abby said. ''No. But he's great at pitching in with the dishes.''

Yvonne studied her. ''I can't believe you. You look so...''

''Pregnant?'' Abby patted her belly.

''Domestic.'' Yvonne smiled.

"So how are the job interviews going?" Abby asked, changing the subject smoothly.

Yvonne made a face. "So-so. This was my third interview, but sad to say I don't think it's a good match. Plus, I'd much rather continue to live in New York than have to move across the country. So...onward and upward."

"How are you doing financially?"

Yvonne sighed and toyed with the glass of wine Tad had poured for her. "Not bad. The main thing is the lack of work. It's driving me a little batty." At age forty-two and with a history of being married to her career, Yvonne would be lost, Abby knew, without an office to go to every day.

"Have you been able to pick up any freelance assignments?" Abby asked.

Yvonne sighed. "Not enough to keep me busy more than a day or so every couple of weeks. It's a tight job market out there. I think there are far too many people like me who've been either downsized or merger-ed right out of a job they love."

"Then you've come to the right place," Tad said from the doorway. He'd changed into a clean pair of khaki pants and a loose knit shirt. His black hair was still wet and scented with shampoo, his closely shaven jaw with aftershave. He walked closer. "Because Abby and I have been talking about expanding the *Blossom Weekly News.*"

"You're kidding, right?" Yvonne plastered a hand across her heart. "Me? Work at a small-town paper?"

Undaunted by Yvonne's not-in-this-lifetime look, Tad grinned. "That's what Abby said." He turned a chair around and straddled it. "Now she's almost busier than I am trying to turn the paper around." His expression sobered. "I'm familiar with your work." He ticked off several series Yvonne had helmed, surprising both Abby and Yvonne with the depth of his knowledge and admiration for her work. "We could use your expertise as a features editor. Think of it this way. It won't pay much, but it'll be an interesting whimsical addition to your résumé while you're waiting for the perfect job to come along."

Yvonne paused, intrigued by Tad's pitch despite herself. "I admit, after looking at how few feature articles there are in the samples of the paper Abby mailed me, that I'm tempted to show you how things should be done in that area. But alas, I have no place to stay."

Tad shrugged his broad shoulders and rested his chin on his fist. "We've got plenty of room."

"It would be nice, having my old friend around," Abby added persuasively.

"All right," Yvonne answered, no match for Abby and Tad's combined argument. She smiled, promising, "I'll hang around for a day or two and advise you—in exchange for the room and board and whatever token salary you can afford to pay. Just understand that if I get a decent job offer or another interview, I'll be out of here, pronto."

RAIN WAS STILL POUNDING on the eaves when Abby and Tad retired to their bedroom later that evening. The sound was cozy and welcoming. Tad couldn't wait to climb into bed and snuggle with his wife.

As he stripped down to his boxers, Tad told Abby honestly, "I invited Yvonne to stay with us, because I figured you might want the company of an old friend while you're making new friends." He climbed into bed beside her, switched off the light and rolled to face her. "Was I wrong?"

"No." Abby turned toward him, and propped herself up on her elbow. "You weren't wrong," she said softly, reaching out to caress the warm solidness of his chest. "I've missed Yvonne and all my old friends at the magazine. But life here is exciting, too," she teased. "I mean, who can beat crawling beneath a porch in the rain and mud to pull out two lovesick pups?"

Tad linked hands with her, then brought her hand to his mouth and pressed a kiss into her palm. "That was pretty funny, wasn't it?"

Abby grinned, loving the coziness of the mattress beneath her and the hard male body cuddled next to hers. "For the record, you looked really cute with a smudge of mud across the bridge of your nose."

"Yeah, well," Tad teased right back, kissing her cheek as he curled his arms around her, "you had some in your hair."

"And you," Abby said, moving even closer, tenderly caressing the underside of his jaw, "had some right here."

Her fingers playing across his skin were more than he could bear. He tightened his arms around her and trapped her against him until she could feel the hard ridge of his arousal pressing her thighs. "You're very beautiful. You know that, don't you?" he said huskily, looking deep into her eyes.

Beneath the thin fabric of her lacy gown, her nipples had tightened into aching buds of arousal. "I feel beautiful when I'm with you," she confessed breathlessly, her heart filled with the wonder and the magic they'd found—and would always find—in their lovemaking.

His eyes held hers with the promise of limitless nights

to come. And then he kissed her until her breath came in quick shallow spurts and he was taking off her gown, rubbing the tender crests with his thumbs and stroking her dewy softness, moving up, in. She surrendered against him helplessly, with a low urgent moan. "Tad..."

"I know." Tad smiled with thoroughly male satisfaction as she pulled off his boxers, rapaciously explored the hot hard length of him, then sat astride him and lovingly drew him inside. The gliding sensation of wet hot silk was more than he could bear. "Abby," he murmured between kisses. "What you're doing to me—"

He groaned again as she slipped free, replaced her body with the softness of her lips and the light gliding touch of her tongue.

He urged her up and over him. "Now," she whispered.

"Now," he said as her breasts brushed his chest.

He plunged inside her, kissing even as they touched and took. Together they learned anew what it was like to be with someone heart and soul. They learned what it was like to need. And take. And give. Until at last their control faltered and they soared higher than either of them ever thought they could go. When the inevitable climax came, they shuddered and clung, appreciating the moment for the wonderful precious tempestuous time it was.

Oh, Abby thought, as their pulses returned to normal and they continued to nestle together intimately, how she needed this, needed him. It might be foolish of her, but she had never felt so loved or cherished, and she didn't want it ever to end.

"I CAN'T BELIEVE it's still raining," Abby said, long moments later on a deeply contented sigh. She was lying on her side, her head on his chest, one leg thrown over his, her knee nestled between his thighs.

Tad wrapped his arms around her, aware if he moved to the left even two more inches they'd both end up sprawled ignominiously on the floor. Knowing he had never felt happier than he did at that moment, he kissed the top of Abby's head. "I can't believe the two of us can actually fit in this bed."

Abby giggled and Tad thought it was the most glorious sound.

Lifting her head, she nodded at his feet, which were hanging off the end of the bed by a good six inches. "It's made for midgets, isn't it?"

"Let's put it this way," Tad drawled, aware he'd had more backaches in the weeks they'd been sharing the bed than he had in his entire life. "It was definitely not designed for someone my size."

Her expression concerned, Abby started to get up. "I know I'm, uh, growing." She indicated the gentle slope of her belly. "So if you want me to get up and sleep downstairs on the sofa to give you more room—"

Tad pulled her back down. "Not on your life. You're sleeping with me, woman, right up to the very moment you run off to the hospital to deliver. So what if my feet hang off the end of the bed?"

Abby chuckled, knowing firsthand how much he liked to cuddle and kiss. She tucked her face into the curve between his shoulder and neck. The warmth of her breath caressed his bare skin. "I've already talked to Donna about incorporating a king-size bed in the redecoration of this room. Unfortunately it'll be another month before we get to it."

Wrapping her arms around him, Abby snuggled closer. Then she caressed his chest with long soothing strokes and finally gave him a leisurely kiss that sent fire sizzling through his veins. "So until then—" she paused and looked deeply into his eyes, letting him know in a glance the many ways she knew they could pass the time spent not sleeping "—we'll just have to grin and bear it."

"I think I can handle that," Tad murmured playfully. He drew her to him and set about making her his all over again. "That," he said, as he bent to kiss the enticing curves of her breasts, "and a whole lot more."

THE GROUP GATHERED around the conference table for the end-of-September staff meeting. These brainstorming sessions were a favorite of Tad's. Abby's, too.

Taking the opportunity to speak out, Cindy said with the ease of an old-timer, "And the reduced price of advertising and stepped-up promotion efforts have tripled the number of ads we're running every week." Tad knew she was doing a good job. The entire staff was.

"Not to mention the fact that circulation has doubled," Raymond said as he poured more coffee for Sadie, seated to his left. "We're now printing twice the number of papers and we still sometimes run out."

"Yes, but we've had a few complaints, too." Sadie frowned as she lifted her coffee cup to her lips. "Some readers feel there is too much hard news in the editions. And not enough on ice-cream socials."

"But people like reading the national and state news, too," Sonny piped up, not afraid to make his case, either. "In particular, we're getting a lot of compliments on Tad's editorials.

"And it goes without saying Abby's home-and-garden features—especially her series on the improvement of the white elephant—are a big hit."

"Even with all that, we're still struggling financially,"

Tad told the group. As much as he'd like to give them all huge raises, it wasn't feasible yet. It was a stretch to keep paying Yvonne's wages, and those were but a fraction of what she would command in the magazine world.

"But we're definitely in a lot better shape than last month," Abby said cheerfully.

Tad grinned at the group. "Thanks in no small part to all of you and the newest recruit." Tad gestured at Yvonne.

Everyone nodded. "The personal profiles on local businessmen are a big hit," Sadie acknowledged.

"Don't look at me," Yvonne said. "Sonny's the one who's been writing them."

Sonny beamed under the praise. "Yvonne helped me shape the material."

"It's always a pleasure to work with talented professionals," Yvonne said.

Everyone grinned. "And now that we've given ourselves a much-deserved pat on the back for everything we've done right—and that's been a lot—we need to address the complaints we've had about the reduced local news," Tad said.

"I have an idea how to fix that," Abby said.

Tad looked at his wife. More and more they were becoming partners in every aspect of their life. To the point he hoped Abby would one day want to give up her search for another magazine job and stay on at the paper permanently. "I'm all for having a happy medium," Tad told Abby honestly, "but I don't want to go back to the gossipy self-congratulatory tone of the original weekly news." That would definitely be a step in the wrong direction.

"Why don't we start a new section of the paper called, say, About Town," Abby suggested. "It'll be for all social events. We'll invite people to submit any personal news and photos they'd like to share with their neighbors.''

''That's a good way to get subscribers up,'' Raymond said.

Beside him, Sadie nodded, putting in her two bits. ''People like to read about themselves and see their photos in the paper.''

Sadie and Raymond exchanged looks again.

''Did I imagine that?'' Abby asked after the staff meeting had concluded and everyone had gone home. She sat on the edge of Tad's desk, crossed her legs at the knee and rested her hand on the swell of her tummy. ''Or were Sadie and Raymond looking pretty cozy?''

''They were pretty cozy. You want to know what else?'' Tad hooked his hands around her waist and shifted her onto his lap.

Abby laced both her hands around his neck and nestled close. ''What?''

''Sadie told me Buster is no longer depressed.''

Abby smiled as she cast a look outside at the pretty September weather. ''Neither is his owner.'' And neither was she. When she'd first come to Blossom, that day she'd learned she'd been let go from her magazine job, she'd worried that, still married or not, unexpectedly pregnant or not, gainfully employed or not, she would never truly be happy here. But all that was beginning to change. She could see having a future with Tad and their baby in Blossom. And she could imagine them being very much a part of each other's life in every way for the next twenty or more years while their child grew up, and that was a very comforting, very exciting thought.

''Aunt Sadie does look happy these days, doesn't she?''

"Very," Abby conceded, her thoughts turning all misty and romantic. "So does Raymond."

"Ready to go home?"

Abby made a low affirmative sound as she bent to kiss him. He helped her to her feet. As they left the building, she fell into step beside him and linked hands with him. "I have a surprise for you."

Tad unlocked the passenger side of the Jeep and helped her in. His blue eyes shone with excitement as he assisted her with her seat belt. "What kind of surprise?" he asked.

"You'll see," Abby promised mysteriously, glad Yvonne had agreed to cooperate with her on this.

Tad bugged her all the way home. "One hint."

Abby laughed and folded her arms. "No way."

"Please."

"Oh, all right." Abby rolled her eyes, her excitement building. "Since you put it that way. Yvonne is staying with Cindy tonight."

"She is," Tad replied slowly.

"Yep. Yvonne's going to tell her all about life in New York City. And they're doing the whole female-bonding thing—facials, manicures, hairstyling, the works."

Tad parked in the drive. Resting his arm on the seat behind her head, he said, "Meaning we have the whole house to ourselves."

"Mm-hmm." At least she hoped they did, Abby thought, if Donna had finished and gotten out of there.

"So the surprise is a candlelight dinner for two?" Tad asked after he circled around to help Abby out of the truck.

"Not exactly."

Tad opened the front door. "Then what?" he demanded as Abby shut the door behind them and took him by the hand.

"You'll see." She led him up the staircase.

Tad winked at her lasciviously. "I think I could get used to this."

"Hush."

"Don't tell me you actually unpacked all your stuff," he teased.

"Not exactly." She had, however, arranged for most of her boxed possessions to be moved to the attic for storage. And that was a start.

"Then—" Tad came to a dead halt in the door to the master bedroom. For once, Abby thought, he was momentarily speechless.

Chapter Nine

"Do you like it?"

"Like it?" Tad echoed, stunned as he moved slowly into the master bedroom. The narrow double bed, mismatched furniture, stacks of books and papers and boxes that had been there since Abby had moved in had all been removed. The walls had been painted a soothing sage green, and a slightly darker sage carpet had been laid. The king-size sleigh bed was covered with a thick feather ticking for extra softness, there were plenty of pillows, and the bed ensemble was a masculine green, burgundy and white plaid. The matching mirrored dresser and cherry wardrobe allowed plenty of storage space for their clothes and possessions, while two deep upholstered chairs, end table and reading lamp provided a cozy sitting area.

Tad shook his head in open admiration. "It's magnificent."

Abby smiled and released an enormous sigh of relief. "I was hoping you'd think so." She'd spent an enormous amount of time secretly trying to please him with the decor.

Tad toured the bedroom, then kicked off his shoes and sat down on the edge of the bed. Grinning, he lay back on the pillows and folded his hands behind his head. "Now this is comfy," he said, sighing appreciably. "Except—" he turned on his side and frowned "—have you actually stretched out on this bed?"

Abby swallowed, wondering what in the world could be wrong. "Well, no..."

Tad shrugged. "Maybe it's just me, then."

Abby glided closer. "If there's something wrong with it, you need to tell me."

Tad studied her. "You try your side and tell me what you think," he said finally.

Abby kicked off her shoes, too. She backed onto the mattress and stretched out on the feather ticking. It felt like sinking into a huge down pillow. It was all she could do not to groan out loud in pure ecstasy. The enveloping softness was exactly the cure for the aches and pains of pregnancy, she thought, not to mention pure sensual comfort.

"Feel anything amiss?" Tad asked.

Abby turned toward him slightly and shook her head. "But you still do, don't you?" she observed, wondering what it could be. A flaw in the feather ticking, perhaps?

"Maybe it's just over here." Tad scooted toward the far edge on his side. "You lie here—" he pointed to the place where he'd been "—and tell me what you think."

He gallantly took her hand to assist her, and Abby scooted over to where he directed. "Now fold your hands behind your head," he said. He waited. "Do you feel it?"

Abby shook her head. Never had she been more aware of the brisk tantalizing fragrance of his aftershave. "I'm quite comfortable."

"Hmm." Tad's frown deepened. "Maybe if you close your eyes and concentrate."

"Okay." Abby closed her eyes.

"Now do you feel it?" Tad's voice was whisper soft.

All I feel, Abby thought, both amused and perplexed, *is a mounting desire for you.* But then, that was nothing new. Whenever she was with him like this, whenever they were in bed together, longing swept through her with disabling force. No matter how tired they were, no matter how uncertain their future, they couldn't seem to get through a night without reaching for each other at least once. And, Abby admitted silently to herself, she wanted it to stay that way. Physical passion might not last a lifetime, but while it was here, she intended to thoroughly enjoy every last nuance of it. And to that end, she thought, as she opened her eyes, reached up and took hold of Tad's tie… "The ticking is really comfortable," she murmured.

"As comfortable as this?" Tad asked softly, roguish amusement sparkling in his blue eyes as he feathered kisses down the side of her face. "'Cause when I lie here, Abby, knowing you've gone to all this trouble to make our marriage bed so very special, I've got to tell you. I feel—" he took her hand and lowered it to the most intimate part of him, then kissed her with a deep possessiveness that took her breath away "—quite a lot of this."

Abby had never in her life experienced such sweet invigorating kisses. Knowing he was her husband, knowing they were expecting a baby, added an extra sweetness to their love play. Still kissing him voraciously, she took off his tie, unbuttoned his shirt, unzipped his jeans. She'd never been the aggressor, but as she helped him shed his clothes and took him in hand, it seemed natural, right. Moving down his body, her hair slipping silkily over his skin, she adored him with lips and hands. Beneath the need to love him was the need to make him hers, in the same way he'd laid claim to her, body and soul, so many times.

She shifted herself higher, ready for a more intimate union. "Whoa there. You're getting ahead of me." He gasped, struggling for control. Gently he turned her onto her back. "Way ahead of me."

"Tad—"

"Let me love you," he said softly, already unbuttoning the front of her short stylish maternity dress. "Let me love you the way you were meant to be loved." His warm breath touched the soft vulnerable skin of her neck, then his lips followed. *Oh, Tad,* Abby thought tremulously as he began to kiss her again. *I love you. I love you so much.*

He deepened the kiss and pulled her close, divested her of her clothes and then loved her as only he could love her until her back arched off the bed and she was trembling, shuddering, begging for release. Bracing his weight fully on either side of her, he settled over her, the tip of his manhood pressing against her delicate folds.

Abby moved to receive him and he slowly, surely, surged upward, then inside her. Gently, gently, he rocked back and forth, until sensations hammered inside her and she strained against him, her body undulating, until she was sure she couldn't bear any more of this, until she was sure they had to find fulfillment. And it was then that he surged against her, wanting her and possessing her until every inch of her wanted every part of him.

Afterward they were, as always, loath to part. Replete and drowsy, Abby snuggled against him in blissful ecstasy.

"What are you thinking?" he asked, running his fingers through her hair.

Abby smiled and lovingly caressed the muscled hair-whorled skin on his chest. "That you are, without doubt, the sexiest most fun guy I've ever met." She propped her chin on her fist and looked up at him, her eyes sparkling. "You really had me going there for a minute, you know."

Tad grinned. "I know." He reached for her hand and pressed a kiss into the palm. "Couldn't resist. You looked so serious, and I wanted to make love to you so much."

Abby listened to the steady drumming of his heart and swept her hand down her body self-consciously. "Even with me beginning to give the term 'pear-shaped' new meaning?" she said playfully. Suddenly, as long as they were being honest, she needed to know. Was this all going to end?

Tad's eyes abruptly turned serious. "This is my baby you're carrying, Abby," he told her in an unmistakably ardent, unmistakably possessive voice. "A part of me and a part of you." He shifted lower and kissed her tummy lingeringly before returning to her lips. All the tenderness and passion he felt for her was in his eyes. "There's no greater turn-on than that."

Emotions soaring, he kissed her again. Still reveling at the happy way things were evolving, Abby kissed him back. And that was the last either of them said—or needed to say—for a very long time.

ON THE WAY to Abby's doctor appointment the next morning, Tad and Abby passed Joe Don Jerome's car dealership. Although the dealership did not open for business for another half an hour, at the side of the building there was most definitely a ruckus going on between Ernest Lee Scruggs, the chief mechanic, and Joe Don himself. Both were standing next to Ernest Lee's new pickup. Ernest Lee was gesturing angrily and pointing to the engine beneath the raised hood of his truck. "I wonder what that's about," Tad remarked as they paused at the traffic light.

"I don't know," Abby murmured as she watched Ernest Lee point out something in the engine. "He sure doesn't look happy." She glanced at Tad curiously. "Didn't you tell me he'd been having a lot of car trouble lately?"

"Mm-hmm. He's broken down a number of times, which is odd, because it's a brand-new truck, and he bought it from Joe Don."

The light changed. Abby turned and saw Ernest Lee stomp off in one direction and Joe Don another. "Well, whatever that was about, they don't appear to have resolved it."

"That's not surprising," Tad said firmly, "since Joe Don doesn't appear to be out for anyone but himself."

Abby cast a curious look at Tad. "Have you had any more complaints about Joe Don's dealership?"

"Nothing concrete," Tad admitted as he directed his attention to the road. "But every time you mention Joe Don's name to someone who's bought a car there—I don't know..." Tad frowned and shook his head. "It's like they want to tell you something and can't."

Abby reached over and squeezed Tad's thigh reassuringly. "Eventually someone will have to trust you enough to tell you what's going on."

"That may be. But it could take a long time. I've been here just a few months. People don't yet have all that much confidence I'm even going to stay. Whereas the Three Stooges have been here, firmly in control, for years."

"Just don't give up," Abby encouraged him seriously. "Sooner or later someone's bound to realize what a good guy you are and trust you enough to confide in you."

As they approached the doctor's office parking lot, Tad reached over and squeezed her hand. "Thanks for asking me to tag along," he said.

Abby was uncomfortably aware she hadn't asked Tad to go with her the first time she'd seen Dr. Ellison, the obstetrician Doc Harlan had recommended. "I'm sorry I didn't ask you the last time."

"That's okay. I know you're used to taking care of health concerns yourself, and that most women don't bring their husbands along for every visit. I'm just glad you asked me this time." Tad paused, looking down at her tummy, then back at her face. "So, I'm really going to hear our baby's heartbeat?"

Abby nodded. She wanted to share this with Tad and so much else. "Yep."

Tad shook his head. "Incredible," he said softly.

Abby's spirits rose even higher; she'd thought so, too. She started to undo her seat belt, then stopped, did a double take and gasped.

Tad's reaction was immediate. "What is it? Are you hurting? Is something wrong?"

Abby gasped again, barely able to believe. Suddenly her pregnancy was more real to her than ever. Face white, she turned to her husband and placed his hand squarely on her tummy. "Tad!" she whispered, stunned. "The baby just moved."

HIS HEART POUNDING, Tad sat with his hand on Abby's tummy. He waited. And waited. To no avail. Nothing.

Finally Abby sighed. She looked every bit as disappointed as he felt. "We're going to have to go in, or I'll be late for my appointment."

"Right." Tad got out of the Jeep.

"I'm sure the baby will kick again soon," Abby said as he helped her out. "I should have gotten your hand over here sooner. I was just so stunned."

Tad grinned down at her, looking every bit the proud papa. "That's the first time?"

Abby nodded. "A couple of times I thought maybe the baby might have kicked, just a little, but I wasn't sure. This time I was sure." She threw back her head and laughed. "It felt like I had a soccer player inside my tummy."

Tad grinned, enjoying the glorious autumn day as much as she was. They linked arms and headed for the building entrance. "So what do you think?" he asked. "Boy or girl?"

"I don't know." Abby snuggled into the warm protective curve of his arm. Tipping her head back, she glanced up at him. "Would it matter to you?"

Tad shook his head. "Just as long as the baby's healthy. That's all that matters."

Abby agreed. She waited while Tad held the door for her. "I used to hear people say that. I never knew what they meant. Now it…well, it makes sense."

"To me, too."

Tad may have missed out on the first kick, but he heard the baby's heartbeat loud and clear on the Doppler, a hand-held ultrasound device Dr. Ellison held against Abby's stomach to amplify the sound.

Ta-dum, ta-dum, ta-dum. The baby's heartbeat filled the examining room, the sound remarkably strong and steady. As their eyes met, Abby's filled with tears, and she thought, but couldn't be sure, she saw an answering sheen in Tad's. One thing was certain, she thought buoyantly. There was no disguising either's happiness.

"Well, everything seems to be in order," Dr. Ellison said after he'd palpated Abby's abdomen, discussed with her how she'd been feeling and checked the chart. "Your weight gain is right on target. Your blood pressure and urine check out fine. Call me if there are any problems. Otherwise, I'll see you again in a month."

The doctor slipped out of the room. Abby started to get up from the examining table. Then she felt it again. Rather than risk Tad losing out, she lifted her blouse with one hand, grabbed his hand with the other and pressed it to her stomach. Like the tapping of fingers on a tabletop, the rapid fluttering moved across the inside of her tummy.

"That?" Tad said joyously. "That's it?"

The baby flutter-kicked again. "That's it," Abby said.

All the love he felt for her in his eyes, Tad bent down to kiss her lips. "Incredible," he whispered. "Just incredible."

"YOU TWO COULD BE an ad for happy parents," the receptionist said as she set up Abby's next appointment.

Abby knew it was true. The baby was bringing them together, closer and faster than she'd ever thought possible.

"I am pretty excited," Tad told Abby as they left the doctor's office and climbed into his Jeep.

"Me, too," Abby said. She rested her hand on her tummy and leaned her head against the seat back. "Now that I can feel the baby moving, it's beginning to seem so-o-o real."

Tad cast her a shy glance. "I know."

Abby watched him fit the key in the ignition. "At first

it was...well, I knew I was pregnant, but I didn't feel any different. I didn't *feel* pregnant.''

In no hurry to start the engine, Tad turned to her. ''And now you do.''

Abby nodded as a car pulled up beside them and a young couple got out. ''Oh, yes,'' Abby told Tad softly. As she looked into his eyes, she knew he was going to make a great dad.

He caught her hand and kissed it. ''I feel it, too.''

Abby's heart soared at the revelation. ''Probably not as much as me.''

''Probably not, you're right.'' Tad cupped her face in his hands, caressed it gently. ''But I absolutely feel something,'' he told her as he lowered his mouth to hers and kissed her with a tenderness that was so real, so potent, it was nearly enough to make her cry. He drew back slightly. ''I feel love.''

Abby gulped, aware she'd never felt such deep all-encompassing emotion or wanted anyone in her life so much. ''I feel it, too,'' she admitted.

Tad regarded her with a thoroughly male satisfaction. And an intimate knowledge of her that was daunting. ''This whole family thing is going to work out, Abby,'' he said firmly, accurately reading the fears that always seemed to lurk just beneath her outward confidence. ''We're going to make it work,'' he promised, kissing her again.

Were they? Abby wished she could believe that even as she kissed Tad back with all her heart and soul. But inwardly she was not as sure that the love they felt for the baby they were expecting was enough to hold their marriage together over the long haul. Her parents had been head over heels in love plenty of times and yet never once had any of their marriages succeeded in the end, she remembered shakily.

Tad slowly lifted his mouth from hers. "This baby is a part of both of us and a testament to our love that no one will ever be able to take away," he said, reluctantly releasing her.

Abby nodded, steeling herself for the worst even as she hoped for the best. No matter what happened, she told herself sternly, she would never forget this time in her life. With the baby, with Tad. She just had to make the most of it while she could, for as long as she could.

Tad grinned and started the Jeep. "Now we just have to figure out a name."

Abby groaned, able to imagine what a task that would be, given the fact that she'd never known a couple who had managed it easily yet. "I've always been partial to Holly."

Tad made a face. "We are not naming our child after a shrub," he stated.

Abby settled more comfortably into her seat. "What would you pick, then?"

He paused, his expression turning very serious. "Corelle, after our first set of dishes."

Abby scowled at him playfully. She should have known he'd horse around. "Be serious."

Tad thought a moment. "Crystal, after our glasses?"

Abby rolled her eyes, then said with utmost gravity, "How about Robin, after the first bird we spotted in our yard?"

Tad's lips curved sexily. "Blossom, after the place where we live."

Abby chuckled. "On to the boys names. How about Lyon?"

Tad shook his head. "Too ferocious."

Good point. Abby studied his profile. "Okay, your turn."

"Boris."

Abby snorted. "Not unless he has a sister named Natasha."

Tad grinned again and at the next traffic stop darted her a look that was even sexier than the last. "I could work on a sister," he allowed.

Abby felt herself tingle from head to toe. "I'll bet you could," she drawled, enjoying the easy banter.

"Maybe we could even start practicing for the next big event now." Tad shot her an openly lascivious look. "I'm free after work. How about you?"

Abby shook her head with mock reproach. "You're incorrigible."

"What can I say?" Tad grinned. He parked in front of the closest storefront and pulled her close. "You inspire me."

"WHAT DO YOU THINK about getting a second car?" Tad asked as they passed Joe Don's dealership for the second time that morning.

"Now?" Abby asked, surprised.

Tad shrugged. "Well, we've been sharing one, and I know there've been times when it's been a pain."

Abby thought about the way the paper had been struggling, and now, with the baby on the way, Tad's finances were probably stretched to the limits, as were hers. "I don't mind walking to work or home. It's only five blocks."

Tad nodded thoughtfully. "True," he said, not looking as happy with her response as she would have expected.

"Besides—" Abby forced herself to be practical even though it was the last thing she felt like doing at the moment ''—if I go back to New York to work at a magazine there, I won't need it.''

The moment the words were out Abby could have shot herself. Hadn't they more or less agreed they'd just take it one day at a time until after the baby was born? But to his credit, Tad's expression remained unreadable. ''True,'' he said again.

Abby gulped, wished she could erase her faux pas and rushed on, ''It wouldn't be cost-effective to buy one only to have to dump it several months later. And financially it's such a big purchase, and we're still strapped for obvious reasons and—''

''You wouldn't mind me looking into it, anyway, would you?'' Tad interrupted.

Because he was already in the process of making a U-turn, Abby couldn't see into his eyes. ''What are you up to?''

''You'll see. Just play along.'' Tad turned the Jeep into a parking space in front of Audrey's Bakery and Café.

It was ten-thirty, and Ernest Lee Scruggs was sitting at a table in the back, the classified ads and a notepad and pen in front of him. He was wearing his mechanic's uniform from Joe Don Jerome's dealership. Neither light blue shirt nor pants had a speck of grease or grime on them. His hands, too, were clean. Which could only mean one thing, Abby thought. He hadn't put in any work thus far today.

''Hey, Ernest Lee.'' Tad waved at the mechanic. He ordered two muffins, two juices and one coffee for him and led the way to Ernest Lee's table. ''Mind if we talk to you a minute?'' Tad said affably. Not waiting for a response, he pulled up a chair and sat down, then pulled up one for Abby, who, like Ernest Lee, was looking a little reluctant. ''We've got a couple of questions,'' Tad continued. "See, Abby and I were just talking about buying a second car. The only problem is we can't afford a brand-new one. I'm a little leery of buying a used one 'cause there's no warranty. And if I pick it out on my own, it's almost a certainty we'll get stuck with a lemon. Not good, when you've got a wife with a baby on the way. So, I was thinking maybe you'd agree—for a fee of course—to take a look under the hood of any car I might want to buy."

Ernest Lee shrugged, looking perfectly willing to help. "Sure," he said.

Tad's brows knit together in a concerned manner. "Joe Don wouldn't mind you advising me on any car he's trying to sell off his lot?"

An angry look came into Ernest Lee's eyes. "You can get a better deal from one of the dealers in Asheville or Charlotte."

"Yeah, I know." Tad sighed. He leaned forward urgently. "The problem is financing. Things are a little tight for Abby and me right now." Tad reached over and patted Abby on the knee. "And since Joe Don has been known to help people who need a helping hand—"

Getting the drift of where this was all going, Abby interjected, "Not to mention it'd be a good way to mend fences with him." Abby looked at Ernest Lee with something akin to an apologetic glance. "You might have heard that Joe Don's been a little put out with us," she said.

Ernest Lee sighed. "Yeah, I know he pulled all his advertising from the paper in the summer."

"So you'll help us?" Tad pressed.

"Look, I—" Ernest Lee suddenly turned very red in the face, stared out the window, then turned back to them. "I'd like to help you folks out. Honestly I would." He crumpled his empty paper coffee cup in his hand. "But I wouldn't buy a used car here in Blossom."

"How about a new car or truck, then?" Tad said. "After all, you just bought one here."

"Yeah, and it's been nothing but trouble," Ernest Lee said darkly. He stood, pushing his chair back with a screech.

"Can't you do something?" Tad stood, too. "I mean, there's a lemon law in this state...."

Ernest Lee blew out a frustrated breath. "The dealer would have to agree the vehicle is a lemon."

"And Joe Don doesn't?"

Ernest Lee wheeled away from the two of them abruptly. "I've got to go."

"If I said something to upset you..." Tad rushed to apologize.

"It's not you," Ernest Lee said. He stalked out without a backward glance.

Audrey, who'd heard everything, came out from behind the counter. Proprietor of one of the most popular places in town, she knew just about everything that was going on. "He's upset because that new pickup he got isn't worth a plug nickel and Joe Don won't let him turn it back for another," she said.

"Why not?" Abby asked. After all, Ernest Lee worked for Joe Don. That ought to count for something.

Audrey shrugged. "'Cause I guess Joe Don doesn't agree it's a lemon. Heaven knows everyone who has the poor judgment to get a car there ends up having trouble with it," she said as she began to wipe down a few of the tables.

"Then why do they go there?" Abby asked.

Audrey sighed. "Because you can't beat the interest

rates, the insurance and sticker price anywhere else in the state.''

TAD DID HIS BEST to keep his feelings to himself, but the knowledge that Abby still wanted a magazine editor's job in New York bugged him repeatedly throughout the day. Part of him believed the life they were building together in Blossom ought to be enough, while another knew exactly what she yearned for, because there was a part of him that missed trotting around the globe for whatever story was currently breaking. There'd been an elusiveness to that kind of life that was appealing, if only because it'd been so darned easy to leave his problems behind him and forget all about them.

That was hard to do in Blossom, where everywhere he turned he was reminded of his yearning for Abby and the baby they were expecting. Where everywhere he turned he was reminded that, no matter how much he wanted her to stay with him, no matter how much he wanted to be what she needed and wanted, his best, just like back in Houston, might not be good enough. In fact, his best might be damn near disastrous.

Fortunately the work of getting out the next issue of the *Blossom Weekly News* kept them both busy from the time they hit the newspaper office until the time they returned, exhausted, to their half-redecorated home and fell into bed.

Still thinking how he might be able to make Abby love him as much as she loved the baby they were expecting, Tad fell asleep. Only to awake short hours later when Abby sat bolt upright in bed.

"Omigod!" she gasped, moaning and groaning and writhing sinuously as she attempted to extricate herself from the comforting warmth of him and the soothing feather ticking.

"What is it?" Tad cried as Abby flung the covers off her and stumbled, still moaning, from the bed.

"Don't touch me!" she shouted back as he followed her, the expression in her eyes as wild and confused as the state of her hair. "Omigod, omigod, omigod!" Abby's breath came out in a shuddering hiss as she did a strange one-legged dance around the bedroom in the moonlight.

"Are you hurt?" Tad bolted toward her. There was only one time in his life he'd ever felt anywhere near as helpless, he remembered, panicking, and that he did not want to think about.

Abby lowered her hands toward the floor, then lifted them toward the ceiling. "No, I'm dancing, you idiot," she pushed the words through her teeth.

Dancing. In the middle of the night. What she was doing looked more like an ancient tribal ritual to him.

Recalling Doc Harlan's advice to indulge his pregnant wife at all costs, Tad figured, what the heck. If she wouldn't tell him what she was doing or why, he'd just do it, too. Moaning and groaning in tandem to her wild sounds, he danced around with her in mirror image, stomping one leg on the floor repeatedly, writhing and moaning all the while.

Abby finally settled down, then she laughed until she cried, and he still had no idea what was going on as she sank onto the floor in a heap. He sank down beside her. "You want to tell me what's up with you?" he asked as she wiped away the tears of laughter flowing down her cheeks.

"I had a muscle cramp," she explained, when she could breathe again. "In my calf. It woke me up, and between you and the feather ticking and the covers, I was so tangled up I couldn't get out of bed. By the time I did, my calf muscle had practically rolled into a circle and the pain was excruciating. The only way to make it stop hurting is to straighten out the muscle, and the only way I've ever been able to do that is to put weight on it. The only trouble is, the process of putting weight on the calf muscle is excruciating, too, and until the cramp stops you can't really stand on that leg.''

"Oh."

Abby peered at him curiously. "Don't tell me you've never had a cramp!'' she said.

"Never." Tad shrugged. "Sorry."

Abby grinned and resumed rubbing her calf. "You really thought I was dancing?''

Tad grasped her leg and took over the rubbing for her. "Babe, I didn't know what to think,'' he drawled.

Tears of hilarity streamed down her face anew. When Abby could finally breathe again, she said, "That was so funny when you started dancing, too. You looked like some jungle tribesman, doing a dance around a fire.''

Tad shrugged, tacitly admitting that was the look he'd been aiming for. "Imitation is the sincerest form of flattery, didn't you know?''

Abby rolled her eyes. "You're incorrigible."

"So you've said."

Silence fell between them, comfortable and affectionate. "Well," Tad said finally, "I'm awake. Wide awake."

"Me, too." Abby sighed, wondering just how long it was going to take them to get back to sleep.

Tad tucked her hand in his, lifted it to his lips, and kissed it gently. "Want to go downstairs and get some milk?''

Abby ignored the tingles. "I'll get it," she said. After all, he'd done so much for her.

Tad shook his head. "Stay right here. I'll bring it up." He returned with a tray of two glasses of milk and two pieces of chocolate cake Aunt Sadie had made for them.

Abby sighed. "We shouldn't be eating something that rich this time of night."

He waggled his eyebrows at her. "We shouldn't be doing a lot of things. That never stopped us before."

Abby laughed softly. Tad was so much fun. If he ever left her, she would miss him terribly. "That's true," she said ruefully as bittersweet melancholy overcame her.

"Hey now, you don't have to worry about your weight," Tad chided gallantly, misinterpreting the reason behind her swiftly shifting emotions. "You're right on track. The doctor said so. Besides, that dance you just did worked off a lot of calories. And I know a way to work off a few more."

"I know you do, sailor. But first things first..." Right now she had a mean craving for chocolate cake.

They sat back against the pillows and munched on their cake. "It's amazing, isn't it," Tad said, "how much our lives have changed since last April?"

Abby nodded. She sipped her milk and looked into his eyes. "To tell you the truth, as much as I wanted to have a child someday, I never really saw myself as a wife or a mom."

Tad's glance softened. "I never saw myself as a dad, either."

"But we're doing it, aren't we?" Abby beamed. "Becoming parents."

Tad nodded.

They fell into a thoughtful silence once more.

"It wasn't that I didn't want a home and family of my

own," Abby said at last. "I did. I just thought it would never happen."

Again Tad nodded, understanding completely. "I know what you mean. Until you and I eloped I never even came close to marrying anyone."

"I know in the beginning it was just fireworks that brought us together. We really didn't know all that much about each other in Paris." And in some respects, Abby thought, knowing Tad still hadn't told her anything at all about his life in Houston, they still didn't.

"Now it's different," Tad said. "Now we're..."

"Friends," Abby finished.

"Great friends," Tad amended.

They forked up the last of their cake. "Do you think it's just the baby and the newspaper making us so close?" Abby asked.

"What do you mean?" Tad put his plate aside.

Abby shrugged. "We're sort of like two survivors of a shipwreck on a desert island," she said, suddenly feeling brave enough to face at least a few of her fears and voice them. "And that, in turn, sort of makes me wonder," she continued, carefully gauging his reaction. "When things return to normal, meaning the paper gets on solid ground and the baby is born and we get used to being parents and all that." Abby swallowed hard and forced herself to keep meeting his eyes and go on. "When things settle down again, do you think we'll feel less close or grow apart?" The way her parents always had in their various marriages.

"No. I don't. What we're building here is going to last a lifetime, Abby. And whatever happens we'll always be connected through our child." He turned off the light, helped her lie back against the pillows and then did the same. As had become their custom every night, they cuddled together in the darkness.

"Tad?" Abby asked eventually.

"Hmm?"

"One more thing." She smiled against his chest, loving his warmth and his strength. "I'm glad it's your baby I'm having."

"Me, too, Abby." Tad sighed contentedly and held her close. "Me, too."

Chapter Ten

"This is probably going to be the best tag sale we'll see for the rest of the year," Donna told Abby as they toured the barn full of antiques, secondhand furniture and all manner of knickknacks, decorator items and recreational gear.

Abby paused in front of a section of baby items. Each day she and Tad thought they couldn't possibly get any more excited about the birth of their baby. And each day they were proved wrong. "I'd love to buy a crib or a changing table, but Sadie made me promise to wait until after the baby shower."

"Well, we can go ahead and get the nursery carpet in and the stenciled border up." Donna paused before a gorgeous writing desk, checked the tag. "What do you think?"

Abby checked the tag. "I think it's way over budget."

"You're probably right." Donna moved on to the selection of paintings. "So how is Tad doing as a prospective papa?"

"Pretty good actually."

Donna smiled and shook her head. "I remember Ron's reaction to my first pregnancy. He had it all," she said, laughing. "Morning sickness, backaches, cravings, sleepless nights. Doc Harlan called it the most advanced case of the couvade syndrome he'd ever seen. Fortunately, by the time I had my second baby, Ron had relaxed enough to take it all in stride.''

Abby paused in front of a his-and-hers bicycle set with a toddler seat strapped to the back of the man's bike. Abby immediately thought about sunny summer days, what it would be like to get on bikes with Tad and the baby and go for a ride around the neighborhood. ''Tad hasn't evidenced anything like that,'' Abby said as she lifted the tag and saw the bikes were within her budget if she stretched.

''He probably will before all is said and done.'' Donna frowned as the cell phone she carried with her began to ring. ''If you'll excuse me…'' She walked a short distance away while Abby continued to look at the bikes. A minute later Donna returned, looking harried. ''My youngest was just hurt at soccer practice. I've got to go. About the lamps and linen chest we picked out for the baby's room…''

''I'll make a bid on them and arrange for delivery.''

''Thanks. See you later.'' Donna hurried off.

Abby went to find the cashier. Before the afternoon was out, she had purchased everything, including the bikes, which she'd had loaded into the back of the Jeep. Figuring she'd surprise Tad, she took them home and set them up in the middle of the living room, then decorated them with big red bows. She got out a stack of articles that still needed to be edited, then sat down to work on them and wait for her husband to show up.

He came home around dinnertime. ''Abby?'' he called as he walked through the door.

''In here,'' Abby called back.

Tad strode in, a smile on his face. His joy promptly

faded as he took in the bikes, complete with baby seat. "What the hell is this?" he barked.

Abby blinked. He'd never berated her over anything she'd purchased before. She couldn't believe he was doing it now. It was so unlike him. She moved slowly to her feet. Head high, she said, "It's a present from me to you and the baby."

His face whitened. He stepped closer, unfairly using his height to force her to lean back to look up at him. "You should have asked," he said in a low disgruntled tone.

Abby swallowed and willed her heart not to pound. She didn't know what was going on here, but clearly something was. "That would have ruined the surprise."

Tad grimaced. "You're going to have to take them back."

"What?"

The muscles in his chest and shoulders flexed as he folded his arms. "We don't need bikes, Abby."

"Says who?" Abby loved to ride. Though she hadn't had much of a chance for years. But now that she lived in a small town, instead of the city, well, why the heck not?

"They'd just sit in the garage," Tad continued.

"So don't ride yours," Abby sputtered, no longer caring they were headed for an argument.

"Look," Tad growled as his eyes zeroed in on her, "I don't want them. Okay?" Giving her no chance to reply, he spun on his heel and stalked out of the house.

"DONNA WAS TELLING ME about husbands who have sympathetic symptoms, but this was ridiculous," Abby told Aunt Sadie tearfully half an hour later as she poured out her heart to Tad's aunt. "I mean, I've heard of mood swings, but…"

Unable to continue, Abby stared at the floor in front of her, where Buster lay on the floor next to a very pregnant Belle. His facial expression looked as mournful as ever, but the way the two dogs were cuddled said they were happy as could be.

"It wasn't a mood swing, dear," Sadie said, casting a glance into the kitchen where Raymond worked preparing dinner.

"Then what was it?" Abby asked, looking at the mingled concern and caution in Sadie's eyes and once again feeling like the odd man out.

"I can't—" Sadie stopped. Her eyes misted. "You're going to have to ask Tad," she said in a strangled tone.

Unfortunately Tad was not likely to tell her anything. And that hurt. She'd thought—hoped—they were becoming as close as she'd always thought a husband and wife should be. She leaned forward earnestly, determined to find out all she could from Sadie. "I did ask him, Sadie, but all he would say is that he doesn't want us to have bikes. He didn't tell me why it was such a sore subject. He just issued this edict and stomped out of the house like the biggest male chauvinist on earth. And you know Tad, Sadie. That's not like him. It's not like him at all!"

Sadie nodded. She didn't approve of her beloved nephew's behavior, but it didn't surprise her, either. "I agree. It sounds as if Tad was unreasonable and overemotional today."

"But?" Abby prodded, sensing there was more.

Sadie pressed her lips together stubbornly. "You still need to talk to him."

Nixing Sadie's offer of dinner, Abby went to the newspaper office. Everyone but Tad had left. He was sitting behind his computer working on the Web site he was creating for the newspaper. "I'm not good company tonight, Abby," he warned, his eyes focused firmly on the computer screen.

"Thanks to you, honeybunch," Abby drawled with provoking sweetness, "neither am I." Determined to clear the air between them once and for all, Abby moved a stack of papers and sat on the edge of his desk, facing him, so he had no choice but to hear her out. "I don't know what I did that was so wrong, but you had no right to treat me that way."

"I know," Tad said, guilt flashing across the features of his handsome face as he saved his material and switched off the computer with a decisive snap.

"I talked to Sadie—"

"Damn it." Tad vaulted from his desk chair and began to pace. "I told her I didn't want you to know about Houston."

Abby drew a breath and plunged on recklessly, "Sadie didn't tell me anything about Houston. But I sure wish someone would."

A silence fell that made Abby's heart thud all the harder. She continued to look at her husband steadily, knowing no matter how difficult it was, these things needed to be said, and said now. "If we're going to bring up a child together, Tad," she told him quietly, "we need to know these things about each other." *And we need to know them because we're married—so very married, in fact—that we may very well elect to stay married even after our baby's born. That is, if we can clear up some of these miscommunication problems before our son or daughter gets here.*

For a second Tad stood very still. With a sigh he turned to her. "I had a brother, Billy, who was two years younger than me.'' Tad swallowed hard and, a distant expression on his face, began to pace again. He paused to stare out the window at the swiftly descending darkness. ''When we were kids we used to do everything together.'' A muscle working in his jaw, Tad turned back to her and said in a low rusty-sounding tone, ''My parents always told me to look after him, and I did—'' he jerked in a breath ''—'cause I was the oldest. But I wasn't that great at it.'' Sorrow tinged his eyes. For a second Abby thought he wouldn't—couldn't—go on.

''I used to be impatient,'' Tad continued self-deprecatingly, ''because he couldn't quite keep up with me.'' Another shadow passed over his eyes. He put his hand up and rubbed at them wearily.

''One day, when I was ten and Billy was eight, we got on our bikes and headed for the empty lot that we used as a baseball field.'' Tad swallowed and forced himself to continue. ''It was just two blocks over on typical suburban streets. We'd ridden there plenty of times. It was no big deal.''

Tad blinked rapidly as tears rose in his eyes and his chest tightened to the point he could barely breathe. ''I wanted to take the lead so I rode on ahead. I knew better,'' Tad whispered hoarsely as he shoved his hands through his hair. He wished he could forever shut out the memory of that awful time, even as remembered images flashed in his head. ''I should have made him go first,'' he said on a tortured breath, ''kept a closer eye on him, but I didn't.'' God help him, he hadn't done so. He shrugged. ''One minute I'm pedaling along as fast as I can go, Billy behind me, struggling to keep up as usual. The next thing I hear is the sound of a car turning the corner and a loud screech, then a smash.'' Tad felt the blood drain from his face. His stomach churned and his knees went weak. "I turned in time to see Billy get knocked off his bike." Tad shook his head. He balled his fists as angry anguished tears streamed down his face. "He never made a sound," Tad said, able to see it every bit as clearly now as he had then. "There was just that instant, his eyes frozen in terror, and then *wham,* he hit the pavement." Tad jerked in a deep breath as more tears streamed from his eyes and nose. "That was in the days before helmets, of course."

Ashamed that after all this time, that even now, he couldn't talk about the accident and hold it together, he wheeled away from Abby. His back to her, he wiped the tears away. Then he sighed and finished numbly, "The head injuries were massive. He died before they could get him to the hospital. And it was all my fault."

He turned to find Abby crying, too. Big gulping silent tears. "Oh, God. Tad..." she said brokenly.

Feeling like a robot, Tad said, "I haven't been on a bike since."

"I'm sorry," Abby whispered. She swept into his arms and held him tight. "So sorry. I didn't know." She sobbed against his chest.

Tad held her close, aware that they were both crying and it felt good. He hadn't cried about Billy since the funeral. "I'm sorry, too," he said hoarsely at length, rubbing the tension from her back with long strokes of his palms. "I shouldn't have overreacted." Tad paused, drew back. "But when I walked in and saw those bikes—" *not to mention the baby seat* "—it was just more than I could deal with."

Abby touched a finger to his lips, silencing him. Compassion lit her golden-brown eyes. "You don't have to say anything more," she told him softly, her very presence, the depth and breadth of her understanding, soothing him like nothing and no one ever had.

"Maybe it's time I talked about it to someone," Tad acknowledged quietly.

"You never have," Abby guessed.

"No." Tad handed Abby a tissue, too. "Donna knew Billy had been hit by a car and killed. I think everyone around here did. But I don't think anyone knew I was with him at the time. Aunt Sadie was pretty good at keeping the details to herself. It was her way of protecting me. Later, when I was older, and she wanted me to talk about it with her—" and she had tried to get him to do so many times, Tad remembered "—I wouldn't."

"What about your parents?" Abby asked curiously as she perched on a nearby desk. "Did you talk about it with them?"

Tad shook his head. "Aside from going over the details of what had happened, no." He met Abby's eyes, remembering the utter lack of joy that had encompassed the rest of the years during which he'd grown up. "You have to understand my family life was shattered by Billy's death. It was never the same again."

He moved to sit next to her. "Did your parents divorce?" Abby asked.

"No." Tad remembered wishing they had. "They stayed married after the tragedy," he reported glumly as he turned toward Abby and she turned toward him. "But their relationship had a hollowness to it that was felt by everyone inside and outside the family."

Abby reached over and linked hands with him. "It must have been hard," she said compassionately.

"It was. Which is why, I think, my dad started taking field assignments that had us living in a lot of foreign countries and moving every few months. Anything to forget.''

"Only forgetting was impossible,'' Abby murmured.

"Right.'' Tad studied their linked hands. "In some respects I think my parents might have been better off if they'd divorced, instead of staying yoked together by promises they'd made to each other but were, in the end, unable to keep.''

Abby moved off the desk and came around to stand between his legs. "You weren't to blame for the disintegration of their marriage, Tad.'' She put her arms around him and tilted her face up to his. "Just like I wasn't to blame for the disintegration of my parents' marriage.''

Tad wished he could believe that. He released the breath he'd been holding. "All I know is that I never want to feel like that again. Like my actions—deliberate or otherwise—robbed someone I love of the life they were meant to have or should have had.''

Abby paused. "Is that the way your parents felt?''

Tad shrugged and forced himself to be ruthlessly honest. "I think my parents resented me for not being able to protect Billy. I know I blame myself.'' *And always will.* "I was faster than he was, older, more experienced. If it had been me bringing up the rear, I could have gotten myself out of the way. Him, too, probably.''

Tears flooded Abby's eyes as they both thought about what a profound impact all this had had on his life. "You don't know that,'' she protested.

"Yeah, I do,'' Tad said sadly, briefly closing his eyes. He pointed to his heart. "In here I do.'' He paused, still struggling with his emotions. With effort he pulled himself together. "Anyway, seeing the bikes in the living room brought it all back.'' The muscles in his jaw tensed.

Abby stepped away slightly and looked up at him. "I'll get rid of them tomorrow," she promised.

Tad touched a hand to her hair, burying his fingers in the silky softness. "I'd appreciate it." He drew a long breath and looked deep into her eyes. "I can't go back there, Abby."

"I understand." Abby caught his hand and kissed it.

A thoughtful silence fell between them.

"Sadie really understands how you feel about all this, doesn't she?" Abby asked finally. "I mean, even if you haven't discussed it."

"Yeah. She knows me pretty well." As Tad thought about his aunt, his mouth crooked up in an affection-laced smile. "That's one of the reasons I wanted to come back to Blossom to finally settle down—so I could be near Aunt Sadie. We're all the family each of us has now. Aside from you and me and the baby," Tad amended hastily. "I wanted to build something real and lasting. I wanted to build the kind of life my parents and I might have had together if only we'd dealt with Billy's death and the subsequent emotional fallout at the time. Because I know now that nothing is ever gained by putting off the inevitable or the painful."

"I agree." Abby thought of her parents' many divorces, and the long-drawn-out falling-apart period that preceded each one. She sighed and linked hands with Tad again. "When it comes to something like that," she agreed firmly, "procrastinating only makes it all the harder."

"EVERYTHING OKAY with you and Tad?" Sadie asked Abby at work the next day.

Abby nodded and confided to Sadie with relief, "We had a serious talk last night." She leaned forward to kiss

Tad's aunt on the cheek, wordlessly thanking her for what she'd done to bring the two of them together. "I understand everything now."

"Good." Sadie smiled and gave Abby a brief motherly hug in return. "He's needed to talk to someone for a long time. I'm glad it was you."

Before either could say anything else, the front door opened and Tim Grau, the owner of the Mighty Fine Restaurant walked in. Though he'd cleaned up the kitchen and managed once again to get an A rating from the health department, his business had been struggling since the salmonella outbreak in the summer. "Can I help you?" Cindy asked from behind the advertising counter.

"I'd like to talk to Tad."

Tad came out of his glassed-in office just behind the bullpen. He shook Tim's hand as if no ill words had ever passed between them. "What's up?"

Tim's cheeks reddened slightly as he met Tad's eyes. "You know that idea you had last summer about me going the community-service route, instead of trying to sweep the scandal under the rug? Well, if the offer's still open, I'm ready to try it now. It's either that or close up shop altogether. So I'll host free classes on safe food preparation at the restaurant if you all will write it up in the newspaper."

Tad grinned. "The next issue soon enough for you?" he drawled.

While the two men went into Tad's office to work out a publicity schedule for the event, Abby went back to work editing the article on fall tree planting. She was almost finished when a phone call came in for her. Listening, she could barely contain her excitement. "No, tomorrow afternoon will be fine. Yes, thanks." She hung up the phone.

"Tomorrow will be fine for what?" Tad asked. He'd just shown Tim Grau out and was heading back to his office.

Abby drew a deep breath. "That was the headhunter I hired. *Chicago Living* magazine wants to interview me for a job as the Home Decorating editor. I've got an appointment set up for tomorrow afternoon. They're leaving an airline ticket for me at the Asheville airport."

The mixed emotions Abby half expected Tad to manifest never came. "Wow, that's great," Tad said, as the other staff looked on in confusion.

Yes, it was great, considering how long and hard she'd worked to make a career for herself in the magazine-publishing world, so why wasn't she feeling a lot more excited? Abby wondered.

Aware of all eyes on her, she forced a smile and went on to reassure Tad brightly, "It's okay for me to fly, by the way. I asked Dr. Ellison, and he said it was okay through the seventh month. And since I'm only six and a half months along..." Abby shrugged.

Tad nodded and everyone else went back to work. "Are you going to spend the night?" he asked.

"Yes. They've arranged for a hotel." And maybe that was a good thing, Abby thought. Maybe that would give her time to think.

Tad touched her shoulder and kissed her cheek. His eyes were filled with kindness and understanding. "I wish you the best of luck," he said, really seeming to mean it.

"Thanks," Abby said softly. She pushed away an unexpected twinge of hurt. Tad was only being supportive and following the agreement they'd established at the outset of this pregnancy, Abby told herself firmly. He

was not—as everyone else around her erroneously
seemed to think—practically shoving her out the door.

"SO HOW'D IT GO?" Tad asked as he met Abby at the
gate upon her return from Chicago two days later.

Abby made no effort to hide her disappointment. "Not
well. I knew the minute they saw me and realized I was
pregnant that I wasn't going to get the job."

"They didn't know you were pregnant before you
went?"

"The headhunter neglected to mention it," Abby said
dryly. "She said it shouldn't have made any difference
to them if they were really interested in my work. And
she's right. But you and I both know how things sometimes work in the real world. Some employers think pregnant women are not to be counted on."

"I'm sorry." Tad enveloped her in a comforting hug.
He pressed a kiss into her hair. "I know you've been
wanting to get back into magazine editing."

"Yes, well—" Abby shrugged "—it's probably for
the best, anyway. Looking at the way the magazine was
structured, I don't think I would have been a good fit for
that job in any case." She just wished she hadn't had to
go all the way to Chicago and spend a night alone in a
hotel room, away from Tad, especially if their time together really was—as it appeared—drawing to an end.

Tad helped her collect her suitcase at the baggage
claim, then walked her out to the parking lot. "How do
you feel? Was the traveling hard on you?"

"Not at all." Abby waited for him to unlock the Jeep.
"I feel fine, really. Physically I'm in great shape."

It was how she felt emotionally that was the problem.
She was relieved and depressed simultaneously. Tad and
the baby were beginning to mean so much more to her

than her career. Knowing that her career was the one thing that had always sustained her, through good and bad times, she couldn't help feeling that letting go of that ambition was almost an invitation to disaster.

And she continued to feel that way all that evening and into the next day. So much so that it was a relief when Tad surprised her by nixing dinner with her to go hang out at the local tavern for a bit and watch the Duke versus UNC football game on the big-screen TV.

Maybe, Abby thought pensively, a little irked to be ditched for a night out with the guys, another night apart was exactly what she and Tad needed.

"WELL, DON'T YOU LOOK like you just lost your best friend," Doc Harlan said to Tad as he made room for him at the table where he was sitting.

"I second that!" Sonny remarked as he walked by, a plate of nachos in one hand, a beer in the other. "After the way you carried on while she was out of town, acting lonesome as all get-out," Sonny teased, "I thought you'd be home with Abby tonight, cuddling like crazy."

If only he could have been, Tad thought, as he reached for a handful of peanuts and began to shell them one by one. "Sadie's got that surprise for her tonight, remember?"

"Oh, yeah. Cindy whispered something about it before she left the office." Still chuckling, Sonny headed on over to the table where the just-out-of-college kids were sitting. "Enjoy your freedom!" Sonny called over his shoulder. "You sure won't get much of it after your baby's born."

"That what has you feeling so blue?" Doc asked. He called the waiter over and ordered a plate of buffalo wings and a pitcher of beer. "The impending lack of freedom?"

Tad shook his head. He explained about the job interview, concluding miserably, "To be perfectly honest, I feel like I cost Abby the Chicago job. If it weren't for the pregnancy, which as you have probably figured out by now wasn't exactly planned..." Tad trailed off as a frosty pitcher of beer was put on the table. He poured a glass for Doc and himself.

Just then, UNC scored the first touchdown of the evening. Doc—a UNC med-school grad himself—signaled a thumbs-up, then waited for the backslapping and high fives to subside before responding to Tad. "Has Abby been complaining about being pregnant?"

"No." Tad studied the bottom of his glass.

Doc broke open a peanut shell and shook two nuts out into the palm of his hand. "Does she seem at all unhappy about it?"

"Well, no," Tad said as he, too, reached for a peanut and broke it open.

"Because she's always seemed really happy about it to me," Doc concurred.

"She *is* very happy about the baby," Tad said quietly. "We both are." *Deliriously so.*

Doc paused, clearly wanting to understand, as their family physician and a friend. "Then...?"

Tad drew a breath. Damn it all, he hated feeling guilty. He'd lived a certain way all his adult life because he'd never wanted to be responsible for anyone's unhappiness and loss again, and yet here he was, up to his neck in soul-deep regret! He scowled. "It's just that, career-wise, for Abby, the timing couldn't be worse," he grumbled.

"Let me tell you something, son," Doc said as he

refilled their glasses with beer. "My first two kids were born while I was in medical school."

"That must've been rough."

Doc grinned and nodded. "It was. I was working ungodly hours at the time. We were five hundred miles from either set of grandparents. And half the time, because I was at the hospital so much, my wife had to be mother and father both to our babies. But we learned something important from all that, Tad, something I've never hesitated to share with my patients and my own kids, as well. Babies don't always come along at the best time, but once they do come along, you realize it is the best time."

Doc gave Tad a moment to think about that, then slapped him on the back and continued compassionately, "This is all going to work out for the best, Tad. You'll see. Once that baby is here, Abby's not going to want to be anyplace but right here in Blossom with you."

Tad hoped like heck that was so.

He didn't know what he would do if Abby did move on and they ended up commuting and splitting custody of their child, as previously agreed.

"WELL, WHAT DO YOU think?" Sadie asked after they'd said goodbye to the last guest and Abby had returned to the living room to admire Sadie's gift to her, Tad and the baby. "Did I or did I not pull off the biggest surprise thus far in your pregnancy?"

Aside from the actual conception? And the fact that every day she was falling more and more in love with her husband?

"You did great, Sadie." Abby hugged her. Returning home from work that evening, sans Tad, Abby had walked into the house to a chorus of "Surprise!" and more gifts and good wishes than she could have imagined. In fact, hours later, she was still reeling from the enormity of it all. Not to mention the timing. Sadie had told her the shower wouldn't be till well after Christmas, just to throw her off.

"I was completely bowled over both by the party and your gift to us," Abby told Sadie gratefully. She leaned forward to give the diminutive older woman a hug. "The cradle is just...well, it's incredible."

Sadie smiled and hugged her back. "It's a family heirloom. I always thought I'd be using it for my own children, but it didn't turn out that way, largely because I kept waiting for everything to be perfect, and that kind of guarantee—the guarantee I wanted and needed at that time—never came." Sadie paused to pick up some plates while Abby did the same.

"Consequently the chance to have a baby of my own passed me by. Although I did have children in my life, lots of them, in my teaching and in my nephews—Tad and his brother, Billy."

"And now you have Raymond," Abby said gently, knowing from having seen them together how much the two were beginning to mean to each other.

"Yes, I do. And I love him with all my heart."

"Are you going to marry him?"

Sadie released a shaky breath. "To be perfectly honest, I don't know. If it wasn't for the nine-year age difference, I probably would."

Abby carried another stack of plates into the kitchen. "You're not going to let *that* stop you!"

Sadie smiled. "From loving him, no. From the possibility that he might have to spend a lot of his best years nursing me through the vagaries of old age, probably, yes."

"Oh, Sadie—"

Sadie raised a quelling finger, then, as the two of them began to load the dishwasher, said, "Now don't you feel sorry for me, Abby Kildaire McFarlane. Raymond and I have lots of good times ahead of us, not to mention a soon-to-arrive litter of the most unusual puppies."

Abby thought about Buster and Belle. The two dogs had become as close as their masters. Abby grinned. "I'll bet those puppies are going to be cute as can be."

"I bet they will, too." Clearly torn between speaking her mind and not interfering, Sadie finally said, "I know you're feeling uncertain. Your marriage to Tad and the baby happened awfully fast. But that doesn't mean you should value either any less."

"Value what any less?" Tad asked, coming in through the back door. He'd walked home in the brisk November air. His cheeks were flushed, his hair windblown. As he shrugged out of his jacket and came close enough to give Abby a kiss, he smelled wintry and sexy and wonderful.

"You." Abby grinned, enjoying the feel of the possessive arm he'd wrapped around her, and snuggled against him. "And the baby."

"I was lecturing," Sadie confessed with a twinkle in her eye. "One of the results of being a teacher for so long, I'm afraid. I feel duty bound to point out the meaning of all manner of things."

Abby took Tad by the hand. "Come on. I want to show you what our friends and neighbors gave us."

Later, after Sadie had left and Yvonne retired to her own room, Tad insisted he lock up while an exhausted Abby went on to bed. He found her in the bedroom, clad in her nightgown, pacing and rubbing her lower back. "Problem?"

"Just the normal aches and pains of pregnancy. My

back aches after I've been sitting for long periods of time," she explained.

"Maybe a back rub would help," Tad suggested.

Willing to do just about anything to ease the discomfort, Abby lay on her side on the bed while Tad went to get her favorite skin lotion. "So what was Sadie really lecturing you on?" he asked as he kneaded the tension from her muscles with hands as warm and soothing as a hot bath.

Abby closed her eyes, loving the feel of his hands on her skin. It was one of many things that she would really miss if they ever parted. "She thinks I've got one foot out the door of this marriage," Abby reported reluctantly.

Tad stopped what he was doing momentarily, then resumed his kneading with slow heavenly strokes. "Do you?"

Abby tried not to wince at the lack of emotion in his voice. "I can't help but feel skittish, Tad," she confided honestly. Aware the ache in her back was gone—to be replaced by one in her heart—she broke free and rolled to face Tad. He looked as if he felt as confused as she did about everything and yet wanted to understand. "After seeing my mother marry and divorce five times, my father marry and divorce six, I feel like I know all the warning signs of a marriage in distress and little else," Abby told him softly. "I don't want our baby to suffer through even one marital breakup."

Tad nodded. "Can't disagree with you there."

"On the other hand—" Abby sighed regretfully "—I don't know anything about the normal happy all-American family you see on TV, either."

Tad rolled her away from him once again. "We're doing fine, Abby." His hands worked magic as they kneaded down her spine. "Between the two of us we'll figure it all out."

Abby didn't know if it was hormones or what, but suddenly she was near tears as he began working his fingers across her shoulders and down her right arm. "There's so much more to it than that."

"I know," he said as he returned to her lower back and continued to work out the kinks.

Abby barely suppressed a groan of contentment. "Tad..." she said as a wave of longing swept through her. Her limbs felt heavy and weak.

"Hmm?" Tad sounded totally absorbed in his work as he made his way down her legs.

"That's not my back."

"Oh." Tad's hands moved upward. "So it isn't," he said mischievously.

Abby smiled and arched against the playful wandering of his hand. "That's not my back, either."

Giving up on the massage altogether, Tad rolled her onto her back. He looked down at her with such intensity she caught her breath. The next thing she knew their mouths were locked in a searing kiss and he was stretched out on the bed beside her. "I forgot to tell you something," he murmured as he divested her of her gown and dizziness swept through her in waves.

"What?" Abby gasped.

He drew all of her against all of him. He kissed her cheek, her nose, her temple, then buried his face in her hair. "When I smell that perfume of yours, I get side-tracked very easily."

Abby kissed his throat. Her fingers slid through the silky mat of hair on his chest, then lower, to the waistband of his low-slung pajama pants. "I'm not wearing any perfume."

Tad smiled. "My point exactly."

One kiss turned into twenty as they touched and tempted and teased, putting everything they had, everything they wanted, into their caresses. Until all that mattered to either of them was the desire sweeping through them both in powerful waves, and he was straining against her, letting her know he wanted her as wildly as she wanted him. And she wanted him that way, all fire and passion, nothing secret, nothing from their pasts, nothing from their future, standing between them.

His kisses were just as sweet, just as filled with longing. As their ragged breaths meshed, Tad taught her what it was to love, not just with hearts and souls, but through touch. He taught her she was just as insatiable as he, that it was better to let their passion build and build. He skimmed her body with his fingers, filling his hands with her soft hot flesh. Then threaded his hands through her hair, pushing it away from her ear, and kissed and caressed his way down her neck. She knew he wanted her just as she wanted him, and she also knew, as he drew back to look at her, his blue eyes alight with unbearably tender protectiveness, that, before they went any farther, he had something to ask.

"Just out of curiosity, Ab—" his voice was rough, filled with the longing for more and the equally important need to know "—are we going to have to stop making love at some point?"

"Soon, yes," Abby said breathlessly as Tad kissed the taut aching crowns of her breasts and the graceful slope of her tummy. "We won't be able to have intercourse. But for right now, for at least the next two weeks," she said as he slid upward, "we can, um…"

"Do this?" Tad guessed as he sat against the headboard, took her with him and lifted her ever so gently, ever so carefully, onto his lap. As she faced him, he delicately, intimately caressed the inside of her thighs. Letting her know, despite the swollen curve of her belly, she was just as desirable—if not more desirable—to him than ever.

"Mm-hmm," Abby confirmed as she shifted and made them one. "We can absolutely do this," she said, knowing he was definitely the sexiest man she had ever met.

"Then we better make the most of it," Tad said hoarsely, kissing her and cupping her breasts until she shuddered in response and her nipples beaded against his palms, "don't you think?"

"Oh, yes," Abby returned lovingly. Overcome with need and yearning, overcome by the tenderness he displayed, she took up the rhythm he started, merging their bodies as intimately and irrevocably as they'd begun to merge their lives. Afterward Tad cuddled her close. "I love you, Abby," he whispered in her ear.

Abby's eyes filled to overflowing. Maybe it was her pregnancy—the surge of hormones flowing through her—but she'd never felt so wanted, nor at the same time more vulnerable, as she did tonight. "I love you, too," she whispered back, holding him close. *So much.*

The problem was, love had never really been the issue for them. They'd both easily confessed to falling in love with each other in Paris. That was why they'd gotten married immediately upon returning to the States.

The problem was, she knew—through bitter life experience—love alone, no matter how passionate or exciting, wasn't always enough to hold a marriage together over the long haul.

There were times when love wasn't nearly enough. She only hoped, desperately so, that this wouldn't turn out to be one of those times.

Chapter Eleven

Abby stood at Tad's elbow, watching anxiously, as he tried to insert a large pinecone into the small end of a rough-barked horn of plenty. "That's the wrong end to be stuffing, isn't it?"

Tad took the pinecone, inserted it in the other end, then added an unshelled walnut and bunch of grapes into the smaller opening of the Thanksgiving centerpiece.

Arms folded, head cocked to one side, he studied his "masterpiece" with a comic expression. "I think I know my cornucopias."

Abby snorted and went to lower the volume of the football game on TV. "That's what you said about the turkey," she reminded him, returning to his side.

Tad shrugged. "So I got the neck and the...well, you know, mixed up."

Abby rolled her eyes. "I'll say!"

"It all turned out all right in the end."

Yes, Abby thought, it had. In fact, this was the best holiday she'd had in ages. Tad wrapped an arm around her shoulders and teased, "Whoever would've thought you'd be standing around in our kitchen, wearing an apron and holding a meat thermometer."

Until she'd met Tad, she'd been a career woman all

the way. "Just don't tell anyone, okay?" she murmured, disgruntled, glad Yvonne—who'd gone home to be with her own family for the holiday—wasn't around to see this.

Tad appeared to consider it. "I could be bribed." He gave her the look that made her blood heat.

Abby blushed as she thought about the many ways they had made love. "Really."

"Really," he said softly.

"What's going on out here in the kitchen?" Sadie poked her head in.

"Exactly what you'd think," Tad said, making Abby's blush deepen. He picked up the turkey baster, put it in Abby's hand and pointed it in the direction of his chest. "I'm being held hostage."

"Absolutely true," Abby agreed. "I'm not letting him out of here until the centerpiece is just right."

"You're having a good time?" Sadie beamed, pleased.

"Oh, yes," Abby said as Tad pulled her close. "How are the puppies doing?"

"Great. They're just starting to wake up. We thought you might want to come and see them."

They all trooped into the mudroom behind the garage and peered into the quilt-lined whelping box Raymond had built for her. Buster was curled in the corner, carefully keeping watch. Belle was lying on her side, all six of her puppies cuddled up against her. As they woke up, they squirmed and began to nurse, making little mewling sounds.

"They are so cute," Abby said.

"They've got the best of both parents," Tad agreed.

A mixture of brown, black, white and buff-colored short fluffy hair covered their compact little bodies. Their faces were tiny and appealing, their ears long and drooping.

Raymond had loaded the box into the rear of his pickup and brought the crew to Tad and Abby's for the day. Sadie was dizzy with delight, watching the new pups. "I don't think she's going to let you take the puppies back home with you," Abby teased.

Tad nodded. "You, Belle, and the pups might just have to move in with Sadie and Buster," he told Raymond, "so Aunt Sadie can keep an eye on them, too."

"Actually," Sadie said shyly as she and Raymond linked hands, "we've sort of addressed that issue."

Raymond grinned. "I asked Sadie to marry me last night."

Sadie held up her left hand, which sported a brand-new diamond ring. "And I said yes."

"Congratulations." Abby embraced them both in turn, and Tad followed suit.

"Have you set a date?" Tad asked, looking as happy as could be for his aunt.

"New Year's Day," Sadie said.

"WHAT ARE WE GOING to give Raymond and Sadie for a wedding gift?" Abby asked Tad one lazy Sunday afternoon a couple of weeks later as they sat in the family room, making wreaths out of pine boughs and red velvet ribbons.

Tad shrugged. "I don't know. A triple leash?"

Abby gave him a look. "Very funny," she told him in the soft playful voice he loved. "And we already got them one when the puppies were born."

Tad paused to give it some serious thought. "How about tickets to the Charlotte Symphony and an overnight stay in a hotel there?" He looked at Abby for her reaction, knowing it was important they get this right, and that it be from the two of them. "They both like classical music."

Abby smiled, as relieved as he was to have that problem solved. "That's an excellent idea."

"Now all we have to decide is a name for the baby."

Instead of the groan Tad was expecting, Abby smiled a secret little smile. She put aside her wreath and came over to sit next to him. "I've been thinking about that. I have an idea."

She was serious, Tad realized. "Go ahead." They'd already discussed—and rejected at least once—every name, male and female, in the baby-name book they'd bought.

"I think the name of our first child should have sentimental value."

First child. Tad liked the sound of that. Nothing would please him more than making more babies with Abby.

Abby took his hands in hers. "I was thinking of your brother. I'd like to name him William if the baby's a boy, and Wilhelmina if it's a girl. Will if it's a boy. Billie if it's a girl."

Not so long ago he would have reacted vehemently to such a proposal, Tad knew. But now he seemed to have made peace with the past, more than he could ever have imagined doing. And he had Abby to thank. "I'd like that," he said softly, looking deep into her eyes. "Very much."

Abby breathed a sigh of relief. "Good," she said, smiling. "Me, too."

They were silent a few minutes more. It was a good feeling, just sitting there together that way.

"So...any word from Yvonne?" Tad asked. She'd

come back briefly after Thanksgiving, helped out a little more at the newspaper, then left again.

Abby shook her head. "Her interview with *Personalities!* magazine was on Friday. She was going to spend the weekend with friends in New York and then head back here on Monday or Tuesday."

The phone rang. Abby got up to answer it. "Well," she said, after greeting the caller affectionately, "speak of the devil." As Tad listened, ebullient congratulations followed. "Of course we understand!" Abby exclaimed. "No. Don't worry about it. I'll take care of everything. All right. Good luck to you—keep me posted. Right. I'll see you on e-mail. Bye." Her back to him, Abby put the phone down slowly.

Tad wondered uneasily what was going through Abby's mind. Since the Chicago-magazine fiasco, Abby had not had any interviews. Mainly, Tad felt, because she had insisted the headhunter tell all prospective employers she was expecting a child at the end of January. Abby wanted no more mix-ups or thwarted expectations on either side. Tad respected her enormously for that.

Feeling the sudden need to hold her, he closed the distance between them. "Yvonne got the job?" he guessed, taking Abby into his arms.

Abby traced the swell of her tummy with the flat of her hand in a protective deeply maternal gesture. "As an assistant managing editor. She's not coming back. They want her to start right away. I'm going to ship the things she left here back to New York." Abby paused, for the first time, her own mixed feelings about her friend's re-entry into the magazine trade evident. Abby continued with a rueful smile, "Yvonne said to tell you she's sorry about the short notice."

Tad shrugged it off. "She always said it would be that

way." *Abby had said the same thing.* At the time he'd told himself he could handle it. Now that the possibility was nearing, he was not so certain of that. Not nearly so certain.

Abby stepped closer. She rested her hand on his chest. "You okay?"

Tad nodded. "Sure," he said.

But inwardly he couldn't stop thinking about it.

And he was still thinking about it the next morning as he told the staff about Yvonne's departure and they tried to figure out how to divvy up the workload and compensate for her leaving.

"Well, I'm happy for her," Sonny said amiably, "but it's really going to leave us scrambling. Every edition leading up to Christmas is going to be jampacked with photos and details of holiday events."

"Not to mention ads," Cindy said, looking just as worried as her younger colleague. "We've got, on average, an additional five pages of advertisements. I think the only merchant in town not advertising with us is Joe Don Jerome."

"His friend at the insurance agency isn't advertising, either," Raymond said.

"No. But Cullen is thinking about it," Cindy replied. "I ran into him at the grocery store last night. He said the number of new homeowner, life and health policies he was writing was down ten percent since he'd stopped placing ads in our paper. The new business was all going to a competitor who was still advertising with us."

"Nowell Haines told his wife the same thing," Sadie said. "She advised him to bring his business back to the *Blossom Weekly News,* but he said he couldn't."

Tad looked thoughtful. "Their loss," he said.

"I quite agree," Abby said. She couldn't believe that

the Three Stooges, as Tad had dubbed the trio of businessmen, were still shooting themselves in the foot over Tad's decision to include consumer reporting and troubleshooting in the paper.

"Who's going to take over Yvonne's slot as Features editor?" Cindy asked.

Tad sized her up. "Actually I was thinking about asking you and hiring someone else to take over the advertising department."

Cindy beamed. "That would be great!"

"Can you sort of pull double duty until I get someone else in?" Tad asked. "I know it's the holidays—"

"No problem."

"Good. And speaking of holidays." Tad stood and disappeared into his office. He returned a moment later bearing five red envelopes. "I wanted to give you all your Christmas bonuses early in addition to the fifteen percent across-the-board raises you'll be getting as of January 1."

He handed out the envelopes. "I also wanted to let you know I've decided to expand the paper so we can go daily by next summer."

Another murmur of approval and excitement swept the group. "Furthermore," Tad went on, "I couldn't have done it without you."

The phone in his office rang. Still grinning from ear to ear, Cindy leaped up to get it. She returned promptly. "Tad, it's for you."

"Who is it?"

Cindy shrugged. "Some lady. She wouldn't give her name. She just said it was imperative she talk to you."

His expression concerned, Tad rose. When he came back, he had his jacket in hand. "I've got to go out for a bit," he announced to one and all. "Hold down the fort for me?"

"Sure," Raymond said.

"What was that about?" Sonny asked Abby.

Abby shrugged, hating to admit it, but feeling a little annoyed. "Darned if I know."

"Should I be jealous?" Abby asked hours later when Tad finally returned to the newspaper. Everyone else was out to lunch. Having eaten a little earlier—she got light-headed these days if she went too long between meals—she'd stayed behind to handle any walk-in business and the phones.

"Frustrated is more like it. That is, if you're sharing my feelings," Tad told her. He plucked their bagged lunch from the refrigerator in the coffee room and took Abby into his office to eat it.

She studied him curiously. "You were working on another troubleshooting story, weren't you?"

Tad nodded. "The same one I've been working on since I took over the paper."

"Joe Don's car dealership."

Tad unwrapped a turkey sandwich on rye and uncapped a thermos of piping hot minestrone soup. "Everyone complains about the quality of the cars, both new and used. And yet they still buy there because of the deal they can get."

"At least at first." Abby opened an individual carton of milk and peeled an orange for herself. "Then a lot of them go out of town to buy their cars."

"Right. Anyway, I've been sort of nosing around quietly, exchanging car-repair horror stories with the locals. Whenever I hear about anyone having anything atrocious happening, I find a way to bump into them and bring it up ever so casually, see if they'll talk about it. More often than not, they get this kind of scared look on their faces and clam up."

Tad wasn't the only one intrigued, Abby thought. Since he'd started investigating this in between all the many duties he had as owner, publisher and managing editor of the *Blossom Weekly News,* she'd become hooked, too. "That lady on the phone just now?" she prodded.

"An assistant over at the vet's. She's young, just out of high school, moved here from another town to start a life independent of her parents. The first thing she did was buy a used car from Joe Don." Tad scowled. "Currently said car is sitting in front of the garage apartment where she lives. The thirty-day warranty ran out on it and she can't afford to get it fixed. I tried to get her to talk about it the other day when I helped Sadie and Raymond take the pups to the vet for their checkup, but no go. I gave her my card, told her if she ever changed her mind, to give me a buzz—and she called this morning."

Abby leaned forward, her pulse racing. "And?"

Tad's frustration deepened visibly. "Like everybody else, when it came right down to it, she panicked and chickened out."

Abby shook her head while she continued peeling her orange. "That is so strange."

"Isn't it." Tad bit into his sandwich.

"After all this time—months—of working on this story, you still have no idea."

"None." Tad perked up. "But on the way back I saw a tow truck jumping Ernest Lee Scruggs's new pickup."

Abby furrowed her brow. "Again?" The pickup seemed to need jumping or had to be towed every other week, which was awfully odd since the owner was a mechanic.

Tad nodded. "Anyway, I stopped to see if I could lend a hand. Told him if he ever wanted to have a beer and trade stories about broken-down cars to give me a call."

"Think he'll take you up on it?"

Tad shrugged. "Hard to say. He's scared of something, too. He looked like he was getting awfully mad, though. When I left, he was kicking the tires on his truck."

"Oh, my."

"Oh, my is right." Tad gave her a once-over that swiftly left her feeling very sexy and very desirable. "So." He leaned back in his chair. "How are you feeling?"

Abby grinned, aware she'd never been happier even if she was beginning to get big as a house. "Pregnant. Very pregnant." And very loved.

"Oh, darlings, there you are!" Sadie burst in from lunch, Raymond behind her. They'd taken to eating over at her house so they could care for Belle, Buster and the puppies before coming back to work. "Raymond and I wanted to give you your Christmas present early." Sadie handed Tad and Abby an envelope, then watched with glee as they opened it together.

"C'MON NOW," Abby admonished Tad hours later in the classroom at the community college. "Be a sport."

"This is silly." Tad stared at the "baby" given to them by the instructor of the parenting class, started to attempt to pick it up to get it ready for its bath, then stepped back and shook his head as if to say, *No way.* He turned to her grimly, very much aware, as was Abby, that she'd already had her turn. "These are baby dolls."

"Lifelike baby dolls," Abby countered.

Tad braced his hands on his waist. "I do not need to practice bathing and diapering a baby doll."

"Obviously," Abby said, picking up their "baby" and handing it to him, "since you just taped that diaper to the baby's hip."

Tad glanced down at the doll, saw Abby was right. Frowning and grumbling something she was just as glad not to catch in its entirety, he put the "baby" back down on the table and ripped the adhesive tab off.

"You just ripped the baby's skin," Abby said dryly. "Little Will or Billie is now howling at the top of his or her lungs."

Tad grinned, enjoying her verbal jab as much as she'd enjoyed delivering it. He poked his thumbs through the belt loops of his jeans and retained his arrogant stance in front of the science-lab table. "No, he/she's not."

Abby arched a brow. "No?"

"Because you would be doing it," Tad said with a teasing grin. "Not me. And you—" he leaned forward to whisper sexily in her ear "—as you have so aptly demonstrated, are as much a pro at this as you are at everything else."

Pulse racing, spirits soaring, Abby drew back. "Flattery…"

Tad ran a hand lovingly over her tummy. "…will get me everywhere?"

Abby warmed beneath the tenderness of his touch and the feeling of the baby kicking deep inside her. "You wish!"

"Class." The teacher clapped her hands again. "Pay attention!"

Tad elbowed Abby lightly and gave her a look of mock sternness that said, *She's speaking to us.*

She gave him a look that said, *I know she is, and you, bad boy, better behave.*

They got through the rest of the class only because Tad decided to pay attention.

"That wasn't so bad, was it?" Abby said as they walked out into the cold clear December night.

Tad backed her up against the side of his Jeep and braced a hand on either side of her. Looking down at her, as if kissing her passionately was very much on his mind, he shrugged and replied, "Depends on how much humor you see in a soaped-up baby landing headfirst in the tub."

"Baby doll," Abby corrected, knowing how embarrassed Tad had looked about that. "And it was only your first attempt," she soothed as she rested both her hands against his chest.

His breath making frosty circles in the air, Tad gathered her close. He looked down at her and brushed the hair from her face. "What if I don't know what to do, Abby? What if I don't have that natural parenting thing that just tells you in here—" he thumped his chest "—what to do and say at any given moment."

Abby slipped her hands beneath the hem of his jacket and ran her hands up and down his back. "Then you read and study and learn," she said.

His quiet gaze said he wasn't sure that was all it would take. "Tad, we can do this," Abby encouraged softly, pressing ever closer. "We can be good parents."

"I know that." Tad opened the door and ushered her inside.

"Then...?" Abby asked after he'd circled around and climbed into the driver's seat.

Tad started the engine and gave it a moment to warm up. Hands resting on the steering wheel, he twisted to face Abby. The lamps from the parking lot bathed them in a gentle golden glow.

Blue eyes serious, he reached over, took her hand and

confessed with unexpected candor, "It just hit me tonight. The enormity of what we're undertaking here. The knowledge that it might not be as simple or trouble-free as I thought it would."

Abby smiled, as mesmerized by his unexpected show of vulnerability as she was by his easygoing confidence and rugged good looks. "I was wondering when it would happen," she murmured, smiling, as other cars around them began to drive off.

Tad's brow furrowed. "What?"

Abby lightly touched his chest as she confessed playfully, "That you'd feel the anxiety I've been feeling all along."

Tad looked as relieved as she felt. "You never said anything."

"That's because most of the time I push those feelings away, just tell myself everything is going to be fine. But sometimes at night…sometimes—usually late at night or very early in the morning—I worry." Realizing they really were in the same boat, after all, Abby smiled at Tad. "Doc Harlan and Dr. Ellison both reassure me it's quite natural. So I know—" Abby took his hand and held it tightly "—it's going to be all right, Tad."

He nodded, accepting that. Then, still looking worried, he glanced at his watch, put the Jeep into gear. "So, what do you think? Is there anywhere we can get a baby doll this late at night?"

FROM THAT MOMENT ON, it was Tad's mission. On Christmas Eve he was still at it. "You've practiced enough, Tad." He'd bathed, diapered, fed and burped the baby doll every night without fail.

Tad bundled the doll in a blanket and returned it to the crib. "I just want to make sure I have everything down pat so that when we bring the baby home, I'll be an old pro," he said.

There was no need to worry about that, Abby thought, amused. He could change a diaper now in nothing flat. And he could give the baby doll a bath with his eyes shut. "Trust me," Abby said dryly as she took her husband into her arms for a lengthy yuletide kiss. "You're going to be as good at that as you are everything else."

Tad bent his head and returned her kiss even more languorously. Abby's heart was pounding when he let her go. "Now this is the way to spend Christmas Eve," he drawled.

Knowing they would make love later—probably again and again—Abby took him by the hand and led him downstairs to the tree. She was eager to give him his gift. "Ready to exchange gifts?"

He nodded.

At Abby's insistence, Tad went first. He was stunned when he saw the framed copy of the first edition of the *Blossom Weekly News* published and edited by the two of them. "It was an important day in our lives," she told him quietly. "I thought we should mark the occasion."

"As well we should," he said as he kissed her again.

He handed her her gift. Inside was a beautiful framed photograph of them together their first night in Paris and another of their wedding day. There was a third frame, one with no picture. "For the baby's first formal portrait," Tad said hoarsely.

Tears sparkled in Abby's eyes. She wreathed her arms around Tad's neck and kissed him soundly. "This is the best Christmas I've ever had."

"Me, too," he said thickly.

"Let's make a promise," Abby said urgently. "No matter what happens, let's spend every Christmas right here together. Let's make sure that our baby has his mom and his dad with him at Christmas.''

"You have my word on it," Tad promised softly.

If he had his way, they'd never be apart again.

"So when are Sadie and Raymond going off on their real honeymoon?" Sonny asked the day after New Year's as the newspaper staff sifted through photos of homes. One had to be chosen for the next makeover project for the newspaper's Lifestyle section.

"They've decided to wait until after the puppies are weaned and our baby is born." In the meantime they'd spent their actual wedding night in Asheville, while the local vet had taken charge of Belle, Buster and the pups as his wedding gift to the new couple.

"I still get all misty thinking about their wedding on New Year's Eve," Cindy confessed as she held up a photo of a Cape Cod house in the country that needed a lot of work.

Abby knew exactly how Cindy felt. Watching the two lovebirds say their vows had made her tear up, too. Tad hadn't said much, but she'd known he was affected, too.

"Look at this one," Abby said, pointing out a sixties-style ranch home. "Think we could update this into something fresh and exciting?"

"It'd sure be a challenge," Sonny said.

"It'd also be something completely different from the rambling white elephant we just did," Abby mused.

"Where's Tad?"

"He took a gift basket of goodies and bottle of champagne over to Sadie's," Abby replied absently, still studying the ranch house. "He wanted it there when they got back."

The phone rang. Sonny went to get it. "Abby. For you!"

Hoping it was Frank at the paint store telling her he'd be happy to donate materials for the fix-up project once again in exchange for free mention of his store, Abby lifted the receiver. She was still on the phone, writing down details when Tad walked in. He took one look at her and said, "You look like you've seen a ghost."

It sort of felt that way. Aware all eyes were on her, Abby shook off her lethargy and said, "Not at all. I'm just stunned." She glanced at the notes she'd made. "That was the headhunter who helped get Yvonne her job. She said *Southern Home and Garden* magazine in Atlanta is expanding their editorial staff and they want to interview me."

Tad cast a look at the faint hint of snow flurries coming down outside. "Now?"

Abby nodded, knowing the weather—and the threat of their first snow of the year—was the least of her problems. "I can't travel," she said. "I'm less than a month from my due date."

Tad was very still. His eyes never left her face. "So you're declining."

Abby nodded curtly, trying not to feel so relieved. "What choice do I have?" At least this time she didn't have to go all the way to Chicago to be more or less turned down at first sight.

The phone rang again. This time Cindy got it. "Abby." She nodded at the phone.

Aware of Tad's eyes on her, Abby picked up her extension. She listened intently, feeling once again like the wind had been knocked out of her. "You're kidding," she said slowly. "No. Well. Of course. Yes. Absolutely.

Tomorrow.'' Abby hung up the phone. Everyone was still looking at her.

"Well?'' Tad said, beginning to look a little impatient.

"That was the headhunter again.'' Abby swallowed, not sure what she felt. Elated. Excited. Scared. Upset. Stunned. With Tad still waiting, she drew a breath and announced calmly, "*Southern Home and Garden* is sending someone here to interview me.''

Cindy grinned, unable to contain her excitement. "What are you going to wear?'' she demanded.

"Beats the heck out of me,'' Abby said. "Absolutely nothing fits me these days except Tad's old shirts and my maternity slacks.''

"We have time to drive to the maternity shop in Asheville before it closes,'' Tad said.

"Now?'' Abby demanded, casting another look at the snow flurries.

"Sure,'' Tad said, his mood remarkably buoyant considering all that was at stake. He had no doubt he could keep her and the baby safe. But he could see Abby needed some convincing. He closed the distance between them and wrapped his arm around her shoulders. "I just heard the latest weather update from the National Weather Service,'' he told her gently. "No accumulation is expected, and it's still early in the day. I've plenty of experience driving in all kinds of weather and road conditions. And if we do run into bad weather, the Jeep has four-wheel drive.''

Tad turned back to Sonny and Cindy. "You two can handle things here, can't you, while I go with Abby to purchase a power suit for her interview tomorrow?''

"Absolutely,'' Cindy and Sonny said in unison.

Tad smiled, went to the hook by the door and grabbed Abby's coat. "Let's go.''

Abby lifted her hair off her collar with one hand, while he helped her on with her coat. As soon as they were outside on the sidewalk, flurries swirling around them, she turned to him and said, "You don't have to do this for me."

"I want to," Tad said, and to his surprise, he meant the words with all his heart. He hadn't been nearly supportive enough of her desire to go back to work in her field the last time and he still felt guilty as hell about that. He'd promised Abby he would never hold her back professionally if they married. No matter how difficult it was, no matter how much he didn't want her to take a job away from him, he intended to hold himself to that vow.

As it happened, luck continued to be with them. The weather held. And Abby found a beautiful cranberry red wool maternity dress and matching jacket in very short order. A long cream, navy and cranberry silk scarf drew attention away from her tummy.

By the time the interview took place at their completely redecorated home, she felt—and looked—like a million bucks. Knowing Tad was waiting to hear, Abby called him as soon as the Atlanta publisher left. He drove right over.

"Well?" he said, coming through the door, an exceptionally happy smile on his face as he paused to kiss her cheek. "Tell me everything."

Abby took his hand and led him over to the sofa. She kept her hand linked with his even after they sat down. "They were very impressed by my work on the Lifestyle section, as well as all my previous work."

"As they should be," Tad said.

Abby sat back against the cushions, looking every bit the capable career woman she'd been when he met her.

"We agreed that the magazine needs a completely new approach and an updated look. So if I decided to take the job, I'd have carte blanche."

As proud as he was, Tad felt himself beginning to panic. "They offered it to you?"

Abby made a seesawing motion with her hand. "They're still working out salary details and my need to commute back and forth from Atlanta on a weekly or biweekly basis with the headhunter representing me." She shrugged her shoulders. "Whether or not we'll be able to come to an agreement, I don't know, but they are very interested."

With effort Tad put his own concerns aside. At least she was willing to commute. At least she wasn't trying to cut him out of her life entirely. "When would they want you to start?" he asked casually, realizing all over again how very much was at stake.

"March."

That was two months away. Tad enveloped her in a hug. "Well, congratulations. I hope you get the job." However they needed to work it out, he decided, they would work it out, as long as she was willing to meet him halfway.

Abby drew back. Her cheeks were flushed, her eyes sparkling with delight and wonder. "You mean that, don't you?" she said happily.

Tad nodded, stunned to find he could put her happiness above his own. "Yes, Abby, I do," he said quietly. "I want you to experience everything this life has to offer. And if that job will make you happy, I'm all for it."

ABBY HEARD NOTHING about the job until the following week when the publisher came in with an offer she found easy to refuse. "It's just not enough money, considering the commute," she told Tad as they got ready for bed that evening. "So I turned it down."

"Just like that?"

"We have to be practical here. It would take a lot of money and effort to maintain two homes for me to commute back and forth. I'll just keep looking."

Tad nodded. His feelings in turmoil, he climbed into bed beside her. He knew she was disappointed things hadn't worked out with *Southern Home and Garden* magazine, but he couldn't help but feel relieved, too. He did not want Abby that far away. He did not want their baby commuting between two different homes. But he also knew he had no more right to deprive Abby of her career dreams than she had to deprive him of his.

Beside him, Abby switched out the light, settled down into the feather ticking and let out a heartfelt groan.

Immediately concerned, Tad shifted onto his side. The softness of her hip collided with his. He touched her shoulder gently. "What is it?"

Abby grimaced and slid a hand beneath her waist. "My back again." She let out a gusty breath and shook her head. "I just can't get comfortable these days no matter what I do."

Tad knew she was tired of being pregnant. He took her hand, turned it palm up and kissed the middle of it. "It's only a couple more weeks."

Abby groaned again and peered at him from beneath her lashes. "Tell that to my aching muscles," she said as he reached beneath her and massaged where her hand had been.

"Maybe we should get rid of the feather ticking," Tad suggested thoughtfully, knowing that people with back problems often slept on harder—not softer—surfaces.

"Try just lying on the extra-firm mattress without the ticking," he said.

Abby rolled toward him, her breasts and tummy colliding with his chest. "You wouldn't mind?"

Tad grinned and pressed a playful kiss to the tip of her nose. "I like the bed either way—it makes no difference to me. Besides, it's not like I'm going to get a lot of sleep if you're tossing and turning all night." He helped Abby to her feet.

"True," she said.

"Besides, this is all part and parcel of being an expectant dad." Tad turned the bedroom light back on. Insisting he needed no help, he made her sit in one of the chairs next to the window while he removed the sheets and blankets and the feather ticking that covered the mattress, then replaced the sheets and blankets. Finished, he helped Abby back to bed.

"Well?" he said as she settled slowly, gracefully onto her back.

She lay there a moment while he gently drew the covers to her waist. She made a comical face. "I still feel like a beached whale."

Tad chuckled as he got into bed. Abby had been saying that for months now, and nothing could have been further from the truth. Her skin was so luminous it glowed, and there was a fundamental warmth and tenderness about her, a certain serenity, that increased daily. "You look—" Tad paused to kiss her deeply then reluctantly pulled away "—like an incredibly beautiful expectant mother."

Abby ducked her head. "You're just saying that."

"No, Abby, I'm not. Right now you are the most beautiful woman in the world to me," he said huskily. He paused to kiss her again. Lifting his lips from hers, he whispered in a voice not to be denied, "Now roll over on your side."

"What!"

"I'm going to give you a back rub. Maybe that will help."

"At this point," she grumbled cantankerously enough to make him chuckle, "the only thing that will help is this baby being born."

Tad was getting anxious, too. But it wasn't time.

"Hush." He turned down the lights, turned on some soft music and slipped his hands beneath the hem of her gown. He knew—from the faint shadows beneath her eyes—she needed sleep—and a hefty dose of tender loving care.

"Close your eyes," he ordered softly.

Abby protested immediately, just as he'd known she would.

"Close your eyes, Abby."

With a sigh she did. Loving the silky feel of her skin beneath his hands, he kneaded the muscles of her back until she moaned. "That feels so good," she murmured, her whole body going languid. "It's even making me sleepy."

Tad grinned. Knowing she needed her rest now more than ever, he put his own desire on hold and kept up the gentle massage. "Just close your eyes and cuddle close."

Abby snuggled into her pillow contentedly. "You really are the best expectant dad a woman could ever ask for."

High praise from a tough customer, Tad thought, recalling that when Abby had first moved into this house she'd refused even to sleep in the same room with him. So who knew? Maybe this *would* work out. Maybe after the baby was born, Abby would decide not to leave, after all.

Chapter Twelve

The phone rang at four in the morning. Groaning, Tad reached for it while Abby got up for what seemed the millionth time that night to head for the bathroom. When she came back, she looked surprised to see him getting dressed. Her eyes gleaming with curiosity, she perched on the edge of the bed. "What's up?"

Tad grinned as he took in the mussed layers of golden-brown hair. Eight and a half months into her pregnancy, her breasts and tummy swollen with child, she had never been sexier or more desirable.

"Ernest Lee Scruggs has finally decided he's ready to talk to me about Joe Don's car dealership." Tad pocketed his tape recorder, notepad and pen, a cell phone and his flashlight as Abby bounded off the bed.

She wreathed her arms about his neck. "Be careful."

"Count on it." He paused to kiss Abby on the tip of her nose, then headed out into the cold.

As expected, Ernest Lee was waiting eagerly. He came out onto his front porch, a jug of moonshine in his hand. Tad greeted him and then hustled them both inside.

"See that pickup?" Ernest Lee pointed drunkenly out the window at his shiny red truck. "A thing of beauty is what it is, and it's also a worthless pile of manure."

Tad turned on his tape recorder, set it down in the middle of the kitchen table and pulled up a chair. "It never has run right, has it?"

"Nope." Ernest Lee dropped into the chair opposite Tad with a clumsy thud. "It sure as blazes hasn't. And you want to know why?" He pounded the kitchen table with his fist. "'Cause it ain't new! Joe Don Jerome rolled back the mileage on it."

Tad took out his notepad. "How'd you find this out?"

Ernest Lee hiccuped loudly. "I tracked down the serial numbers through the company that made it. When I said I was the original owner, they thought I was somebody else, so I did some more hunting on my own and found out that the reason Joe Don has so much trouble with so many of his cars is that he's been buying up all the known lemons on the market dirt cheap, rolling back the mileage a'fore they get to his place and then selling them as great deals. Only they aren't such good deals, are they—" Ernest Lee hiccuped again "—if they never run right from day one."

"Why doesn't anyone complain to the state attorney general?" Tad asked as he got up to make some coffee for the drunk mechanic.

"'Cause they can't." Ernest Lee's red-rimmed eyes filled with despair.

Tad leaned forward urgently. "Why not?"

Tears rolled down Ernest Lee's wind-burned cheeks. "'Cause they lied, that's why."

"NOW WE KNOW the whole scam," Tad told Abby as soon as he got home some five hours later. "Joe Don Jerome sold the lemons to unsuspecting customers at what appeared to be cut-rate prices, Nowell Haines the banker encouraged customers to falsify through exaggeration or outright lies the information on their credit applications whenever necessary to push through the loans at a higher-than-market interest rate, and Cullen Marshall took care of the insurance. Together they made sure people got more expensive cars than they truthfully would have been qualified to purchase, and if anyone complained, they'd point out that they'd lied on their credit applications, and if found out, could go to jail for fraud.''

Abby put aside the Lifestyle article she'd been editing while she waited for him and accompanied him to the kitchen.

"No wonder people were too scared to kick up a ruckus."

Tad helped himself to a bowl of the cinnamon-raisin oatmeal simmering on the stove. "Fortunately I now have the ammunition to stop them. I talked to the district attorney on my way home. He's going to launch a criminal investigation after he reads my article. He's not going to prosecute anyone who fudged on their credit application."

Abby sat opposite him. "That's wonderful, Tad."

Yeah, it was, he thought as he picked up her hand and kissed the back of it.

Just as suddenly Abby tensed. "Oh, no..."

"What?" Tad asked, baffled.

One hand on the tabletop, Abby levered herself upright. "Don't look now, but my water just broke."

"TAD, WILL YOU JUST calm down?" Abby said after putting on some dry clothing and telephoning the obstetrician.

"I'm calm."

Like an erupting volcano is calm, Abby thought. "It's

going to be fine. My labor has barely started. The pains aren't even regular yet. We have plenty of time to get to the hospital." Plenty of time. She was not going to panic.

"That's good," Tad said. "Because I don't want you having our baby in the car en route to the hospital."

Abby smiled, amazed how calm she felt now that the moment was finally upon them. She'd thought she might fall apart. "All right. Just hang on while I get the articles I edited this morning while I was waiting for you. I want to drop them off at the newspaper on the way to the hospital. It'll just take a second."

Tad regarded her in exasperation. "Abby, I'm going to feel much better.when I get you and the baby to the hospital over in Asheville."

"Then help me here." Abby collected the edited papers she'd left strewn across the living-room coffee table. "And we can leave all the sooner."

"CAN YOU BELIEVE she was worried about dropping off some work at the newspaper?" Tad asked Sadie and Raymond, who'd driven to the hospital to be with them. His adrenaline pumping, Tad paced the corridor floor as, inside the private labor room, the nurses prepped Abby for the birth.

Raymond smiled. "Sounds like Abby. Hardworking and practical to the bone. And she was right. It did just take a second. You had to drive right by the office, anyway. And you got her here in plenty of time."

Sadie patted Tad's arm and brought him back to the sofa to sit between her and Raymond. "Now, honey, you just calm down," she said, rubbing his back. "Everything is going to be fine."

Tad reminded his aunt and her husband tensely, "The baby isn't due for another two weeks." What if he or she wasn't quite ready? What if something goes wrong during the delivery? What if, what if…?

"Babies come early all the time, Tad," Aunt Sadie said as a nurse appeared, held up a sterile gown and cap and motioned Tad to come with her. "Everything's going to be fine," Sadie added reassuringly.

And for a time Abby's labor was textbook perfect, if a bit slow. Over the course of the next eight hours, she went from one stage to another, with nary a complaint. Handling the pain and the brand-new experience well, she even managed to joke with Tad and Dr. Ellison and the nurses. But as soon as their baby's head emerged, everything changed.

Tad saw it on the obstetrician's face even before the doctor stated urgently, "We've got a nuchal cord times two and it's tight."

The nurse's expression turned gravely serious, too. She grabbed Abby's shoulders. "Stop pushing, Abby."

Perspiration streamed down Abby's face. "But I feel like I have to push," she protested breathlessly, still clutching Tad's hand and struggling to sit up, to see what was going on.

"Don't push," the nurse repeated. "The cord is wrapped around the baby's neck. The doctor has to release it. *Don't push.*"

"Tad," Abby whispered, looking to him for help. Tears of pain and terror streamed down her face.

"Hold on, Abby," Tad whispered against her ear. "I'm right here. I'm not going anywhere." He put his hands around her shoulders, and held her all the tighter, infusing her with strength and being careful not to dislodge her IV or get in anyone's way. "Everything's going to be fine," he repeated firmly. It had to be, he thought as a lump appeared in his throat and tears gathered in her eyes. They couldn't lose their baby. They couldn't.

Dr. Ellison swore. "I can't get it." He grabbed a pair of large bent-angle scissors from the sterile table. He struggled for what seemed to Tad like an eternity but was probably really more like half a minute—then abruptly exhaled in relief. "I got it." He placed the scissors down on the table. "Okay, push, Abby."

The nurse echoed Dr. Ellison. She lifted Abby's shoulders slightly. "Push, Abby, push!"

Abby gave it her all. Two pushes later the baby slid out.

But instead of the healthy pink or red they'd been led to expect in Lamaze class, their baby son was tiny and bluish-gray. And he wasn't crying and he wasn't moving. The silence in the cold and sterile delivery room was deafening. Quickly Dr. Ellison cut the cord. "Call the neonatal resuscitation team, stat!"

Abby's obstetrician carried the baby to a warming table with short glass walls and a bright light. The doctor and two nurses clustered there. Tad and Abby could see and hear the frantic activity as the nurses and doctor rubbed the baby vigorously with towels, trying to get him to wake up and breathe on his own. "Do you have a heart rate?"

The nurse replied, "One hundred and falling."

"No spontaneous respirations," Dr. Ellison reported grimly. "Let's bag him."

Clinging to each other, Tad and Abby watched as an oxygen mask was fit over their son's face. The nurse began to squeeze the bag ever so slightly, and at that point a new medical team rushed in.

"What's the story?" the doctor asked and Abby's obstetrician filled him in.

"We had good fetal heart tones up until the moment of delivery," Dr. Ellison added.

"Keep up the manual stimulation. Let's get ready to intubate and prepare a dose of epinephrine." One nurse scrambled to get the epinephrine, the other the intubation tube. With his thumbs the pediatrician opened the baby's mouth, inserted a silver instrument and tilted the baby's head back so he could see down the throat. He put the tube in, pulled out the silver scope, put on his stethoscope, listened to both sides of the baby's chest. "Good aeration," the pediatrician reported briskly. "Heart rate?"

"Sixty and falling."

One nurse put the epinephrine down the breathing tube. The other continued with the chest compressions.

"Heart rate's going up. Eighty. Ninety. It's over a hundred."

"We're getting spontaneous respirations."

Thank God, Tad thought. He noted with relief their baby's chest was at last moving on its own.

Still clinging to each other, Tad and Abby watched, barely daring to breathe. They knew, although doing better, their son was not yet out of danger.

"Heart rate?" the pediatrician asked.

"One hundred twenty and strong."

Tears of joy streamed down Abby's and Tad's faces as they saw their baby's feet and hands were at last moving, too.

"Well, he looks like he's coming around," the pediatrician said with satisfaction. "Let's try to extubate him and see how he does." With the nurses' assistance, the pediatrician removed the tube. As soon as he did, the baby let out a lusty cry that echoed throughout the room.

Tad and Abby laughed and cried and hugged each

other all at once. Tad knew the sound of their son exercising his tiny lungs for the very first time was the most beautiful sound in the world. And he knew he'd remember it the rest of his life, as would Abby. And one day, when their son was much older, a teenager maybe, they'd tell him what a scare he'd given them.

The nurses smiled. "Let's get him a dry blanket." They removed the blanket beneath him and slid in another, then put a white knit cap on his head. All the while their baby—who was now a healthy pink—continued to cry and carry on as if furious at being yanked from Abby's warm womb into this cold world.

"Okay, let's get him over to the special-care nursery where I can keep an eye on him," the pediatrician told the nurses assisting him.

The nurses transferred the baby to a glass-covered incubator and wheeled him out. The doctor headed for Abby and Tad, introduced himself as the neonatologist and briefly explained what would happen. "Your baby's breathing on his own now and his heart is beating, but we need to keep a very close eye on him for the next few hours, so I'll be moving him to the special-care nursery." The doctor's eyes were kind. "Depending on how he does, we'll decide whether we can move him out to the regular mother-baby nursery or if we need to keep him here and do some testing." He held up a cautionary hand. "Most babies who suffer this sort of insult recover completely and there are no residual damages, but we won't know exactly how your baby's going to do until he gets through the next few hours."

The nurse looked at Tad. "When you're ready, we'll take you over and show you where it is and how you can visit your son."

ABBY, EXHAUSTED from the birth, stayed awake just long enough to get stitched up and be moved to a private room. Then she fell asleep, her hand clutching Tad's, tears of joy and relief still rolling down her face.

Tad knew Abby believed the worst was over. He wished he felt the same. Deciding to check on the baby again—hoping that would waylay his anxiety—he left the room and headed down the hall to the special-care nursery. As he neared the glassed-in area, he saw Doc Harlan—who'd told Tad he'd be by to check on Abby and the baby—inside, consulting with the nurses and the neonatologist.

Tad moved closer to the window. Little William was in a warming bed. He was dressed in just a diaper and his color was still good. He was motionless again, but this time it was because he was sleeping. Tad noted he had a full head of black hair and looked a lot like Abby. As Tad thought about what had almost happened back there in the delivery room, guilt assailed him anew. He didn't care what anyone said. He knew it was his fault Abby had delivered early. They'd both been pushing hard at the newspaper. Too hard, he now saw.

When Doc finished consulting with the neonatologist, he strode out into the hall. "How's Abby?"

Tad swallowed hard around the ache that had been in his throat since things had first started to go wrong. "Sleeping." *Please, God, don't let her wake up to bad news.* "How's baby William doing?"

Doc clapped an immensely comforting hand on Tad's shoulder and confided gently, "They've done two tests on the baby to see how much oxygen is circulating in his blood—which tells you how well he's breathing. The first one, taken right after he was revived, was not as good as we'd like to see. However, it was consistent with the type of trauma the baby suffered at the time of delivery.

"He seemed to be breathing well on his own, so the pediatrician held off on reintubation and repeated the test twenty minutes later. The second test showed marked improvement, and the pediatrician feels comfortable just observing the baby in the special-care nursery for the next twelve to twenty-four hours.

"If William continues to breathe easily, then Abby will be able to come in and start feeding him in the next few hours. But if he's struggling for air or breathing too fast," Doc cautioned, "we'll have to hold off on starting feeding and do follow-up testing." Tad regarded Doc warily. "Doesn't the baby need to eat?"

Doc nodded. "If we can't feed him, we'll start an IV and feed him that way for the time being." Doc went on to explain that babies breathed through their mouths only, so the pediatrician didn't want to do anything that would make it harder for William to breathe.

The fear gripping Tad's heart squeezed a little more. More than anything he wanted to protect Abby and his son. "You're worried about my son, aren't you?" he asked grimly.

"Some, yes," Doc admitted honestly. "But William's a fighter, Tad, and he's holding his own for the moment. There's a lot to be said for that." Doc studied Tad with a physician's eye. "I wish I could say you looked as good."

Taking Tad by the arm, Doc led him down the hall in the direction of Abby's room. "You've had a really rough time of it, too, haven't you, son?" he asked compassionately as every wrong thing Tad had ever done came back to haunt him with crushing speed.

Years ago he'd let his kid brother down, with an error

in judgment that had ended up costing Billy his life. Now, years later, he'd done it again, this time with his wife and son. And he was just as powerless to do anything about it after the fact. Instead, he had to wait it out and see if his son was going to be okay. The way Billy hadn't been.

With effort Tad pushed the torturous memories away. His dreams for the future fading faster than a shooting star, he knew he had to unburden himself. And who better to talk to than Doc, who'd often said that in his thirty-some years as a healer he'd seen and heard it all?

"I never should have pressured Abby to move here. But I did because—God help me—I wanted her with me. Not just as the mother to my child but because I wanted her to make my dream hers."

"Sharing a dream can bring a couple closer together," Doc said gently.

"But it wasn't just that," Tad said grimly, his shame mounting. "I needed her skills, her insight, to make the paper what it is today." Tad shoved a hand through his hair. "I couldn't have garnered anywhere near the success without her input." And therein lay the trap he'd created for them. "Don't you see, Doc? I'm the one who got her excited about newspaper work. Not enough to want to do it forever of course—I don't think that's possible—but enough to want to put in way too many hours." *Like she had that very morning,* Tad thought guiltily. "And now, because of that, our baby is here early, and I can't shake the feeling that in my selfish need to have everything my way I might have gotten us into a bad situation that I can't fix." What if—because of his damned selfishness and self-centeredness—things went wrong again and he and Abby lost their son? Tad had read between the lines enough to know that although William was stable, he was not out of danger yet.

The silence that fell between the two men was more indicting than any tribunal. Hand on Tad's arm, Doc directed Tad past Abby's hospital room to a deserted waiting room a little farther down the hall. Once there, he propelled Tad onto one of the sofas and made him sit.

"The last thing Abby needs is to hear you talking like this," Doc told him gruffly.

"Maybe," Tad allowed grimly, ashamed. He wished like hell he'd had something more noble to report. "But it's all true. I took advantage of Abby at a real low point in her life." *Was this—Will's condition—punishment for that?*

Doc folded his arms. "Abby strikes me as a young woman who knows her own mind. She wouldn't have come to Blossom with you if she didn't want to be here."

That wasn't quite true, Tad thought uncomfortably, as pain and regret tightened like a vice around his heart. He had backed her into a corner when she lost her job at *Trend,* and he knew it, even if no one else here did. Until now he'd believed he'd do it all over again in a flash if it meant he and Abby could have the chance to make their marriage a real one and be together again, but now he wasn't so sure he hadn't brought this all on them himself! He swallowed hard. If anything happened to their baby, if he was at fault, he knew he would never forgive himself. And neither would Abby.

Doc moved to the bank of windows and stood opposite Tad. "As far as the baby coming early goes, that could have happened if she hadn't worked at all. So you needn't blame yourself about that." Doc paused, trying to see if he was getting through. "Look, son, you and Abby and the baby have all been through a lot today. It's going to take time to recover. Talking to Abby about any of your doubts or regrets about past misdeeds is not going to do any of you any good, particularly at this juncture, so I want you to promise me you'll let that go for now,'' Doc said firmly. ''Save it for later, after William is home, if you must discuss it.''

Doc seemed to think by then it would no longer be necessary.

''Right now, just concentrate on getting some rest yourself. And helping Abby and baby William do the same. It wouldn't hurt you to get something to eat, too. Not to mention a shower, shave and fresh set of clothes.'' Doc placed an arm around Tad's shoulders. ''So here's what we're going to do....''

Chapter Thirteen

Abby awoke the following morning, not sure how long she'd been asleep, only knowing that every part of her ached with the need to be with Tad and see her baby again. Shakily she tried to sit up, only to discover she still had an IV in her arm and was woozy as all get out. Worse was the fuzzy memory of Tad talking to Doc Harlan, telling him he regretted ever bringing her to North Carolina. Or had that been a nightmare? Abby wondered, confused.

Closing her eyes, she sank back against the pillows. And that was when she heard it, the quiet heavy footsteps, then Tad's voice, low and urgent, and the brisk purposeful voice of the neonatologist.

Tad and William's pediatrician came into the room. To Abby's surprise, Tad was showered and shaved. He even looked as if he'd had some rest. But there was a distant regret-filled look in his blue eyes that hadn't been there before she went to sleep—which made her think that her memory hadn't been a nightmare at all. And there was something else going on here, too, she thought. Otherwise, the faces of both men wouldn't look quite so reluctant and grim, and she wouldn't be feeling quite so panicked.

"Hello, Abby," the pediatrician said gently.

Abby swallowed around the lump in her throat as every self-protective instinct she had snapped immediately into place. "How's the baby doing?" she asked as Tad sat beside her on the edge of the bed and took her hand.

William's pediatrician smiled at her, but the expression in his eyes was grave. "Abby, I'm a little bit concerned about him. He seemed to recover from the initial birth incident quite well, and we checked some tests on his blood to see if he was getting enough oxygen, and those looked good. But since that time he's started to breathe a little fast again and his temperature dropped a bit."

"I don't understand." Abby shot Tad a fearful look before turning back to William's pediatrician. "What does that mean?"

"When you or I get sick, we get a fever. When a baby this young gets sick, sometimes the temp goes down a tiny bit, instead of up," he explained, his serious expression telling her everything she didn't want to hear. "The first thing we do when that happens is check the baby's blood sugar and infection count. William's blood sugar was fine. But his infection count showed too many of the cells that indicate he might be getting sick."

The pediatrician went on to explain they'd ordered a chest X ray, which had looked normal, and then drawn blood for cultures. "In the meantime we've started William on antibiotics and IV fluids."

Abby struggled against the panic that threatened to envelop her. "When can I see him?" She had to get to William, let him know they were there.

"Right away. As for feeding, as long as his respiratory rate reminds high, as I've explained to Tad, I can't allow you to breastfeed him. We'll give William all the nutrition he needs through an IV so that we don't hinder his breathing."

They were doing everything they could. She had to have faith. Abby drew an unsteady breath and worked to keep her voice even. "How long is he going to be in the hospital?"

"If the blood cultures remain negative, his breathing slows to a normal rate, and he continues to do well, then he can probably go home in seventy-two hours. If the cultures are positive, William will have to stay here in the special-care nursery anywhere from ten to twenty-one days."

Still struggling to understand, Abby asked, "Did he get sick because he was born early? Or was he born early because he was already sick?"

"Most of the time these infections just happen, and we're unable to relate it to any specific event if there's no infection in the mother. You, Abby, have shown no signs of fever or infection, so we'll probably never know why this occurred."

Abby could deal with that. As long as William got well. And he would get well, she thought fiercely. She and Tad would see to it.

William's pediatrician talked to them some more, promised to come back to see them again that evening, then left to continue his rounds. Together, Tad and Abby walked down to the special-care nursery. A nurse showed them how to scrub their hands for several minutes with a rough bristly brush and some brown antiseptic-smelling soap, then ushered them in.

Abby teared up when she got her first good look at her son. He was so beautiful. He had a head of black hair, long-lashed eyes, rosebud lips and one heck of a determined chin. He was nineteen inches long and weighed six pounds five ounces, according to the identification card on the outside of his isolette. He was lying on his back in the warming bed clad in just a diaper. An IV line had been inserted into his foot, and a clear plastic helmet had been placed over his head. Abby felt frightened and reassured all at once. He was alive, and as long as he was alive, he had a chance to pull through.

Her heart pounding, she glanced at the nurse. "What's the helmet for?"

"That's an 'oxy hood.' We're giving him a little extra oxygen to help him breathe."

Abby leaned against Tad, aware she'd never needed his strength and determination more than she did at that moment. "He's so tiny," she whispered. "So defenseless." She wished she could hold him.

Tad nodded and tightened his grip on her. "But he's one heck of a fighter, Abby. The doctors have said so."

THE DAYS THAT FOLLOWED were indisputably the roughest in Abby's entire life. As the pediatrician had suspected, William had a positive blood culture that confirmed the presence of an infection in his tiny body. A second chest X ray also showed a small pneumonia in his lungs, and another weighing showed a loss of three ounces. They continued the IV and the antibiotics, and prayed the powerful medicine, combined with the essential nutrition, warming bed and oxy hood, would do the trick. And all the while Abby and Tad paced and prayed. Twelve hours after being on antibiotics, William's breathing improved somewhat. A second blood culture showed the same bug that the first culture had. Convinced they'd selected the right medicine, William's pediatrician continued the antiobiotic, and within thirty-six hours of the baby's first becoming sick, a very grateful and blissfully happy Abby was able to hold him in her arms. And, taken off oxygen, William was able to eat for the first time. Hours later, his IV fluids were discontinued and he was moved to a crib.

Tad and Abby both had reason to rejoice when repeat blood cultures, drawn several days later, were negative. It meant, William's pediatrician explained, that they had suppressed the bug. Nevertheless, William had to finish a fourteen-day course of antibiotics.

During that time Abby was discharged from the hospital.

Abby's parents—notified by Sadie—sent telegrams and flowers to the hospital, expressing their good wishes, but—otherwise engrossed in their work—did not offer to come and visit or help out. Tad felt badly for Abby. Surely, he thought, if ever there was a time when a grown woman needed her parents, this was it. But Abby wasn't surprised. She told him she'd expected as much and not to worry about it. *She* wasn't going to. Instead, she focused her every thought, her every ounce of energy, on helping their infant son get well. As did Tad. Until finally, day by day, William improved, and they heard the news they'd been waiting to hear.

"You can take your baby home."

Tears of joy streamed down Abby's face as she looked at the infant in her arms. A huge knot of emotion grew in her throat, making speech impossible. Tad kissed her forehead and his son's tiny fist in turn, and for a few minutes he too seemed unable to speak. Finally he thanked William's pediatrician profusely for all he'd done.

"Anytime," the doctor said with a smile and a wink. "And maybe next time," he said, playfully hinting there might be other newborns of Tad and Abby's for him to take care of, "the whole thing will go a lot easier."

Next time. Abby jerked in a quick breath at the thought.

Would there be a next time? Another pregnancy?

She faced Tad awkwardly, wondering where they went from here. Their agreement only covered the period until their baby's birth. Now William was here. He was finally out of danger. And the future loomed ahead of them uncertainly.

The doctor left, and a heavy silence fell between Tad and Abby. At last Tad braced his hands on his hips, then offered matter-of-factly, "I'll go down to the business office and take care of the paperwork necessary to sign Will out."

Abby nodded. "I'll get our things together and wait for you here."

ALTHOUGH WILL SLEPT peacefully the whole time, the forty-five-minute ride home seemed interminable. Abby felt odd, sitting in back, while Tad sat in front and drove. Odder still was hearing about the newspaper. Although Tad was still very much caught up in the goings-on in the office, it seemed ages since she'd worked there. Even longer since she and Tad had shared anything remotely like the fiercely passionate relationship they'd once enjoyed. *It's not my imagination,* Abby thought as she stared out at the cold blustery February day. The two of them were united in their love and concern for their child. But as for everything else...

Tad had been keeping a very tight rein on his emotions and withholding every bit as much as he said since the birth of their child. She knew he loved their baby, too, and had been devastated by little Will's illness. But it was more than that. She didn't know how or why it had happened, but there was an emotional wall between them now, keeping them apart. A wall she couldn't ever see herself scaling.

Maybe, though, she thought dispiritedly, she shouldn't be surprised by that. He'd married her on a whim, because of the passionate nature of their whirlwind love affair, and stayed married to her because of the baby and because of the paper. Now the baby had been born and the newspaper was on solid ground. Tad had to realize, as did she, that it was time they thought about going their separate ways again, just as they had once promised each other they would.

As Tad turned the Jeep into the drive, Abby sighed. The only problem was she wasn't sure she wanted to leave, even to go back to work in the magazine field. Given a choice, she would much rather work on getting their relationship back to the happy state it had been in before Will's birth. Unfortunately she couldn't do it alone. And right now she wasn't sure Tad was all that driven to help her.

No sooner had he cut the engine, than Sadie and Raymond were rushing out the door. They brought the baby in. Sadie had the house warm and the cradle waiting. For a few minutes they oohed and aahed over the still-peacefully sleeping William. Then Sadie, remembering an urgent telephone message for Abby, abruptly went to get it.

Abby left to return the call, then rejoined the group several minutes later, still in a state of shock. "The editor-in-chief of *Southern Home and Garden* magazine has just quit to take a job in London. They've offered me the position." Abby named a salary that was twice what she'd made at *Trend*.

"What are you going to do?" Sadie asked.

"I don't know and I don't have much time to decide. They'd need me to start in six weeks, and they want an answer within forty-eight hours." Abby swallowed and looked at Tad. "If I don't take it, they want to start a full-fledged search."

"Congratulations," Tad said with what sounded like real enthusiasm. He hugged her warmly, clearly impressed. "That's a huge career leap."

"Yes," Abby agreed woodenly, "it is."

Sadie and Raymond looked at each other and stood. "I'm sure you two want to discuss this alone." Sadie kissed Abby's cheek, as did Raymond. Both offered their congratulations.

"Thanks," Abby said, knowing now what she hadn't known before Will's birth—and Tad still didn't know—that she couldn't take a job that would take her away from her baby, even for a few days at a time.

William was only going to be young once; she wanted to cherish this time with him. And she wanted to find a way to rebuild her marriage to Tad, to get over this crazy distance between them, however—why ever—it had come about. But only, she thought, if he was willing to meet her halfway.

Sadie and Raymond left quietly, and Tad went to get

the bottle of champagne they'd received as a gift in honor
of William's homecoming. While she watched, dread
weakening her knees, he searched the kitchen cupboard
for two glasses. Finding them, he set them down on the
counter. "I don't see how you can turn this job down."

*Just tell me you love me and want to stay married to
me forever, and watch how fast I react.* "The job is in
Atlanta," Abby reminded him, putting aside the crushing
hurt she felt and carefully gauging his reaction. *His needs
and desires were just as important as hers. This had to
be about what he wanted, too.*

His expression impassive, Tad shrugged. Meeting her
glance, he said gently, "It's only an hour and a half flight
to Atlanta. We can figure out a way to share the care of
Will and both still have what we want in our careers."

Abby thought back to the promise they'd made to stay
together only until after the baby was born. Then the
nightmarish conversation in the hospital. What was it
she'd thought she'd overheard Tad say to Doc Harlan? *I
never should have pressured Abby to move here...but I
did because... I needed her help in making the paper
what it is today... And now that our baby is here... I
can't shake the feeling that...I might have gotten us into
a bad situation...*

She hadn't wanted to face it then, or ask him if he'd
had second thoughts about the marriage. It had been just
too painful. Now she had no choice.

Having seen her parents' bitterness and disillusionment
at the end of every one of their many marriages, she'd
rather she and Tad end their marriage while they were
still friends. Like it or not, she told herself firmly, following his cues, he was doing them all a favor by react-

ing this way. This job was the graceful way out for both of them.

"So it's true. Abby is leaving the *Blossom Weekly News*," Cindy said sadly the next morning.

Tad put the finishing touches on the ad for Abby's replacement. "The opportunity is incredible." *And I'm the last person in the world who should stand in her way.* Hadn't he promised himself, when Billy died, that he would never be responsible for depriving anyone of the life they should have had again? In the background Sadie and Raymond exchanged concerned glances. Catching them, Tad frowned.

"But she just had your baby!" Sonny protested with all the youthful naïveté of a recent college grad.

Secretly Tad had hoped Abby would want to stay there with him, especially after all they'd been through together, building the paper to its current level of success. But, he reminded himself sternly, Abby had been honest with him from the start, telling him that, as much as she wanted to be fair about the baby and give their child a mother and father he could count on, she was not going to sacrifice the career she'd spent the past ten years building for his dreams of a permanent home and life in North Carolina.

Besides, if she didn't want to continue their marriage by now, she never would. Tad didn't want to lose Abby altogether. The only way he could keep her in his life without the acrimony of divorce, as in her parents' relationship, or the coldness and strain and unspoken resentments in his own parents' marriage was to muster all his courage and let her go gracefully. So that was, he thought resolutely, exactly what he was going to do.

ABBY WAS IN THE KITCHEN when Tad came in the back door, a cardboard box of her belongings in his arms. Raindrops dampened his shoulders and glistened in his hair, and his cheeks were rosy from the cold March air. He also looked like he'd had as rough a day as she had, trying to explain to everyone why they were splitting up. "Where do you want these?" he asked.

Abby struggled to hide her melancholy. "Dining room, I guess."

Tad carried them in there, set them down gently and then returned.

"Is Will sleeping?"

Abby nodded, wishing this wasn't so awkward. "Yes. I just put him down."

Tad made several more trips. By the time he'd finished, he'd carried in six boxes that were filled to overflowing. Abby surveyed the jumbled mess. "I had no idea I had so much stuff at the newspaper."

Tad shrugged out of his coat and looped it over the back of a chair. "So, when are you going to Atlanta to hunt for a place to live?" he asked casually.

"Personnel is going to call me tomorrow after they've received my signed employment contract." Which she still hadn't sent. "I'll set up a house-hunting trip then."

"But you're expecting it to be when?" Tad pressed.

He sure was anxious to get rid of her, Abby thought irritably. She shrugged. "Next week sometime—at least that's what I hope." Studying the slightly aggravated, very distant light in Tad's eyes, Abby thought maybe he was right. Maybe the sooner she wrapped up the details on this, the better.

Tad poured himself a cup of freshly brewed coffee. "Will you be leaving Will here?"

"For that particular trip, yes." Abby turned away from the stack of thank-you letters she'd been writing. She tried not to think about how difficult it would be to be separated from William even for a few hours, never mind a few days. She studied Tad. "Unless you want me to take him with me."

"No." Tad lifted his cup to his lips. "I'd like to take care of him here. I can grab a couple of days off from the paper."

Another awkward silence fell between them. Finally Abby shook her head. "I feel like I should say something to ease the tension between us," she said quietly.

Tad turned and stared out at the bleak March day. The sky was gray. A light rain was falling and had been all day. "It's hard to be comfortable when a marriage is splitting up."

"True," Abby allowed, irked that he could take this in stride so much more easily than she could, when it had been she all along who'd insisted they stay together only until after the birth.

Aware he was now watching her as carefully as she'd been watching him, Abby stubbornly marshaled her pride and steeled herself not to cry. Hearing the clothes dryer buzz, signaling the end of the cycle, she headed into the utility room. "Although I guess we should have known that our romance was way too passionate to last, at least the level it was in Paris." It was just too bad, Abby thought as she pulled a load of warm baby clothes from the dryer, that she'd wanted it to be that way forever.

Tad watched her carry the clothes into the kitchen. She sat down in a chair and began to fold them. "I don't know about that. Our sex life here was pretty damn passionate," Tad said matter-of-factly, "at least when you were pregnant."

So much so, Abby thought, that she'd allowed herself to be completely fooled about the direction of their future.

"That's because we were both romanticizing the pregnancy and awaiting the birth of our baby," she told him as she neatly folded a blue print sleeper. "Now William's here and it's a different kind of joy we're feeling. One that is a lot more...parental." Abby drew a bolstering breath as she turned a tiny undershirt right side out and stacked that, too. "Anyway, I love my career and know it will sustain me through life's ups and downs, just as the newspaper will ground you in any number of ways. And," Abby continued pragmatically, warming to the task of getting out of this marriage with at least her pride intact, "it'll be easier for William this way."

Easier for all three of us, she amended silently.

Abby returned to the laundry. She plucked the damp clothes from the washer and tossed them into the dryer. "Perhaps it was the impulsive way we married or the wonder of expecting our first child together, but whatever the case, you and I romanticized marriage to a ridiculous degree. And marriage isn't a fairy tale," she concluded as she switched on the dryer and returned to Tad's side. "People just don't live happily ever after these days."

Tad finished the last of his coffee and set the mug down with a thud. "You're right about that," he said gruffly.

Abby looked at him, her heart sinking. If only he knew, she thought, how very much she wished he would argue with her about this, tell her she was all wrong, that marriages did last, and theirs could, too. Because she wanted to live happily ever after with him, and William, and maybe even have another child or two. But she couldn't do it alone, she thought, studying his squared shoulders and girded thighs. She couldn't do it at all without his help. And that, she realized reluctantly, was obviously not going to come.

"I'm going back down to the paper," Tad said curtly, picking up his coat. He looked at her like he had the hounds of hell on his heels. "If anyone needs me—" he was already striding out into the rain and the cold "—I'll be there."

Chapter Fourteen

"I couldn't believe it when Abby told me you'd gone back to the office tonight. But then I couldn't believe it when she told me she was taking that job in Atlanta, either."

Tad swiveled away from his computer screen and faced his aunt with exasperation. It had been one heck of a day. The last thing he needed was familial interference. "Aunt Sadie, you know I love you—" he began irritably.

"I love you, too." His aunt paced, waving her arms excitedly. "But that doesn't mean the two of you aren't the most stubborn shortsighted people I've ever seen. Furthermore, Tad McFarlane, I never thought I'd see the day when you'd be afraid to go after what you want! But here it is, anyway!"

"I'm not afraid," Tad said grimly. Grabbing his mug, he went over to pour more coffee into it. "I'm keeping a promise I made to Abby." *Even if it was costing him dearly.* He'd told her he understood her devotion to her career—and he did. He'd told her he'd support her decision to go back to work as a magazine editor as soon as the baby was born—and he had. The fact that it had come just weeks after William's birth was a shock, but that did not in any way negate the promise he'd made. And now it was up to him to honor that promise. It didn't matter if it felt like his heart had literally been ripped in two.

Sadie perched on the edge of his desk. Her frown deepening, she followed his gaze, then demanded, "Will you stop looking at Abby's formal letter of resignation and listen to me? You're going to end up looking as mournful as Buster on a bad day for the rest of your life if you aren't careful."

Figuring this conversation had gone on long enough, Tad tore his eyes from Abby's letter and gave his aunt a warning glance. "Don't you think you're exaggerating just a bit?" he said dryly. After all, it wasn't as if he and Abby would never see each other again. They'd agreed to rear their son together. They would likely see each other all the time. So what if it wasn't quite the same? So what if he might not ever make love to her again or hold her through the night or enjoy the morning sunrise and the first cup of coffee of the day with her? She was going to be happy. She was returning to work she loved almost more than life. And for that reason he had to put his own selfish concerns aside and be happy for her.

"No, I do not think I'm exaggerating a bit. And quite frankly I'm furious with you. I never thought you'd let life pass you by the way I did for so many years. But I was lucky. I found Raymond and fell in love and married him."

Tad smiled at his aunt gently. "And I'm happy for you, Aunt Sadie."

"I know you are, honey." Sadie watched him kick back in his chair. "But think of all the time I wasted earlier in my life by being so shortsighted and foolish and picky and afraid to really invest myself in any one relationship.'' She paused, her expression mirroring the sadness he felt deep inside. ''You and Abby have a child, Tad. You have a marriage. Don't let either of them go.''

''I HAVE TO TELL YOU, Abby,'' Yvonne said as Abby tried for the hundredth time to put the signed employment contract into the envelope that would be express-mailed to Atlanta first thing the next morning, right after she had spoken to the publisher and accepted the job. ''The magazine-business rumor mill is going crazy! Is it true? Are you going to be the new editor-in-chief of *Southern Home and Garden* magazine?''

Abby finally put the employment contract down and switched the telephone to her other ear. ''They've asked and given me forty-eight hours to decide.'' Briefly Abby filled Yvonne in on all the perks that came with the job. ''If I accept, I'll have to cut my maternity leave a little short and head for Atlanta right away, but they'll let me bring the baby to work for the first year.'' Abby paced over to the bassinet, where William slept soundly.

''Wow.''

Yeah, wow, Abby thought as she lightly, lovingly smoothed William's soft cheek. The job was a dream. The perks were incredible. After ten years of working nonstop for just such an opportunity, she ought to be walking on air. But instead, all she could think was that she was leaving Tad and taking their baby with her, and that Tad was more than willing to have her go.

Not that that should've been a surprise to her, though. She'd known from the outset that Tad's dream of one day owning and running his own newspaper had meant more to him than she did. The two of them had split up less than twenty-four hours after they'd first tied the knot for just that reason. Had it not been for the fact that she was carrying his baby, they never would have lived together and stayed together for all those months.

"You don't sound excited."

Tears blurring her eyes, Abby paced away from the bassinet. "I'm not."

"Because of the baby?" Yvonne prodded gently.

"It's everything," Abby said, and then to her horror, burst into sobs.

"Oh, honey," Yvonne clucked sympathetically.

"It's hormones," Abby sniffed, trying to stifle her tears with her fist. "Postpartum ones this time." That had to be it. She could not be falling apart just because the marriage she'd never for one minute really expected to last was breaking up.

"Well, you know what they say," Yvonne said. "Pregnancy is supposed to be one long roller-coaster ride. And you had one heck of a time, seeing William through his illness and waiting for him to get better."

"You'll get no argument there." Abby plucked a tissue from the box and blew her nose. Her life with Tad had been a roller-coaster ride from start to finish. And she was so sorry it was over. She'd gotten to like—no, love—having Tad in her life.

There was a brief silence on the other end of the line. "How is Tad taking all this?" Yvonne asked gently.

Abby swallowed around the growing knot of emotion in her throat and tried to get a grip on herself. "He doesn't seem to care what I do either way."

"Now, Abby, I am sure that's not true!"

Abby thought about Tad's immediate assumption she

would take the job in Atlanta, never mind that their baby had just been born and they'd have to live in two different cities. If that wasn't pushing her out the door with both hands, if that wasn't letting her know her days as his wife were over, she didn't know what was. "Unfortunately it is."

"Then steal a page from his book and seduce him into changing his mind," Yvonne said, practical as ever.

Abby flushed. "He never seduced *me* into anything!"

"I beg to differ. Any man who convinces a woman to marry him during a whirlwind weekend romance in Paris has also *seduced* her into wanting what he wants."

"Not really," Abby murmured wistfully, as she thought back to the weekend that had so changed her life. "To tell you the truth, I wanted all that, anyway," Abby confided. "The husband, the home, the baby. A personal life aside from my work." And for a brief time, she'd had it.

"Aha! I *thought* you were a closet romantic."

Abby massaged her temples. "Yeah, well, I was always afraid to admit it for fear I'd get it all, then have it taken away." She hadn't wanted to feel deeply or let herself be vulnerable or love a man more than life. But she had.

"And you did have it all with Tad, didn't you?" Yvonne asked gently.

Suddenly the lump was back in Abby's throat, bigtime. "You saw us together. You know we did."

"Then what are you doing talking to me," Yvonne demanded in exasperation, "when you could be going after what you really want, right this instant?"

HALF AN HOUR LATER Abby was headed for the phone again when the doorbell rang. Sadie and Raymond stood on the other side. "I was just going to call you," Abby said as she fastened her earrings.

Sadie cast an admiring glance at the sexy black cocktail dress Abby hadn't worn since that fateful weekend in Paris. "You were?"

Abby paused to slip on a pair of heels. "Yep." She searched through the front-hall closet for a suitable wrap. "I need a baby-sitter. Pronto."

Raymond helped Sadie with her raincoat and took off his. "William asleep?"

Abby nodded. "And he's just been fed and diapered."

"Sounds like we're all set, then," Raymond said. Because Tad had the Jeep, Raymond handed Abby the keys to his sedan.

"Might we ask where you're going?" Sadie asked.

Abby looked Sadie square in the eye. "To find that husband of mine. He and I have some straightening out to do."

IT WAS TEN in the evening and Tad was still toying with the wording on the newspaper advertisement he was composing when the door opened and shut. In stormed Abby, looking incredibly beautiful and loaded for bear.

Slim as the day he'd met her, thanks in no small part to the stress of the past few weeks, the only change in her willowy form was the added lusciousness of her breasts.

Pausing long enough to hang her coat on the rack next to the front door, she strode toward him resolutely, her high heels clicking on the polished wooden floor. Her expression both defiant and determined, she reached in front of him, picked up her letter of resignation, ripped it up with a flourish and then dropped the pieces of it in front of him.

Tad stared at her, aware she'd never looked more feisty or beautiful than she did at that very minute, in the short and sassy black cocktail dress.

His heart pounding, he looked at the papers she'd so dramatically shredded in front of him, then back at her face. He hoped like heck this all meant what he hoped it did. But with Abby, and the way her moods had been going up and down lately, there was no telling.

He sat back in his chair, determined to play this every bit as mysteriously as his wife. Blue eyes sparkling with unbridled mischief—and challenge that matched her own—he looked her up and down slowly, his eyes lingering on the fullness of her breasts and the slenderness of her hips, before once again returning to her face. "Mind telling me what the meaning of that little gesture was?" he drawled lazily.

"I'll tell you what the meaning was," Abby said as she dropped unceremoniously into his lap and wreathed her arms about his neck. "You are not pushing me out of your life, Tad McFarlane. I am here to stay."

"Oh, yeah?" Tad shot back, liking the unabashedly amorous light in her golden-brown eyes. It felt so good to have her in his arms again. He'd missed holding her and making love to her so much.

"Oh, yeah," Abby echoed as all the hopes and dreams he had once had for them and thought were dead surged to new life. "Because I realized tonight that the months we've spent together have taught me something."

"And that would be?" Tad prodded, realizing he never wanted to let Abby go. And yet he knew there was still so much they had to clear up before they could go on. As he looked into her eyes, he realized she knew it, too.

Abby rubbed her hands thoughtfully across the soft cotton fabric of his shirt, molding her trembling palms to the muscles of his chest. "That I have to go after my marriage and a life and a love with you with the same tenacity and faith and commitment I've always given my career."

Tad rubbed his thumb across her face, tracing the shape of her cheek and jaw. "I have to say I'm all for that," he murmured as he bent his head to kiss her. Then he drew back. "But before we rush ahead and recommit to each other, there are some things we have to talk about."

"I agree," Abby said quickly, a determined edge to her tone. "And first on the agenda is the job, Tad. Before I came over here, I turned down the job at *Southern Home and Garden*. And I told the headhunter I'm withdrawing from the job search permanently."

Tad tensed. "I told you before, Abby—I don't ever again want to be responsible for robbing someone else of the life he or she was meant to have." He cupped her hands in his. "I know how much your career has always meant to you, and I don't want you to look back later and regret passing up this opportunity."

Abby gazed deep into his eyes. "Is that why you told Doc in the hospital you regretted having me move here and work on the paper?" She briefly explained what she'd heard.

Tad grimaced. "I realized that night how selfish and self-centered I'd been. I felt guilty about forcing my dreams on you and wanting you with me—not just during the pregnancy but for all time—no matter what the cost to you.''

Abby moved closer in a drift of perfume. "What did Doc say to all that?"

Tad stared into her long-lashed golden-brown eyes. "He told me you wouldn't have been here with me if you didn't want to be."

Abby's lips curved softly. "Doc's right, you know. Baby or no baby, I never would have stayed married to you all those months if I hadn't loved you or hoped a miracle would happen and we'd find a way—with time— to work everything out." Abby paused, still studying him, gauging his reaction. "But there's one thing I don't understand. If you felt that way, why didn't you just tell me you wanted me to stay here rather than go to Atlanta?"

Tad regarded Abby seriously. "Because I wanted you to make the decision about your future based on what you needed in terms of your career and your life, not on what I needed. I felt it was only fair, since we spent most of last year chasing *my* dreams."

When Abby heard that, she knew Tad really had changed, as had she. Both of them for the better. "And if I had chosen the job in Atlanta? What then?"

Tad turned his swivel chair to the left and directed Abby's attention to the computer screen on his desk. Aloud she read, "'For Sale. Thriving newspaper in Blossom, North Carolina—'" She turned to him in amazement.

"That's as far as I got," he said, "but you get the gist."

She looked at him, stunned. "You were going to sell the newspaper?"

Tad nodded, feeling a lump in his throat the size of a walnut. "And follow you to Atlanta. And, if necessary, win your heart and your attention and your love all over again. Because as Sadie pointed out," he told Abby gruffly, looking deep into her eyes, "our love for each other is worth fighting for." He held Abby close and stroked her hair. "So if you want to call the publisher, tell him you've talked to me and I've agreed to move, and you want to take the job, after all, then it's absolutely fine with me."

"Oh, Tad. Thank you." Abby embraced him. "That means so much to me. But… I don't want to do that."

He studied her face carefully. "You're sure?"

Abby nodded. "I realized as soon as I thought about what it would be like to take such a challenging high-pressure job that it wasn't something I could do without working twelve- to sixteen-hour days. And while that would have been fine while I was still a single woman, now I'm a mom and a wife, and I want to be with my family a lot more. Plus—" her lips lifted in an affection-ate grin "—word has it that the editor-in-chief of the *Blossom Weekly News* is a *very* understanding guy. He's so understanding, in fact," Abby continued, "that he lets his wife work at home whenever she wants or bring their baby to work so the baby can be with the two of them as much as possible."

Tad grinned and sifted a hand through her hair. "Funny," he drawled, his eyes sparkling mischievously too, "I'd heard exactly the same thing."

"So it's a deal?" Abby wreathed her arms about his neck. "We'll stay here, stay married and continue to build the *Blossom Weekly News* into the finest newspaper North Carolina has ever seen?"

"Agreed." Tad kissed her fiercely. "But only on one condition," he said.

Abby cuddled against him, content. "Anything."

Tad cupped a hand beneath her chin. "This whole misunderstanding has made me realize that I have to talk about things. Not gloss over our problems or run from them the way my parents did after my brother's death. Because my parents and I should have talked about things. Not just after Billy's death, but all along, even if it was painful. Instead, we kept it all bottled up inside because we didn't want to hurt one another. And we ended up hurting one another all the more in the process by becoming permanently emotionally estranged. And then I did the same thing in my marriage to you, in my attempts to protect you. When all my silence on the truly difficult emotional issues really did was end up hurting you," he said softly.

"You weren't the only one who was afraid." Abby drew a ragged breath and looked at him with serious eyes. "I said my vows, never really believing it could or would last. And I held a part of myself—the most vulnerable part of myself—from you all along. Only when I was about to lose you did I realize I had a lot more to give than I thought." She leaned forward to kiss him tenderly. "I love you with all my heart and soul, and I always will."

He held her tenderly and looked deep into her eyes. "And I love you with every fiber of my being." He tugged her closer and indulged in a long steamy kiss that left them both feeling very content, glowing and alive. "Don't ever doubt that."

Abby's spirits soared and she knew there was only one thing left to say. "Then I, Abby Kildaire McFarlane, once again take thee, Tad, to be my lawfully wedded husband…''

''And I, Tad McFarlane, once again take thee, Abby, to be my lawfully wedded wife…''

''Forever…'' Abby said softly.

''And ever…'' Tad agreed.

''And from this day forward, I promise to keep the lines of communication open between us, speak always what is in my heart and on my mind. And I expect you, dear husband, to do the same.''

''I think I can handle that,'' he replied.

Abby kissed Tad soundly once again. ''Good,'' she said, cuddling against him, '''cause we have a long and happy life ahead of us.''

''And maybe,'' Tad said as he kissed his way down the slope of her neck, ''given a little time, maybe even another baby or two.''

Abby kissed the strong column of his throat. ''William would like that, I'm sure.''

''As would Sadie and Raymond.'' Tad sighed, content.

Abby drew back. ''Think we should go home and tell them the good news?''

''Absolutely.'' Tad nodded vigorously. ''But first—'' Tad kissed her ''—you and I have some catching up to do.''

And they did.

Tyler Brides

It happened one weekend...

Quinn and Molly Spencer are delighted to accept three bookings for their newly opened B&B, Breakfast Inn Bed, located in America's favorite hometown, Tyler, Wisconsin.

But Gina Santori is anything but thrilled to discover her best friend has tricked her into sharing a room with the man who broke her heart eight years ago....

And Delia Mayhew can hardly believe that she's gotten herself locked in the Breakfast Inn Bed basement with the sexiest man in America.

Then there's Rebecca Salter. She's turned up at the Inn in her wedding gown. Minus her groom.

Come home to Tyler for three delightful novellas by three of your favorite authors: Kristine Rolofson, Heather MacAllister and Jacqueline Diamond.

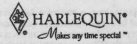

HARLEQUIN®
Makes any time special ™

Visit us at www.eHarlequin.com

PHTB